Going
the C

LINDA TAYLOR

WITHDRAWN

ARROW

Published in the United Kingdom in 1999 by
Arrow Books

3 5 7 9 10 8 6 4 2

Copyright © Linda Taylor 1999

The right of Linda Taylor to be identified as the author of this work has been asserted
by her in accordance with the Copyright, Design and Patents Act, 1988

First published in the United Kingdom in 1999 by William Heinemann

Arrow Books Limited
The Random House Group Ltd
20 Vauxhall Bridge Road, London, SW1V 2SA

Random House Australia (Pty) Limited
20 Alfred Street, Milsons Point, Sydney, New South Wales 2061, Australia

Random House New Zealand Limited
18 Poland Road, Glenfield
Auckland 10, New Zealand

Random House South Africa (Pty) Limited
Endulini, 5a Jubilee Road, Parktown 2193, South Africa

The Random House Group Limited Reg. No. 954009

www.randomhouse.co.uk

A CIP catalogue record for this book is available from the British Library

Papers used by Random House
are natural, recyclable products made from wood grown in
sustainable forests. The manufacturing processes conform to
the environmental regulations of the country of origin

Printed and bound in Norway by
AIT Trondheim AS, Trondheim

ISBN 0 09 927233 4

Acknowledgements

My sincere thanks to everybody who has stuck by me with love, friendship and support, and to all at Darley Anderson and William Heinemann who have worked so hard to pull it together.

And with deep gratitude to three inspirational women: Patricia Mackridge of Tonbridge Girls' Grammar School; Ann Mann of Harris Manchester College; and Gillian Carey, Senior Tutor of Harris Manchester College, for her majestic ability to send a beam of light through the fog.

Chapter One

'Oh my God!'

It was Monday morning. But that wasn't the half of it. It was very *late* on Monday morning.

Louise squashed her face into the orange cushion, then the red one, then the rust one. She wriggled until she found the limp pillow buried underneath. She flattened her cheek against the cool cotton and opened one eye. The psychedelic yellow and green sunbursts on the pillowcase put a bomb under any lingering sensations of tranquillity. These colours were supposed to turn her into a positive thinker, according to an article she had read. This morning they were burning out the backs of her retinas. She groaned, pulled a face and struggled into a sitting position in bed. She pulled the duvet up around her shoulders, stuck an Ultra-Low cigarette between her lips and thought about lighting it.

Something else struck her as her arms waved around in front of her body. They ached. Not only that, her throat was raw, her nose was defunct as breathing apparatus, and her head was about to explode with pain. She gave the cigarette a regretful look before flinging it aside, collapsing back against her pile of cushions and closing her eyes. So the tickly nose, sore throat and hot head of the previous evening had not just been the usual Sunday night list of complaints brought on by the thought of Andrew and Jez's Monday morning faces, alight with manic cheer brought about by a frenetic need to keep Party Animals afloat. She really did have a cold. A horrible one. And that would explain why she'd over-slept.

She let out a low, earthy groan, pausing to appreciate her own Mariella Frostrup husk, and let her eyelids droop. She groped for her radio alarm and felt her way along the buttons. What had she left it on? She hoped it was Virgin. She needed to be rocked right out of bed. It was Classic FM. She clicked it off again quickly, lay still, and then frowned. The television was on in the corner of the bedroom. It was getting on her nerves.

She prised open an eye in time to see Ainsley Harriott giving her a broad grin while gyrating his hips and flipping a selection of seafood medallions into the air from a non-stick frying-pan.

'Oh, sod off.'

So she had fallen asleep with the television on. And the finger of guilt prodding at her solar plexus was telling her that she had overslept by a lot this time. She wasn't going to be able to make up for it by bursting into the Party Animals office clutching scraps of paper covered with ideas that she had hastily scribbled down on the tube and pretending that she had spent the morning on 'project analysis'. There was no way she was going to make it in today.

She wanted a cup of tea, but the flat was freezing and she couldn't face getting out of bed. But she'd have to get out of bed any minute now and ring work to simper her way through her explanation. They'd never believe she'd over-slept because she was actually ill. Analogies of little boys crying wolf sprang into her mind. Andrew was looking for an opportunity to fire her, she felt sure of that after the last warning he gave her. It was her own fault. She'd just never felt at home in that company, just as she'd never felt at home anywhere else. So she'd taken too much time off, despite knowing that it would rebound on her later.

2

She'd joined Party Animals as a project manager. Andrew and Jez had both interviewed her. They were an Exciting and Young company, they'd explained. Great, she'd enthused, feeling personally neither exciting nor young, but overwhelmingly jobless. Everybody wanted parties, everybody went to them, everybody paid for them, and was prepared to pay a great deal, they said. Especially in Cambridge, where they had been under-graduates together, and where they had both got the idea. At the time, the philistine thought had occurred to her that everybody in London was too drunk, too knackered or too pissed off to go to parties, and that in Cambridge it might have been different, but she had smiled in an Exciting and Young sort of way and got the job. In practice, her job as project manager involved sitting in the office trying to sound like a receptionist if somebody rang and making clicking sounds with her plastic lighter to feign the machinations of an expensive switchboard before handing the phone over to one of her bosses. She was starting to think that the Exciting and Young company was a Not Very Well Thought Out company.

She dragged her eyes away from the figures jiving about on the television screen, wound the duvet around her body and slid her legs over the edge of the bed. Her feet flopped about until they met the carpet. The ground felt more solid than usual today. She had a vision of herself melting into the floor like an ice cream. Perhaps she would stay there all day. Perhaps she would die of dehydration, and nobody would know. Not until Harris upstairs smelt something funny coming from her flat, and then she'd be uncovered, rolled up in her duvet, her glassy eyes still fixed longingly on her unlit cigarette.

She paused with a hand outstretched towards the phone while she planned her own funeral. She wondered what music they might play. Perhaps Jon would insist that they

3

played 'You Sexy Thing'. Her father had liked that, except he had always sung, 'I believe in marigolds' for the first line. Then Jon, wiping away a tear in the front pew, would be sorry that he was scared of commitment and had made her agree that what they really needed was space from each other. If he could only see the state that she was in today, he would realise how much he loved her. The reality, however, was that none of those thoughts would sprint across his agile mind.

He didn't exactly want things to end between them completely, he'd explained, it was just that it wasn't healthy to live in each other's pockets. She'd been in this situation before, and the alarm bells were pealing melodiously. They had spent a year and a half on an association which she, at least, had thought of as a relationship, but which he'd seen as a cool and modern arrangement. It had jogged along, at first in a fairly sprightly manner, becoming somewhat red-faced and wheezing after a time, and had eventually suffered a coronary and collapsed in an ungainly fashion on a park bench. If she had ever joined the joggers round the corner in Gunnersbury Park she could have produced a dramatic representation of the whole affair in a mere fifteen minutes. It was over. But what was really irritating Louise was that Jon hadn't had the courage to say this. Instead, he'd talked about space. Space, Louise was well aware, was infinite. Jon wasn't talking about cutting down on their occasional pub visits, curries, nights in her flat. No, he meant, You have that universe, and I'll just leap into my rocket and jet off to this one. Bye then.

With a pout, she decided to finish her funeral plans. She got to the part where her coffin was trundling away on the conveyor belt towards the flames with Jon hanging from the brass handles yelling, 'Come back! I forgot to tell you I adore you!' when her father came to mind. She pushed the memory away quickly, staring at the television for distraction.

She found herself fascinated by the man with 'Can't' emblazoned on his chef's hat as he tried to grate an orange and succeeded in grating the ends of his fingers instead. The audience howled with laughter. Ainsley's eyes opened into planets as he gave the camera a knowing look. They should have made a daytime programme about men which women everywhere could enjoy, she decided, burning an acid look at the two guys fumbling with whisks. Something like *Can't Commit, Won't Commit.* It could be a masterclass, hosted by a man in a contented relationship.

'No, don't do it like that! What are you like! Ring her up, go on. Yes, I know you only rang her three days ago, but she won't mind, really. You've got no idea, have you!' (Shrieks of female mirth from the audience.)

Louise inched herself in her duvet cocoon across the carpet towards the telephone, reached it and fell on top of it. She pulled up the receiver and poked her fingers at the buttons, then lay back and waited for Andrew to answer in his exhaustingly keen voice.

'Party Animals, this is Andrew speaking, how can I help you?'

'Andrew.' She paused, her breath coming in short rasps. 'Andrew, my aunt's dead.'

'Louise?'

For a moment, she had a sudden urge to be somebody else. It was something that had started in the fifth form when she used to sneak off to the copse down by the hockey pitch for a fag. Miss Hicks would creep up on the other side of the trees, then yell through the branches, 'Is that Louise Twigg and Sally Birlington?' For some reason, Louise would always deny it, while Sally would jump fifty

5

feet in the air and levitate there, nodding. But Andrew, just like Miss Hicks, knew it was her.

'Yes,' she said.

'Louise, you told us your aunt died over a year ago. You can't come up with that one again. Where are you?'

'I'm at home, and it's a different aunt.' Now her throat hurt even more. That was Andrew's fault, for making her raise her voice.

'Look, we've had everything under the sun from you. I got in this morning, and Jez and I looked at each other and do you know what he said? "Monday," he said. "What will Louise come up with today?" So what is it?'

'I've got the flu.' Louise rolled over and landed on her face. Unfortunately, it was where she'd left a hunk of uneaten nan bread. She nudged the plate to one side with her nose.

'Are you saying you can't come in?' Andrew sounded bored.

'I'm saying I can't even get to the kettle. I can't even turn the telly off because I can't reach the remote control. I'm saying that I'm genuinely ill, and even saying it makes my throat hurt more, and makes me iller.' She coughed roughly, her eyes streaming.

'Sounds like you've had a night on the piss and sixty Marlboros,' Andrew said heartlessly. 'No point in expecting you in this afternoon, I suppose? We've got a couple of urgent orders, and Jez and I have to go and inspect a venue. I suppose we'll have to ask someone else to cover the phones.'

There was a long, intolerant pause. Louise remembered that she'd once thought Andrew fancied her. If he had, he was certainly getting over it.

'I'm sorry,' she said.

'You always are, Louise. Will we see you tomorrow, or is this a three-day hangover?'

6

'I'll be in tomorrow. I promise. If I can just sleep this off, I'm sure I'll make it—'

Andrew hung up.

She lay back on the floor. It was a relief to have made the phone call. At least now she was authentically off sick even if Andrew and Jez, intent upon world domination in their party facilities emporium, didn't believe her. They'd just have to survive without her. And now that she had freed herself for the day, she had a strong urge to fight the germs and do something more fun than lying in bed with the curtains closed.

She rang Sally at work. After a long debate with the switchboard operator, she was put through.

'Louise Twigg?' Sally sounded ridiculously polite. She had someone with her. 'Could I possibly call you back?'

'It was only a quickie,' Louise raced on. 'You know, as we haven't seen each other for a while now. I wondered what you're doing for lunch?'

'That would be a little tricky.'

'This evening then?'

'Er, I'm afraid I have a fairly full timetable for the immediate future.'

'Fergus,' Louise declared.

'Yes.'

'You're not meeting him at lunchtime, are you?'

'That would be correct, yes.'

'God, that's just so – keen. And tonight too?'

'Yes, that is the current plan.'

Louise rolled her eyes to the ceiling. What was the matter with men these days? Didn't Fergus have a life of his own? What had happened to football and lager and strippers and men-only fortnights in Tenerife? Not that she wanted to go out with a man like that herself, but at least if Sally would oblige they could spend their

7

lunchtimes looking for cushions in Habitat, and evenings chatting up men who weren't in Tenerife.

'Bye then Sal.'

'You could call me later in the week if that's convenient.'

'And you'll pencil me in a window. I know. Talk to you soon.'

She hung up.

'Selfish cow,' she uttered into the air, and sniffed hard. She supposed that if Jon were as adoring as Fergus, though, she and Sally would have even fewer opportunities to meet up over the full-blooded red, and they might spend more time just heaving contented sighs at each other when they did. As it was, whenever they squashed themselves into wine bars to discuss Jon, Sally always gave her a funny look. As if it were all Louise's own fault. But it wasn't just Fergus. It was also the fact that Sally was busy being a brilliant solicitor. She couldn't work out for the moment which of Sally's areas of total fulfilment she felt the most peevish about.

Anyway, she consoled herself, her legs might not have carried her as far as Chancery Lane. Perhaps later she'd go shopping on her own. Some new clothes would show Andrew and Jez that she meant business, and tomorrow she'd turn up at Party Animals with a fresh attitude. After she'd had another hour's sleep. She climbed back on to the bed, ran a hand vaguely through the tangled strands of her dark blonde hair, and collapsed back on to her mountain of mismatched cushions, caring not one iota if she snored like a lion.

When Louise woke up again, her first image was of Jon climbing over his desk and reaching for Kelly's breasts. She tried to swallow, failed and didn't even try to open her eyes. It must have been a dream. One of those dreams that tells you what's really going on.

With men, there had always been one casually dropped name that caused her palpitations and night-sweats. Jon's one was called Kelly. Louise had never met her, but she had spoken to her on the phone once when she'd rung him at work. She sounded pleasant, fun, bubbly and single. She was 'harmless', according to Jon. Louise knew that Jon slept with every woman he called 'harmless', but forgot to tell her about it. It was a code of his. He was so sure of his own wind-chill factor he didn't even realise he had a code, but Louise did. For some reason, something was telling her that at this moment he was grabbing somebody's breasts. She knew, even in her state of semi-delirium, that they weren't hers.

'Right!'

She cast herself out of bed and fiddled with the radio until she hit upon something loud, discordant and energetic. It was time to make some changes. And the first day of the rest of her life would start with a trip to the shops. Later, when she felt really good about herself, she would sort things out with Jon once and for all.

In Flickers, her favourite candle shop, she pondered over the aromatic oils. She'd heard the lavender was good for seduction. She put that one back. Lemon would be bracing. At least it would go with the pillowcase. Cinnamon might be a nice one to burn when she was eating her way through another take-away from Aziz. And she could spread eucalyptus all over the cushions to clear her nose. She hummed to herself and collected a range of tiny bottles in her palm before ambling towards the till. She stopped abruptly and smiled at the bemused face of the woman painstakingly planting price labels on to scented night-lights at the counter. She glanced down instinctively at her clothes. She'd wanted to wear the maroon sweater with this rather short pink skirt, but that had been at the bottom of the laundry basket, so she'd had to make do with the long cardigan she'd bought to wear with trousers. With her coat open to let some cool air make contact with her flushed skin, she supposed it probably looked as if she'd forgotten to put anything on the bottom at all. But then, the tights were opaque. And her boots came up to the knee. It wasn't that obscene, and yet the woman's small features were definitely crumpled with dismay. Louise smiled more broadly and was met with an overt frown.

'Is there a problem?'

'Don't move!' the assistant issued and slid from behind the counter.

Louise obediently froze.

'The belt of your coat, dear. It's caught on the candelabra. You'll bring the whole thing crashing down if you twitch a muscle.'

'Ah.'

'It's caught quite firmly. You need to shift a bit to the left.'

'Okay.'

They smiled at each other while the woman worked slim, pointed fingers on the obstruction.

'No, you need to move the other way.'

'Right.'

'But slowly—'

Louise winced as the top of the candelabra made contact with her head. The mobile above the shop door tinkled. She cast an idle glance at the figure that had just strode in and wriggled back to yank at the belt of her coat.

'It's a nice coat,' the assistant said. 'These long ones are quite fashionable, aren't they?'

'Are they?'

'Oh yes. I think you're supposed to wear something underneath, though.'

Louise managed a laugh and flipped up her cardigan to reveal the pink pleated skirt. She glanced down and realised that she was flashing her tights and a pair of hip-hugging white knickers underneath to the customer who was waiting patiently at the till.

'Louise?' a naggingly familiar voice queried.

She looked again, more closely, as the wrought-iron candelabra was yanked up into position, taking with it several strands of her hair. She winced, and made full eye contact with the man who was now leaning on the counter and drumming his fingers.

'Andrew?' she breathed, as if there could possibly be some doubt. He raised an auburn eyebrow at her in reply.

'Andrew, this isn't what it looks like. I came shopping to get some oil. For my nose.' She wrinkled her nose to show him how red it was and strained to make her eyes run again. They'd been running when she'd arrived at the shop. The icy November wind had ensured that. Now the buggers wouldn't oblige. He seemed uninterested in her, and as the assistant trotted back to the counter, began a conversation about outside lanterns.

'So – so what are you doing here?' Louise shuffled forwards, her face reddening, her collection of bottles rattling in her hand. He looked over his shoulder at her with a studied lack of urgency that was ominous.

'You recommended Flickers. Remember? For all our lighting needs? It was a shame you were too ill to come to work today, because one of the things I was going to ask you to do this afternoon was come down here and check out the range we could use for garden parties. And obviously, in your depleted state, you'd never have managed it. Would you?'

Louise opened her mouth and prayed for a sneeze. Hopefully a really wet one that would cover him from head to toe, give him her germs, and ensure that in due

11

course he would have to take his sarcasm right back. Nothing happened. She closed her mouth again.

'Been shopping?' He eyed the carrier bags by her feet.

She put her sore nose in the air and decided that braving it out was the safest option. 'If you must know, Andrew, I've been buying myself a new outfit for work. I realised that I should be more professional. I've realised a lot of things about the way I do my job. So despite the fact that I feel dreadful, I dragged myself out so that I could turn over a new leaf. And if you really must know everything, I was on my way to the counter to ask about outside lighting when you walked in. It's just that I got my belt caught on the candelabra.'

She realised it didn't justify showing him her knickers, but that would have to go unexplained for now.

'Whatever you say, Louise.' He sounded bored as he glanced over a folder which the shop assistant had handed him and tucked it under his arm.

He turned to go. For a moment she thought he was just going to sweep out without another word in her direction, but he stopped, looked her up and down, and lingered for a little too long on the expanse of thigh between the bottom of her cardigan and the top of her boots.

'Just a hint, Louise. Save the Miss Whiplash look for the bedroom.'

He nodded at the assistant, assured her he would be in touch and left the shop. The bell tinkled long after he had disappeared. Louise let out a long breath.

'Sadistic swine.'

'Oh dear.'

Louise slammed the bottles down on to the counter with a crash. 'I have decided that things are no longer going to go wrong.'

'That's seven pounds forty then, dear.'

'And what's more, I'll take the candelabra too. We seem to have bonded.'

Later that evening, Louise was treated to the sight of Harris leaning against her door-frame with eyebrows matted thunderously. She didn't know much about him even though he'd lived in the flat upstairs for a good few months, but she did know he was an actor. He had managed to mention his moment of fame in *Casualty* each time they'd banged into each other. For that reason, she was never quite sure whether his range of expressions displayed genuine emotion, or if he was getting himself into character. This evening, though, he was doing thunderous quite convincingly. She pulled a rueful face.

'I'm sorry, Harris, is it the piano?'

He was attractive, she had to admit. She hadn't really appreciated him in full view before. Each time they'd met, he'd always had a woman on his arm, or was on his way out to meet one. When he'd knocked a few weeks ago to ask if he could borrow some bubble bath, she'd spent the evening in the kitchen listening to squeals, splashes and ultimately groans coming from his bathroom upstairs. She wasn't naive enough to imagine that it was simply the aroma of midnight musk that had sent him into rapturous flailing. No, he'd definitely had company. But it wasn't just the fact that he was clamoured for, that put her off. It was something to do with the fact that he just knew he was attractive. His clothes shouted it. Tonight he was in crisp chinos and a powder-blue shirt with the collar flipped up. And she could bet that the shirt had been chosen because it was exactly the same colour as his eyes. The brows that were still drawn together were as boot-polish black as his hair. She'd often wondered if it was a rinse. And he might have been wearing mascara. Either that or he was blessed with the sort of thick black lashes that she could have murdered him for.

13

However, she flushed as she remembered that the last time they had rubbed shoulders in the hall, he *had* laughingly asked her if she'd actually been playing her piano or standing on the keys while she changed a light bulb.

'It's the piano,' she confirmed flatly. 'It was too loud.'

'No, Louise. There's a small village in Venezuela that can't hear you. They've emailed me to ask you to sing louder.'

'You don't like it then?' She opened her eyes appealingly.

'It's not possible to do it *without* the singing, I suppose?' He folded his arms. She took a moment to admire his biceps covertly. Not too bulbous. Bigger than Jon's. She wondered if everything he possessed would be bigger than Jon's. She cleared her throat.

'It wouldn't be the same without the lyrics. The chorus is too repetitive.'

'But it's repetitive anyway,' he explained patiently. 'You've played "I'm Going to Wash That Man Right Out of My Hair" six times in a row. I know. I counted.'

She let out a hefty sigh and didn't care that he saw. Her nose started to run, and before she could stop herself, she sneezed violently at him. She grappled with a tissue and stuck it over her face.

'You see the problem?' she said in a muffled voice. 'I'm ill. My ears are bunged up too. I can't tell what volume I'm playing at.'

He paused to assess her. She squirmed under his gaze. She hadn't bothered to change when she'd got home, and the short pink skirt was still hidden somewhere inside the long cardigan. He seemed to have only just noticed, and had visibly brightened. He shifted himself in the doorway, looking at her legs from a different angle, and when his eyes returned to hers there was a smile lurking there.

14

'I'd say bed was the best cure,' he said slowly.

'Oh yes, I'm going there in a minute,' she nodded. 'Once I've done a few things.'

'Like washing your hair?'

'Oh, is it that bad?' She raked her hands through the limp strands. She'd caught her hair up behind in a scrunchie, but it was at a length where nothing stayed where it was supposed to.

'No, Louise, I was referring to the song. Your hair looks delicious.'

She eyed him over her tissue. Delicious? Her hair? What had got into him tonight? She blew her nose heftily and stuck the tissue back up her sleeve.

'Well, if that was all, Harris, I'd better get back to—'

'What's that wonderful smell?' He poked his head through the doorway.

'Search me. I can't smell a thing.'

'Something's very . . .' He savoured his words. 'Erotic in here.'

'Oh that. Must be the Chicksticks I grilled earlier.'

'No, I'll swear it's not pre-packaged food.' He was edging himself inside her flat. Attractive or not, she wasn't in the mood for this. She had been planning her letter to Jon while she thumped away on her second-hand upright. Phrases like 'All men are bastards' had been skitting through her head. 'It's lemony and fresh. Very stimulating.' He flared his nostrils at her.

'Are you rehearsing for a washing powder commercial?'

'Sharp, like you, madam. Have you been buying smelly candles again?'

'It's the oil burner. Don't tell me you can actually smell it?'

'I expect the village in Venezuela can smell it as well. You're only supposed to put a few drops in, you know.'

15

'I know.' She grabbed his elbow and nudged him back towards the door. 'Well, thank you for that, Harris. It confirms that I have no sensation in my nose at all, which will be useful evidence to put to my employers tomorrow.'

'You know what's good for colds?' He popped his head round the door as she began to close it on him.

'Enlighten me.'

'Sex,' he said without blinking.

'Sex?'

'It's all the sweating you do. One of the extras on *Casualty* had a stinking cold when we were filming the accident scene. We did it over three days. She said—'

'Good night, Harris. Thank you for your concern.'

She shut the door firmly, leaned back against it, and drew in a noseful of lemony fresh air. She remained unstimulated. She gazed fondly at her new candelabra. At some point, she would go back to the shop and buy candles to go in it too, but there were lots of bits sticking out to put them in, and money was tighter than she was admitting. There was still the unpaid phone bill to contemplate. She wandered over to the piano and gently shut the lid over the keys. She would return to *South Pacific* tomorrow evening, perhaps with a little less gusto. She supposed she was being ambitious expecting the neighbours to put up with her playing. They were small flats, after all, in a row of terraced houses. Just like any part of suburban London, there wasn't much chance to get away from the noise.

She dragged herself through into the kitchen. Didn't they say 'Feed a cold, starve a fever?' She was still hungry. She yanked open the fridge door and squatted while she assessed the contents. A half-drunk bottle of South African white, a foil container with the left-over sag aloo from Sunday, a jar of pizza topping, some mature cheddar cheese, four wilted spring onions. She frowned and

16

worked her way along the shelf in the door. Tahini? Ah yes, from the night she'd made hummus and eaten so much of it she'd never been able to face it since. Some char siu sauce, chilli sambol, wholegrain mustard, mayonnaise and American blue-cheese dressing. And there was something with Paul Newman's head on it that she'd bought and hadn't known what to do with.

She tutted, pulled out the mature cheddar, and took a bite out of the side. Today may have been the first day of the rest of her life, but there was always tomorrow. Then she would wow them at work, and what's more, go to the supermarket and buy some things that she could actually eat. And all this she would do in a skirt that was visible below the line of her jumper. She was in too good a mood to write to Jon tonight. Tomorrow she'd flash off the letter without a second thought.

She smiled to herself, flicked the kitchen radio on to Classic FM and waltzed around until she was exhausted and knew she would sleep like a baby.

Chapter Two

'We've got to let you go, Louise.'

'Oh no, Andrew, you can't mean it!' Louise followed Andrew around the table in the middle of the office, the lurex bobbles of her plastic antennae bouncing in front of her eyes. 'I'm committed. I'm sorry. I'm here, aren't I? Jez, talk some sense into Andrew, will you?'

Jez cleared his throat nervously and looked down at the brochure he was flicking through on his lap as he lolled in his chair. Louise could tell he was agitated.

'I can't believe you'd do this to me without any warning!' Louise turned back to Andrew, who had paused on the opposite side of the table to rearrange his tie and deliver his most managerial glare. 'It's just because you saw me in Flickers yesterday, isn't it?'

Andrew didn't answer, but raised his eyebrows.

'Listen,' she went on. 'I've still got the most horrible cold, but even so I tried to get out yesterday and do something positive for Party Animals. I bought this skirt.' She waved her hips at them. It was modest enough, in a demin-and-press-studs kind of way. And they'd never told her to be formal. 'I was checking out the range in Flickers when Andrew walked in, Jez. You've got to believe me. I'm really thinking myself into my role here. I even bought these on the way to work.' She wiggled her antennae. 'Guys, you must understand. I shouldn't even be here today. You should see my tongue.'

She opened her mouth wide and threw back her head to give them a good view. Jez cleared his throat again. She could hear the pages of the brochure flicking at alarming speed.

'Stop it, Louise,' Andrew said in a cutting voice. She looked at him appealingly. He reached down to tuck his ample shirt into his less-than-ample waistband. 'It's no good getting remorseful now. We've been thinking about letting you go for a while. Yesterday just helped us to make up our minds.'

'Please don't fire me.' Louise abandoned her physical pursuit of Andrew and sank back against the wall. Suddenly, the lurex antennae didn't seem like such a good idea. She removed them carefully, letting out a small squeak as a strand of hair wound itself around the plastic hairband. 'I mean it. Please don't. I know I haven't been an ideal project manager, but things are different now. I really want to make something of this job.'

Andrew gave her an unimpressed look.

'If you fire me, I won't even be able to sign on. Can't you at least give me notice so that I can find another job? A month?' Jez looked over his brochure at Andrew. His eyes were sympathetic. He kept silent. That was the way it usually worked. Andrew was the bombastic one. Jez was the quiet one. When it came to nasty, management business, like firing unreliable employees, it would be up to Andrew to make the pronouncement. Louise sighed and dangled her antennae from her fingertips.

'I'm sorry, Louise,' Andrew said, holding out his hands as if he was trying to persuade a psychopath to give him the gun. 'It's not just the way you've done the job. It's to do with our turnover as well. Things aren't going brilliantly.'

'That's an understatement,' Jez murmured, dropping his eyes back to his lap.

'Okay, things are awful. The bank's going to call in the loan unless we come up with something drastic.'

There was an uncomfortable pause.

'I'm with you so far,' Louise said. 'Firing me is drastic. For me, anyway.'

'It's not just that.' Andrew fiddled with his waistband again. Louise was tempted to observe that if he'd taken a reduction in his own salary and cut down on his consumption of Double Whoppers there might just be more funds to go round. She watched him brush back his hair in agitation. And to think she'd almost seen him as attractive in a big, burly, rugby-playing sort of way, and had even called his hair strawberry blond. It was clear now. He was fat and ginger. Andrew glanced at Jez, who obviously wasn't going to help.

'What is it?' Louise asked, standing up straight again. 'There's something you're not telling me. It's not just my salary, is it?'

'Spit it out, Andrew,' Jez said under his breath.

'We're going back to Cambridge.' Andrew put his head back to look down his nose and four of his chins disappeared. 'We should have stayed there in the first place. London isn't right for our type of business. We know the demand in Cambridge, and we've already discussed it with the bank. So that's all there is to it. There won't be a need for a project manager there.'

'Oh,' Louise said.

'We can't afford the overheads here. We're going to rent a house in Cambridge and run the business from the ground floor.'

'Oh. I see.'

'It makes perfect sense.'

'Yes, it does.' Louise blew out slowly and meandered over to the bin. She dropped the antennae and heard an empty clink as they hit the bottom. 'Well, I'm sorry about that. For you guys, I mean. No doubt you've been worried about this for a while.'

Jez looked up. He blinked at her.

'I mean, I can see your point.' She sat on the window-ledge and gazed across the tiny room. It was piled high with rubbish. Paperwork was balanced on boxes of coloured lights, champagne glasses, party balloons by the hundred. There seemed little point in arguing.

'Well, it's good of you to take it so well.' Andrew dropped his four chins back into place. 'It never really worked between us, did it?'

She shot him a direct glance, and his cheeks coloured.

'I just meant—'

'I know what you meant.' She smiled at him. 'But all I'm asking is that you make me redundant. If you fire me I'll find getting another job almost impossible. And I won't have anything to fall back on until I do. Just let me go nicely, if you would, and give me a reference when I need one. Then we'll all part on good terms, won't we?'

'Sounds fair enough.' Jez looked at Andrew again. Andrew bristled, squashed his shirt into his waistband again, and sniffed.

'I don't want it to rebound on us if I write you a reference,' he said.

'How could it? You don't have to tell any lies. Just say you've let me go because you're relocating. That's true, isn't it?'

'Yep,' Jez said, holding Andrew's eye with his. 'That's what we'll do. It's fair enough, Andrew. Being fair is part of good management, isn't it?'

'I'm not sure if we have to do this, legally, I mean,' Andrew said.

'I'm not sure if you can let me go without any notice, legally, I mean,' she replied as pleasantly as possible.

'I don't confuse the professional and the personal,' Andrew said, his breast rising. 'I'm a shark when it comes to the boardroom, and saving this company means making ruthless decisions.'

21

Louise wanted to fall over with exasperation. She could have pointed out to Andrew that nobody knew what he was like in a boardroom seeing as he'd never set foot inside one, but it wouldn't help her to achieve her objective. Let him think he was a shark, even if she saw him more as a whale.

'Just give me a break, and write me a decent reference when I need it.' She eyed him firmly. 'Please?'

Andrew looked from her to Jez, who had his eyebrows raised.

'Louise,' Jez said, blushing and laying the brochure down on the desk. 'It's really nothing personal. You've been really great with the clients. You're good with people. They liked you. C'mon, Andrew, you've said so yourself loads of times.'

'Not so good at timekeeping,' Andrew muttered.

'Nonetheless, I'm sure if you find the right niche there'll be no stopping you. And a good reference will help you no end.' He turned his eyes back to Andrew, who chewed his cheek, but the matter was decided.

After she had collected her belongings and shoved them into a plastic bag, Louise wandered away down the corridor with the half-empty bag swinging against her legs. She couldn't even storm out. Jez was too nice to be rude to, if he was a bit of a wimp, and she needed Andrew on her side. She heard the door to the Party Animals office open and close behind her. Heavy footsteps followed her down the corridor. She stopped and turned round. It was Andrew, looking ruddy faced, his blue eyes bright.

'Listen, Louise, about all that.'

'Yes?' She gave him a brittle smile.

'Er, I don't want you to think . . . you know.'

'What?'

'It's just . . .' He took her arm and pulled her gently to the side of the corridor. As nobody was in sight it seemed a

22

little strange, but she allowed herself to be repositioned. 'You know, about us. It was nothing to do with anything. It's just that we're going to Cambridge.'

She nodded, and waited for him to go on. He seemed to have stopped. She found her voice.

'I'm not quite sure what you want me to say. I didn't think for one minute that it had anything to do with anything at all, other than your bank balance.'

'Good.' He searched her face, and seemed happy that she was being straightforward. 'Good, that's fine then. I didn't want there to be any bad feelings. That's why I was a little overbearing in there. In front of Jez, you know. I didn't want him to know anything.'

'Anything about what?' She widened her eyes.

'Right.' He squared his shoulders. 'Great. I see you understand. I wouldn't want Jez to doubt my professional integrity. It's, um . . . You know, getting involved with employees, and all that.'

'Don't worry,' she reassured him. 'I'm sure Jez has the utmost respect for your professionalism.'

He watched her carefully. She fixed a smile in place.

'Yep, I'm sure you're right.' He relaxed. 'Jez has always admired me, I know that. He expects me to be the tough one. But it's not always that easy. I'm a big softy underneath this iron exterior, you know.'

Louise wondered how she could ever have thought that being squashed by him might be quite nice. She maintained her smile until her cheek muscles began to ache. Flattering men was not the first thing that had popped up on her agenda that morning, but it was practical.

'It's no problem, Andrew. I wish you both luck in Cambridge. I'll keep checking the FT. I'm sure I'll be buying shares in you one day.'

'Yep.' Andrew's eyes acquired a glazed, happy look.

23

'That's the way I want things to be. Once we're big enough to expand.'

'Oh, you'll get even bigger, don't worry about it.' She patted his stomach affectionately and turned back on her way. It wasn't until she was halfway down the stairs that she heard the door back into the Party Animals office swing shut.

'Ah, Louise! How are you?'

Louise wasn't sure if being recognised on sight by the senior consultant in her old temping agency was an insult or a compliment, but she seated herself comfortably and prepared a willing smile.

'I'm really well, Judy. And how are you?'

'Hmmn. Okay.' Judy was already at the computer keys. Louise had prepared a speech, but for the moment she kept it to herself. Judy tutted through pursed lips as she scrolled through the screen. Every so often she stopped to make a noise as if she was deep in thought.

'Hi, Louise!' A young woman she recognised, with small eyes and a big nose, danced past, grinning. 'Still on the hoof then?'

'Well no, actually, it's been over a year since you set me up with a job. Don't you remember?'

'Oh right. A year, was it? That was good going.' She grinned again and disappeared.

'*Over* a year!' Louise asserted to the empty space she had occupied. She turned her attention back to Judy.

'The problem is . . .' Judy began, her eyes on the screen. 'That . . .'

'They're relocating. Party Animals, that is. It's not my fault.'

'Hmmn?'

'They said I was really good with people. The clients loved me.'

24

Judy raised middle-aged eyes from her computer screen and dropped them on Louise. It was like being sized up by a teacher from the grammar school where she and Sally had been classmates. Whatever she'd claimed, they'd always known her better than she knew herself. She resigned herself to the truth.

'It's your record, Louise. We have our own reputation to think of. It's no good us sending a temp if we have to send another one in her place in a matter of days. Do you see my point?'

'Yes,' Louise considered carefully. 'But I'm older now. I'm thirty-two, you see, and my attitude to so many things has changed. I really do want a chance in a proper job now.' A vision of her phone bill tangoed through her brain. 'And I'd like that chance as soon as possible.'

'Let's see. Drunk on reception, timekeeping, time-keeping,' Judy heartlessly read from her screen. 'Insolence to the managing director?' She looked at Louise quizzically. 'What on earth happened there?'

'She accused me of fondling her husband's bottom at the Christmas party.' Louise was defensive. 'She was completely wrong.'

'Ah.' Judy looked sympathetic.

'It was her son's bottom I fondled.'

Judy rested a level gaze on her.

'Not an inspired idea.'

'I was drunk.'

'Ditto.'

'Look, is there any chance for me here or not? I'm so broke it would make you cry if you knew the whole story.'

'This is just the attitude that causes you problems.' For a moment Louise thought that Judy looked motherly. 'You need to sort out your priorities. You *are* good with people, but you're too chaotic.'

'Not any more.' Louise sat up efficiently. 'I've made

some important decisions about my life, and from now on, nothing's going to take me by surprise. And once I've made a decision, then, well, that's it.' She nodded affirmatively.

Judy tapped her pen. There was a pause while she nibbled on her lip. Then she smiled, revealing that she had coated her front teeth with lipstick.

'All right, Louise, because I like you I'll probably be fired myself for this, but I'll give you another chance.'

'You will?' Now she seemed more motherly than ever. It made Louise want to hug her own mother too. She'd ring her soon and see how she was.

'I'll put you on the books and let you know as soon as something comes up. You're a fast typist, good admin skills, and yes, I have to admit, among your mis-demeanours you have managed to impress a few people with your communication skills.'

'Judy, you rock!' Louise stood up and grabbed the older woman in a hug. 'I don't suppose you could find me something that's just a tiny bit creative too?'

'I'll see what I can do. But don't expect it to be tomorrow.'

That was fine, Louise thought at home that evening. It meant she could kill off her remaining germs with a snifter of brandy without worrying about having a hangover the next day. And a glass or two of brandy was helping her to compose the perfect letter to Jon.

She'd seated herself in the kitchen, wrapped up in a big red jumper and a pair of jeans to fight off the arrival of winter. The flat was supposed to be centrally heated, but the boiler never really worked up enough steam to be convincing. She had stuck the radio on in the background, and after a quick boogie around the kitchen, glass in one hand, Ultra-Low in the other, was just in the mood to clarify her feelings. She'd slapped a writing pad, envelopes and a booklet of stamps on to her kitchen table to make sure she went through the whole process. And she'd exhumed her Filofax from underneath a pile of bills and magazines to make sure she'd get his postcode spot on.

'Dear Jon,' she began, and stopped to giggle. She pulled a straight face, took another sip of brandy and tried to continue. She wrote another line, and stretched back in her chair. She could remember the very first time she'd seen Jon.

She and Sally had lurched into the Punch and Judy in Covent Garden after work. She'd stood next to him to order drinks for them both, and he'd turned round lazily to assess her. They'd caught eyes. She'd looked away, her pulse thumping, her skin glowing. It had been a lust-at-first-sight moment, and she'd known, from the way his pupils had widened when he'd seen her, that it had been mutual.

Sally had looked sophisticated in the sexy-librarian-about-to-rip-her-glasses-off-and-shake-down-her-hair way, a view which annoyed her intensely, but didn't stop every man around her following it through in their imaginations. Louise had been dressed in the house style of Party Animals, as they'd politely requested since she'd worked there. Wacky-smart-casual. She'd never quite got to grips with what wacky-smart-casual really was. She'd produced various combinations of suits, multicoloured tights, lurex and elegant black court shoes. On the night she'd met Jon she'd been in a red Lycra dress with additional purple streaks in her hair which Andrew and Jez had said were going a bit too far. Jon hadn't minded. After all, he'd said it was all in her eyes. Come-to-bed eyes, he'd said, in a husky, come-to-bed-*with-me* sort of voice. It had melted her knees into pools of water. Of course, they hadn't that night. He'd asked her out for a drink the following Friday, and they *had* that night. That had been the beginning.

Louise stood up and paced around her kitchen. Maybe, just maybe, he might be wondering if she would phone. After all, did men these days want to do all the running? Or not? Who knew? She lit another cigarette, downed another glass of brandy, and before she knew it was yanking the phone through from the bedroom on its extended lead and pressing out Jon's number.

As soon as it began to ring, she froze in horror at her own actions.

'My God!' she whispered to herself. 'What am I doing?'

She was entering the Glenn Close school of spurned women. Jon had asked for space. But he could have been lying. She was drunk. She didn't care. After several rings he picked up the phone. She gulped.

'Hi,' she breathed at him. 'It's me. How's life?'

'Kelly! I was wondering where you'd got to!'

It could have been the result of her cold, the brandy and the cigarettes that had fatefully disguised her voice. It didn't have to be that he'd completely forgotten who she was.

'No, it's Louise.'

'God, Louise, I'm sorry. I'm expecting Kelly to ring about a customer. She's got some details that I need.'

'I bet she has.'

'What is it you wanted?'

Louise thought for a moment. What did she want? Right now she wanted to dig his heart out with a frozen chicken drumstick. It was a sign.

'Just to tell you that it's completely over. Whatever we had. Which wasn't anything. So I don't expect either of us will notice, will we?'

There was a long pause. He was probably stabbing at the buttons of his electronic personal organiser so that he could get on to Kelly the moment she rang off. She heard him exhale.

'Louise? Are you sure about this? I didn't exactly say that I wanted us to finish.'

'Piss off,' she said and hung up.

As soon as she'd put the phone down she thought of a string of fine insults that she could have thrown his way. She hopped across the kitchen and returned to her letter with renewed enthusiasm. Once she'd finished it, she dribbled another measure of brandy into her glass and drank it. Drinking a lot of brandy suddenly seemed like a very good idea.

Then she flicked through her battered Filofax to find his address. Other names and addresses jumped out at her like old photographs.

'Lenny!' she breathed in wonder.

What had been wrong with Lenny? She chewed the end of her pen and tried to remember. He was a flirt, yes. A big flirt. But compared to Jon, he'd been a saint. She thumbed through more names. Some sent an electric bolt of shock through her. She hadn't, had she? But she had, it was just that she'd forgotten. She continued her survey, and after another fortifying glass of brandy decided that she'd write to Lenny the disc jockey and Giles the accountant too while she was at it. Well, she was single now, wasn't she? What did it matter if she reunited with a couple of old flames? And just to make sure she didn't change her mind about any of it, she decided she would go out and post the letters right now.

As she stomped out to the post-box in her boots and overcoat, her breath coming in vicious rasps, she couldn't help wishing that her last words to her boyfriend of nearly a year and a half hadn't been 'piss off'. In her letter to Lenny, she'd apologised that her last statement to him had been, 'And if you impale yourself on your stunted little microphone, I'll laugh.' With Giles she had been more succinct. 'Get out of my life, arsehole.' Perhaps in another two years, after another cyclical failure, she'd be lurching out to post a letter to Jon. 'I'm sorry I told you to piss off. I was drunk. I wasn't myself.'

'Oh no, no, no.' She jammed the letters into the box and zigzagged back to her flat.

She paused for breath in the hall before she put her keys into her flat door. She gazed up the stairs. There were muted sounds coming from Harris's flat.

Instinctively she climbed up the stairs and stood outside his door. She pulled off her gloves and rapped sharply.

He opened it an inch. His eyebrows shot up at the sight of her.

'Hi!' she hiccuped at him. 'Can you turn the music down, please?'

'It's really low already, Louise. It can't be disturbing you, can it?'

'Oh, okay. Then shall I turn mine down?'

'I can't hear anything.'

'So, um. Do you want to borrow some bubble bath?'

She gave him a lopsided smile. Just why she had floated up the stairs and decided to pester him right now she wasn't exactly sure, but it was probably associated with drinking half a bottle of brandy. The word 'rebound' shot into her mind and shot out again. She batted her eyelashes at him.

'Louise . . .' Harris slipped outside on to the landing and pulled the door to behind him. She realised that he was wearing nothing but a towel. His chest was damp. And very hairy. She stared at it fixedly.

'Louise, shall we talk about this tomorrow?'

'That's a nice chest you've got there.'

'Now's not a brilliant time.'

'Nice amount of hair. A sprinkling, but not shag-pile. If

30

you see what I mean.' She slapped her hand over her mouth and giggled. 'Ooops, I said—'

'Look, why don't I pop down to see you tomorrow night?' He smiled, but he looked tense. He was hopping from one foot to the other as if he needed the loo. She raised a finger at him in understanding.

''Snot a problem, Harris. I'll just go away again. Tomorrow will do fine.'

'It's just that—'

'Big Boy?' a female voice called from inside his flat. Louise frowned and then hiccuped again, but it came out as a belch.

'Oh, I see.' She tapped the side of her nose. 'You've got company, Big Boy.'

'Yes! It's, er, an old friend.' He seemed happy that she'd worked it out, whilst still in some sort of pain. She turned to go, then glanced over her shoulder.

'Big Boy? Is that your real name? Does that mean that Harris is only a stage name?'

'Bugger off, Louise.'

'Blimey. Must be an old friend.' She stood to attention, then began her descent of the stairs. 'I know where I'm not wanted. Never mind.'

'We just have some catching up to do.'

'Of course you do.' She nodded at him understandingly, maintaining a fixed smile as he slunk back into his flat and closed the door. She was grateful that he'd disappeared before she fell down the last two steps. She lay in a heap in the hall and wondered what she should do next. She should go to bed, of course.

She let herself into her flat, threw off her coat and headed straight for the bathroom. She didn't even want to stop to peruse the bottle of brandy on the kitchen table. Her surreal state confirmed that she'd worked herself through most of it without the need to produce a ruler.

31

She pushed her way into the bathroom and started to hum. She fumbled with her pot from Corfu and tried to extricate her toothbrush. Being single was great. She could join a club. Or something. She was a free agent. Maybe she could even live her life like Harris did. She paused to chew on the bristles of her toothbrush and glance up at the ceiling. Perhaps the idea of his oozing testosterone would be just as appealing when she'd sobered up. And Sally would get fed up with Fergus at some point, and they could go out and do some serious flirting. Or something. She looked devastatingly attractive tonight, she assured her own reflection in the bathroom mirror. Her normally blue eyes were a little pink, and the blonde hair was somewhat flyaway, but the raw material must be there. Hadn't Jon fancied her once? And Harris? And maybe even Andrew? And a few others? She couldn't be that repulsive. She wouldn't be alone for long. Oh no.

She sat on the side of the bath and gazed around contentedly. Her eyes fell on a stock of Tampax under the sink. She chewed harder on the bristles. She was late, yes. Quite late. But not that late.

She did a fuddled calculation. Actually, she was that late. She stood up and fiddled around in the plastic biscuit tin she used for embarrassing medical supplies. If she wasn't deluding herself she had half of a test left somewhere. It would just clear things up. She pulled out the box, and from it a plastic wand wrapped in foil. She tried to concentrate. The effect of the brandy was definitely peaking. Ah, yes. She knew what she had to do next.

After she'd managed to aim almost straight, she put the wand on the edge of the bath and continued with her ablutions. It was difficult not to sing when she was in such a good mood. And, as usual when she was poleaxed, the songs of the musicals her mother had taught her at the piano were the first to spring to mind.

She picked up the wand from the side of the bath and examined it carefully. Then she threw it in the bin under the sink with relief. She yawned at herself and rolled out several yards of dental floss. She made a cat's cradle with it while she sang the opening lines to 'Getting to Know You'. Then she remembered she was supposed to be doing something with her teeth. As she flicked the cotton strand in and out of her mouth and tried to hum at the same time, a thought occurred to her.

'Blue line, good; no line, bad. No, hang on – no line, good; blue line, bad.'

She stared at her flushed face in the mirror, a knotted mass of dental floss hanging from her front teeth.

'What was it again?'

She dropped to her knees and pulled the instructions on the box out of the bin. She read them aloud, this time with forced concentration.

'No line, good; blue line, bad.'

She retrieved the plastic wand from the bin.

'Oh shit.'

There could be no doubt about it. She was pregnant.

Chapter Three

'God, Louise. You look a bit odd.'

Louise opened her front door for Sally Birlington, her best friend since she was eight, and gave her a withering look.

'What did you expect, Sal? I've got a streaming cold and I'm three and a half weeks pregnant.'

'Blimey. I still can't believe it.' Sally pulled her jacket lapels together in front of a thin silk blouse as they wandered into the flat together. She stopped in the living room, her chin dropping.

'What the hell is that?'

'What?'

Sally gave Louise an ironic look and pointed at the candelabra.

'That.'

'Oh, it doesn't matter any more. It was only an idea anyway. Come through.'

'You're going to have to stop impulse buying, Lou. You know you always get it wrong. And it's chilly in here. You've got to keep warm, you know. I'll put the kettle on for you. You go and put your feet up.'

'Well, if you will walk around in evening wear in November, of course you'll be chilly.'

'What, this?' Sally plucked at her blouse. 'I have to look the part.'

'I know, ignore me. I'm just jealous.'

'Tea's what we need.'

Sally flashed a smile and took charge of the kettle,

leaving Louise standing pointlessly in the middle of the kitchen. She'd changed into her daisy leggings, a roll-necked jumper and thick socks since her visit to the doctor, and twisted her hair up into a topknot. Next to Sally she felt like a Teletubby.

'So tell me all the gory details.' Sally fumbled around in the washing-up bowl for mugs, pausing just to inch up her sleeves. She ran the mugs under the tap and frowned as she tried to find a clean tea cloth.

'I'm really grateful you rushed round, Sal. You'd better not stay long, though. You don't want to get into trouble at work.'

'Hey, I'm a partner now, remember? I can fiddle my timetable if I want.'

'Oh yes.' Louise shuffled around in her socks, un-decided about whether to sit down or not. It was funny that since this had been confirmed, she had lost all capacity to make decisions. She felt as if her thought processes had left her head and were zooming around with the clouds earning air miles. She remembered that Sally would think she was a disaster area. Sally, who had done law at King's, way back then when she herself was dawdling through the biological science degree she hated. Sally, who had gone to university at eighteen, ginger and unexceptional, had apparently literally worked her freckles off and come out the other side stunningly beautiful, while Louise had sped in and out of Leicester in a revolving door. Sally, who was now a solicitor. A very good one. A partner, in fact. Sally, who at school had worn a brace and red hair in bunches, but now had perfect teeth and hair clamped in a delicious auburn ponytail by a stylish gold clasp. In a figure-hugging suit and neat heels, she looked fantastic. Louise suddenly wished that she hadn't rung Sally up and begged her to rush round.

'What did Jon say? Is he coming round? I don't want to

35

be here when he arrives. You'll have so much to talk to him about.'

'I haven't told Jon yet.'

Sally raised an eyebrow, wiped the mugs, and set them next to the kettle.

'I tell you what, Louise. After all these years I swore you'd lost the ability to surprise me, but you've gone and done it again. It's just so . . . amazing.'

Louise decided to sit down before she fell down. Sally said 'amazing' in the way she might if Monsoon were selling off their stock at an eighth of the price. She pulled the long strands of her fringe out of her face and tried to hook them behind her ears.

'I just can't believe it! How can I be pregnant? I don't feel any different. It was only because I did a test, just on spec, you know, to reassure myself. If I hadn't done the test, I wouldn't be pregnant at all.'

Sally slid herself into a chair and gave Louise a funny look.

'How did you feel when that thin blue line actually appeared?'

'That's the thing, Sal.' Louise shook her head, stunned. 'Up until now, I swore those bloody things didn't work. It's the first time I've ever had value for money from a home-testing kit.'

'Can I see it?'

Louise struggled up, trotted out to her bathroom, and picked up the wand from the sink where she had left it. She placed it on the table in front of Sally's glowing amber eyes. The blue line was more blurred than it had been when she'd first realised it was there, but it was still, undoubtedly, there. Louise's first instinct had been to Tippex it out, but a modicum of logic had told her it wouldn't change things.

'Wow,' Sally breathed. 'It really is true, then.'

'Yep.' Louise threw her hands in the air. 'But God Almighty, Sal, I feel exactly the same. Not sick, or hungry, or fat, or any of those things.'

'Shit.'

'Exactly. So what I want to know is, why have women been lying to us all these years? They always say you know when it happens. But you don't know. It's a lie. Take it from me.'

'Perhaps you know the second time.'

'How?'

'By the fact that you don't know. If your period's late, and you feel completely normal, you know you're pregnant. That must be it.'

Louise paused to wonder what feeling completely normal was like but didn't dwell on it for too long.

'I only felt a bit tired. And once, a week or so ago, I felt dizzy but I thought that was just my hangover.' Sally blinked at Louise. 'I'd been out with Jon the night before and drunk more than I ought to have done. He spent the whole night eyeing up a woman with much bigger breasts than me. It was when the thought occurred to him that he needed space.'

'Ah, I see.' Sally turned her attention back to the blue line. 'And the doctor says it's definite.'

'Absolutely.'

'So now what?'

Louise sat back in her chair feeling hot and cold again. When she didn't answer the question, Sally got up and made them both tea, sniffing at the milk and pulling a face before slopping a millimetre into the mugs. She delivered Louise a mug, and looked down at her with a sympathetic expression.

'You are going to have to tell Jon. You know that, don't you?'

'Of course I do. He's got to know.'

'And what about your mum? Have you told her?'

'Mum?' Louise gazed at Sally. 'I can't tell Mum. It's only just over a year since Dad died. She's too wrapped up in her own problems at the moment. I'm not likely to see her for a while anyway, and by that time I'll have done something about it.'

But how was she not going to tell her mother? The thought flipped through her mind. It backflipped again. She just wouldn't. She left the thought doing acrobatics inside her head and concentrated on Sally who was pouting her lips as if she was trying to form a tricky question.

'What *are* you going to do about it, Lou?'

Louise grabbed at her mug and sipped the tea. Time passed while fireworks continued to explode in her head. Sally was still watching her when she put her mug down and looked up. Sally was a loyal, wonderful friend. She and Sally had their differences. In fact, they hadn't got anything in common, but maybe that was why they'd remained friends. What they usually did was each try very hard to understand what the other was doing, even if she privately thought it was insane. But now, for the first time, Louise was in a situation that Sally couldn't understand even if she strained until she went purple. Only someone who'd never found herself pregnant could ask somebody else who just had what she was going to do about it.

'God, I don't know what I'm going to do, Sally. It's the most incredible, appalling, unbelievable, unearthly thing that has ever happened to me in my whole life!' She stood up and flapped her hands in the air.

'I'm thirty-two! If there was ever going to be a mistake, why would it happen now? Why not earlier? Why should it wait this long to present itself, just when I'd persuaded myself that my ovaries had shrivelled up into walnuts after years of wasted effort? All I can say is that I feel surreal, I feel cosmic, I feel . . .' She ran out of adjectives.

Sally patted her wrist. Louise stiffened for a moment. It was so long since she and Sally had bothered to touch each other, it was a strange feeling. But she allowed herself to be pulled into her friend's arms.

'You've got to wash your hair before you see Jon,' Sally said cautiously. 'You don't want to look like a disaster area when you deliver a piece of news like this, do you?'

Louise thought about it all again as the hot-water tank emptied into the bath, filling the room with steam. She plopped into the water full of tangerine essence and lay there. She had rung Jon at work, surprising him immensely judging by the minor falsetto in his voice. She told him she wanted to meet him. She didn't say why but had been so firm that he'd agreed. She'd suggested a pub in Kensington where they sometimes met after work. It was neutral territory, and it would do.

What she would say when she got there was another thing. How did one announce something like this? With fanfares? If her old upright piano was more portable, she could wheel it over to the pub with her and sing him her news. Something like 'I'm just a girl who can't say no'. Maybe strings would be more soulful. A lone cellist hacking out Elgar's Cello Concerto in E Minor as Jon wept into his beer. Or perhaps she should approach the whole thing with a little more aggression. The LSO crashing out Tchaikovsky's '1812', complete with firing cannons. That would be symbolic. Then she could make an oblique announcement in time to the blasts. 'Jon, you know your cannon? Well, the good news is that it's loaded.'

Whatever she said, he would have to deal with the same volcano of reaction as she was. But let him erupt too. Then, when she had sent him away to distribute molten lava all over East Putney, she could get on with deciding what the hell she was going to do.

She wallowed in the water for another ten minutes, her hands laid over her stomach. It wasn't until she tried to sit up that she realised that she had put her hands on her stomach. She squeezed the flesh there. It wasn't bulging, wobbling, growing, or any of the things she had imagined it might be. It was just her tummy, sitting there, being a tummy. And yet, underneath all that pointless flesh was a little hive of activity, stirring itself, becoming something.

She threw herself out of the bath in a panic and attacked her body roughly with a towel. She rubbed the steamy mirror and peered at herself in the clear space. It was odd that at the only time in her life when an independent jury would declare that she had finally produced some evidence of being grown-up, the face that stared back at her in the mirror was that of a girl.

Half an hour of make-up application later, she no longer looked quite so girlish. As she fled through the hall on her way out, she heard Harris thundering down the stairs. His arms were outstretched in a welcoming fashion, his eyes were flashing, and she was nearly knocked sideways by the stench of cologne. She glanced around in confusion before she realised with a shock that he was actually heading for *her*. And he was wearing leather trousers.

'Not now, Harris,' she said, letting herself out of the front door.

Jon was already in the Churchill Arms when she arrived. She paused at the door, allowing a handful of glamorous men and women to laugh their way past, and looked at his back. He was leaning on the bar, and had already ordered himself a pint.

He looked gorgeous from behind. Broad-shouldered and dashing in a charcoal-grey wool suit that was dull

40

beneath the tawny streaks of his hair. She could almost feel the soft, bluntly cut ends on her fingertips as they glowed under the muted red lighting of the bar. He was nicely built. Slim, but tall, and elegant. Full of promise. And look where it had got them both. But she had to deal with this maturely. She stuck her tongue out at his back and made her way over to the bar. She ordered herself a drink and paid for it, only realising as she put her purse away that she hadn't bothered to say hello first. She turned to find Jon giving her a curious look.

It hadn't occurred to her to plan everything in advance, including instructions for her facial muscles. Whenever she met Jon, she always, always, broke into a bright smile. That had been the persuasive instinct in her. 'We *are* going to have a fantastic time tonight, Jon, and aren't you pleased that you chose to spend it with *me*!' But this evening, she just stared at him, because she felt a strange tug inside that had nothing to do with lust. It was something to do with union. It was very, very odd. Jon shifted his elbow on the bar beside her to look at her properly. She blinked back into his eyes. Lovely eyes. A sort of dark tawny shade with little brown flecks. Would the baby have them too? But he was talking to her.

'You look nice tonight. You've got a good colour. You must be keeping yourself well.'

There was no answer to that. Instead she said, 'Shall we go and sit down?'

'Sure.'

He seemed very calm considering that she'd told him to piss off less than twenty-four hours ago. She wondered why as they walked through to the back of the pub, finding a seat to one side in an area surrounded by framed mounts of exotic butterflies. She sat down and shrugged her thick coat on to the back of her chair, pulling at her jumper to reveal her shape. She wanted to remind him that she was a woman. Not that he'd be in doubt for much longer. He settled himself down, pulled out his cigarettes, and offered her one.

'Er, I'm not sure.' He shrugged, and took one for himself. 'No, I will have one,' she said, taking one from the box.

He held out his lighter for her, but she delved into her bag and found her own, not looking at him. She blew a plume of smoke away from them, and rested her hand around her glass. For the moment it was nice just to sit away from the bustle of the bar, to feel warm, to gaze at the pinned-down dead things on the walls. Jon sipped at his beer, settled himself again, crossed a long leg, and waited. She shouldn't really be smoking, she mused. But then again, she shouldn't really be pregnant either. She realised that Jon was watching her and swivelled her eyes to look at him.

'So, Jon,' she began, leaning forward. 'Last night I said we were finished.'

'I remember.' He raised an eyebrow. He almost smiled, but he didn't. He looked far too calm to be told that he was a father. Even if only for a week or two, she qualified quickly in her head, thoughts see-sawing.

'Didn't you go to work today, then?' he continued, eyeing her faded jeans. 'I take it Andrew hasn't taken to letting you come to work in those.'

'Er, no, I didn't.' She wasn't about to tell him she was pregnant *and* jobless.

'Because of your cold?'

'That and one or two more minor problems.'

'Really?' He set his pint down.

'Hmmn. This cold's been a bummer. But it's loosening up now.' She sniffed to make the point. A glance at his face confirmed that she hadn't needed to offer him a demonstration of her cold in the loosening-up stage. Jon

42

had always been a bit funny about illness. Probably because it was something that generally happened to other people. It struck her that for the same reason he was bound to be a bit funny about pregnancy. She took a tentative drag of her cigarette.

'Should you be smoking?' he said. She shot him a startled glance. 'If you've got a bad cold. It makes it worse, you know. I always stop if I feel a bug coming on. But I've got more self-discipline than you, I suppose.'

She wanted to quip that his self-discipline obviously hadn't permeated as far as his sperm. It would be one way of telling him. She couldn't decide whether that would be better than a stark announcement. In fact, now that they were facing each other, she couldn't think of any way whatsoever to put it to him. She was on the verge of scribbling it on the beer-mat and flipping it over to his side of the table with a karate chop, when he was off again.

'So, why did you want to meet up, Louise? I guess you've got some things to say to me. Just shoot. I probably deserve it all.'

She searched his eyes. He was so charming, laconic, at ease with himself. She suddenly had the desire to put a bomb under his complacency and dive for cover.

'I'm pregnant.'

She was pleased with herself. It came out without a tremor. She sniffed again and fished around in her jacket pockets for a clean tissue. She blew her nose hard, and paused when she was out of breath. Then she settled again, and looked at him. He had stopped with his glass halfway to his mouth. If it wasn't for his cigarette burning away unsmoked in the ashtray, he would look at that precise moment like one of the exotic butterflies on the wall, captured in a moment of life, pinned down, mounted and framed. She noticed that he looked a little pale. Finally he unfroze himself and drank several large mouthfuls of

43

his beer. He glanced over his shoulder several times, as if to make sure nobody had heard.

'Are you sure?' he asked eventually.

'Yep.' She wiggled her nose to try to stop it itching.

'Oh God,' he said.

Well, at least he hadn't asked her who the father was, she consoled herself as she pecked at her beer and examined the butterflies on the wall again. For a moment she could imagine Jon with his charcoal suit and spectacular brown hair spreadeagled on a background of card and hung on the wall. With exactly the expression on his face which he had now. Terrified.

'Don't get me wrong, Louise – but, are you sure who the father is?'

Ah well. She pursed her lips around her cigarette end. So far, apart from a temporary blip, it was all going as she had imagined it.

'I don't think I'm even going to answer that,' she said. 'Except to say that you always make the mistake of assuming I'm like you.'

He chewed his lip as he regarded her. His eyes mirrored guilt. But it wasn't relevant now. She hadn't brought him here to demand to know the gory details of his meanderings.

'Sorry,' he said. 'It's just that I always thought you and Andrew had a thing.'

'What?' She almost spat her cigarette across the room.

'Well, he's a handsome bloke. I assumed that's why he employed you.'

'What? Because he's handsome?'

'Because he fancied you. It's what I thought.' He gave a half-laugh. 'Well, it wasn't on account of your organisational skills, was it?'

'For God's sake, Jon, it's gross that you should assume they took me on as a bit of skirt to have around the office.'

44

They paused and looked at each other. There was no way on earth she was going to admit to him now that she'd thought Andrew fancied her too.

'So have you told Party Animals this is why you're off work?'

'I wouldn't dream of telling them about this. It's far too private.'

He puffed on his cigarette. 'So, er. How pregnant are you, Louise?'

'Completely.' She was confused by the question. His eyelids fluttered.

'No, how far gone – I mean, when did it happen?'

Perhaps he wasn't checking out her dates to see that they coincided with his, but it certainly felt like it.

'Three and a half weeks. It was the last time we had conjugal relations.'

He looked unenlightened.

'We went to the pictures in Leicester Square and back to Ealing for a curry. Is that any help?' He still looked blank. 'My name's Louise. Is that the clincher? You know, five foot eight, dark blonde hair, blue eyes, size twelve? Mother you disapprove of because she's common, sister you approve of because she's not.'

'But how, Louise? I mean, why that night?'

She stopped to count to ten. She got to ten, and went on to twenty. It was amazing that she was doing all the justifying, seeing as this was one event that demanded without fail the participation of two people.

'You knew I had come off the pill. You knew that the doctor had advised it. That's why, if you remember, we were using other methods.'

'Jesus Christ. Why the hell didn't you stay on the pill?'

'Because I did what the doctor told me to do. She said I'd been on it too long. Why the hell didn't you know how to put a condom on properly?'

45

'Pack it in, Louise.'

'No, you pack it in. I assumed you knew what you were doing. If you hadn't known you should have said so, and we both could have practised on a banana until you got the hang of it.' She sat up. 'Why don't you start saying the right things. Or is it too much to ask?'

'Like what, for God's sake? You've just blown my world apart.' He fingered back his fringe in agitation. 'I was going to tell you tonight that the bank's agreed to grant me an MBA loan. Everything's just starting for me. I can get a place next year at Cranfield, and my whole career begins properly from there. It's all kicking off, don't you see? And then you land this on me.' He shook his head at her, eyes disbelieving. 'It's just that your sense of timing is almost sadistic. If I didn't know you better, I'd think that you enjoyed telling me. Especially after last night.'

'Why?' She mouthed the question, stunned by his monologue.

'Because you knew damned well that this thing was bogging me down. I needed to be free to think about leaving London, being mobile, without any ties.'

'But you said you didn't want us to finish,' was all she could think to say.

'Shit, Louise. Of course I did. What did you expect me to say? Oh, that's good? Terrific, I was dying for you to finish with me? I didn't want to upset you, and you seemed so set on things. I wasn't going to argue with you.'

'But you did argue with me.'

'Oh, stop it, Louise. I can't get more honest than this, can I? Give me credit.'

She watched him crush his cigarette in agitation and immediately light another. The display of angst in front of her made her feel calmer. He was gorgeously handsome, his hair was still thick and touchable, and his face still arranged in a heart-stopping manner, but his body

46

language was a definite turn-off. She'd never seen him behave like this before. It made him seem very weak. She realised that by comparison it meant she was stronger than him, but that hadn't occurred to her before.

'So please explain why you rang me last night to finish, then brought me here tonight to tell me this. Why not tell me on the phone?'

'The answer to that is completely bloody obvious,' she yelled at him. 'I didn't know until today.'

And there was the letter that was going to land on his mat tomorrow, she thought, her courage buckling. And there were the letters to Lenny the disc jockey and Giles the accountant asking them to contact her with a view to sex.

'Oh my God!' she said, her hand flying to her mouth.

'Jesus, what is it now?'

She stared at him, and pulled her face back into a mask of serenity.

'Nothing.'

'I'm getting another drink. Want one?'

She nodded. While he was away, she played with her beer-mat, pulling the top layer of paper from it, and setting fire to it in the ashtray. She stopped when the barman gave her an arch look as he was collecting empty glasses. It was just then she felt in her own world at the moment. Jon returned and set a beer down for her. He took a deep breath as he sat down again. He seemed more peaceful. She wondered if he'd downed a triple whisky at the bar.

'I've just realised something,' he said in a more pleasant voice. 'I'd got you all wrong for a moment there. I'm sorry I was harsh. It's been a long day, and I was so excited about the loan. But you're obviously going to deal with it, aren't you? You wouldn't be drinking and smoking like this if you were thinking about keeping it.'

47

She sipped the froth silently from the top of her beer. Jon gave a short laugh.

'God, for a moment I thought you were going to demand marriage and security and all that crap.'

'Crap?' She raised her eyes to his.

'C'mon. You've got the same view of all that baggage as I have.' He lit another cigarette and looked at her through the smoke with one eye half-closed. It was his 'canny' look. She knew that he used it in sales. It had never worked on her. She'd fallen in love with him despite his affectations, not because of them.

'You're wrong, actually,' she said quietly. 'I would like nothing better at this moment than to know that I had someone to rely on.'

'Well, don't think I can be that person.' Then, as if regretting his abruptness, he softened momentarily. 'Look, I know I've been a bit harsh, but this has come as a real shock to me. I've told you what's happening in my life. You've got to respect that. We had some good times together – some great times – but neither of us was really committed. And certainly nothing like this was ever meant to happen.' He took a deep breath. 'I'm sorry, but if you go ahead with it, you'll be on your own. I want to make that perfectly clear.'

She paused for a moment to stub out the cigarette she had just lit.

'I didn't say I wanted to go ahead with it. All I said was that I wished I had someone to rely on.'

His shoulders slumped with relief.

'You've got Sally,' he said reassuringly. 'And your sister. She's a strong woman. She'll help you through it all. She knows what it's like to want a career without all the hassle of nappies and sick. She'll understand that you don't want it. She's never wanted kids, has she? Why should she? This is the nineties.'

48

'She has Hallam's children. They're over most week-ends.'

'But they're not hers, are they?' He leaned forward again intimately and put his hand over hers. 'And by the time she got together with Hallam, his kids were past the nappies-and-sick stage. All I'm saying is that she'll help you through it. You're not on your own, Louise. You mustn't think that you are.'

She allowed a silence to fall between them. After several minutes of turning her glass around and around, she studied the framed butterflies again. She had a vision of them throwing off their pins, bursting through the thin glass of their cases, and fluttering across the pub and out the door.

'Louise?' She looked up. 'Are you all right?'

'Of course I'm all right. Why shouldn't I be?'

'If there's anything you need, you only have to ask.'

'Like what?' She threw the question at him and waited for the answer. He was in control of himself again, she noticed. And now he thought he was being munificent.

'I know you won't want me there for the actual thing. Don't worry, I understand that. You'll probably want your mother there for you. Girls stick together at times like this, don't they?'

'Girls?' She stared at him incredulously. He seemed surprised by her ejection.

'You know what I mean. Let's not get stupid about semantics.'

'No, let's not. Here are some very sensible semantics for you. You are a selfish git, Jon, and I wish to God I'd never laid eyes on you.'

'That's not exactly fair, Louise.'

'I could sum you up in a few words. In fact I did, last night. You'll get the letter tomorrow morning. I think you might be surprised by how accurate it is.'

49

'Look, just calm down, will you? I've said I'll back you up if you want to get rid of it. What more do you want me to say?'

'Nothing,' she said, standing up and stopping to blow her nose ferociously into a tissue that was already soggy and full of holes. 'Bye then.' She picked up her coat and carefully pulled it on. She wasn't in any hurry. She was on her way out, but in her own good time.

'Is that it then? At least you'll tell me when you do it, won't you?'

'You want me to send you an itinerary so that you can hold a wheels-up party?' She shook her head at him. 'No, Jon. No information, no contact. You've just forfeited your right to any of that.'

She pulled her handbag on to her shoulder, shuddering at the thought of the cold journey home but warmed by the prospect of her big, cushion-strewn bed. She picked up her lighter and cigarettes, and walked away from Jon without looking back.

Chapter Four

'How does music publishing grab you?'

Louise flicked the switch on her radio–cassette player and T-Rex were silenced abruptly. She squashed the phone to her ear, her pulse drumming.

'Are you there, dear?'

'I'm here, Judy.'

'Thank God for that. I thought you'd fainted on me. You need to get yourself round there quickly, this afternoon to be precise. They've been left in the lurch, and it could be temp to perm. It's a good company, Louise, small but successful, and if you got yourself in the door you could be on to something. You'll have to be reliable. No time off. Definitely no sickies. Be there all day, every day and you've got a real chance. Can you smarten yourself up sharpish and show them what you're made of?'

Louise snapped up the pen she'd been doodling with. Her fingers paused over the envelope from BT which was already decorated with flowers, squiggles, zigzags, and the phrase 'Oh shit'. The nib of the biro wavered, her answer sticking in her throat. A job in music publishing? Right now, this afternoon, when she was still lurking in an emotional bomb-site? How on earth was she going to find the time and space to work out what she was going to do next? How could she take time off to deal with it?

'It's, um.' She tutted, drawing another daisy and adding another phrase to match the others, this time in large capitals.

'Louise? Isn't this exactly what you want?'

'Yes, yes it was.'

She blew her fringe out of her eyes and screwed up her face.

'Was?' Judy's voice rose. 'Don't mess me about. Yes or no. I've got at least a dozen good candidates on my books who'll leap at this.'

'Judy, it's just that . . .' Her stomach twisted itself into a double helix. 'It's only that . . . Could I start in a week or so, do you think?'

'No.'

'No chance of that at all?'

'Now or never.'

Louise played with the pen until it flipped out of her fingers and landed in the washing-up bowl.

'Yes or no, Louise.'

'Look, something's come up, it's only temporary but it means I can't work exactly right now. Another week –' She thought of what Sally had said. Sorting this out wasn't going to happen in a hurry. There were waiting lists, even for women lurking in emotional bomb-sites. '– or two and I'll know where I stand.'

'This afternoon. Yes or no.'

Judy had ceased to be motherly and became mother-in-lawly instead. Louise drew a big tulip and hatched over it. A big chance in the industry she'd love to be a part of. Not now. It couldn't happen now.

'Louise?' Judy barked.

'I'm sorry, Judy, I'm going to have to say no.'

'Right,' Judy said in a thin voice and hung up.

The Jobcentre ascended into the swirling grey and white clouds. Louise peered at it from the cocoon of her scarf. The wind was nipping at her legs, but she'd worn a skirt out of habit despite the onset of an early winter. She wiggled her toes inside her shoes. Her DMs probably would have been more practical than high heels, but she'd never been into a Jobcentre before and she wasn't sure what the dress code was. Better to look professional in a way that suggested potential. Potential that could begin in a few weeks when she'd resolved her predicament. That was the idea.

She wasn't even quite sure what she was going to do inside, but it had struck her that sitting at home writing pertinent obscenities on the backs of her bills wasn't achieving much. She needed a bit of time to sort things out, but for the moment she had no job, and no money coming in. Instinct told her that if Party Animals was in dire straits, paying her what she was owed wasn't going to be a priority. She had to find something that would start in a month, perhaps, but in the meantime, she had to sign on.

She pulled her scarf up to cover her nose and peeped over the mass of scarlet wool at the face of the building. She'd never signed on before. She'd never had to. She'd always managed to sweet-talk her way into a new opportunity the minute the door slammed on the previous one. Her father would be staring at her in bewilderment if he could see her now.

There was one other tenuous option but something inside her still rebelled against it. Rachel was always nagging her to get a proper job. She'd offered more than once to put her name forward for temping options that came up in the record company she worked for. But music was Rachel's thing. She did it brilliantly. She'd blazed her own trail in the company and was doing exactly what she loved now – talent spotting and signing.

Louise stamped her feet impatiently and gazed up at the grey and white vault above. Were they snow clouds? Not in November, surely, but they were doing a good impersonation. Rachel's office was lovely and warm. It would be nice to be sat in the corner now, sticking labels on CDs and making coffee for superstars, or whatever it was temps did there. She could picture herself batting her eyelashes and saying huskily, 'One lump or two, Jarvis?' But working in Rachel's shadow would be just like being at school in Rachel's shadow. She'd been three years above her, and Louise had been called 'Rachel's little sister' by staff until she wanted to prise their eyes out with the corner of her protractor. No, she'd find her own way to where she was going, wherever that was.

'Wing it,' she whispered into her scarf, dropping her eyes on the entrance to the building.

It was like walking into an airport lounge, without the epithet of travelling in hope attached. Long, thick overhead lights ran along the ceiling, and the warm-air vents sent a hum of background noise reverberating through the building. Somebody was saying something over an intercom. She pulled her scarf down to her neck and stopped to listen. It was like being at the supermarket. Clients were being told that there was a special offer on aisle six. She wasn't sure whether it was the clients or the jobs which were on special offer. Rows of stands littered with white cards confronted her. The faces she could see were grey, drawn and lacking in humour. And they were the staff. She wondered what she was going to tell them. Paranoia filtered through her system.

Should she say she was pregnant? Would she be allowed to sign on if she told them the truth? What if she got a job and threw up everywhere? Wasn't that what Sally had warned her about, that the feeling that nothing was happening would soon be replaced by the feeling that everything was happening? She squashed her fingers into her palms, and realised that they were cold with sweat. What if she wasn't entitled to anything at all? What if Andrew changed his mind, and pretended she'd been fired for misbehaviour when he was asked?

There was nobody to tell her what to do. Even the woman at the reception desk was too busy sorting through papers to look up. Louise wanted to hurl herself at the desk and blurt it all out, but then she might end up saying the wrong thing. The woman would look up, brush her short bob away from her chin, and tell her that she was on her own.

She walked carefully to the side of the room and took a moment to lean on the stand labelled 'Catering'. Nobody else could share this confusion with her. Not her mother, her sister or her best friend. Jon was right, Louise was on her own.

Her weight seemed to increase as she hung on to the stand. She grew colder and colder. It was several seconds before she realised that she was in the process of fainting.

'Oh blimey . . .'

The world became a mass of purple and blue blotches. For a moment, it was blissfully peaceful. If she was dying then everyone else would have to sort everything out on her behalf. She could just sink to the floor, murmuring, 'Bye, guys. Don't forget to ring BT about the late bill, will you? I'm off now.' Perhaps her father had felt like this? 'The life insurance policy's under the mattress, but thank God I'm not the one who's got to work out what it means.' The blotches turned completely black.

'Hey, you all right in there?'

Louise opened her eyes and stared up. It must be a dream. One minute she'd been standing in the Jobcentre contemplating the meaninglessness of everything she'd ever known, the next she was cradled in Ewan McGregor's lap.

If she had died, she knew for sure that this was heaven. As sensation found its way into her lips, she realised that she was smiling. She hoped he wasn't going to fade away and become her ceiling. If this wasn't death, she sure as hell didn't want it to be a dream either. It wasn't. The pale, wide eyes looking straight down into hers stayed right where they were.

'It's okay,' his voice said. 'She's come round now. I'll sit her up. Can somebody get a glass of water or something?'

'I'm not really sure. We only have a staff room. We don't supply beverages to clients.'

'Get a fucking glass of water, will you? Or do I have to do it myself? If it costs you too much in shoe leather or breaks into your time-management survey, you can put it down as "Client feigned death to get attention", can't you? Jesus Christ, forget it, I'll take her to a café.' The pale eyes looked at her, gentle again. Louise examined them in minute detail. They were the sort of mint green that ran through a set of marbles she once had, and very calm considering the force of the outburst. 'Can you stand up? I'll get you a cup of tea somewhere.'

'I think perhaps I should stay here for a minute,' she murmured. Moments like this didn't present themselves often in anybody's lifetime. She was going to make lying in Ewan McGregor's lap last as long as humanly possible.

'Okay, you just take your time.'

A sigh escaped her lips. A flicker crossed his eyes as if it was a thought. She wondered what it might have been. Time passed. He brushed a strand of hair out of her eyes and looked at her intently again. Was it possible to faint lying down after you'd only just fainted standing up? She guessed she might be about to find out.

'Do you think you could sit up now?'

'Oh, I'm not sure.'

'It's just that I'm getting cramp in my leg.'

'Oh.' She pulled a noble face. 'I'll see what I can do.'

She reluctantly dragged herself into a sitting position and looked down. Her legs were askew, her skirt ridden up to her thighs, her emerald green opaque tights displayed to the occupants of the Jobcentre right up to the gusset. There was a small crowd around her. The woman with the bob from reception seemed to have developed a nervous tic, several older men were bending over, apparently fascinated by the emerald gusset, and Ewan McGregor was on his haunches, rubbing vigorously at one of his thighs through torn jeans. Very torn, she noticed, wondering if it was a fashion statement or the result of fighting off hoards of women with long nails. She watched him rub away, bewitched, and stopped herself just before she offered to do it for him. She should stand up now. She heaved her skirt over her thighs and tipped herself on to her knees. She gave her audience a reassuring smile and made it to her feet, teetering on her heels and causing the crowd of fascinated men to stick their arms out ready to catch her. She opened her mouth to apologise, and sneezed instead. Her nose chose this moment to run uncontrollably.

'Oh hell. Hang on a sec.' She fumbled around in her pockets for a stringy tissue. The receptionist pulled a face.

'Well, if you're sure you're all right,' she concluded, glancing longingly over her shoulder at her empty chair wedged behind the safety of the reception desk. She trotted away and busied herself with a man in overalls who was waving a white card at her. Louise heard her distantly explain that there was no need to remove the cards and that she didn't know why nobody ever understood that, and looked at her assortment of older men over her tissue.

'It was kind of you to help. I'm fine, really. No breakfast. I should really eat breakfast, shouldn't I?'

'I'll take it from here,' Ewan McGregor said. The other men smiled sympathetically at Louise and dispersed slowly. Louise pinched her nose through the tissue. She groped in her pocket with her left hand and came up with the foil wrapper of a long-eaten packet of extra-strong mints. If he would go away she could fold it into a little triangle and perch it on the end of her nose until she could buy some tissues.

'Need another tissue? I've got one in here somewhere.' He began a search in the pockets of his denim jacket. He came up with a folded piece of lined paper with something scribbled in biro on the back. 'Will this do for now?'

She took it thankfully and wrapped it around her nose.

'Look, why don't I get you into a café and you can blow your nose on some loo paper. It's no wonder you felt groggy. You've got a bastard of a cold, haven't you?'

'That's right.' She sniffed as heartily as she could without making everybody around her gag and allowed herself to be quietly led from the building. The receptionist looked up, and went back to her loud explanation of something called JobClub to a middle-aged woman who was explaining equally loudly that she thought it was a bloody stupid idea.

Louise walked out into the cold air and stopped to take a deep breath through her mouth, holding the pyramid of paper firmly over her nose. She hoped the café wasn't far. She didn't want Ewan McGregor to glance at her again and find she had mucus dribbling from her chin.

'Just up here,' he said, nodding along the road.

'Right,' she puffed.

He stopped at a small café which she hadn't noticed before. It looked wonderful inside. It was bright, cheerful and very relaxed.

'You don't mind a greasy spoon, do you?'

She shook her head and followed him inside. The threat of winter vanished as she was hit by the smell of hot coffee, toast and bacon. The warmth enveloped her face. Before long it would even work its way down to her toes. A puff of steam burst from a tea urn. At the back was a doorway signposting the toilets. She wandered off in that direction, forgetting to mention that she really fancied a plate of toast as well.

In the toilet she removed the piece of paper from her nose. She could hardly give it back to him, whatever it was. She shoved it in her coat pocket instead, and blew her nose on a banner of soft pink loo paper until it felt safe to stop. She wrinkled her sore nostrils at her reflection. Her eyes were watering and her nose had a definite border of orangey-red, but she didn't look as frightening as she'd feared. She ruffled the strands of dark blonde hair that hung over her eyebrows. The Rod Stewart look, she'd joked to the hairdresser after she'd finished her experiment. The hairdresser had laughed and accepted the tip. When Louise had got home she'd put off ringing Jon until she'd found a way to pat it all down with mousse. But thank heavens it was growing out now.

Her trip to the hairdresser with the alternative sense of humour was just another occasion when she'd swallowed her feelings. Perhaps she'd done it far too often? Perhaps this was the time for all that to change? But the strange man in the torn jeans with the wide-apart green eyes was sitting out there, waiting for her to come back and explain herself.

She glided back into the café and looked around for her saviour. He was picking up a tray from the counter and taking it over to a table near a window. No she hadn't been deluding herself, he really was terrific. Out of the corner of her eye she could see a tiny white flake of skin on the outside of her nostril. She rubbed it away quickly and followed him, and after he'd made himself comfortable on the black plastic seat, she sat down opposite him and slid her coat from her shoulders.

'Hi!' He looked as if he wanted to laugh. 'You look like a laboratory mouse.'

She gave him an offended look.

'In a fluffy sort of way, I mean. I got you some toast, and a pot of tea. I'll grab a cup with you, if you don't mind. It's fucking freezing today, isn't it?'

Not backward in coming forward with the expletives, she noted. But he hadn't struck her as one to stand on ceremony. And he'd ordered toast. He was gaining Brownie points by the minute.

'Yep, sure is. It's brilliant in here though.' She sighed contentedly and loosened the collar of her sweater to let more warm air in. 'It's really kind of you to order this, but you must let me pay.'

He gave her an assessing look.

'I assumed you would pay.'

'Oh. Yes, I would. Obviously.'

'Fine. You're in work, aren't you?'

'Sorry?'

He nodded at her clothes. 'Smart coat, skirt. I noticed that.'

'And the gusset, no doubt.' She picked up a piece of toast and bit into it. It was heavenly.

'No, I missed that. I think Jim got an eyeful though.'

She expected him to say 'Lucky bloke', or something like that. He didn't. She wasn't sure whether she was disappointed or whether she'd have been more annoyed if he had.

'Anyway, I've been fired,' she said, cramming the toast into her mouth, and only realising once she saw the surprised look on his face that she was eating it like a pig. 'God, I'm sorry. I'll slow down. You should have a bit too.'

'No, I'm fine. I never eat until the evening. Why were you fired?'

'Because my ex-boss is a fat prat,' she said, helping herself to tea. 'No, I'm wrong actually. It turns out he's a tart with a heart, or something like that.'

'A fart with a heart, perhaps?'

'Yes, that's more like it.' She stopped to swallow her mouthful of toast and to take a sip of tea. 'So you know him, then?'

He smiled. He had a lovely smile. She stopped chewing, her mug poised in the air, and stared at him.

'I used to have one like that. Not any more. I'm a free agent, now.'

'Oh.' A free agent. That was one way of putting it. It was better than being a statistic. She peered at him as he emptied a sachet of sugar into his mug. She blinked and looked again. It was an odd phenomenon. Each time she looked at him he became more gorgeous. And of course, her luck being what it was, he would turn up and rescue her when she was three and a half weeks pregnant and wearing a comedy red nose. She let out an involuntary giggle.

'What's up? It's not exactly tea at the Ritz, but this place is clean. And it's dead cheap. Which is just as well, if you've lost your job.' He sipped at his mug and crossed one knee over the other. Several glimpses of solid leg showed through the rips in the denim. 'I usually pop in here for a cuppa after signing. You'll have to get used to that. It's a pain in the arse, but you just have to know what to say. The pressure's right on, you know.'

'But this is all new to me. How are you supposed to know what to say?'

He eyed her steadily. She tried to hold his gaze without growing hot. With every second that he maintained that long, calm look he was shooting up the top twenty of all-time gorgeous men, heading for number one. She cleared her throat squeakily.

'I mean—'

'You are looking for another job, aren't you?'

'Sort of. Soon. Yes.' She twiddled her teaspoon. 'Not this week or next, at least.'

'You do know you've got to prove that you're actively seeking work to sign on, I suppose?'

'I have?'

'Bugger me, you are a novice, aren't you?'

She gazed into her tea, and suddenly wished that he would go away. Just at this moment she didn't want to be reminded of what an all-round twit she was by the most gorgeous man in London. On the other hand, there was such an enormous thing happening in her life that she felt as if she was looking at him through the wrong end of a telescope. Not that she wanted to stop looking.

'I can give you a few tips, if you like. I've been signing over six months now. Hopefully not for much longer. But that depends on what happens. Still.'

He stopped to stretch lazily in his seat. He was sturdily built under his jacket, with a round-necked T-shirt plastered with the name of a band she hadn't heard of, also ripped, just below the breastbone. Perhaps he was moonlighting as a lion tamer? She had an ill-defined instinct that he was moonlighting as something, but she wasn't sure what. He seemed too lively, too awake, to be somebody who had spent six months watching *Countdown*. She picked up the second piece of toast, forgetting to offer it politely to him first, and set about eating it. She tried to form questions in her head that wouldn't seem silly. She didn't even know his name. But then, he didn't know hers. He drained his mug.

'I've got to go now, I'm afraid.' He stood up. She gripped her mug tightly and watched him in dismay. 'Thanks for the tea. I'll repay you one day. You sure you'll get home all right?'

'Er, yes. I live locally. It's not far. Thank you for looking after me, back there. I'm not quite sure what happened. I think—'

'Well, you take care of yourself.' He nodded down at

her. 'And make sure you don't miss out on breakfast. You don't want to go fainting all over London, do you? Next time, you might not have me to pick you up.'

'No. I'll try not—'

He sauntered out of the café. She looked back to her tea and toast, fighting the urge to shout 'Come back!'. There was no need for that. And once he'd left it was almost as if he'd never been there. It was a pantomime moment. One flash of pink smoke, and he'd vanished. She sat on her own, suffused with her own thoughts, the world outside becoming more distant. She was pregnant, and that was everything.

It had just been another day on planet Tharg. She'd turned down the career break of a lifetime and fainted in the Jobcentre. Then a gorgeous-looking man with less-than-gorgeous manners had dragged her into a café and been beamed away. As she stared at the mutant toast crumb that was floating around in her mug she vowed that she would make it back to the Jobcentre. She'd pick up some forms, and she'd find a way through it, all without displaying her gusset to anyone.

Chapter Five

'I'm fifty-five,' Olivia announced to Sarah, the temp, who was crouching over the computer as if she'd slipped a disc. Olivia marched on to her desk. Sarah looked up.

'Is that all?'

Olivia wasn't sure why she'd announced that fact as she'd arrived at the office. She hadn't been sure where such an opening gambit might lead a conversation either, but that certainly wasn't the response she'd wanted. Now she wanted to wrap her hands around Sarah's slender throat and squeeze until her face went blue right up to the roots of her feathered, bleached hair. That was probably something to do with getting so little sleep this week. And it was all down to hearing from Katherine Muff again.

It was years since she'd thought about the old school, but one phone call had brought it all flooding back. Louise and Rachel had followed her path through the same school but they didn't ramble on about it. Olivia had tried to put it all behind her. She had been trying so hard to move on after Bob had gone. But Katherine Muff wanted her to go back, to a class reunion at a restaurant in the town, in only a few weeks' time. The thought of it sent a chill creeping over her. She couldn't face all those girls again. They'd all be satisfied women in their fifties now. What would she say to them? What had she done with her life?

'You do my 'ead in, you do,' Sarah said, Olivia swung round as her reverie was broken. It was nine in the morning, and she was at work. Carol would be here soon. For the moment, Sarah was grinning. 'Sometimes I don't think you're on the same planet as the rest of us. I said I thought you was much older than fifty-five.'

'You're still so young,' Olivia said grittily. 'I expect everyone over thirty looks like an old lady to you.'

'Nah, my nan's older than you and she looks like that one out of Abba.'

'Abba?' Olivia ransacked her memory. 'Oh, really? The blonde girl with the blue eyes?'

Sarah guffawed loudly. 'Come off it. I mean the haggard one with the red hair. But she still don't look her age. Terrific she is.'

'Well, that's nice for her.'

Sarah sniffed, fingering the keyboard, unsure whether or not to look away as Olivia fixed her with a hostile glare.

'I've got to get this memo typed before Cow-bag comes in. I should have sent it yesterday, but I got confused.'

Olivia nodded. She wanted to get the mail opened before Carol arrived. But there were other things on her mind as well. Sarah's face brightened as if she suddenly understood something.

'God, I'm a plank! I get it. You're fifty-five *today*. You should have said it was your birthday. We can go for a drink at lunchtime. Apart from Cow-bag. Don't tell her.'

Olivia opened her mouth and shut it again. Of course it wasn't her birthday, but when it had been her birthday three months ago, she hadn't told anybody at work about it so as not to make a fuss. Nobody had noticed that she'd been sulking all day, and she'd gone home feeling churlish and unappreciated. She'd had a card from Louise which arrived a day early, and a card from Rachel two days late. Since Katherine had rung, being fifty-five seemed important. Why shouldn't they all go to the pub? They hadn't done it on her birthday, and she hadn't been inside a pub for years.

'Yes, let's do that.'

'Nice one.' Sarah looked close to happy now. 'We'll go to the Queen's Head. I'll see if anyone else wants to come.'

Smiling unsteadily, Olivia returned to her desk and attacked a pile of brown envelopes, listening to beeps and boops coming from the computer Sarah was attempting to use. Carol, who Sarah had neatly christened Cow-bag after her very first day, had told them to treat it with respect. She said it was a Pentium. Olivia had wanted to tell Carol that she found a Pen Tidy technologically challenging, but she'd kept quiet. They'd had the new computer for a week and Carol showed no sign of planning any training time for them. The only one with any idea was Shaun, one of the social workers, but he only dropped in from time to time to file notes and pick up case studies. He was trying to do what he could for them, but he soon tiptoed out of the office whenever Carol appeared.

Olivia worked her way through the mail, stacking a pile of letters for Carol to read as soon as she got in. She insisted on seeing everything before Olivia got a chance to attach it to a file. She got a kick out of writing 'File' in red ink on the tops of the letters, without the word 'Please'.

'Aw, fuck. I think I've done something to it.'

Olivia turned, clutching an envelope, and wandered back over to the computer. Sarah picked up a paper-clip, unwound it and began to pick her teeth thoughtfully with the end.

'What did you touch?' Olivia asked in a horrified whisper.

'Nothing. I was miles away, and when I looked back at the screen there were these psychedelic boxes coming at me.' She bent forwards and pulled a face. 'I'm too scared to touch anything now just in case I mess it up. It could be a virus, or anything. I was all right with Windows three one.'

'Could it be that thing? You know.' Olivia could feel

herself getting hot as Sarah turned wide brown eyes on her with rapt attention.

'What thing?'

'The thing – that does that sometimes.'

'Does what? This?'

'Yes.'

'I think this is something to do with the Internet.' Sarah turned back to the screen and took a pained breath. 'I expect the computer's going to dissolve now. It's no good. We'll have to ask Cow-bag when she gets in.'

'Somebody's in my parking place again.' Carol entered the room like an avalanche.

They jumped to attention, Sarah physically levitating from her seat and all but clicking her heels together behind her. Olivia frowned at her. Sarah was young. She was employable. Olivia was stuck with it. Carol was so pleasant to look at, with scraped-back black hair, a petite ballerina's face and full, sweet lips. But within this innocuous body was the personality of a T-Rex with chronic PMT.

'What is the current problem?' Carol ranged her ice-blue eyes over the two women.

'Good morning, Carol,' Olivia said. She was a different generation, but that was where the day usually started. Carol ignored the snivelled attempt at civility, leaned over the keyboard, pressed a button, and the psychedelic boxes disappeared. Sarah's half-finished memo reappeared. Carol pulled herself back up to five foot four. When she did that, Olivia, who was a stately five nine, always felt that she should kneel so she didn't appear taller. For some reason it seemed to add to Carol's aggravation to have to look up at her.

'The screen saver,' Carol issued at them through tight lips. 'I set it on Friday. Now it will come into action every two minutes.'

They stared back.

'That way,' Carol explained tartly, 'I shall know when anybody's daydreaming. I can hear it setting in from my desk, and I can see it. Although why you should have problems understanding a concept as simple as the screen saver, I do not know. Especially you, Sarah.'

'The pattern's different from the old one.'

'You're supposed to be IT literate!'

'I was all right with the old one. I didn't realise they all had different patterns. The screen just disappeared. I thought it was a virus.'

'The young are supposed to have supple minds, aren't they? Surely I don't have to say everything twice. Not to you, at least, Sarah.'

Carol gave an elaborate sigh. Olivia's grip on her envelope tightened. So Carol was saying that Olivia's mind was not supple, and she had to be told everything at least twice, because she was old. Certainly her brain wasn't considered supple enough to know that the pattern was the screen saver, although that was what she had been trying to explain to Sarah. It was just that she'd called it a thing instead.

'Is that the memo I wanted sent yesterday, Sarah?'

'Er—'

'The one I specifically asked you to send as an attachment to the email I dictated, before you left?'

Sarah peered at the computer screen as if there could be some doubt.

'This is no good to me at all. Now I shall have to ring Roger and explain why my suggestions weren't with him last night as I promised.' She pinned Sarah to the wall with the ocular equivalent of a javelin. 'If you continue like this, Sarah, I will think about asking the agency for a replacement.'

'Couldn't you show me how to do attachments again? I didn't quite grab it first time round.'

'Why don't you know your way around a tool bar, for heaven's sake?' Carol's voice froze over. 'You're supposed to be a competent typist.'

'Administrative assistant,' Sarah corrected in a mumble. 'There are three thousand buttons on the tool bar. How was I to know which ones to press?'

'Because I showed you, perhaps?' Carol put her nose in the air.

'Only the once,' Sarah murmured. 'It's not like proper training.' She shot Olivia a glance which showed that she'd been daring in bringing up the subject of training. Olivia bit her lip and turned with her envelope back to her desk. When she unclenched her palm, she found that she'd screwed the brown paper into a ball. All she needed to do now was to set fire to it and lob it at Carol's head. Her hairspray would feed the flames, and they could sit back and have a cup of coffee while they watched.

'I'll look at the post now, Olivia.'

Carol slipped off her overcoat. It was very chic, high around the collar, fitted around the waist. It would look good with jackboots, Olivia thought. Carol hung it on the standing rail and made her way over to her desk, the king-sized one at the back of the room. Olivia watched her out of the corner of her eye as she slid into her rotating chair and disappeared from view. She got up quickly, tutting impatiently, and played with the plastic controls until the seat was high enough. Then she seated herself again, patting the sides of her hair into shape. Balanced on her elevated chair, she reminded Olivia of Rachel in her high chair, staring imperiously at a bowl full of mashed banana whilst making noises of disbelief. Olivia thumped the post down on the king-sized desk.

'What happened to this letter?' Carol picked up the creased evidence.

'It met with a clenched fist,' Olivia said obliquely. A

pair of cold blue eyes challenged hers. Olivia looked away first.

'I think I need a cup of coffee.' Carol turned her attention to her diary and ran a Mont Blanc pen down her notes. 'Not as strong as you usually make it.'

Olivia rested her hot head against the door of the small kitchen where she and Sarah took it in turns to make coffee. If she closed her eyes now, she could fall asleep standing up and stay there until it was time to go home. But she had the day to fight through first. Nobody would care that she had private worries. Sarah was too young to think that Olivia's thoughts were anything other than killingly boring. Carol was too much of a Cow-bag to give a damn what her thoughts were. Carol was only thirty-six, the same age as Rachel. Rachel was bossy too, but she had so many redeeming qualities that it didn't matter. Olivia often wondered what would happen if she left her manager and her eldest daughter in an airless room and locked the door. With that thought, she smiled, filled up the kettle and switched it on.

'Hi there, Mumsie. How are you doing?'

'Do you mind not calling me that, Sally?' Louise shifted the hot-water bottle that was wedged between her Thin Lizzy T-shirt and her father's old green jumper and pulled a chair up to the phone. 'You can't be bored, surely? What are you doing ringing me from work?'

'I wanted to know if you'd thrown up yet.'

Louise smiled and tutted. It was all about clichés to Sally. She paused to glance over at the kitchen table strewn with paperwork she'd been reading her way through. She had advice on everything now. How to claim jobseeker's allowance, how to jobseek, and how to have a termination. The latter had been given to her on her second visit to the doctor. The doctor had told her that

70

she shouldn't make a decision too quickly, but at the same time reminded her that time was of the essence. In other words, she had to rush into making a sensible decision. And all the time she just couldn't believe that any of it was actually happening.

'Hey, Sal, something occurred to me.'

'What's that then?'

'It's four weeks now and I can't feel a thing. Can I sue them for making me believe I was pregnant when I wasn't?'

There was a long pause.

'What are you on about?'

'I can't be expecting a baby. It's ridiculous. First, this sort of thing happens to women in dungarees and flat shoes who live in North London and eat Marmite for years in advance, not me. Second, there's absolutely no evidence that it's true. I'm not sick, I'm not eating gherkins, I'm not pressing my stomach up to *Panorama*. The only overwhelming instinct I've got is to stay in bed until people stop telling me I'm pregnant. Now you're a lawyer, you tell me if that would stand up in court?'

'Oh, you're in denial.'

'Of course I am!' Louise grabbed at her packet of Ultra-Lows and lit one in agitation. 'And I'll stay in denial until I have one shred of evidence that it's not a big joke.'

'Are you smoking?'

'What if I am?'

'Well, it shows you don't feel maternal. That should help to clarify things.'

'I don't feel anything, that's the whole flipping point!' She stared at her cigarette end ominously. 'Surely if you have a very late period you must build up loads of hormones that shouldn't be there? That would show up on the test, wouldn't it?'

'Nope. General knowledge, Lou. The blue line doesn't

71

appear unless there's a special pregnancy hormone present.'

'Right then.' Louise paced around the kitchen with the phone tucked under her arm, thinking hard. 'Right, got it. Even if I am pregnant, I'll lose it. That's what happens. Nature will sort it out in a week or so, and I can get on with my life.'

'Louise, darling, you're the biologist.'

'Yes, but I spent three years analysing dead frogs. And what's more, I did it very badly.'

'It's really unlikely you'll lose it. Face it. You're up the duff.'

Louise frowned, playing with her cigarette. She dumped it in the ashtray.

'Say that again,' she instructed.

'You're up the duff. You've got a bun in the oven. You're in the club.'

'Okay, I get the picture.'

'Um, up the spout. In the family way . . .'

'All right, Sal, you can put the thesaurus away now.'

'I just want to help you come to terms with it all.' Sally's voice softened. 'Lou? There's only going to be one way out of it. You know I'll come with you, don't you? You won't be on your own.'

Louise closed her eyes and pressed the receiver to her ear. The words of comfort washed over her. Right over her.

'Thanks, Sal.'

'Let's see, when can we meet again . . .' Sally let out a thoughtful breath. 'Saturday? I'm supposed to be going to the ENO with Fergus but I could make some excuse and come round to you instead. How about that?'

'Okay.'

'And let's get this show on the road. You're not getting any younger, Lou. You need to get yourself into a good job, and soon. You can't keep on turning your nose up at things just because Rachel did them first.'

'What—?'

'You want someone to tell you how it is, don't you?'

Louise rolled her head backwards and stared up at her ceiling until it went pink in front of her eyes.

'Bye then. Talk to you soon.'

'And keep washing your hair. It's important to work from the outside in when you're feeling a bit low.'

A bit low? To Sally, feeling a bit low was finding that the newsagent had run out of *Observers* on a Sunday morning, or that Waitrose were fresh out of quail's eggs. And this was definitely something that started on the inside and worked its way out. Louise had learned that much in biology.

'Tell you what,' Sally concluded. 'I'll take you for a curry on Saturday. How does that sound?'

Louise's stomach gave a sudden, violent rumble.

'Right, you're on.'

'So are you doing something nice tonight?' Sarah asked as she dived into a gin and tonic.

Olivia had opted for an orange juice. If she wasn't mentally alert enough to deal with the distribution of the agenda for the meeting in the afternoon, Carol would blow a gasket. If she had any gaskets left to blow. One day, she told herself, Carol would have a visionary experience which would result in her recommending Olivia for an MBE for services rendered to the unit. One day.

'And then, pigs might fly,' Olivia muttered, wincing as a chink of ice caught in her molar and wedged itself there.

'Ah, shame. Not going out then?'

'Sorry?'

'Not going out,' Sarah repeated slowly. 'Are you all right today? You look cream crackered.'

Olivia smiled. Acknowledgement, at last. Even if it did come from Sarah. And as she looked at Sarah, she decided that she was sweet really. It was just that she was so different, so young, so strange to Olivia. The greenish tinge of her bleached hair was testament to that. And her confidence was awesome. When they'd walked into the pub, Olivia had instantly felt too old to be there. There was nobody in the building who looked under forty. There was one other man in a suit whose hair was as grey as hers, but even he had given her a cursory glance and turned his attention to Sarah's legs instead. Sarah had stormed up to the bar, ordered drinks for them both, insisted on paying, and found them a table. It was as if she felt at home. Like her girls, Olivia mused. They were at home in the world too.

'I am knackered,' Olivia said.

'Ah, well, never mind. You have to spoil yourself on your birthday, don't you? I always get rat-arsed, and I tell Neal to surprise me. He always comes up with something. Last year it was a Chinese at that place that brings you a birthday cake. Does your husband surprise you then?'

Olivia sipped at her orange juice again while she considered the question.

'He did surprise me, once.'

'That's nice. What did he do?'

'He died. But I think that was the only time he ever did anything surprising.'

Olivia fixed her eyes on a palm set on a window-ledge which looked like an Areca, and was wilting through lack of care. It worried her.

'Don't they water their plants in here?' she asked Sarah. It was then she noticed that Sarah's mouth was hanging open. 'What's the matter? What did I say?'

Sarah's hand flew to her mouth to cover it.

'I'm so sorry. I'm really sorry, Olivia. I had no idea your husband was – had . . . you know.'

'Died?'

'Yes. That's it. God, the last thing you want to do on your birthday is to think about that. You want to enjoy yourself, don't you? Think about nice things. Look, why don't I get us both another drink. You just stay here and make yourself comfortable, and I'll be back in a tick. I'll get us something to eat as well. What do you fancy? A sandwich? A nice lasagne or something like that?'

'Er, lasagne sounds lovely. I'll give you some money.'

'No, no. We'll worry about that later.'

Sarah fled.

It was funny that whenever Olivia did want to think about the nice thing which was her husband, everybody stopped her from doing it. She wished somebody would let her talk about him. But nobody would, and she couldn't bring the subject up with Rachel or Louise, the only people in the world now who had known Bob almost as well as she had herself. There were other things she also wanted to say to her daughters, but she couldn't mention them either.

'Room for a small one?' The sound of Shaun's voice had her smiling before she'd looked up. 'I'm in a dreadful rush, and I can't stop for a drink, I'm afraid, but I couldn't let this occasion pass without dropping in myself to join the fun.' His impish grin tightened as he gazed vaguely around the bar, possibly wondering if he'd been too hasty in opting for the word 'fun'. 'Not on your own, are you?'

'No, no. Sarah's here too. She's gone to get some lasagne.'

'Great!' Shaun touched his hands together. He was too gentle to go for the hearty clap-hands sort of gesture, but the enthusiasm was there. Olivia liked him. He was kind. The younger women in the office paid him no attention at all. He had a hook nose, eyebrows that met in the middle, and hair that was trying to escape out of a skylight. He was somewhere in his forties and single. Olivia often thought that it was a pity that the younger women she saw around her didn't seem to appreciate kindness. Sarah only talked about Brad Pitt, and how her boyfriend of three years looked a bit like him if you closed the curtains, turned all the lights out, and put a bag over your head. Part of Olivia wondered what Brad Pitt would look like when he was fifty-five. Another part of Olivia had sat and watched a film starring him, and seen Sarah's point. But Shaun was no Brad Pitt.

'It's very nice of you to come,' she said, shifting along the cushions on the bench to allow him to sit down.

'I'll just perch for a bit. Then I must be on my way. I have to visit the Sheldons again.'

'Oh, you poor thing. It's a difficult one, isn't it?'

'Hmmn.' Shaun fell into thought. He never discussed his cases, but Olivia read all about them as she was working. Shaun was a sensitive man. She knew he was struggling with the emotional-detachment aspect of his career profile. 'Still.' He beamed at her, eyebrows lifted in one unified act. 'You're the birthday girl, so let's be happy about that.'

'Yes.' Olivia dutifully pecked at her orange juice again. She had a bizarre urge to giggle.

'So, you're a scorpion.'

She gazed at him. In a moment of bewilderment, she thought he had paid her a gross insult. But he looked so happy as he sat there, he couldn't be insulting her.

'I am?'

'Yes. Tempestuous and strong-willed, but brave and passionate.'

'Really?'

'You know. Smacks life right between the eyes. Mind

you, it's more effective that way, I think. I'm not like that myself. I'm a sideways-on type. I'm a Cancer, you see.'

'Oh.' She laughed loudly. Several heads turned to stare. In fact, she was a Leo. She'd never thought she was like a Leo at all. She was a sideways-on type too, like Shaun. Perhaps she had Cancer rising in her heavens or something. 'You sound as if you know a lot about it.'

'Just a bit. I do birth charts, you know, as a hobby. I could do yours for you.' He considered her for a moment. 'Yes, of course, why don't I do that? I never got you a card, did I? And I've got to go in a minute, so I could do your chart, as a present.'

'Oh no, really.'

'Yes, I insist.' His eyes sparkled. 'The computer does the chart and I interpret it. I bought a computer on HP for home, you see. You can get software to do the astrology map. But it's amazing how accurate it is. I do it for therapy, and it seems to be therapeutic for other people too, so what's the harm, that's what I say.'

'Of course. There's no harm in anything that's therapeutic,' Olivia said with feeling.

'So I need to know your time and place of birth.'

Olivia shifted on the bench. She wasn't only an impostor at her own birthday celebration, she was also about to have a fictitious life presented to her on an astrology chart. Her lips twitched. It would be like going home from the launderette with someone else's washing. It was nothing like the reality of her own life. It brought her back to the school reunion again. What was she going to say to them all, if she went to it? What would they say to her? What did they know?

But she had to answer Shaun. She glanced at him, her thoughts wavering as she concentrated on the small scar on the end of his nose. It wasn't *her* birth chart, and if it made Shaun happy there might not be any harm in it. Poor

77

Shaun. He had such a stressful job. He looked as if he could do with some therapy.

She gave him the time and year of her birth, then added, 'And I was born in London. My parents were hop pickers. It's what brought us down to Kent.'

'That's fascinating,' he said, as if it really was fascinating. For a fleeting moment she felt important. It made the birthday charade worthwhile. Perhaps she should do it more often. Just once every three months, perhaps, to allow time for everyone to forget the date, and for another young temp to arrive who was looking for any excuse to go to the pub at lunchtime. Bob never used to take her to the pub, and the thought of going without him was unthinkable. But it was nice to be here now. She instantly felt a flash of guilt.

'Well, I'll give it to you when it's ready.' He grinned at her. 'By the way, no skeletons in the cupboard, are there? You should let me know, just in case it throws up something unusual.'

Olivia gripped her orange juice. Then she remembered that she was going to go home from the launderette with someone else's washing.

'Here y'are. Lasagne. And another orange juice. But I've slipped a vodka in there to cheer you up.'

'Thank you, Sarah.'

'And I must be going, I'm afraid.' Shaun leaped up. 'Sarah, Olivia, see you soon. And happy birthday again.'

He looked for a moment as if he might swoop down and peck her cheek. Olivia leaned away from him. Her cheeks were too dry to be kissed. Sarah watched Shaun weave his way out of the pub, his long neck waving above the heads of others. She tutted.

'Couldn't bend wire that shape, could you. Poor Shaun. D'you reckon he's gay?'

'What? Shaun?'

'Still single at forty-three. Either that or he's got appalling foot odour.'

'Do you think so?'

'Eat up then. We don't want Cow-bag tanning our arses for being late back, do we?'

Olivia obediently tackled her lasagne with a knife and fork. She'd never got used to eating out in public. She hadn't done it often enough. Not like Sarah, who was launching noisily into a chilli con carne beside her, breaking off lumps of garlic bread, and dipping them in the sauce. And not like her girls. She stopped to wonder for a moment what they were both doing. At lunch somewhere, probably. Rachel at a fashionable brasserie, Louise probably curled up in the corner of a café somewhere with a cup of tea, a sandwich and a paperback. They were in control of their own lives now, she told herself sternly. And they certainly didn't need her any more. She shouldn't worry about them so much.

Louise threw open the piano lid, heaved the stool into place and thumped herself down on it. She pushed the loud pedal down to the carpet as if she was racing down a straight and launched herself at the keys.

She banged out Handel's 'Largo' with as much bad temper as she could, and trilled along with gritted teeth.

'La – LAH!' she concluded.

She slumped, breathing unsteadily. Why couldn't anyone say anything right? Why was it that at the most crucial times in your life, when you most needed somebody to talk to, there was nobody who was just the right person to talk to about it, whatever it was? Then she realised that someone was knocking at her door.

She flung the door wide and growled into the hall. A pair of blue eyes smouldered into hers. She frowned at Harris. His black hair seemed to have been assaulted with hair gel. Why in God's name was he looking at her like that? The noise? She had been yelling, and it had been a pretty defiant version of 'Largo'.

'I'm sorry, Harris, I'm in a bad mood this evening. Can't you get earplugs or something?'

His grin tightened as if she'd surprised him. She realised he was wearing very snug denims and a loose white shirt – unbuttoned to the waist. He was obviously halfway through getting dressed.

'Look.' She rubbed at her head. 'Just go and get dressed and I promise I'll be quiet. Okay?'

'Get dressed?' He reclined against the door-frame at an unusual angle. It made his hips stick out sideways. She watched curiously. 'I was thinking of getting undressed.'

His teeth flashed white.

'Oh, I see. Are you doing odd hours again? You should warn me. You go off to bed, and I promise I won't play any more tonight. Okay?'

'No.' He beamed at her. 'I want to go to bed, yes. But not alone.'

She squinted at him as he raised his eyebrows, lowered them and raised them again. The penny finally dropped.

'Oh God, I'm sorry. I've ruined your seduction scene. It must be pretty awful trying to get somebody in the sack while a mad woman's caterwauling in the flat below you.' She gave him a sympathetic smile. 'Sorry. You go back to whoever it is, and I'll just – just hide under the sofa or something until it's all over.'

She closed the door on him. She caught a waft of aftershave as the latch clicked. She sniffed at the air. A nice one. He had good taste. What a shame he was a love-rat. And if she hadn't been pregnant, she might just have allowed him to be a love-rat on her time. But that was a distant thought now. She'd just have to put up with the thumping from upstairs and accept that it was all happening to someone else who was more focused on sex than on the consequences.

She decided to ring Rachel. It was Sally's fault for making her think about her again. Now she had to risk being sucked into the black hole of Rachel's answering machine. Louise knew all about filtering calls, but Rachel just substituted 'filter' with 'ignore'. But there was just a small chance they'd launch into a warm and sisterly conversation which would end in Rachel offering wonderful advice.

She picked up the phone and pressed out Rachel's number. After three rings, she got the answering machine.

Rachel Twigg and Hallam Merton can't take your call right now. Please leave us a message, and one of us will get right back to you.

'Bloody liars,' Louise mumbled.

She wasn't about to deliver a monologue about her present state to a machine. Rachel might have the volume turned up. She might be announcing her predicament to a room full of hairy musicians, all smarming up to Rachel in the hope of her getting them a deal. She might blow her sister's credibility completely, and Rachel was second only to Andrew in her need to be considered professional. She hung up.

She could always call her mother.

Louise pictured her, at home with a book or a magazine, or in front of the nine o'clock news, with a cup of tea or a glass of wine, her eyes gazing mistily over her father's photographs on the mantelpiece, and the one of herself and Rachel looking like a couple of aliens with gapped teeth and bunches. She dialled her mother's number.

'Mum? It's me. Just ringing to say hello.'

'Is everything all right, dear?'

'Of course. I just wondered how you are.'

'I was just going to watch the news with a cup of tea. Did you need to talk to me right now?'

'No, no. Just thought I'd let you know I've had a bit of a cold. Just in case it occurred to you that I might not be well. You'd better go and watch the news if it's so important to you.' She finished with a resounding snap.

'You sound prickly. Are you premenstrual?'

Louise laughed, and stopped herself just before it turned into a shriek.

'No.'

'I could send you a vest. I've bought one for you, but I didn't like to send it without asking you again. You seemed so against the idea.'

Louise stared at the wall with round eyes. How was it that her mother imagined she applied her emotions so ardently to issues such as vests? She had been against eating meat in her time, against fascism, and against Soft Cell, but never really against vests. The thought of teasing an ounce of reaction out of her at the moment on the subject of vests was surreal.

'Please send it if you feel you must.'

'Did I tell you that Betty phoned a while ago? Frank's flu seems to be on the mend now. The doctor says that as long as he stays warm and finishes his course of antibiotics, his chest should clear up in no time.'

'That's just great news, Mum.'

'I think I'll go and watch the news. I can't really talk to you when you're in this sort of mood. Shall we try again another time?'

'Why not.'

Half an hour later, Louise was stirring up a vat of spaghetti to have with cheese sauce when her doorbell rang. She stopped, holding the wooden spoon perfectly still, and waited to see if it would go again. It did. It was her doorbell. She tried to rationalise it. That meant somebody was outside the house, ringing, because they wanted to see her.

Jon. The thought of him turned her hot and cold. She couldn't see him tonight. Not with a whole packet of spaghetti on the go. She'd have to pretend that she was having people round so that she didn't look greedy, but with her hair twisted up and stuck in place with a biro she didn't exactly look as if she was expecting anyone.

She flew to the bathroom and stared aghast at her reflection. Her eyes were glowing and her hair looked like a Mohican that had been arranged sideways. With a shaking hand, she drew a line of lipstick across her lips and pressed them together. Her T-shirt was hanging below her jumper. She tucked it in quickly.

She trotted out into the hall as the ringing came again. She stopped in the darkness to take a deep breath and focus blearily on the shadowy figure looming through the frosted glass. She flicked on the hall light. It wasn't until she'd already half-opened the door that she glanced down and saw that she was wearing her Marks and Spencer slippers. The ones her mother had bought for her last year. The ones she had sworn never to wear because they were very long, and very thin, and made out of Axminster carpet. The ones that made her look like a circus clown. But it was too late. The figure on her doorstep had turned round to face her with a broad grin stretched across his face.

She gulped. Her mouth dropped open. It was impossible to disguise the dreaded realisation that hit her like a mallet. A pair of brown eyes twinkled back at her from a sea of black dreadlocks. And he was still wearing the same crocheted rainbow hat that he'd had on the last time she'd told him to impale himself on his stunted little microphone.

'Hi there darlin'. I was passin', an' I thought I'd drop in. You know, havin' got your letter, an' all.'

83

'Lenny!' she squeaked, trying to ignore the way he was suggestively rotating his hips. 'How the – how nice to see you again.'

Chapter Six

'So what the hell did you do?'

Sally waited with gaping eyes while Louise forked another mouthful of sag aloo and prawn biryani into her mouth. She chewed and swallowed.

'God, this is gorgeous. I swear by this restaurant. Did I tell you I saw Neil Kinnock in here once? These guys know their ghee from their Swarfega. Orgasmic. Have you tried the mung dhal?'

'Louise! Will you spit it out?'

No danger of that, Louise thought. First she would plough through her own plateful, then edge her spoon bit by bit over the halfway line on the serving dishes that Sally seemed to be ignoring, then she would finish off the nan, and if she was still hungry, work through the napkins.

'Hang on. Pass me that bit of bread, will you?'

Sally picked up her side plate and handed it to Louise.

'What did you do with Lenny, for God's sake?'

'I didn't do anything with Lenny.' Louise took a swig of water. 'He likes his women the same way he likes his cigarettes, with a bit of zing. I don't think I could have been more lacking in zing that evening if I'd been on display in a coffin. He was really nice, and stayed for about five seconds to catch up on old news, then he was off.'

'And you think it was the circus clown slippers that did it?'

'The combination of those and the Rod Stewart hair seemed to do the trick. When I was seeing Lenny, my hair was quite nice. Much longer.'

'I remember. I don't know why you ever had it cut,' Sally said, cruelly flicking her lustrous auburn locks over her shoulder.

'This is so typical!' Louise declared, fork in hand. 'I go to the hairdresser, come out looking like an upturned spring onion, and everybody thinks I did it *deliberately*. What on earth makes you think I'm such a masochist?'

Sally considered as she delicately nudged a piece of chicken tikka across her plate. 'Your hair will grow though, won't it?'

'That and everything else,' Louise said, tearing at her nan bread and staring thoughtfully across the restaurant at a handful of men wearing white T-shirts and jeans who had just wandered in. 'Oh God, not them again.'

'Trouble?'

'Just a pain in the bum. They call all the waiters "Abdul" and order chicken phalls all round. Last time I was here with Jon they had a belching contest. It was lovely. Especially when Jon joined in. But he was very drunk.'

'Well, we could have met somewhere more central . . .'

'No, Sal. I really appreciate you sacrificing *Don Giovanni* for me, but I couldn't make it into town on the tube. I had my first burst of sickness today. It was gruesome.'

'You seem all right.' Sally watched Louise shovel another hillock of biryani into her mouth. 'Although I notice you're off the hot stuff.'

'Couldn't face waking up tomorrow with a bottom like a dragon's nostril.'

'But you're not too sick to eat?'

'Eating seems to cure it. That's the weird thing. I thought eating would make me feel sick, but it's the other way round. I think that might have put Lenny off as well. I took him through to the kitchen, and while I was talking to him I was picking bits of soggy spaghetti out of the saucepan and chewing on them. I didn't even realise I was doing it.'

'Fine.' Sally sat back in her chair and picked up her wine-glass. 'So that's Lenny sorted. Now what about Giles? You wrote to him suggesting oral sex as well, didn't you?'

'Haven't heard a word from him.' Louise dabbed at the corners of her mouth with the stiff napkin. 'With any luck, he's emigrated. Or married Sophie. Or both.'

'She was the one he left you for, wasn't she?'

'Excuse me!' Louise sat up indignantly. 'I left him, or don't you remember?'

'Yes, after you found out he'd been taking Sophie to Paris with him on expenses.'

'So? I was still the one who did the dumping.'

'But it doesn't count if you have to dump him because he's already going out with someone else.'

'Well, he fancied me first. It took me ages to agree to go out with him. I don't like beards. I should have trusted my instincts.'

'Oh, Louise.' Sally sighed and shook her head. 'Some-times I feel that we haven't moved on from the fifth form. I still remember coming in all excited that Monday morning and telling you about Guy.'

'He was the one who put his hand down your school knickers on the train to Paddock Wood, wasn't he?'

'Please! It was more romantic than that.'

'Sorry.' Louise suppressed a burp, smothering her mouth with her napkin. She would look a bit of a hypocrite if she was the one to kick off the belching contest this time.

'Guy was lovely. A real boy next door. I don't know why we ever finished.' Sally's face crumpled into a frown of concentration. 'Come to think of it, why did we finish? I bet he's gorgeous now. He was very tall, you know, with lovely thick arms. I bet he's a real hunk.'

'We had a boy next door too,' Louise mused. 'Paul Fisher.'

'I remember. You got him drunk in his parents' caravan when he was thirteen, he pinged your bra strap, you slapped him and he threw up on the stowaway table.'

'What about Fergus?' Louise played with the idea of eating the last of the sag aloo, and went for it. Sally looked pensive.

'Fergus is . . . nice. He's attractive, sincere, sensitive, cultured, ambitious, good in bed, rich,' Sally nodded at Louise, 'good sense of humour, independent . . .'

Louise dropped her spoon as she attempted to deliver half a serving dish of sag aloo to her plate in one go.

'Charming, witty, thoughtful, titled. Did I mention that? His father's the Earl of something. Just found out last week.'

'You're lying.'

'Okay, maybe not an earl. Sir someone or other. And he's stylish, attractive—'

'You've done attractive.'

'Okay, he thinks the world of me. He thinks we have a future together,' Sally finished, looking blank.

'And?' Louise was agog.

'It's not so much "and", as "but".'

'Okay, but?'

'But . . .' Sally pursed her lips and focused on the flock wallpaper.

'But . . . don't tell me. He doesn't know the words to "Hotel California".'

'No, no. Nothing so trivial. It's just—'

'His fresh pesto just isn't the same as the stuff out of the jar?'

'Stop it.'

'Well, what do you expect?' Louise stared at Sally in horror. 'How can you say this is like the fifth form? You've

88

got a man who has absolutely everything that a girl could ever want, and you still say a word like "but". What is it you want, for God's sake?'

'Perhaps I'm too fussy. Perhaps it's because I've been single for too long. It seems as if there's something wrong with all of them.'

'Fussy!' Louise threw her napkin down on the tablecloth. 'Bloody hell, Sal, if I'd ever met a man who had just one of those qualities I'd have died of shock. I mean, let's just get this in perspective, shall we? I get the rejects that even the Reject Shop wouldn't stock, and you get hampers from Fortnum and Mason. And you don't even order them. Just don't expect any sympathy.'

Sally pulled herself up straight and rearranged her jacket.

'I was hoping you'd understand. I mean, you haven't settled, have you? Even when you were with Jon, you weren't just with Jon, were you?'

Louise licked her finger and stabbed it around the poppadom basket.

'What exactly do you mean?'

'I mean . . .' Sally leaned forward to be heard as the men at the window table began a chorus of 'The First Time Ever I Saw Your Face' without using their vocal chords. 'All I mean is that you didn't settle, did you?'

'You've started, so you'd better finish,' Louise mumbled, feeling her face becoming hot.

'Look, I don't want to say anything dreadful. Especially not now. It's just that you did tell me about . . . things.'

'I hadn't spoken to you for a month before I rang you about this, remember,' Louise said. 'You can't draw any conclusions about anything.'

'No, I know.'

'Jon was behaving like such a git then. When did I speak to you?' Sally raised her eyebrows. 'Okay, he always behaved like a git. I think I was entitled to give some thought to other people.'

'I know that.'

'So . . .'

'So,' Sally continued. She was being careful now, Louise thought. Tiptoeing over a minefield. 'So, nothing really.'

''Ere, Abdul, bring us the pickle tray or I'll give you a slap.' The summons was accompanied by raucous laughter. Louise aimed a disdainful look towards the table, and froze with horror as she met eyes with half a dozen men.

'Oy, Blondie. Sit on my face and tell me that you love me!'

She looked back to Sally quickly.

'See? Your hair can't be that bad,' Sally said, a little stiffly. 'The men still go for you. They always did.'

'And I'm so delighted,' she retorted flatly. 'That's just what I need right now. A gang bang with six paralytic scaffolders.'

'So.' Sally pulled a face at Louise. 'Shall I get the bill, or do you want a bucket of kulfi to finish things off?'

Louise paused guiltily with the last shred of spinach wrapped around her fork. Sally was smiling again. Louise relaxed and smiled back.

'It's really nice of you to treat me to a meal, Sal. You know I can't afford to do this now.'

'I can't remember a time when you ever could,' Sally said, gazing over her shoulder to attract the waiter's attention. 'That's what you've got to remember. If you're ever going to have a decent standard of living, you've got to do something about it now. Before it's too late.'

'Too late for – what?' Louise was troubled as Sally flicked open her leather wallet and pulled out a credit card. Images of Sally striding up and down Oxford Street wearing a sandwich board with 'The End is Nigh' scrawled on it danced in front of her eyes.

'Everything.' Sally gave her a direct look. She put her elbows on the table and leaned forward sombrely. 'You can't even think about keeping it, Louise. You haven't talked about it all evening, you know. You haven't made any plans, have you?'

Louise shook her head.

'The longer it goes on, the harder it's going to be for you. Believe me, you've got to act quickly on this. You have to get two opinions, then wait for an appointment. And allow time afterwards in case of complications.'

'How do you know so much about it?'

'It happened to a girl at work who told me all about it. She said I was the only one she felt she could confide in.'

'Oh God.'

'Deal with it, Louise,' Sally said. 'Just let me know where to be, and when. They owe me a few days' leave. I'll come and sleep on your sofa.'

'Thanks, Sal.' Louise put her hand over Sally's as she turned her attention to signing the slip. Sally looked up in surprise. 'I want you to know that whatever happens, I'll never forget this.'

Olivia jumped as a hand appeared in front of her eyes clutching a flat brown envelope. She had been lost in her own world. Tomorrow they would all be into December. It meant Christmas was creeping up again. She had been pondering over it all day, with Sarah leaping out at her every few minutes and asking her why she looked so startled seeing as they worked within pissing distance of each other. Olivia had tried to look reprimanding, but had found it difficult. Sarah had a way of saying what they were all thinking.

Now it was well after six, and the last person she

expected to see in the office was Shaun. She had actually been enjoying herself, without Carol hanging from her heels like a vengeful hamster and without Sarah musing about the funny rash on Neal's left testicle. A cold, heavy rain was battering at the window, and it had been calming. She didn't intend to leave before it let up a little. It had been nice to lose herself in her own thoughts while she could still occasionally hear footsteps from the office above, or a door swinging down the corridor. It wasn't like being alone at home.

She took the envelope from Shaun. He perched on the edge of her desk, swinging his leg a little over-cheerfully, she thought, and waited for her to open it. She glanced at his face. It was all expectation, his shaggy eyebrows raised in what looked like hope.

'What is this, Shaun?'

'Something for you,' he said. 'Go on, open it. I promised I'd do it for you, remember?'

She frowned at him as her brain ticked quietly into action, then she remembered. A warm flush spread up her neck.

'Oh good grief! You don't mean my horoscope.'

'I do. It's fascinating. All your life there for you to see.'

'Oh no. I couldn't accept it.' She tried to squash the envelope back into his hand. He pushed it back towards her.

'Yes, you can. It didn't cost me anything. Just a bit of time, which is nothing really.'

As she tried to refuse again she noticed that his cheerful leg had stopped swinging. Her conscience teetered. It was mean of her to disappoint him.

'Go on then.' She buried her confusion under a silly laugh. 'It's just that I'm feeling old, Shaun, and you doing this reminds me that I'll be sixty soon.'

'You don't really think about it like that, do you?' he

92

said. 'Surely age is immaterial. That's what I say. It's what you feel inside that really counts. Who you are. What you're all about. The things you long to do. The hopes, fears, passions, ambitions, all those things that you never breathe a word of to anyone else, in case . . .'

He had been speaking to the corner of the room, but he suddenly dropped his eyes as if he'd remembered Olivia was there. She was all attention.

'In case?'

'In case they think you're stupid.'

'Yes.' She clutched the envelope between her fingers. 'Yes, I think I know what you mean.'

'I know you do,' Shaun nodded. 'That's why I wanted to do your chart. I don't offer my services to just anyone, you know.'

She must have held his eye for a little too long, because he turned very red and looked down at his dangling Hush Puppy. Olivia's face grew warm too. She knew he hadn't meant to say anything quite so suggestive. Sarah would have given him a crude response, they both would have cackled, and he would have bounced out of the office, with Sarah waiting until he was out of earshot before saying, 'Now, is he gay, or what? I can't make it out.'

'I'm very grateful,' she said.

There was a pause. He was waiting for her to open the envelope but she had no intention of looking at the chart with him leaning over her like this. She wasn't good enough at acting to carry it off. She'd played Henry Higgins once, at the grammar school, but even the addition of a moustache the size of a doormat hadn't convinced the audience.

'The rain's getting heavier,' Shaun said, standing up and wandering in an indirect trajectory towards the window. 'And it's pretty cold. Christmas coming. I suppose your daughters will be down again this year?' Shaun had his back to her. He was bouncing up and down on the balls of his feet as he followed a particularly conspicuous raindrop down the glass.

'Er, I'm not sure yet. They're both very busy. Rachel's always rushing around, you know, with her job, and she's got Hallam to think about, and his children. And Louise is always, well, doing something. She's got a boyfriend. Very smart type. In sales. I think she might want to spend Christmas with him this year. They've been together quite a while now.' Olivia stood up and started to clear the papers on her desk into a plastic tray.

'Don't you like him?' Shaun turned round to bounce with his back to the window.

'Who?'

'Louise's boyfriend. It's the way you said it. I got the feeling you didn't like him.'

Olivia smiled at Shaun. 'I've only met him once.'

'And no grandchildren?' Shaun raised his eyebrows at her again.

'Er, yes, in a way. I've met Hallam's children. They're very sweet.'

'But no real grandchildren yet?'

Olivia packed her tray away in the metal cupboard against the wall. 'I try not to think about it. The girls have their own lives to lead.'

'But is it what you'd like?' Shaun took a step forward, his eyes questioning. 'It's just that my mother goes on and on about it. Do all women of a certain age go on about grandchildren?'

Olivia shut the cupboard firmly, and twisted the latch.

'I suppose it's to do with being alone, feeling that there isn't anybody to make a fuss over. When your own children grow up, they don't need you any more. There's something about small children that makes you feel wanted.'

Shaun moved towards the door as Olivia slipped on her

raincoat and hooked her umbrella out of the rack in the coat stand. She frowned as she gazed over the empty office. She'd forgotten something, she was sure of it. Shaun hesitated beside her.

'Got the chart?' he asked.

'Oh yes. It's in my bag.'

'Good.'

Of course, it was just that Shaun had come in and upset her usual routine. She made her way around the desks to the king-sized one at the back and dropped the seat of Carol's swivel chair as far as it would go. She patted the seat, and stood up again, smiling brightly at her companion.

'There! All done.'

'What was that for?'

'Oh, just in case the cleaner forgets. One of us always tries to remember.'

'Er, are you intending to get a bus in all this rain?' Shaun said as she flicked off the lights.

'Yes.' She walked with him along the corridor.

'It's just that I could give you a lift home if you wanted.'

'It's very kind of you.' She patted his arm. 'But I've stood at that bus stop through rain, wind, sleet, hail, you name it. I shall be here tonight, as usual. We women of a certain age like our little routines, you know.'

She parted company with Shaun in the road outside the building, and waved as his Citroën lurched away like a temperamental racehorse. She watched his tail-lights disappear, wondering if she'd been too stubborn in refusing a lift. It was very cold. In the past, Bob would have picked her up if the weather had been so unforgiving. Now their old Ford Escort sat in the garage like a monument. She hadn't minded Bob driving her around, but she didn't want other people doing it. It made her feel like a bag of shopping.

She walked down the steep hill into the town, the squalling wind massaging her calves. No, it was better to be getting the bus. It meant that she could sit with other passengers, gazing through the rain-spattered window at the images of the town as they drifted past. She liked the quiet companionship of the journey.

Before she reached the bus stop, she stopped to stare at the bright window display that always caught her eye. She held her umbrella tightly while the traffic in the High Street threw splashes on the back of her fawn tights, and read the notice that had been intriguing her for the past two months. Somebody in there had a sense of humour.

Why don't you go away?

It was written with red marker pen on fluorescent green paper. Below it, white cards were dotted on a display showing cheap fares to destinations all around the world. She read them all again, then glanced at her watch. If she was quick, she might just make the half past.

Louise waited in the doctor's surgery idling through *Hello!* magazine and trying to ignore the toddler who was standing next to her knees, staring at her.

'Come 'ere, Alexander!' the woman opposite her with a baby balanced on her knee leaned forward and hissed across the room. 'Leave that lady alone.'

'It's all right.' Louise gave a curt smile. 'It's very flattering to get so much attention from a male. Even if he is a bit diminutive.'

The woman stared at Louise aggressively. Louise turned back to the magazine quickly. Whatever she'd said, it hadn't been taken in the spirit that it was meant.

The doctor's surgery was turning out to be a fascinating place. This was her third visit, and she was starting to get the feel of things. She knew that the surgery was run by a husband-and-wife team. They were both Sri Lankan, the receptionist had told her on her first visit, and *he* always had more free slots than she did. Louise couldn't possibly have contemplated seeing a male doctor about this, so she had been added to the list of names waiting to see Dr Balasingam, female. The first morning she had waited two hours for the privilege, and it had been worth it. Dr Balasingam was on the button, that was for sure. While Louise had been waiting she had been curious to see every patient who arrived being offered an immediate slot with Dr Balasingam, male. All had hedged, and opted for his wife.

On her second visit, Louise had felt sorry for Dr Balasingam, male. She'd almost wished she had something gender unspecific to deal with. The measles or a bad ear infection. Surely, she'd thought, gazing around the surgery at the stacked bodies who all looked like malingerers, one of them might have had the decency to boost Dr Balasingam, male's, confidence, and opt for a slot with him. But it was not to be.

She had been sitting next to an elderly woman who was wheezing violently and pausing every few seconds to produce a puffer spray from her coat pocket and squirt it down her throat. Choosing a moment when the woman did not seem in imminent danger of choking to death, Louise had leaned sideways, and whispered to her.

'What's wrong with Dr Balasingam?'

The old lady had wiggled her eyebrows and contorted her face meaningfully.

'He's a bit eccentric. Mrs Burton came in with corns, and ended up having her whole diet changed to nothing but potatoes and them lentil things. Nobody's quite sure about him.'

'Ah, I see.'

'He doesn't give prescriptions.'

'Ah.'

'Nor them antibiotics.' The old woman lowered her voice and added vehemently, 'Never.'

'Oh. Dreadful.'

'Yes. And he takes hours. It's not what you want, is it? Hours of claptrap. You want a bottle of pills and out the other side.'

'Oh yes, indeed.'

'But *she*'s very good. Yes, very good. She knows her stuff, that young lady. I don't care what they say about foreign doctors, she's very good.'

'I see,' Louise had nodded.

'Did wonders for me,' the elderly lady had concluded, dissolving into a coughing fit which had the whole surgery sliding to the edges of their plastic chairs ready to pounce and do mouth-to-mouth if required.

But today Louise had turned up, prepared to wait her full two hours to see Dr Balasingam, female, and had been told that she wasn't taking a surgery that afternoon. There was only *him*. Even the receptionist seemed vaguely alarmed at the situation. Louise had thought about putting off her appointment, but had decided that Sally was right. This needed to be dealt with as soon as possible. And there was no need for a physical examination. All she needed to do was follow on from her past conversations, and tell him that she'd made a decision.

Dr Balasingam, female's, absence from the surgery explained why it was so empty today. Louise used her peripheral vision to analyse the woman with the baby, trying to rise above the fact that the toddler next to her was now banging a plastic truck against her ankle. She wondered which of them needed the doctor. Since this had happened to her she hadn't been able to see anything wrong with anybody at the surgery, apart from the elderly lady and her incredible collapsing chest. Everybody else seemed happy, sprightly and just plain attention seeking.

98

Not like herself, with her real problem, and her real condition.

The banging on her ankle became agonising. She glared down into the gnome-like face of the child in the most scary way she could muster. He stared back, unfazed.

'Get lost!' she hissed. The child frowned back, trying to read her lips. 'Go on, sod off!' she mouthed as clearly as possible.

'You're a tart!' The toddler shouted at her, and ran across the room to dive into a pile of Lego.

Louise burned her eyes back towards her magazine. Her fingers were twitching to deliver a playful slap. She tried to calm herself.

It was a sign. Somebody out there was telling her that she was no good with children. She didn't understand children. No, it was even simpler than that. She didn't like children. Where on earth was the dilemma?

A male voice came drifting over the intercom. It was pale, with lilting tones. Louise perked up, intrigued.

'Mrs Daversham, pick up thy bed and walk to consulting room number two!'

The intercom crackled.

'How does this turn off? Oh, I've got it—'

The intercom went silent, as did the waiting room. The receptionist raised her head slowly like a ghoulish butler, and nodded slowly at the woman with the baby perched on her knee. She picked herself up hesitantly from her chair and headed, white faced, down the corridor, with the toddler sent by Lucifer hanging from her iron grip, his fluorescent trainers dragging along the thin carpet.

Louise looked quickly down to her magazine again, her heart pounding. She was next. In a matter of minutes, she would be walking down the corridor, and announcing the most important decision of her life to an extra from *Rocky Horror*.

99

She waited as the minutes rolled by. An awed hush had descended on the waiting room. Even the receptionist seemed to be ducking behind her desk, as if she expected a cry of terror or abject pain to arrow down the corridor and shiver in the air over their heads. Mrs Daversham had been in for twenty minutes. She thought about going home and was on the verge of making a polite excuse at reception and saving her revelation for another day, when Mrs Daversham reappeared, complete with two very subdued children, and exited from the surgery without so much as a nod in anybody's direction.

The intercom crackled. Sparks of electricity shot through Louise's body.

'Miss Twigg, kindly be so good as to transport yourself in the direction of room number two where your consultant awaits.'

The receptionist peeped over her appointments book. 'Good luck!' Louise heard her whisper as she walked past.

Louise pushed open the door, and walked inside. She closed it behind her. A tiny man was crouched over a wide desk, evidently reading through her medical notes. He seemed much older than Dr Balasingam, female. His bald head gleamed like a dimpled Malteser under the yellow arc of light cast by his desk lamp. He didn't seem to notice that she'd arrived. She cleared her throat.

'Yes, yes. I know that you're here. I have to know all about you, don't I, before you can tell me what ails you today? Please, do seat yourself and be comfortable. I shall be with you in two beats of an eyelash.'

Louise slipped into the leather chair opposite his desk and watched him read. He seemed completely engrossed, as if he was reading a great work of literature. Every so often he stopped to sigh, or to nod, or to raise his eyebrows, but he didn't look up until he had scoured every scrap of paper before him, and when he did, Louise was taken aback. This terrifying character had none of his wife's efficiency or abject professionalism. His deep brown eyes were spiritual. They shone out of his small head like beacons. She found herself smiling at him.

'Ah, my dear, you have little to smile about, I think. You are contemplating the great question of life.' He put his hands together in front of his compact body. 'It is such a difficult thing, to face oneself in this way.'

Louise stopped as she was about to open her mouth. She was confused. Her conversations with Dr Balasingam, female, had been nothing like this. The other doctor was herself a thoroughly modern woman, probably in her late thirties, and Louise had felt that she had covered all the ground that she should do under the circumstances. She had been given leaflets, told of her options, and it had all been done with enormous sympathy. But this wasn't the same.

'You see . . .' Dr Balasingam got up from his chair and walked across the room. Louise decided that it was better if she stayed seated. It would be embarrassing to stand up and to end up speaking down to his shiny bald head. 'This is an important moment for you. You have no support from the man involved, but still you must decide what your feelings are towards your infant.'

'Infant?' The word was odd.

'I only say this because I have seen such sadness. You must think for yourself at this time. People will try to tell you what to do. They feel more relaxed, you see, if the people they love take the same decisions as they would do themselves. That is only natural. But there is only one thing that you must consider here, and that is yourself. How do you feel?'

Louise waited for him to go on. It was a full minute before she realised that he had asked her a direct question, and was pointing his eager brown eyes in her direction.

'I feel . . .' Louise searched her mental thesaurus. The word she came up with was disappointingly ordinary: 'Sick.'

'Oh dear. There is a basin here, and I will not watch if you are embarrassed.'

'No, I mean sick as in tired, if you know what I mean. It's as if this has been going on for ever, and I'm trapped in limbo.'

'Ah! Limbo. Yes, I can see why you might feel that.' He wandered over to the window and played with the folds in the net curtain until he had knotted it tightly around his finger. It took him some minutes to extricate himself. Then he turned around with more purpose. 'So, Miss Twigg. You have made a decision.'

'Er . . .'

'I think that you have come here because you are decided upon something. If not, I feel you would have wished to speak to my wife.'

'Yes.' Louise readjusted the strap of her bag. Of all her conversations to date, this was the most boggling. 'Yes, I'm going to go ahead with it.'

'With . . .?' He opened up his brown eyes and waited.

'With a termination. I have to. It's what I've got to do.'

He nodded, showing neither relief nor dismay, and popped into his chair again. He picked up his pen.

'So, Miss Twigg, perhaps you will tell me why you feel that you must do this. I have to make notes, you see. I apologise to you for the intrusive manner in which medicine is conducted, but it is the way of the law.'

'I understand. Your wife explained it all to me very clearly.'

'Yes, yes. She would. She is clear, is she not?' He lapsed into a whimsical smile. An absurd thought struck Louise.

He was in love with his wife! And she could see now why she would be in love with him too. For a moment, she felt stupidly romantic. Where might they have met? At medical school? Through their families? On a moonlit beach fringed with palm trees? She gave the doctor a sloppy smile.

'Miss Twigg?'

'Yes.' Louise cleared her throat and pushed the image of Dr Balasingam in a sarong, down on one knee, from her mind. 'The thing is, I'm thirty-two, and I haven't got a job. I haven't got a boyfriend either. My – er – immediate prospects are somewhat limited.'

'Ah, your prospects.' Dr Balasingam looked up with a light of hope in his eyes. 'That is an interesting use of vocabulary. You are a lover of Jane Austen, I think? Have you been a student of English literature?'

'Er, not really. I did biology at university.' He seemed crestfallen. 'I watched Colin Firth on the television, though.'

He put his head on one side like a sparrow analysing a crumb.

'I was speaking of the six great novels.' He waited, but as she didn't offer any encouragement, straightened in his chair. 'Please carry on. Your prospects are not good.'

'That's right. And I can't do this on my own. Besides, I'm not even sure . . .'

'Yes?'

'. . . if I can afford to support myself, let alone another human being.' Louise let out a long breath. 'It's just no good. I didn't ask for this to happen. Everything's wrong. The more I see children around me, with fathers and mothers, with a ready-made family to support them, the more I know I can't do this. It's just not fair. And I haven't done anything with my own life yet. I can't impart any advice, or wisdom, or anything to a child.'

'I see.' He turned his attention to her medical card, scrawling notes in a wild hand which seemed to take up half a page per word. 'And is there anything else?'

'Isn't that enough?' Louise pulled herself up in her chair. 'Please don't make me feel guilty about this. It's so difficult. You have no idea how painful this is. You have no right to make it worse. I've never felt so confused in my life.'

His brown eyes studied her as he listened. Louise felt her emotions rising to the surface. She had under-estimated herself. She had been suppressing any violent reactions she might be having, but that didn't mean they weren't there.

'Can you imagine how incredible it is to be pregnant? That after years of being autonomous, you're no longer a single being, acting selfishly, only for yourself and your own interests? And to know at the same time that it's impossible to carry it through?' She swallowed hard. 'And what's more, I'm condemned if I have an abortion, and condemned if I become a single mother. Don't you see that? That's what having a choice really means. Which would you prefer to be castigated for?'

'This is how you feel?' He looked at her sorrowfully.

'Of course. Would you want to be pigeon-holed? I'm a statistic whatever I do now. That's what nobody realises.'

She reached into her pocket for a tissue, her eyes brimming. She pulled out a crumpled piece of paper with biro scribbled on it and stared at it for a moment. The man with the wide green eyes flashed across her memory. The paper was stuck together where her nose had run all over it as she'd walked from the Jobcentre to the little café up the road. She'd forgotten that it was still there. She pushed it back, and accepted instead a tissue from the box that the doctor passed her over the desk.

'I'm sorry.' She blew her nose and took a shaky breath.

'I've been bottling that up. It's just the most unbelievable thing that has ever happened. I've never wanted to cry so much in my whole life.'

'In which case,' the lilting voice of the bald doctor came back, 'you must cry until you have drained yourself entirely of tears. And while you are doing that, I will make us both a cup of instant coffee. That's if I can find the kettle. I know it's here somewhere.'

'Oh.' Louise watched him as he searched through a series of cupboards and finally produced a kettle, waving it at her in triumph.

'One thing I do have, Miss Twigg,' he said, grinning at her cheerfully, 'is time.'

Chapter Seven

The following morning, Louise woke up and found that the sun was slanting across her bedroom from a small gap in the curtains. It highlighted a million particles of dust on its way over to a heap of ancient newspapers teetering on the edge of her chest of drawers. She lay very still. Gradually, her conversation with the doctor came back to her. She turned over and snuggled into her fluorescent pillowcase. She would just lie here for a moment, then she would get up, clear up the kitchen, and cook herself poached egg on toast.

Buttery toast, with the egg really gooey in the middle. Two eggs, in fact, and two slices of toast. She hadn't eaten poached eggs since her mother used to cook breakfast for them before they went to school. Why had she forgotten how good it was? And then she would get ready and go down to her interview at the Jobcentre, with all her forms correctly filled in. A sense of well-being came over her. It was all going to be all right. She only had to take things a step at a time, and stay calm. She gave a satisfied sigh and glimpsed her radio alarm to check the time.

'Oh my God!' She sat bolt upright. 'Oh no, oh no, oh no!'

She threw herself out of bed and yanked open the curtains. The sun streamed in, dazzling her. She charged through the particles of dust and ran to the bathroom, ripping off her T-shirt and twisting the shower handle as she jumped into the bath. The water was cold. She screamed and twisted the knob the other way until boiling water pounded at her shoulders in a cloud of steam. She squirted shampoo on her head while she hopped around rubbing soap under her arms. She stopped in horror at the sensation under her fingertips. When had she last shaved her armpits? A neat little gorse bush had rooted itself under each of them. But then again, she reasoned as she grabbed at her toothbrush while trying to rinse the shampoo out of her hair, it didn't matter any more. What mattered was that she'd made a decision, and that her life had changed.

She sprinted back through the kitchen, stopping only to open the fridge and stare longingly at the contents. That was another thing that was going to change. From now on, she was going to have a well-stocked fridge. Full of healthy things. She'd go shopping on her way home. She raced on to the bedroom, sorting through her pile of unwashed clothes like a threshing machine, and pulling on a thick green jumper and a pair of button-up red jeans.

Everything still fitted her in all the right places, she thought, wincing as her hands brushed her breasts inside her bra and sent a shiver of pain through to the nerves in her teeth. That was a new development. Painful boobs. PMT boobs were painful enough, but these things felt as if they were about to launch rockets. Just what might Jon, or Lenny, or Giles, think if she thrust these weapons in their eyes now? But it didn't matter any more. And what's more, she no longer cared that it didn't matter.

'I'm a woman, W-O-M-A-N,' she sang, wiping her foundation over her nose and stabbing at her eyes with the mascara brush, 'I'll say it again. I'm a woman . . . Ow.'

She grabbed her jacket, collected her forms together, put them in a Co-op carrier bag (hoping that the receptionist with the bob would feel more sorry for her than if she turned up with her forms in a Hatchards bag), zipped on her knee-length boots, and tromped out of the house.

It was clear and bright outside. And it was December. She flung her scarf over her shoulder and paced up the South Ealing road admiring the whiteness of the buildings in the winter sun. The sky was a crisp blue. She pulled on her gloves and wiggled her fingers. Christmas was coming soon.

Christmas. The second one to be faced at home without her father around. She could see his photographs now, perched on the mantelpiece, delicately arranged on her mother's dressing-table. Her father as a young man with a hod of bricks over his broad shoulder. Her father with his face whipped into ruddiness and health by years of exposure to the elements. Her father with his arms around her, squeezing the breath out of her in a bear-hug. What would he think of her now?

'Grandad,' she murmured into the air.

She'd found a way round it after all, thanks to Dr Balasingam. He made a lousy cup of coffee, but he was a fantastic listener. From now on, she would make sure she saw him for anything that didn't involve personal probings or sore nipples. He had let her talk and talk until she had found her own way to a conclusion. He'd asked questions that hadn't occurred to anybody else. She was glad now that he had a reputation for being insane. Nobody had interrupted them.

She reached the Jobcentre and danced through the door. It seemed much less daunting now. All she had to do was to be sure of her story, and she would get through to the next stage. After that, she would make other plans.

'Short-term goals,' she chanted under her breath as she set the receptionist with the bob in her sights. 'One step at a time. Be confident. It's going to be all right.'

She flashed a happy smile at the woman who looked up, gave her a suspicious look, then seemed to suffer a dim bout of recognition.

'Louise Twigg. I'm here to talk about being destitute. I've got an appointment.'

'One moment, please.' The receptionist dropped her head to search through a handwritten appointment book. 'Yes, you can wait in the waiting area. Your name will be called. If you can give me your forms, I'll hand them to the officer.'

Louise pulled her forms from her bag, flashing the Co-op logo in the woman's face, and presented them. She found a row of chairs and sat in one, trying to look poor and downtrodden, yet at the same time keen. She had a sudden empathy with actors going for auditions. 'I can do happy, I can do sad, I can do active jobsearch!' It struck her that a good start would be to wander around and look at the cards. She got up, making sure she was steady on her feet this time (to faint twice under the Catering board would look a little contrived) and headed for Office and Secretarial, adopting an expression of fascination.

She scanned the cards. She stopped to focus on one and blinked in disbelief at the offer of four hundred and fifty-five pounds an hour before she realised that the decimal point was in the wrong place. It was a shame. It would have been worth doing, even for just a day.

There was a gentle tap on her shoulder.

She stiffened, remembering to put her active-jobsearch face on before she turned round to impress the benefits officer. A pair of wide green eyes stared into hers. A hot flush instantly covered her entire body. Her first thought on seeing Ewan McGregor again was that she had gorse bushes in her armpits. She clamped her arms to her sides as if he would be able to detect the horror lurking there.

'Hi!' she said. It came out a little operatically. She swallowed hard. 'What are you doing here?'

He smirked at her. She remembered that he wasn't big on social graces.

109

'Sightseeing. I usually bring a packed lunch and a thermos. What about you?'

'Oh, I'm here for an interview.' She cringed. Why hadn't she said something witty? She'd have to try harder. He looked casually unimpressed. But then, he was the one who'd tapped her on the shoulder. She raised her eyebrows at him questioningly.

'Listen,' he said. 'I don't want you to think I'm stalking you or anything, but I have been hanging around hoping to see you again.'

'Yes?' Oh joy. Oh thank you, God. Louise decided to forget about being pregnant for the next thirty seconds. A girl had to be allowed to dream.

'The thing is, you know that piece of paper I gave you?'

Louise's hand shot guiltily into her jacket pocket. She fingered the crumpled paper, firmly stuck together with dried mucus.

'I can't say I remember.'

'Yeah, the piece of paper I gave you to hold over your nose? You had a cold, and no tissues. You must remember.'

'Oh, *that* piece of paper.' She nodded, feigning enlightenment. 'Yes, now you mention it, I do remember. It was very kind of you to help me out.'

'Well, the thing is, I need it back. There isn't any chance at all that you hung on to it, is there?'

Her fingers tightened on the paper like steel pincers. No way. No bloody way. She was not about to stand in front of the most gorgeous man in London and present him with a piece of screwed-up A4 paper covered in her own snot. Not in her wildest nightmares. Eating soggy spaghetti out of a pan of lukewarm water was like wild flirtation by comparison. And dashing though Lenny had been in his time, he had nothing on this one.

'God, no, I'm so sorry . . .'

'Shit.' He looked thoroughly crestfallen. He pushed his hands up through his pale brown hair, leaving it sticking out in spikes. If anyone else had done that they would have looked stupid. It made him look even more sexy. He turned away, stared around the room, and came back to face her again. He chewed his lip.

'Do you know where you put it? I mean, it couldn't still be in a bin at your house, could it?'

She gazed at him, curiosity needling her. What was on this piece of paper that was so crucial? She'd assumed it was a shopping list or a page of doodles, but judging by the anguished look on his face it was a matter of life and death.

Excitement tickled its way down her spine. Her fingernails dug into the much-coveted paper, proving that it was firmly stuck into one amorphous mass. Whatever she was holding, the tragic thing was that it was no use to him now anyway. Unless he was into modern art, and wanted to display it in a glass case in the Serpentine Gallery. 'Snot on A4 feint, by Ewan McGregor.' No, he couldn't be an artist. He wasn't wearing tie-dye leggings. Just the neatly fitting denims that he'd had on before that were nicely crumpled in all the right places. She dragged her eyes back up to his.

'I'm afraid I threw it away. I'm not even sure where. I empty my pockets all the time, you see. I'm a bit neurotic like that. Can't stand pockets full of gunk.'

She smiled, remembering that she'd produced a medieval peppermint wrapper right in front of him to wrap around her nose. With any luck he wouldn't remember. But he was giving her such a disappointed look, and she wanted to keep him talking to her. Perhaps she could give him a glimmer of hope, just to see him smile again.

'Look, I'll tell you what I'll do. When I go home, I'll

check through all my waste-paper baskets and see if it's there. I suppose it's just possible I chucked it in one and forgot about it.'

'So you don't empty your bins as often as you empty your pockets?' He gave her a short smile.

'No, bins are different,' she said, as if there was a logic to any of this.

'I did ask at the café, once I realised what I'd given you, and they checked the loo at the back. No luck. So trying to find you again was my only hope.'

'What was it you gave me?' She tried to look curious in a hypothetical way. 'Just in case I find it, and don't realise.'

'Oh, it was just something I scribbled. It won't mean anything to you, but it's important to Ginger and the rest of the guys.'

'Yes,' she breathed quietly. This was starting to sound dodgy. Who were Ginger and the rest of the guys? A team of bank robbers? Kidnappers? Terrorists? And she had blown her nose on the only copy of the plans?

'Louise Twigg.' A voice hailed her from across the building.

'Oh, that's me!' She held up her hand and a shower of rubbish fluttered out of her pocket and sailed to the floor. She squatted quickly to scoop up the stringy ends of dried tissue, sweet wrappers, and the cellophane off her last packet of cigarettes. She squashed them into a ball in her palm and shoved them back into her pocket. He was still watching her thoughtfully.

'I'll give you my number,' he said, casting a glance over his shoulder at the suited man who was waiting with scarcely concealed impatience for Louise to follow him. He fished around in his denim pockets and found a cigarette packet. It rattled. He took out the cigarette, put it in his mouth, and ripped off the top of the packet, flattening it out against the Office and Secretarial board while he wrote a number down. He handed it to Louise. She glanced at it.

'I don't know your name,' she said.

'Ash.' He gave a short laugh. 'It's what the guys call me.'

'You can't smoke in here!' the receptionist with the bob screeched across at them.

'Fucking people,' Ash muttered. 'I wasn't going to light the bloody thing. See you around, Louise.'

He sauntered out of the building, stopping to clap on the back one of the old men who Louise recognised as having been fascinated with her gusset. Then he was gone.

Ash, she mused as she trotted obediently over to the benefits officer in the suit who was glancing agitatedly at his watch. It could be a gang member's name. Ash the Knife. Ash the Acid Bath Burglar. Ash the Great Train Terrorist. She vowed to herself that she would attack this piece of paper with a chisel if necessary to see what was on it. A burst of anticipation danced over her body.

But this was reality, she reminded herself as the benefits officer led her to a desk, invited her to sit down, and paused to crack his knuckles and scratch the end of his nose with his biro before sitting down opposite her.

'Good God, what are you doing here?'

'That's a fine way to greet your little sister,' Louise replied as she shivered on Rachel's doorstep. 'You might at least ask me in.'

'Of course you can come in. You're lucky I'm here. Hallam's in Brussels – again – and I've got the place to myself. You didn't come all this way on the tube, did you? What would you have done if I wasn't here?'

Louise stepped into Rachel's hall, stopping to close her eyes briefly and savour the merits of central heating. She began to sway gently.

'Louise? Are you drunk?'

'No. Wish I was.'

'Great. I'll open another bottle then. Come through to the kitchen. You could have called me, you know.'

Louise plodded after Rachel, watching her tall body gyrating ahead of her into the bright kitchen. She'd had her dark hair cut very short again. It suited her. She'd always had more than her fair share of eyes and cheekbones. Her eyes were a deep brown, her hair thick and black, and she'd turned heads since she was about fourteen. She was more like their grandmother than either of their parents. She'd been dusky too. Louise had been lucky enough to inherit her mother's eyes and her father's biceps, but none of their grandmother's sultry charm. But she hadn't come here to be churlish about Rachel's looks. She'd come to be churlish about the fact that she never answered her phone.

'How could I have called you? You never answer the sodding phone. There might be an emergency or something, and you'd never know. I did try calling you, actually.'

Rachel turned round with a chilled bottle of wine rescued from the fridge. She opened her eyes wide.

'So it was you who left messages saying "No, you won't" and "Bloody liars", then?'

'I said "Bloody liars" but I didn't say "No you won't".'

'That's odd. I wonder who that was?' Rachel had the bottle open in half a second. Years of practice, Louise noted.

'Probably one of your cocaine addicts finishing a sentence he'd started three years before. I won't have wine, actually. Can I have something soft? Just a glass of water will be great.'

Rachel's fine eyebrows levitated in the air.

'Shit, you're not on the wagon, are you? I was hoping we could get pissed.'

'You can get pissed if you want.' Louise smiled, but

114

Rachel was still staring at her in horror. 'Er, I've got a pig of a hangover, if you must know,' she lied. 'I can still taste the gin today.'

'Ah.' Rachel nodded with understanding. 'Well, if you will drink spirits, you'll feel like shit. Best to stick to the soft stuff, like I do.'

Louise watched Rachel throw wine into a glass the size of the FA cup. When she put the bottle down again it was half-empty. She took a deep sip of it, sloshed tap water into a glass for Louise, handed it to her, and motioned her to follow.

They went through into Rachel's sitting room. Louise instantly started to relax. Sometimes she'd wished Rachel and Hallam would adopt her. Whatever her flat was lacking seemed to be present in Rachel's house. She had artful lighting, tasteful throws all over the two sofas and the armchairs, a spattering of ethnic rugs, and real paintings around the walls. Louise had the same ideas, but in Rachel's house everything actually matched. If only she'd earned some money, Louise taunted herself, just what sort of life might she be living now?

Rachel collapsed into an armchair. Louise frowned, wondering how many FA cups' worth of white wine her sister had got through before she'd turned up. She'd always had a drink on the go since Louise could remember. But Rachel worked hard. She guessed she'd earned the right to play hard too.

'Actually, I'm really glad you came,' Rachel announced, curling her black-stockinged legs under her tight skirt. 'I had a weird message from Mum the other day asking me if I wanted a vest. I think she's cracking up. And Hallam's being a git at the moment. He's never here, he never wants to talk, and the only time we spend together we're being mobbed by those two little bastards. He's besotted with them, Christ knows why.'

She stopped to light a cigarette. Louise sat back in the floppy armchair, pointing her nostrils at the clean air at the back of the room. In the last couple of days the smell of cigarette smoke had suddenly made her stomach lurch. Rachel didn't offer her a cigarette, which saved another feeble excuse. She seemed too preoccupied. She swept her dark, silky fringe from her eyes.

'His company are downsizing. He thinks he might be on the hit list. As for me, I'm surrounded by no-hopers. I'm pissed off with everyone looking to me for an answer. They all think I'm the oracle. Really, they do. I'm drinking too much, smoking too much, and I haven't had sex for three days. You know the sort of thing. Bloody horrible life this is.'

Louise took a sip of her water and loosened her coat. This could be a long night.

'It's not just the money. We'll manage on my earnings. I've been doing really well, and as long as he gets the redundancy package he deserves, we'll struggle on. But that's all we do, Louise. Struggle. I'm getting a bit hacked off, to be honest with you.' She took another slurp of her wine and a drag of her cigarette. She gazed distantly at the far painting of a woman with three breasts that Louise had never had the courage to say she didn't understand.

'Do you know what? Sometimes I just want to throw it all in. Everything I've built up. I just want to give it all two fingers and do something really relaxing. I do get tired, you know. I mean, physically tired. Everybody's so used to me staying up all night at gigs, working all day to make it work for those ungrateful, smelly little objects.'

'Hallam's children?'

'The bands.' Rachel sounded irritated. 'They're so bloody full of themselves, so keen to show that they can do it on their own. They cling round your neck like drowning men before they make the big time, and afterwards they lie around in mirror shades with a week's worth of stubble, and complain about the deal they've got. No, Louise. I'm really glad you came. It makes me realise what's wrong with it all.' She leaned over the tiled coffee table and flicked her ash in the drip tray of the Hedera ivy. 'I just want to be a zoo keeper.'

'You do?' Louise clutched her glass of water to her chest.

'Yes, or a swimming pool consultant.'

'I don't think you'd actually get to lie around in swimming pools all day if you were a swimming pool consultant.'

'Don't be pedantic,' Rachel snapped. 'I just mean that sometimes it all gets too much.'

Louise shifted uncomfortably. Rachel was so good at what she did, and so powerful. She was just having a funny turn brought on by several crates of white wine. She was usually so big hearted, if mercurial. She seemed more agitated than usual tonight.

'You'll be fine,' Louise reassured her, after a suitable pause. 'Don't worry about it. Hallam loves you, doesn't he? And you love him.'

'So?'

'So I think that's something to be happy about. I really do.'

'God, Louise, if I want saccharine, I'll watch *Richard and Judy*,' Rachel tutted dismissively.

She inhaled again on her cigarette, narrowing her eyes across the coffee table. Louise wiggled around in her seat. Any moment now she would be warm enough to take her coat off, then she wouldn't feel quite so frumpy and stupid.

'All I was trying to say is that Hallam loving you is quite important. I think it is, anyway.'

'I know that. It's just all gone wrong and I don't know why.'

117

'But he's so much nicer than all the others that came before him.'

'*All* the others? Make me feel like a slapper, why don't you?'

'No, I just mean that you've got a real relationship. You live together. You've got this lovely house. It's not just a house, it's a home. He pays half the mortgage. When you get a water bill, you discuss it. You split your phone bill down the middle.' Louise conjured up the image of her own unpaid bill just to torture herself even further. 'You play with the children together.'

Rachel squirmed into a straighter position and peered at Louise closely.

'You have been watching *Richard and Judy*, haven't you?'

'So what if I have?' Louise stuck her chin out. 'You only knock it because you haven't seen it. You don't know what it means to millions of people.'

'The reason I slag it off,' Rachel explained elaborately, 'is exactly because I don't have time to watch it. That's the point. Jesus, Louise, if anyone's got time to sit down and watch Nicky Clarke do perms for the cast of *The Bill* for two hours every morning, there's got to be something missing from their lives, hasn't there?'

'And if you couldn't get out?'

'What, if there was a tube strike, or something?'

'I mean, if you broke your leg.' Louise struggled to get her coat down over her shoulders. She was feeling very warm now. 'Or, I don't know. What if you were at home all day, for some reason?'

'Waiting for the French polisher?' Rachel quirked a sarcastic eyebrow.

'Something like looking after children. What about all those women, stuck at home, washing nappies and clearing up sick? Why shouldn't they watch Nicky Clarke doing perms for two hours?'

'I didn't realise you felt so strongly about it,' Rachel said, looking amused. She sank back into the sofa again and continued to consider Louise. 'You've lost your job again, haven't you?'

'Oh, leave it out, Rachel.'

'You have.' Rachel blew out a long trail of smoke. Louise bit back a nauseous lurch. 'You're bloody hopeless. How long at that last place? A couple of months?'

'Well over a year. Anyway, they're downsizing.' Louise emphasised her point with a widening of her eyes. 'It happens to the best of us, you know. They don't need me any more.'

'Oh, Lou.' Rachel shook her head. Louise stared down at the ethnic stick figures on the rug, wishing that Rachel would never have cause to say 'Oh, Lou' to her again. She wavered. She hadn't been sure whether she would tell Rachel about the baby or not. A raw, familial instinct inside her was urging her to rush the information out. But her rational head stepped in and warned her away. She knew what she was doing now. She wasn't going to let anyone else muddy the waters for her.

'So that's why you came here.' Rachel pulled a face, sticking her glass into her mouth at the same time. She swallowed a little too noisily for a sober person. 'No wonder you've got a hangover. I'd have a hangover, if I were you. So are you going to let me help you at last?'

'I'll sort it out. Just don't tell Mum, please. I don't want her to worry about it.'

'Okay. Deal. I won't tell Mum. Does that mean no, you don't want me to help you?'

'Music's your thing, Rachel. It always was. I wouldn't be as good as you.'

'How do you know if you don't give yourself a chance? There's a slot for you, that's all I'm saying. I can introduce you to the right people and give you a break. You could actually have a career instead of a string of Saturday jobs.'

'Rachel!' Louise frowned at her severely. 'Just let me work this one through for myself. Please.'

'Okay.' Rachel shrugged. 'Be a hero then. I've got other things on my mind.'

There was a silence. Rachel lolled back on the sofa and stared at her ceiling. Louise glanced up. It was devoid of cobwebs. But the credit for that was due to the woman who came in twice a week and got rid of them. Louise would have to clamber up on a stool to get rid of hers. That was another thing on the agenda for tomorrow.

'To tell you the truth, Louise, I think Hallam and I have reached the end of the road.'

Louise pulled herself up in her chair, her attention grabbed.

'Oh no, Rachel. You can't mean that.'

'I do. I'm sick of it all. His ex-wife, maintenance claims, what's good for the boys. I mean,' she dropped chocolate eyes on Louise, which were genuinely soulful, 'I never asked to be a stepmother, did I? I never said that I was maternal. I've tried, I really have. But I tell you what really pisses me off.' She waved a long, slim finger. Another glorious feature that Louise had failed to inherit. 'Just as I get used to them on a Sunday night, they bugger off again. It happens every time they're over. It takes me all weekend to get in the mood to have them here, and then they're gone. Whisked away again.'

'I thought you liked them being whisked away.'

'Not on Sunday nights. I have to go through all that adjustment to get used to them, to be interested in their lives and what they think, then they evaporate. Sometimes I think the only reason I've put up with it for so long is for Mum.'

'What?'

'You know, so that she's got some surrogate grandchildren. I'd feel so sorry for her otherwise, with Dad gone, and nothing else to live for.'

Louise paused to absorb the series of opinions that Rachel had produced, most of which were new to her.

'But – but she hardly sees the boys!'

'She knows they exist, doesn't she?' Rachel sighed, her head flopping against the loose cushions. She spoke again, slowly. 'The thing is, Louise, I've met someone else.'

Louise swallowed. This was seriously dismal news. Rachel and Hallam were good together. Hallam was nice. He brought out the best in Rachel. And Louise was growing to like the boys too. Rachel gave Louise a secretive smile.

'You'd better tell me about it.' Louise's voice came out as a sigh.

'Well, I was at a gig keeping an eye on a new band we've signed, and there was a man in the crowd. A doctor. Twenty-seven, blond hair, amazing orange eyes, six foot three. He bought me a drink, and we got talking. What do you think?'

'I think he's younger than Hallam, blonder than Hallam, and more orange eyed than Hallam.'

'Don't be obtuse. I mean, what do you really think? We talked about me, my life, my job. He was really interested. He asked me why I put up with it all.'

'Original,' Louise muttered into her water, wishing heartily that she was in a fit state to drink something strong and neat.

'He's specialising in psychiatry,' Rachel said, her eyes glowing, her legs swinging from the sofa. She leaned forward, her face intense. 'I gave him my card.'

'And?'

'I think I'm going to see him again.'

Louise leaned forward too. It seemed to be the thing to do.

121

'Is this room bugged?' she asked.

'No.'

'Why are you whispering then?'

'God knows.' Rachel threw herself back on the sofa and drained the FA cup. 'Guilt, I suppose. Though why I'm supposed to feel guilty when Hallam never asks me what I feel about anything, I don't know. I just don't know what to do, Lou.'

'Well, what are the options? You cheat on Hallam, feel awful, and get back together, or you cheat on Hallam, feel awful, and leave him.'

Rachel tutted. There was another long pause.

'I thought you might understand. I mean, you hop from one relationship to another, don't you? You're not settled?'

Louise was glad that she was sitting down. To be told by her best friend and her big sister in the space of a few days that she was some sort of role model because all of her relationships had been abject failures was a little difficult to grasp.

'You've got to decide, Rachel.'

'You could tell me to go for it.'

'Why?'

'Because life's too bloody short, that's what you could tell me.'

'Sounds like you've already made your mind up.'

'God, you sound just like Mum!'

'Have you told her about this?'

'Of course not. I can't talk to Mum about anything. She can't even talk about Dad. All she wants to do is send me vests. Vests! That's just what my somnolent sex life needs. A fucking woolly vest!'

Louise sat quietly while Rachel catapulted herself from the sofa, stalked out to the kitchen, retrieved the bottle of wine, and brought it back with her. There was no mention of circus clown slippers. Even in her naive enthusiasm, Louise couldn't see her mother trying to persuade Rachel to wear circus clown slippers.

'Mum, by the way, has got to get her act together,' Rachel continued. 'I'm damned if I'm spending another morose Christmas down there. Either she comes here, or she spends Christmas by herself. All those bloody photographs of Dad all over the place. She's got to move on.'

'I like the photographs.' A shard of defensiveness shot through Louise.

'It's like a shrine,' Rachel steamed, holding the bottle upside down over her glass. 'I can't stand it. It's not as if he was so bloody wonderful.'

Louise stood up. She hadn't even realised she'd done it until she saw Rachel's eyes widen in alarm. Now that she was on her feet, she supposed she should say something important. Rachel burbled on.

'Calm down, Louise. I wasn't being disrespectful. Just honest. Dad was nice, but he wasn't ever going to set the world on fire, was he? I just think Mum could realise that while she still has time to do something with herself. She could meet someone else. She could get a decent job, instead of putting up with that sadistic bitch who bosses her around day after day. She could bare her bum to the whole bloody lot of them. I'm just being honest. I loved Dad, but he was . . .' Rachel cast her eyes over the woman with three breasts, thinking deeply, 'well, Louise, in honesty, he was a bit uninspiring, wasn't he?'

'Rachel, how can you say that?' Louise breathed. 'I had nothing but admiration for him. He built that business up from nothing. He could have stayed a brickie, but he set up on his own instead. Who do you think paid for our school uniforms? You've forgotten too much. You get your business head from him.'

'Don't get hysterical. I know you and he were bosom buddies, but I loved him too. I just don't think there's any need to get schmaltzy about somebody just because they've died.'

'Schmaltzy?' Louise heard her own voice rising.

'I just think that before we canonise him we might just look at the facts. He was great fun, yes, but he'd have loved it if we'd both left school, got jobs in Tonbridge and got married by the time we were twenty-one. He'd have loved it if we were just like Mum. You know that's true.'

'He was a family man. It's not a crime. And Mum was happy. If Dad was still around, she'd still be happy. It was what she wanted too.'

'Are you sure Mum was happy?' Rachel gave Louise an even look.

'Of course she was.' Louise was thrown by the question. 'I don't know what to say. He was kind. He cared about other people. He didn't go on and on about himself for hour after hour like you do.'

'Hooray.' Rachel stood up unsteadily, her glass in her hand. 'So I'm selfish. Fine. The truth is that I've had to learn the meaning of the word "ambition" out of a book. Neither of our parents ever had it. If I'd been as willing to jog along as you have, I'd never have had any of this. They never inspired me to do anything different, to go against the grain. I'm not like you, Louise. I can't put up with normality like you can.'

'Fine,' Louise said. 'If this is normality, then I'm Luther Vandross. The real reason I came round tonight was to give you this.'

Louise tossed the piece of paper that Ash had given her at the coffee table. It skimmed across the tiles and landed on the floor. 'It's a song. I wanted you to have a look at it and tell me what you thought. It was because I wanted to do something for someone else. It had nothing to do with me losing my job. The truth is that if I ever had a problem, ever, you'd be the last person I'd turn to, Rachel, and that's why you're so different from Dad.'

'Well, I'm sorry if I can't replicate that special relationship you had.' There was an edge to Rachel's voice. She almost sounded jealous.

'You can't!' Louise pulled her coat back over her shoulders, pausing briefly to note that she'd only ever got it down as far as her elbows, and turned to stomp away. It was satisfying. She thought she'd lost the ability to stomp, but Rachel's attack on her father had revived it. He was probably hovering, somewhere above the woman with three breasts, and banging a couple of bricks together in applause.

'Where are you going?'

Rachel walked unsteadily after Louise as she headed down the hall.

'Away.'

'You can think of this as home, Louise, you're always welcome here.'

'Sod off.'

'Why don't you stay? We can talk this through.'

'No.' Louise stropped towards the door. 'I'm going home.'

'If you need money, I can lend you money.'

Louise twisted the door handle and let in a blast of cold air from the outside. It was better to get used to the idea of being freezing again as soon as possible. She turned back to Rachel. She knew Rachel would lend her money. She knew she'd help her in a real career. Her sister had always been generous. But what she needed her to say right now was that she wanted to be an auntie.

'I don't want money, Rachel.'

'What's this? Somebody who doesn't want money? It must be Louise. Ah, it is!' The deep tone that washed over

Louise from the doorstep had her squirming inside her clothes with pleasure. It was Hallam, his key outstretched, his bushy eyebrows, half chestnut, half grey, raised in evident delighted surprise to see Louise standing on his hall rug. She wanted to throw her arms around him and tell him that everything was going to be all right. She smiled into his safe, sure, brown eyes and he glinted back at her as only a very cold man can. They were distracted by Rachel losing her balance behind them and falling into a nest of tables. Hallam pulled a comical face at Louise.

'Pissed again, is she? Well, I won't be away so much in the future. If I can just get in and warm up, I'll tell you both what's happening.'

'I've got to go,' Louise said. If she stayed in Hallam's presence too long she just might blurt it all out, and then Rachel would have another chance to tell her how hopeless she was. No, she had to be strong, for the baby. 'Bye, Hallam.' She pushed a kiss against his icy cheek. 'See you, Rachel.'

She headed past Hallam, down the path, and out into the street, stopping only on her way to the tube station to admire a frozen pile of dog turds arranged in an artistic heap and wondered acidly if Rachel would have bought them for the coffee table had they been up for auction.

Chapter Eight

'Your life is at a crossroads. It is for you to decide which road you wish to travel down. Others will try to influence you, but you must follow your instincts. Like Robert Louis Stevenson, a famous Scorpio before you, you are an adventurer, and may find that opportunities to travel overseas present themselves. The stars show distress in the recent past due to the death of a loved one, and confusion. This may soon be replaced by a time of great opportunity. You must listen to your heart.'

'What a load of cobblers,' Olivia muttered, leaning back on the sofa and sipping her glass of wine. She finished the page.

'Both anguish and joy are promised as the year draws to a close. There may soon be a happy announcement from someone close to you. Above all, your chart shows that your independence is increasing, and that you will find that you have confidence in yourself to take on tasks which you have been putting off.'

She squinted at the foot of the printed sheet where Shaun had scribbled a note in his own handwriting. She tilted the paper to one side, and then back again.

'Olivia,' she read aloud hesitantly, 'I dope you don't spink I've been nude to men-tion a decent death. Perhaps louse will marry her – toyfriend.' She put her glass down and gazed at the television without seeing it. 'She'd better bloody not.'

Her eyes wandered over to Bob's photograph. It was one she'd taken herself. He was leaning against his cement-mixer and smiling genially at her. She could be talking to him, of course. It didn't mean she was mad.

It was all there, as she'd expected. Travel, romance, death and a happy event. Of course she travelled. She got the bus to work every day. There was no romance, but she often thought of Bob and their early years together. Perhaps 'romantic' was not a word she would have used to describe their relationship. They had been comfortable with each other. He had made her feel safe, and she had been a part of his team. Death was obvious. Everybody died at some point. If it hadn't been Bob, it could have been his mother, just three years before, or her own mother, fifteen years ago. It still felt recent to Olivia. She'd never got used to her not being around. Sometimes she even caught herself thinking 'I must tell Mum that', only to realise that she wasn't there to tell.

· She lay back against the sofa. A happy event was whatever you wanted it to be. Rachel and Hallam were clearly never going to marry. Somehow she couldn't picture Louise announcing her betrothal with shining eyes. She hadn't even mentioned the boyfriend the last few times they'd spoken, and Olivia hadn't liked to ask. If she was happy with him, she would have talked about him.

Olivia picked up her glass again and took a sip while she rested her eyes on Trevor McDonald. She'd turned the sound down, having watched the BBC news, but she still liked to look at him. She'd like to have met a Trevor McDonald. Years ago, of course. But she hadn't really time to be courted by anybody. It had all happened so fast. She looked away from the television screen and turned her mind back to Shaun's chart.

Perhaps the happy event referred to her reunion dinner. She slipped the chart back into the brown envelope and placed it on the cushion beside her. She had to ring

Katherine Muff. She was putting it off. She took another sip of wine. Words from the chart played around her head.

Increased independence. It was a bit cheeky of him to put that in. Being left on your own after your partner of nearly forty years had died could be looked at as increased independence. And what tasks was she putting off, for heaven's sake?

She glanced around the small, spotless sitting room, hoovered and polished until it glowed. Even the piano was gleaming, and that was always the first thing to gather dust. She had the garden under control, and it was December now anyway. Bob had dug around the borders so neatly that it was only a question of mowing in the summer, doing a bit of pruning when the roses got carried away, and shoving a few bulbs under the ground in the autumn. Apart from that, there was only the garage.

Olivia's skin tingled. There was the garage, and more importantly the Ford Escort that was sitting in it, untouched since Bob had died. She kept meaning to sell it, but she couldn't face that. She didn't know what she should charge for it. It was stupid, leaving it sitting there. Bob had talked her into applying for a provisional licence when he knew he was ill, but it was in a drawer upstairs. If only Louise would drive. She'd passed her test, years ago, but she always said that there was no point in having a car in London, and anyway she'd forgotten which one was the clutch. She'd have given it to Rachel, but she didn't need it. She and Hallam had their own cars, and they were much more impressive.

Annoyed to have discovered the task that she'd been putting off, and even more annoyed that she had allowed herself to be seduced into the idea that anything on Shaun's chart could be pertinent to her life, Olivia tipped another small measure of wine into her glass. She'd deal with the car eventually, but she wouldn't do it now. Why should she? Just because she'd lied about her birthday and because Shaun found astrology therapeutic were not reasons to sell the car.

There was too much to think about first. Including the bloody dinner.

Trevor McDonald had disappeared and was replaced by a series of adverts showing couples lavishing Christmas presents on each other. Olivia's jaw tightened. She flicked the button, the screen went black, and she picked up her wine and took it through to the kitchen to ring Louise. She was going to screw up the courage, somehow, to mention the dinner to her. At least if she brought the subject up it might jolt her out of this inertia.

As she dialled Louise's number, Olivia had visions of the other women arriving at the restaurant. There would be Geraldine Fletcher in an off-the-shoulder satin number, with her flowing chestnut hair and big bosoms; Jane Kerr, diminutive in glasses and a velvet suit, snapping at her chauffeur as she climbed out of the limo; Audrey Hamilton, blushing furiously and mumbling under her breath while flicking back a long plait; and of course, Katherine bloody Muff, surrounded by photographers, stopping to sign autographs, waving away her driver and taking the arm of her glamorous escort. Somewhere up the road, Olivia would be stumbling off the bus, brushing the dust from her one nice dress, shivering under the quilted mac she wore to work, and grappling with her umbrella. Olivia held the receiver in a stranglehold as she waited for Louise to answer.

'Yes?' Louise sounded bright. That made a nice change.

'It's Mum. How are you, dear?'

'Oh. Hello.'

'I've caught you off your guard. Are you just going out?'

'No, no.'

'Is Jon there?'

There was a pause. Olivia thought she heard a snort.

'No.'

'Are you in the middle of your dinner?'

'No!' Louise yelled, starting to laugh. 'Nothing was happening, and then the phone rang. How are you, Mum?'

'Oh. Well, I'm all right.'

'Hang on, let me get comfy. I've got the phone in the bedroom. It's a bit nippy tonight so I thought I'd get under the duvet and listen to the radio.'

'Are you cold?'

'Not any more I'm not. Snug as a bug.'

'Did you get the vest?' Olivia started to worry.

'Er, no, not yet. When did you send it?'

'Two days ago. By parcel post. I wonder if it's got lost. Or been stolen.'

'Unlikely, Mum. There are far more interesting things to nick at Christmas than frilly vests, aren't there?'

'I suppose so. But it might have arrived during the day. You'd have been at work. They've probably taken it back to the depot. Unless they just put it on your doorstep. They do that sometimes. Diane Fisher next door had a parcel delivered once, and it was stolen because they just left it outside her porch. Are you sure they didn't leave it outside and somebody took it?'

'How the hell would I know?' Louise giggled.

'You could check. You could ring them and ask if they've got it.'

'Why don't we give it a couple more days and see if it turns up?'

'Well, all right.' Olivia frowned. 'If you do ring them, you'll have to say what else was in the package. It was a bit bulky, you see. It might have come open. I wanted to surprise you, but I'm going to have to tell you.'

'A bottle of gin?'

'Gin? Why would you want a bottle of gin?' Olivia thought carefully. 'Are you drinking a lot at the moment? Rachel is. I'm sure she's drinking too much, but neither of you like spirits, do you?'

'It's a joke, Mum. What else have you sent me?'

'Well, I was in Marks and Sparks getting your vest and I saw that they had some of those lovely warm slippers that I got you last year. I bought some for you. The fleece on the inside of your old ones must be worn out by now. They won't be warm if there's no fleece inside.'

'And they're the same? Long brown and orange canoes crafted out of carpet tiles, with pointy toes and little bells on the end?'

'These didn't have bells.' Olivia gave a short laugh. 'You haven't really seen any with bells on, have you?'

'I don't need another pair, Mum. Honest.'

'They can be a spare pair, then, can't they?' Olivia suggested as helpfully as possible. Louise was silent. But she'd answered the phone in such a good mood. Olivia wanted to hear her laugh again.

'How do you con a sheep?' Olivia quipped.

'What?'

'It's a joke. Sarah told it to me at work.'

'A joke? You don't tell jokes.'

'Shut up, Louise.' Olivia closed her eyes. Now she was snapping. It must have been the extra glass of wine. 'I said, how do you con a sheep?'

'I don't know, how do you con a sheep?'

'Pull the wool over its eyes,' Olivia said through gritted teeth. There was a long pause. Now she felt really silly. She shouldn't try telling jokes. Bob used to tell bad jokes, and the girls always teased him about it, but she couldn't be Bob, even if she tried.

'That was really sad, Mum.'

'Well, blame Sarah, not me. Neal told it to her. I thought

132

it was corny too, but I was just trying to cheer you up. Perhaps I shouldn't bother.'

'It sounds as if you're the one who needs cheering up. Are you sure you're all right?'

Olivia took another sip from her wineglass. 'I'm just a bit – bit worried about something. That's all. That's what I rang to tell you.'

'Oh?' Louise sounded very alert now.

'It's silly, really. It's just that Katherine Muff rang and wants me to go to a dinner, and I can't go.'

'Muff?' Louise gave an explosive laugh.

'You know, I was at school with her. Katherine Muff.'

Louise went off like a hyena. Olivia leaned against the kitchen cupboard and listened. No, she wasn't like Bob. Her girls only laughed at her when she said something in earnest.

'So why can't you go?'

'It's just . . .' Olivia thought of all the reasons that she didn't want to go. She opened her mouth and tried to formulate a concise summary. It was difficult. She didn't want to blackmail Louise emotionally into offering to come with her. She didn't want to use words like 'alone' and 'insecure'. She was starting to wish that the girls respected her, just a little bit, for the person she was. 'I – I haven't got anything to wear.'

Louise collapsed into giggles again. Olivia smiled to hear it. Perhaps she'd met somebody? It was ages since she'd heard her younger daughter so cheerful.

'Blimey, Mum. There's not going to be anybody from the press there, is there? Just a load of women with bubble perms complaining about their corns. Just wear what you're comfortable in.'

'I haven't got a bubble perm.' Olivia tried to joke, fingering the soft waves of white hair around her face, but she was wounded. 'Or corns. If I went, I'd like to look nice.'

'Why bother dressing up? It's just going to be a mothers' meeting, everyone going on about how much their kids earn. You'll probably be bored senseless. In fact, why go? You've never kept in touch with anyone from school, have you?'

Olivia's mouth wobbled. Why go? That wasn't what she expected to hear. But then again, Louise had a social life. She had friends in London. She went out, to nice places. She was always meeting people in pubs. Olivia stood up straight and frowned at the cupboard door.

'I want to go!' she asserted. 'And I want you to help me decide what to wear, not to talk me out of it. Don't you understand? I never go anywhere. Nobody ever asks me.'

'You went to see Betty recently, didn't you?'

'I want to go to a restaurant!' Olivia realised with a shock that she was almost shouting. 'And what's more, I want you to come with me! It's not much to ask, Louise. I think it's the least you could do!'

There was a silence. Louise was perfectly still on the other end of the line. She wasn't used to her own mother issuing orders at her. Not for many years.

'Louise? Are you still there?'

'When is it?'

'Less than two weeks' time. On the Saturday night. You could come down on the train, and we could go together. You could even go back the same night if you wanted to.' Then she added quickly, 'But you could stay over. You know you could sleep in your old room.'

She heard Louise blow out as if she was thinking hard.

'Okay, Mum. I'll come with you.'

'It's all right dear, I understand.' Olivia put down her wineglass with a clatter, her voice rising an octave. 'You'll come with me?'

'Yes, yes. I haven't see you for a while, have I? It might be a good thing. And it'll give us a chance to talk properly.

134

Yes, why not?' Louise's voice gained life. 'Why the hell not? I'll come with you, and we'll take the piss out of the bubble perms together. How about that?'

'Oh, good grief!' Olivia put her hand to her mouth. She could feel tears in her throat. They must not show in her voice. Louise would feel pressured, as if it was a great event.

'Okay, Mum, I'm going to crash out now, but why don't you ring me nearer the time, and we'll sort out the details.'

'That's, that's fine.' Olivia cleared her throat. Her lips had spread into a wide grin that she couldn't control. It was stupid to be so absurdly happy. 'Thank you, darling. I think we'll have fun.'

'Oh, and Mum? I've got some good news for you. I won't tell you now. I'll tell you when I come down.'

Olivia had begun to jig around on the kitchen tiles but now she stopped. Her brows knitted into a frown.

'You're not getting married?'

Louise laughed again.

'I thought all mothers wanted their children to settle down, start families, and all that stuff.'

'Not to Jon?'

'Don't panic, Mum. I need Jon like a haemophiliac needs a leech. No more clues. I'll speak to you next week.'

After she'd put the phone down, Olivia finished her glass of wine, pondering over Louise's statement. It was worrying. Was she getting married? Who might she be thinking of marrying? Who could she possibly have met in the few weeks since she'd last mentioned Jon? It was far too quick. She couldn't know what she was doing.

She took herself up to bed, watching her slippers slide over the swirls on the carpeted stairs. For now she wouldn't worry about Louise getting married. She was going to dinner, and she would show off her beautiful blonde daughter who lived in a flat in London. That

135

would show them. And it struck her finally as she tiptoed into Louise's old bedroom and gazed at the *Malory Towers* books lined along the shelf that Bob had put up, that Shaun's chart had been bizarrely accurate. She *could* feel a surge of increased independence. She had made a stand and got what she wanted. And she had a warm feeling inside telling her that things weren't going to stop there.

Rachel rapped on the wooden door and stood back. From the outside, the building looked like a squat. She flashed a smile over her shoulder to her companions. She knew what she was doing, even if they didn't – yet. The door was opened. A bouncer wearing black tie and a stony expression stood barring their way, his figure filling the doorway.

'Rachel Twigg,' she said. His face twitched into a smile of recognition.

'Nice to see you again, Rachel.'

'And you too, Adam.'

He stood aside and an explosion of colour appeared in his place. Rachel hopped through the doorway and motioned the four men in leather jackets to follow her. The band she had recently signed loped into the Caribbean restaurant after her, gazing around with white faces that were trying hard not to look overawed. The cocktail bar area where they stood was ablaze with gaudy lights and cluttered with huge, bright paintings. Down some wooden steps ahead of them, the restaurant area had the solid, earthy appeal of an Elizabethan tavern. Bob Marley pulsed warmly through the air. Rachel shook off her coat and an elegant waitress draped in a bright cotton print arrived to take it from her.

'Cocktail first, gents?'

'Wow!' the drummer managed, losing his cool first. 'I

never knew there were places like this in Camden Town. Magic.'

'You'd better be paying,' the lead singer quipped, flicking back a long fringe and grinning.

'Of course!' Rachel laughed at them. 'All you guys have to do is eat and drink what you want and think about writing fantastic songs. The rest is up to us.'

'Cool.'

'Shall we go to our table and drink there?'

There was general consent. Rachel relished it while she could. The multicoloured waitress showed them to their table, smiling broadly at the appreciative gazes she was receiving. If only, Rachel thought, they would stay like this. Appreciative, grateful, happy. There was just a chance that these guys might. But it was more likely that in a couple of years or less they'd be slagging off everything their first deal had brought them, and looking elsewhere. She gazed around at the new band affectionately as they blinked at menus the size of road atlases. They were dynamic on stage – she wasn't taking any chances in that department – but socially they were still gauche and spontaneous. It was like taking a gang of Muppets out to dinner.

'Isn't it a shame they have to grow up?' she murmured, smiling as she picked up her own menu.

'Rachel? Bugger me, I thought it was you!'

She swung round as her back was slapped heartily. Dave Forrester's face loomed up against hers and planted a wet kiss on her mouth. He'd once been something big in a band that had two number ones, and had since spent his time touring with new line-ups, getting stoned and getting old. But she'd heard that the company were going to back him for a coming tour, and enthusiasm was the name of the game. She stood up to interrupt the kiss and appear delighted at the same time. It was a move she'd perfected.

'Davey! How are you, sweetheart?'

'God, you're a gorgeous woman!' He clasped her waist and she neatly sashayed to one side, tutting at him.

'And practically married, as you well know, you old lech.'

'Yeah, well I can try, can't I. We're going back to the hotel for some beers and a jam. Want to pop in later?'

She kept a grip on her smile. Impromptu jamming sessions in small hotel rooms were what put record company executives on Prozac.

'I'll see what I can do. Meet the boys while you're here.'

She neatly introduced them. As Dave leaned over the table to shake hands with each of them in turn, Rachel couldn't help noticing that he'd got an angry spot on his neck, and his complexion was gaining the quality of used kitchen foil. But the band were drop-jawed when they realised that it was *the* Dave Forrester who they'd happened to bang into in a restaurant.

'Fuck me!' the lead singer whistled as Dave staggered off with a long-haired bass player and two top-heavy brunettes in tow. 'Rock and roll!'

'So *that*'s what happened to Spinal Tap,' the lead guitar muttered wryly. He wrote the band's lyrics. Rachel could see why. She kept a straight face.

'Well, he's got a platinum Amex.' She raised her eyebrows meaningfully. 'You keep writing your brilliant ditties and one day soon you too—'

'– could have a face like a dog's rectum,' the lead guitar finished for her.

Rachel sat down again and allowed herself to laugh. It took the tension from her limbs. All day she'd been dreading this, not because she didn't like the band – they were truly adorable – but just because she was so damned tired. Still, successes like this gave her the buzz that kept her on her feet, even when all she wanted to do was go home, kick her shoes off, collapse on the sofa and ruffle Hallam's hair.

A spring of emotion danced in her throat. They'd been like that once. But he'd stopped asking her questions. Just when she wanted to give him answers, he'd suddenly stopped asking the bloody questions. It was no good thinking about Hallam tonight. In any case, he wasn't even going to be there when she got home, whenever that might be. He was in Paris this time, sorting things out. All she had to look forward to was a dark house and an empty bed. It wouldn't be so bad if the place wasn't so incredibly silent when he was away.

She thought of Louise, living alone. It was all right for her. She was used to it, and it was her choice. She was happy, bumbling along with casual jobs, with a casual life. She never seemed to encounter any real problems. She hit temporary blips all the time, but they were never real obstacles. She had a bubbling humour which got her through everything. But it seemed that the more Rachel fought for her life to be simple, the more complicated it became. And she hated being alone. She loathed it. She was exhausting herself with her lifestyle, but anything was better than being on her own while Hallam was away.

Sometimes she wished she shared a house with a bunch of nurses. She liked being around boisterous life. It was even a nice feeling when the boys were over, if only Hal would give her a chance to get close to them. But they were *his* children, after all. She was always on the outside, looking in. Just as she'd stood watching her father laughing with Louise. Her stomach muscles tightened.

She looked up and smiled brightly at her increasingly euphoric troop. She took a deep slug from her glass as the drinks appeared on the table, and waved her hands at them.

'Come on! Keep up! You're out to enjoy yourselves

tonight. Last one standing has to appear on *Richard and Judy*.'

Louise disentangled a basket at the supermarket and headed straight for the vegetables. They looked so good. How could she never have noticed that before? Especially the broccoli. She chose a large floret. She tried to move on, but the broccoli called her back. She loaded more into her basket and went for Brussels sprouts and cabbage. And potatoes too. Mashed. With a pork chop. And very thick gravy. Her basket sagged on her arm as she staggered around, piling in her ingredients. By the time she got to the cleaning materials, she was having to wedge J-cloths and bottles of bleach under her arm. But it felt so good. The new Louise. Healthy, clean, organised, and full of broccoli. She picked up another floret on her way back to the till.

Chocolate. She didn't normally eat much chocolate. Why not? It was fantastic. She grabbed a handful of Mars bars and sprinkled them on top of her load. So this was what being pregnant was all about. Eating whatever you felt like, with no reason to feel guilty. And as the regular assistant recognised her and reached for a packet of Silk Cut, she shook her head, trying not to look as smug as she felt.

'No?' The colour drained from his face.

'No,' she said decisively. 'But if you can hang on a second, I think I need a Black Forest gateau.'

She found a note wedged under her door when she got home. She pushed her way into the flat, dumped her shopping bags, and unfolded it.

It looked as though somebody had been trying to get a pen to work, but there were words there if you looked closely. It was from Harris.

'Louise,' she read, puzzled that he had bothered to write to her when he only lived upstairs, 'I am on fire. Harris.'

Her hand dropped to her side clutching the note. She stared up at the ceiling.

'On fire?'

She walked around and thought about it. On fire? Really? She sniffed the air.

He was an actor, and their ways were different from the rest of the population, but wasn't the reaction to being on fire a fairly universal one? Wasn't running away and screaming the usual form? Just who would calmly look for their most expensive writing paper, take up an ink pen and compose a note to a neighbour at a time like that?

She wandered out into the hall and peered up the stairs. There was no smoke, no sign of panic. And Harris was bright enough to use a telephone directory. Why weren't the fire brigade axing down his door? She looked at the note again. Something did actually smell a bit strange. She put it to her nose and drew in a deep breath. It was aftershave. What a smoothy. She shook her head. He probably sprinkled aftershave on everything, including his rent cheque.

There was nothing else for it. She'd have to ask him if he was all right. Perhaps he'd had a chip-pan fire, and was panicking about what to tell the landlord? But Harris didn't eat chips. He was a muesli-and-exercise-bike man. She hammered at his door.

'Harris?' she yelled through the wood. 'Are you all right in there?'

Silence. She put her ear to the door. He must be out.

'Oh, Big Boy!' she called coquettishly, making herself giggle. The door flew open. She jumped, clutching her chest. 'Good God, Harris, don't ever do that again!'

Then she realised that he was naked. Completely naked. And he wasn't attempting to hide the fact. He put an arm up against the door and reclined seductively. It was simply impossible not to stare at his body. He was tanned all over and sprinkled with black hair, and he had a fantastic set of equipment. She took a quick step back and stared at his face for an explanation.

He gave her a long, slow smile, his eyes glowing like coals.

'At last, Louise. Now I've got you.' She thought he was going to lunge for her, but he didn't move.

'But I thought . . .' She swallowed nervously. 'I mean, where's the fire, Harris?'

'Here, Louise.'

Her eyes could not have grown any wider as he indicated very graphically exactly where the fire was. And she was obviously provoking a reaction.

'Oh my God!' she breathed in shock.

'And you want me too. I know you do, Louise. That's why you came to me.'

'I, um.' She took several small steps towards the top of the stairs. 'Actually, I came to you because I thought you were burning to death. That's why.'

'I *am* burning. Burning with desire for you.'

'Look, I'm really flattered,' Louise gulped, backing her way down the stairs. His erection seemed to follow her every move. It was like the probe on a Dalek. 'But now's not a good time.'

'Now is a *very* good time,' he countered, glimmering at her passionately. 'When's a better time than this?'

It was logical, she supposed, as he pointed down at himself. But she was already halfway down the stairs.

'I'm sorry,' she whimpered up at him. 'Perhaps another day?'

'So you're going to leave me burning?' he called after her. He sounded a little petulant. She'd guessed a while back that he had a pretty good success rate.

'Yes.' It came out very lamely. 'Sorry.'

She reached the bottom of the stairs. He appeared at the

top, unabashed. The sight of his nakedness did very odd things to her. She could feel her temperature shooting up.

'Perhaps I should have given you dinner first,' he said thoughtfully.

'Maybe,' she nodded at him. 'It was a little direct.'

'Okay. I'll give it some thought.'

He turned, allowing her a prime view of his firm, tanned buttocks, and walked back into his flat.

Perhaps it was sheer adrenaline, but she had never applied herself with such vigour to cleaning her flat. The cobwebs disappeared, undiscovered corners were hoovered, and entire populations of spiders were rendered homeless. As she scrubbed and wiped, Louise tried without success to blink away the image of Harris's erection. It was imprinted on her retinas. She could only imagine what he might have been doing upstairs after she'd left him. The thought made her feel peculiar. Tension pricked at her. Later in the evening she heard him thundering down the stairs and she stiffened, wondering if he was going to knock on her door. She'd open it, and he'd be there in a wet-look thong massaging himself with baby oil. But no. She heard the front door slam on his way out and heaved a sigh of relief.

Mother Nature was an odd creature. She was pregnant, for heaven's sake. There was no biological imperative for her to think about men just at the moment. But she was. And amid the jumble of disconcerting images in her mind were Ash's wide green eyes. She had a wild urge to speak to him again. And, being practical about it, she needed advice.

It was a new and strange thing to be applying for the dole. She still didn't have a clue what she was supposed to be doing in order to qualify, but it was clear she was supposed to be doing something. She wanted to work as soon as she felt well enough, but for the last few days she'd been assaulted, always at the least expected time, by violent attacks of sickness. And she needed to think, to work out a longer-term solution. Ash had been signing on for six months. He could help.

What if she rang him, just to confirm that she'd found his piece of paper, but wasn't prepared to give it to him because she'd blown her nose on it? Could she follow that up with an appeal to him for help? No. What if she told him the truth, that she'd opened it and read it, realised that it was a song, and given it to her sister to look at?

She thought about it while she picked the cherries off the top of the Black Forest gateau. Was Ash's song any good? It had musical notation scribbled all over it, but she could only read music, not guitar chords. It made sense for him to be in a band. He was probably signing on while he waited for his big break. Rachel just might be able to help, and didn't Louise owe him a favour in return for his kindness? He had picked her up when she'd fainted.

She made a decision. She sorted through her jacket pockets until she found the piece of cigarette packet with Ash's number on it. Then she dragged the phone through to her bedroom and flopped on the bed.

She picked up the receiver. She took a deep breath. He was gorgeous. She put the phone down again.

She stood up and checked herself in the mirror. The make-up she'd plastered on in the morning was smudged, and her hair looked more like an optic-fibre light than an upturned spring onion. It didn't matter. It was the phone. She brushed her hair anyway, put on another layer of mascara and sank to the level of admiring the bulbous lumps which were now her breasts through her jumper. Then she tried again.

He answered the phone himself, but she had to pretend that she didn't know it was him. She couldn't just say

'Ash!' as if she'd remembered every semitone that his voice was capable of.

'I'm sorry to bother you. Could I speak to Ash, please?'

'Yeah, speaking. Is that Louise?'

She almost threw the phone across the room. How did he know?

'Yes. It's a Louise, I'm not sure if I'm the Louise you're thinking of.' She gave a girlish giggle and pinched the skin on her wrist really hard until it hurt, for punishment. 'I'm the Louise from the Jobcentre.'

'I know which one you are. I only know one Louise, anyway. Not that I really know you. But I don't know anyone else called Louise.' He paused. 'They called your name out while I was there. Louise Twigg. It's an unusual name. Easy to remember.'

'Ah, yes. And I know your name's Ash because you told me.' She cringed with embarrassment. The conversation was limping around on crutches already, and she'd only been on the phone for thirty seconds.

'Right. So, did you find the bit of paper I gave you?'

'There's good news and bad news.' Now she had to think on her feet. How could she have known that her mind was going to go blank the moment she heard his voice again? 'I've found it, but—'

'You have! I can't fucking believe it. You've saved my life. Oh, Louise, you're a star. You brilliant woman. Have my babies.' She could hear him laughing into the air. At the same time, she could feel herself going cross-eyed with the permutations of possible responses to his kind offer.

'But—'

'So, can I meet you? Or you can send it to me, if you'd rather.'

'Oh no, I can meet you,' she said. 'I'd like to talk to you anyway. About something completely different.'

He was still laughing. He had a fascinating laugh.

145

'Great. I could see you in the café again, tomorrow. We can talk about anything you want.'

'It's just about—' She yanked up the verbal handbrake. It made an ugly squeal of rubber on fresh air. She couldn't stall this moment when he was so exuberant with her boring request to be advised about her jobsearch. She would find a suitable moment tomorrow to be boring. And overnight, she'd think of a way to put it that didn't sound boring at all, but wonderfully sexy and enigmatic. That way, he'd forgive her for showing his song to someone else without asking him first.

'See you there tomorrow.' She could hear him grinning through his voice. 'About eleven do you?'

'Do me?' Oh, yes please, a little voice cried. 'Eleven's fine.'

He hung up.

Chapter Nine

'So, I was wondering if you could help me with my jobsearch,' Louise finished, fluttering her eyelashes across the Formica table top. Ash looked at her while he stirred his tea slowly with a bent teaspoon. He'd been very quiet while she'd related the tale of yesterday's interview to him. Too quiet. He hadn't laughed at the funny bits she'd practised over her pile of bacon sandwiches that morning. She sneaked a hand up to the strands of hair that were falling in her face and tried to tuck them behind her ears again. She'd intended to turn up looking as if she'd just stepped out of the salon, but she'd fallen asleep on her wet hair last night, and it was disobeying orders.

'Do you see what my problem is? I need to know how *not* to get a job just at the moment. It won't be for long. I thought you might give me some tips. You seem to know what you're doing.'

He frowned and dropped his eyes to his tea. She watched avidly as he lifted the mug, sipped from it, winced, put it down again and added more sugar. He was probably a bit put out that she'd turned up at the café, found him at the table, and launched into her resounding monologue in answer to the simple question 'How's it going?'

'Why don't you want to get a job?' he asked. She kicked herself under the table. She'd just assumed that it was part of the unemployed thing, to try to outwit the Jobcentre. There was a logical answer, of course, which involved morning sickness for three hours every afternoon and a need to work out a long-term solution, but she could hardly tell him that. If she'd met him under any other circumstances they might just be on to their favourite pubs by now.

'It's just – you know. Timing.'

'Ah. Timing.'

'Yes.'

He pulled a squashed packet of tobacco out of the pocket of his denim jacket, arranged a Rizla on the table, and began to roll up a cigarette. She took a quick slug of tea. It wasn't the sort of café where you could object to someone smoking. She leaned away from him, towards the door which was constantly swinging open, and prayed that she wasn't going to produce an overt gag when he lit it.

'Timing of what?' he asked, watching her again as he fumbled around in an attempt to find his lighter. He patted all of his pockets in turn, fingered his jeans and swore under his breath.

'Oh, I've got one. Hang on.' Louise flipped open her handbag and found her lighter nestling in the bottom. She flicked the flame for him and he leaned forward, putting up his hands to cup hers and hold them steady.

She jumped as his skin touched hers, knocking the end of his thin cigarette upwards so that it bent in the middle and formed a perfect right angle. Slowly, he raised his eyes to hers and pulled the crooked cigarette out of his mouth. He assessed it silently.

'I'm so sorry. You can have one of mine instead. Here.' Fumbling pathetically, Louise found her packet of Ultra-Lows where she had last left them in her bag. 'In fact, have them all. I've given up.' She tossed the packet over the table. 'There you are.'

He paused again, picking up the packet and peering inside.

'There are fifteen left in here.'

'I don't care. Have them.'

'Impulsive, aren't you?'

Louise produced a wobbly smile. The smell of cigarette smoke now made her feel horribly ill. Rationale didn't come into it.

'Think of them as a thank-you present for scooping me up when I passed out.'

'Thanks. I'll keep them for emergencies. I tend to stick to rollies. Cheaper.'

She watched him straighten out the cigarette she had bent. She bit her lip and stuffed more hair behind her ears, then attempted to hold out the lighter for him again. He put out his hand and gently prised the lighter from between her fingers.

'I'll do it, shall I?'

'Yes,' she breathed. 'Why don't you?'

'So,' he asked again as he blew a thin jet of smoke away from her, 'what did you mean about timing? Are you doing something else that you don't want them to know about?'

'I just need a bit of thinking time, to sort myself out. You know how it is.' She tried to look conspiratorial. She had the feeling it wasn't very convincing. The look on his face said that he was either bored witless or deeply unimpressed with everything about her. It could have been her corrugated hair or it could just have been the fact that she was behaving like a twit.

It shouldn't have mattered, but he was wearing a chunky black jumper under his denim jacket which stopped just above the waistline of his jeans and left a small expanse of his stomach visible. She could see a layer of soft brown hairs there, and it was doing strange things to her. She'd realised he had nice eyes when she'd woken up from her faint and stared up into them, but until now

149

she hadn't taken in just how appealing the complete package was. That was all Harris's fault. She'd probably never be able to hold a conversation with a man again without expecting him to drop his trousers and point his equipment at her.

'Why don't you tell me how it is.' He gave her a brief smile.

'It's – it's difficult, at the moment. I need to work out what I really want to do. I'm a bit like you, I suppose.' He raised his eyebrows at her. 'You know, with your band. You obviously need time to get your – songwriting off the ground. I assume that's why you're not working.'

'My songwriting,' he murmured, picking up his mug and fondling the handle. Louise stared longingly at his thumb moving rhythmically up and down the strip of china. 'So you've brought the song, then? I was starting to wonder.'

'Well, that's what I wanted to talk to you about,' she said hurriedly, trying to get the upper hand again. 'I'll do you a favour if you do me one.'

He raised his eyebrows again. 'What sort of favour?'

'I need to buy some time. I need somebody to show me how to deal with all these jobseeking requirements so that I don't balls it up.'

'And if I do that, you'll give me my song back?'

'I'll do even more than that. I'll show it to someone who knows about bands. My sister, Rachel, works for a record company. They're always on the lookout for new talent. If she saw your song, I thought she might be able to help you.'

'Right. Have you got it on you now?'

'I – I've already given it to her, actually. I hope you don't mind.'

He lay back in his chair and crossed one knee lazily over the other. He looked at her distantly. Her pulse seethed slowly under his scrutiny. She had an odd feeling that she'd done something wrong.

'You're a strange one, Louise. I can't work you out at all.'

'Really?' She blinked. Enigmatic was good. Probably.

'Yeah, you've got everything going for you. Smart, lively, articulate. You could be making a decent living. You could probably walk into another job tomorrow if you really wanted to. Not like the blokes I see down here most days. Some of them don't stand a hope in hell of getting another job, however hard they try.'

The finger of guilt returned to jab her in the eye. She tried not to think about her father, her mother, her sister, all of whom would raise their eyebrows disapprovingly. They didn't know she was pregnant. Neither did he.

And on top of that, she'd just offered him an exclusive introduction to someone in the music business, and he didn't seem to have heard her. Surely he wanted a break. Didn't all bands want a break like this?

'Er, my sister works for this record company,' she repeated limply, 'and I've given her your song. I hope you don't mind.'

He responded this time with a philosophical wave of his hand.

'We've been through record companies. We've sent demos all over the place. We've forced ourselves into people's offices. Of course I don't mind if you've given your sister our song, but you're obviously not in music yourself.'

'Why do you say that?'

'Because a song scribbled out on a scrap of paper, however much detail there is, won't give her a bloody clue what we're like live. That's all. I'm sorry, Louise, but she'll probably bin it.'

'But I thought—'

'Don't worry about it. It was nice of you to try. It'd be helpful if you could get the song back, though.'

'You want it back? But what if—?'

'It's the only version of the lyrics Ginger worked out. I can remember the music, but he's going mental about it. Please get it back for me.'

She sat quietly, feeling silly. There was a small silence between them. She assumed he was quiet because he was frustrated with her. She had simply run out of things to say. He shifted himself, and gave her a direct look.

'So why don't you want a job when you're perfectly capable of getting one?'

'And what about you?' she retaliated. 'If you didn't insist on walking around like a maypole, you might land a job yourself.'

'Maypole?' His eyes captured hers. She steeled herself against lust, and returned the stare.

'Yes. All those bits and pieces hanging off you. I could just see you in a suit. You'd knock their socks off. What's stopping you walking into a job tomorrow, if you really wanted to?'

'Can you see me in an office?' he asked, still looking relaxed.

'Yes, if you can see me in one.'

'I am trying to do what I'm actually good at.' He leaned forward, speaking slowly. His eyes had become intense. 'And what I want to do doesn't come with a safety net. You either go for broke, or you never do it.'

'You're talking about your band.'

'I don't just mean the band. Nothing I do pays. It doesn't mean it's not a contribution to society, if that's what you're angling for.'

'There's no need to take a moral tone,' she said, getting hot under her layers of clothing. 'I only put the question back to you. I've got my reasons for not being able to get a

152

job just yet. You don't know anything about my circumstances, so don't lecture me.'

'I wasn't lecturing you.'

'Yes, you were. You said I should go and get a job tomorrow. But I can't.'

'Why not?'

'I'm not telling you.' She cringed as her answer landed with a soft thud. She could have phrased it a bit more elegantly.

'Hey, I was only asking you what the dole office is going to ask next time you go in.' He smiled at her and she almost slid off her chair with delight. 'You're going to need a lot of coaching. You haven't got a clue how to handle it, have you? Off like a firework at the first question. That's the one thing that's guaranteed to get you into trouble.'

He seemed genuinely amused by her. It was confusing. Everything about him was confusing.

'Have you been testing me?'

'Something like that. You even turned up to see me in a skirt.' He leaned around the side of the table to gaze at her legs. 'And a very nice pair of shoes. And tights. Pink ones. Interesting.'

She pulled her legs quickly away from him. He sat up again, his lips twitching.

'I was just checking. If you go in to sign on looking as smart as this, they're going to punt you straight off for an interview for a job you'll probably get. If you really do need some time to work things out, you're going to have to be a bit more – downbeat.'

'So what do you advise? Taking a pair of gardening shears to all my clothes?'

'You'll have to be a bit more subtle than that.' He took another swig of his tea. 'So you're not going to tell me what all this is about, then?'

'No,' she answered.

'So, what is it, I wonder? You want to finish *Lord of the Rings*? The kitchen needs redecorating? You've always wanted to teach yourself Chinese, and now seems like an ideal time to do it?'

Her face grew hot again. He was lolling on his chair, his rolled-up cigarette resting between his fingers, quite at ease with himself. He wasn't the one who was bloody pregnant, was he? Her temper flashed.

'Let's see if I can remember. Your band, Ealing's answer to Oasis, has spent a year writing a song that starts "Rolling on the bed with Viola"? Even if I did want to teach myself Chinese, can you tell me why that would be any more pointless than what you're doing?'

'Would you give a fuck if I explained it to you?'

He still looked calm. She was mortified. She'd been rude, and the last thing she wanted was to scare him off. In fact, in the secrecy of her flat, she'd been quite intrigued by the song, but as she sat opposite him her nerve endings were stripped and sticking out all over the place. He was just so damned intriguing. Why was it fair that she'd met him now? Just when her life had taken a dramatic turn that didn't involve getting off with hunky unemployed men? She didn't regret her decision. She was excited about it. But she wanted him to like her too. It was perplexing.

'I'm sorry,' she said, not meeting his eyes. 'I didn't mean to be so rude about your song. It obviously means a lot to you.'

He laughed at her, swinging in his chair.

'So, you showed my song to your sister as a trade for me helping you out. But she's already got it, hasn't she, and I haven't agreed to help you polish your job-dodging skills? That was very trusting of you.'

'No,' she said, 'that was to say thank you for picking me up when I fainted under the Catering stand. So we're quits now. I've got your number. If my sister's interested in seeing you live, she'll let me know.' She buttoned up her coat and drained her mug. Pride, she urged herself. Baby first, lust later. Probably much later, when everything had healed up again and there wasn't an attractive man in sight, but she wouldn't dwell on that now. 'Good luck with your songwriting. I might bang into you over the giros some time.'

Louise stood up, hoisted her bag over her shoulder, and turned to go.

'Hey, hang on there.' She glanced back at Ash. Annoyingly, he was still smiling at her. 'I said I'd give you a few tips if you needed them, and I will. Your place or mine?'

'It's not a date,' she said through tight lips, her hormones getting up to boogie again.

'I wasn't asking for one.' He dropped his smile and looked at her earnestly. 'I don't know what your problem is, Louise, but I'll help. Why don't you give me your address, and I'll drop round some time? In fact, if you're not doing anything now, I could go through things with you. I've got something I've got to do this afternoon, but I'm free for a couple of hours.'

'A couple of hours?'

'Well, that's if you want to put together a CV that makes you unemployable. Temporarily, of course.'

Louise hesitated. She'd invited strange men to her flat before, but at the moment she wasn't drunk. 'If you really do want to help me out, we could meet again on neutral ground.' She tried to make her prim suggestion sound casual. As her words boomeranged back to her from the yellow gloss on the café walls, she wanted to die.

'Neutral ground's expensive when you're on the dole. I can brew us up a cuppa at my house if you want.'

She stood stupidly, trying to think of something to say.

'I'm not sure.'

He sat back and folded his arms.

'I thought you wanted me to help you.'

'Yes, I do. But . . .'

'But you hadn't thought it through. You didn't think that me helping you would involve any actual contact.'

'It's not exactly that.'

'So you'd rather we established a correspondence, perhaps? You could send me your queries and I could answer them by post? I can see it now. *The Letters of Louise Twigg and Ashley Carson-Brown, the de Beauvoir and Sartre of West London.*'

'Ashley Carson-Brown?' She stared at him. 'Is that really your name?'

He let out a long breath, as if he was tired of the debate.

'Do you want help with this or not? C'mon, Louise, this is all a bit coy, isn't it? Would it help if I answer that question you're mulling over?'

'What question?' The colour rose in her cheeks again.

'You're wondering whether this is all innocent.'

'Well, of course it's innocent. I don't know what you mean.'

'I'm seeing someone. Okay? So my offer to help is humanitarian, not some perverse way of trying to get you into a compromising situation.'

He stunned her into wordlessness. She felt relieved and gutted in equal measure. He was still watching her quizzically. For a moment it occurred to her that he was trying to make sense of her, just as she was trying to make sense of him.

'I can assure you that I wasn't angling for a seduction,' she fibbed.

'Good. So we know where we stand. Do you want help or not?'

She had to go. None of it made any sense. She got as far

as the door, and turned back. He was watching her without expression.

'I'll ring you,' she blurted out, and fled.

'You're completely bloody mad,' Sally blurted down the phone. 'I don't know what you're thinking of, Louise. You just can't do this. You can't.'

'Why not?' Louise was perched on the edge of her bed eating her way through a plate of salad sandwiches. 'Just because you wouldn't do it, doesn't mean I can't.'

'You're just not thinking straight. I know it's difficult at the moment, but – sorry, hang on, Lou, I'll be with you in a tick.'

Louise was put on hold. She launched into another sandwich, wincing as she chewed a piece of grit. She knew she'd forgotten something. She should have washed the lettuce first, but it looked so fresh and natural and edifying that she'd just thrown it between two slices of brown bread and got stuck in. Sally clicked back on to the line.

'It's okay now.'

'Are you really busy? I could ring you tonight.'

'No, don't do that. Fergus is cooking for me. I can talk to you now. Listen, you just can't do what you're suggesting. You'll be in such a state. You'll be tied down with no money, no prospects, no social life. You'll be lonely, sad and desperate. And what will you have to offer your baby, for God's sake?'

'Right, get this, Sally. I have lots to offer a baby. I'm going to find a decent job once I've worked out what I want to do, I'm going to have money, and I'm going to have a baby too. Who knows, I might even have a social life. I want to do this, Sally. I'm really happy about it.'

'But you hate Jon. You told me you wished you'd never clapped eyes on him. And what's he going to think about this? Christ, Louise, you're just not thinking.'

'He doesn't have to know about it.'

'Yes, he bloody does.'

'Okay, so I'll tell him, but that's all. He can come and visit if he wants. We can be friends, can't we?'

'You'll be tied to him for the rest of your life. Have you thought about that? You'll never be able to move on. Every sodding week for ever you'll have Jon turning up on your doorstep and claiming his rights as a father.'

'I think that's a tad optimistic, Sal. He doesn't want to know about it. He's going to be really relieved if I tell him to stay out of it.'

'He might feel like that now, but how will he feel when he knows there's a little baby out there carrying his genes? He'll be curious, at least. You'll never shake him off.' Sally paused for breath. 'No, Louise. The answer's no. You can't.'

'What do you mean, no?' Louise put down her half-eaten sandwich and stared at her chest of drawers.

'I mean, no, you can't do this.'

'But, Sally . . .' Louise blinked into the air, choosing her words carefully. Friendships teetered at moments like this. 'I wasn't asking for your permission. I was telling you what I was going to do.'

Sally was silent. Louise could hear her shuffling papers on her desk.

'I thought you wanted my advice,' she said huffily.

'I have wanted your advice, and I've valued it, really. But I've made my own decision now.'

'I'm sorry, Louise, but as far as I'm concerned, there's no decision to be made. You haven't done anything with your own life yet. What's your baby going to think of you? And you'll be on your own, with nobody to support you. How are you going to feel when you're walking around like a beach-ball on two cocktail sticks? Who's going to be there for you through all the false alarms? Who's going to drive you to the hospital and go through the experience with you?'

Louise thought hard.

'The midwife?'

'God, Louise. Stop joking.'

'The taxi driver, perhaps? I might get one like John Travolta in *Look Who's Talking*. That would be fortuitous, wouldn't it?'

'Louise, be serious.'

'I am being bloody serious. When I say I'm going to do this on my own, I mean exactly that. I'll get myself to hospital. It's not so sodding difficult, is it?'

'Don't kid yourself, Louise. It's going to be a living nightmare. And you might as well count sex out from now on. You'll be a virgin for the rest of your life.'

'I don't think virgins normally have children unless the Holy Spirit gets involved.'

'You know what I mean.'

'You mean a single mother. Go on, Sally, you can say it.'

'Well, yes, that is what I mean actually. Any man you meet is going to run a mile from you. Is that what you want?'

Louise let out a long breath and closed her eyes.

'I am not going to be a statistic, Sal. I'm only signing on temporarily. Soon I'll have a good job and I'll be independent and happy. What's wrong with that?'

'Just listen, Louise. You'll meet someone. When you get a proper job and mix in a stimulating social group, then you'll find someone who's really right for you. Do you want to blow that chance out of the window?'

Louise put her plate of sandwiches on the bed and stood up. She paced around, dragging the telephone cord after her. It was important to stay reasonable. She'd known Sally for so long.

159

'Look, I didn't ask for this to happen. I didn't even think for one minute that I wanted to keep it at first, and I'm sure that in my position you wouldn't want to, but that's irrelevant. I can't say what's changed, but I've made my mind up. I'm happy, Sal. Don't you understand? I've been fingering packs of disposable nappies in the supermarket. I've talked to the doctor about pre-natal classes. I might even crochet something.'

'What the hell are you going to crochet?'

'I don't know yet. I only just thought of that one.'

'I'm going to have to come and see you,' Sally tutted. 'What about Friday night? Shall I bring a bottle round and we'll get a take-away?'

'I'm not sure.'

'Why?'

'I – I don't know what I'm doing on Friday.' Louise winced at her feeble excuse. The last thing she wanted was an entire evening being lectured by Sally.

'Listen to you!' Sally exclaimed urgently. 'You can't just carry on as if nothing's happening. And what are you going to do when you've actually got a baby? You won't be able to go flinging yourself around pubs like you do now. Not without paying for a babysitter, which you won't be able to afford. Bloody hell, Louise, you're just heading for obscurity. I thought you were more sensible than this. You've really blown me away.'

'Thanks.' Louise paced towards her chest of drawers, looked at herself in the mirror, and pulled a face.

'I suppose you'll go all pro-life now, and judge everybody who isn't as dewy-eyed as you. I remember you ranting and raving about choice. You've certainly changed your tune.'

'This *is* about choice. That's what nobody seems to understand.' Louise glowered at the phone. 'I'd be the first one to chain myself to the railings if they changed the laws,

160

but that doesn't mean that I can't make my own sodding mind up, does it?'

'You're shouting.'

'I'm not,' Louise shouted at the receiver.

'Yes, you are. Don't shout at me. I'm only trying to help.'

·'I didn't shout. I just have stronger feelings about my own life than I thought.'

'So.' Louise heard Sally breathe out. 'You tell me how you're going to support yourself, then?'

'I told you. I'll find a good job – a proper one. And what about my mum? She's alone down in Tonbridge. I'm sure she wouldn't mind if I stayed there for a bit if things are difficult.' Sally was disdainfully silent. Louise regretted her statement instantly.

'Oh, right. So you're going to whiz back to the metropolis of Tonbridge, to the house you grew up in, and spend your days boiling nappies and pushing a pram up the high street. Just like the girls we used to feel sorry for when we were at school. Brilliant. You have come on from the day we got our O level results, haven't you? You got nine of those, remember? Good ones. Just so that you could go back to where we came from and fester.'

Louise sank back on to the edge of her bed. She could remember weaving through the town with Sally, both of them vowing that they wouldn't be pram pushers. Not, at least, until they'd proved something to the world. But that had been a long time ago. Things changed. Her attitude was changing daily. She wasn't sure that she liked the word 'fester'. It certainly wasn't going to apply to her. She would make sure of it.

'I'm not asking for your approval any more, Sal. I'm sorry, but if you can't say anything more positive, I'm going to have to ring off.'

'Fine,' Sally snapped.

'Fine,' Louise snapped back. Sally crashed the phone down first.

Louise's new purchase – a book of babies' names – cheered her up. It was incredible how the most ludicrous names could seem elegant once you understood their derivation. But you couldn't expect a child to go through life with a paragraph of explanation to countermand the sniggers.

'Hi, I'm Gerald, from the Old German meaning "spear rule". It's an ancient name, probably introduced into Britain by the Normans.' Or, 'Beryl is actually derived from the gemstone, a name related to the Arabic for crystal.' The poor child would have enough to deal with being a Twigg. Louise knew. It wasn't the most distinguished of surnames, but she'd survived. No need to add to the burden.

She could go for something really simple. Fred. Or Dot. Or, on the other hand, she could see what the baby looked like, and wait for inspiration to dawn. She could picture herself heaving her body up in the delivery room to peer into the wrinkled face. 'Clementina! It has to be!'

She smiled to herself, rubbing her hand on her stomach. A little person. She would do all she could to make life happy for them both. And that meant staying on top of her plans. If she could just fight through this period of nausea, sign on for a short time to make sure she didn't lose the flat, and work her way into a promising career, the stage would be set. She thought about Rachel's suggestion again.

She'd first offered to give Louise an opening in the music business when Louise was trying to find a niche for herself after university. She hadn't taken it too seriously. Rachel had gone into her profession early and worked her way up. And it had taken very hard work and long hours. Two factors that Louise had never equated with the concept of the ideal job. They'd always been a musical family in their own funny way, but Rachel had been the first to turn it into a career. It made sense, but she'd done it first. The last thing Louise wanted was to creep around in her shadow.

They'd always had a piano at home. Her father used to shout requests from the garden while her mother sat at the keys and obliged. She played music from Lerner and Lowe, Rogers and Hammerstein, and occasional short classical pieces, but Louise's memories were of them cramming on to the piano stool and crooning along to 'How to Handle a Woman' while her father chuckled through the window. At school, she'd had the opportunity to learn the piano properly. Her father had worked like a Trojan to make sure they could afford it. She could still remember her very first lesson. Her piano tutor had dropped her a note telling her to bring something along that she liked to play so that he could judge her level.

She'd jogged into the tiny room with *Oklahoma* under her arm, and delivered a fine rendition of 'The Surrey with the Fringe on Top'. Complete with vocals. A long silence had ensued. Mr Benson – who wore a tight suit, spoke in a whisper, looked like the Tefal Man, but played the piano like a dream – had coughed with embarrassment and suggested they get started on scales right away. Perhaps that was when the fun had gone out of it. Rachel, on the other hand, took guitar lessons with the trendiest teacher in the school. He was known as Jake, had long hair in a ponytail and played sax in a jazz band. He disappeared in the middle of one of the terms. So did Gina, the raunchiest sixth former in the school. The older girls thought there was a connection.

But before she launched herself into a dazzling career, Louise had to stop feeling sick and be sure that she wasn't going to be evicted. And that brought her back to Ash. He had offered to help her tackle the Jobcentre. In which case, she could just pop round, take some newspapers and her forms, and have a cup of tea with him. That might be friendly.

It hadn't taken long to persuade herself. She was back in the bedroom before she knew it, picking up the phone, dialling his number, and breathing erratically into the plastic. There was a click as it was answered.

'Ash?' she said quickly.

'Er, I'll just go and get him. Hang on.'

It was a woman's voice. A *woman's voice*. Louise stared at the brick view beyond her window. Of course, not all men were like Jon. When she'd pictured him and his girlfriend she saw them meeting at the pub, parting company at the tube station unless it was one of those lucky nights. They lived together, obviously. It happened to normal people. She heard scuffling from a distance, and he was there on the end of the phone.

'Hi.'

'It's Louise,' she said. She stopped, waiting for him to explain that now wasn't a good time, that he had just flung on a pair of boxer shorts during his late-afternoon sex romp, that he was covered in glazed apricots and couldn't keep a grip on the phone, that his girlfriend was exploring his inner thighs with her tongue, and could she ring him back in five minutes. No, forty-five minutes. She had the feeling that he would take his time over things. She suddenly felt like a gooseberry.

'Great. I'm really glad you called. Did you change your mind?'

He sounded almost genuine. His girlfriend must have left the room. Gone back to bed, probably, to wait for him in the position he liked the most. But, Louise tried to reason calmly, she was pregnant, and was going to have a baby. She was in an awkward position herself.

'If you think you can help me, I could meet you tomorrow.'

'Yeah, brilliant. Can you make it early afternoon?'

'That's fine.'

'Why don't you come round here?' he said.

She chewed on her cheek. She wanted to ask him if his girlfriend would mind but it would sound as if she saw herself as competition. Better to be blasé. Why should his girlfriend mind? She couldn't know that Louise wanted to steal her boyfriend.

'Is that all right?'

''Course. I'll give you the address.'

Louise picked up a pen and scribbled down the details. As she did, her doorbell rang.

'Is that your bell?' he asked.

'Er, yes.' She frowned across the room.

'Right. Well, I'll see you tomorrow.'

'Yes, probably,' she answered, and hung up quickly before she could make more of a fool of herself.

The bell rang again. Louise glanced at her watch. Sally was at work. Jon was at work. Rachel was at work. The whole bloody world was at work apart from her. And Ash. And his girlfriend, she added mentally, as she padded out to the outside hall. But, she remembered, she was expecting a frilly vest and a pair of circus clown slippers from her mother. It was about time they arrived. She flung open the front door.

A bunch of flowers appeared with a pair of short grey legs beneath them.

'Flat two?' a nasal voice asked.

'Yes.'

The bunch of flowers was flicked to one side. A strange man grinned at her.

'Who's a lucky lady then?'

'I don't know.' Louise gawped at the flowers.

He consulted a form in his hand.

'Louise Twigg?'

165

'Er, yes, but—'

'For you, madam.' He grinned again. Then, unexpectedly, he began to sing at her. 'Somebody loves me, I don't know who, maybe, maybe, it's you!'

Louise shook her head at him.

'There's been a big mistake.'

'Nope.' He dropped his grin and looked at her with impatience. 'Can you take the blimmin' things, please? I'm on double yellows and this is a wheel-clamping area. I've got three more deliveries to make before half past five. If you find out there's been a mistake, you can always chuck 'em in the bin, can't you? Ta!'

Louise took the flowers and the man trotted off, muttering under his breath. She closed the front door and searched for a label. She found a small white envelope and pulled out the card. It was printed in biro. She leaned against the wall as she read it.

To my sweet Louise. Thinking of you. With all my love, Jon.

Chapter Ten

'Bastard!' Louise issued through her teeth as she ploughed her way through the back streets of Ealing the following day. 'Git. Sod. Bastard.'

She was going at such a speed that she'd reached the end of the road that Ash lived in before she realised it. She stopped and glowered at a passer-by simply because he was a man.

What was she doing here? She gazed back down the road. She'd hardly even noticed what the area was like. Once they might have been smart family houses. Now they were scruffy apart from the odd façade here and there that had been renovated. Judging by the number of bells clustered around most of the doors, she was in bedsit land. All this had passed her by as she'd marched down the road the first time. She'd been more interested in her plans to booby-trap Jon's boxer shorts.

She'd taken the flowers into her flat and sat and stared at them. Jon hadn't rung to ask if she'd got them. There was no letter this morning from him. Just that one, cute little message and enough tiger lilies to buckle the top table at a wedding reception. Finally, out of simple pity for the flowers, she'd stuffed them in a bucket and put them on the floor. Vases were not her usual style, and she hadn't thought to get one just in case her ex-lover chose the big-bunch-of-flowers tactic to assuage his guilty conscience. First she'd propped the message up against the bucket and read it over and over. Then she'd taken it with her when she'd gone to bed and propped it against her clock radio so that she could consider it some more.

What exactly did he mean?

Without any clarification, she could only think the worst. He would think it was all over by now. It was his equivalent of a bottle of Lucozade, except there wasn't an InterLucozade service that he could ring up and pay to deliver a bottle to her door. It was his way of saying 'Get well soon', but from a safe distance.

Louise sniffed in a noseful of freezing air, wiggled her fingers in her knitted gloves, and began to walk back down Ash's street, musing over her boots. She got a whiff of something dreadful. Tarmac? Oil? Whatever it was, quite suddenly her stomach turned over, a burst of sweaty heat washed up her body, and she knew she was going to be sick.

'Oh, no . . .'

She dived into the nearest garden, yanked the plastic lid off the dustbin sitting at the bottom of a row of clean white steps, and bent over it.

'Urghhhh!'

She tried to stand up straight, panted miserably, and retched all over again. Inside the bin was a neatly tied-up Sainsbury's bag. She could see an empty bottle of olive oil pressed against the thin plastic. Olive oil.

'Oh yuk, urghhhh.'

The front door opened at the top of the white steps.

'Just what the bloody hell do you think you're doing!'

Louise held on to the sides of the bin for support, her knees flexing and straightening ominously. Her forehead was clammy and her fringe was sticking to her eyelashes. Through bleary vision she identified one of the houses that had been renovated. That would explain why the indignation was so profound.

'I'm really sorry,' she gasped.

'Get away from my dustbin!' a woman in a caftan screeched at her. 'Go and do that in the gutter. You're disgusting.'

'It's not my fault. I'm so sorry.' She wiped her glove over her eyes and took a breath of air. It was going to be all right now. The feeling was going away again. She picked up the lid and placed it back on top of the dustbin. She offered a weak smile. 'You'd never know there was anything in there.'

'Bloody drug addicts! Take your needles with you!' The woman took a step towards her, waving a billowing sleeve. Louise decided to back away. She'd never wrestled with a woman in a caftan before, but it hadn't ever been on her list of things to do before she died.

She staggered away as she heard the door slam above her. She reached a low wall at the front of the next house and sank on to it. The branches of a fir pricked at the back of her head. She didn't care. She would just sit here enveloped by an overgrown Christmas tree and think about what to do next. Her Co-op bag with the local newspapers and her Jobcentre forms inside was still hitched on to her wrist, but now she wasn't so sure she should visit Ash after all. What if she threw up again? What was her body saying to her? Don't visit Ash. You're going to have a baby, and that means no fantasies.

She closed her eyes and let her chin flop on to her chest while she pondered. No fantasies. If Sally was right, she might as well take a vow of chastity now.

But then again, if she couldn't actually *do* anything, might it not be possible just to have a last, fleeting glimpse of what it felt like to have a crush on someone? Couldn't she just play with the idea a little bit longer until a big bump appeared and scared everyone away? Then she could do the decent thing and get herself to a nunnery. If they'd have her, of course.

'Louise?'

She jerked her head back. Ash was standing right in front of her, hopping from leg to leg and shivering. Not surprisingly, seeing as he was only wearing his aerated jeans and a T-shirt – the one with the unknown band on the front and a rip just under the breastbone. She swallowed back the urge to yell in shock.

'Blimey. How long have you been standing there?'

'Just a few seconds. I thought you'd fallen asleep.' He grinned at her. 'I, er, saw you from the house. It's just opposite. That one there, with the green door.'

'Oh.' She tried to regain her dignity by sitting up straight. The Christmas tree was still framing her head, but it was too late to worry about that. 'Oh, I see, I'm sorry. I just had to sit down for a moment.' He looked at her with his head at an angle. 'It's a long walk from my flat, and I suddenly felt tired. It must be this flu virus I've had.' She dazzled him with a smile.

'Right. Do you want to come in then? I've put the kettle on.'

She nodded and followed him back across the road, admiring his thick-soled climbing boots. Very masculine. They went up a row of steps, more yellow ochre than white, and into a dark hall. She stopped inside as he closed the door behind her and wandered away to a kitchen at the back of the house.

'This house is bigger than it looks on the outside. It's really nice inside.'

'Not so big when everyone's home,' he called back. 'We share the first two floors here between five of us. Come through. It's only me and Karen here at the moment. She's upstairs, but I think she's asleep. We can just sit in here if you like.'

She went into the kitchen and gazed around. All the units were cluttered. A mountain of washed crockery was balanced on the draining board. Nobody seemed to have the time, or the motivation perhaps, to put anything away. She concentrated on the labels on the jars and bottles ranged near the cooker. Somebody enjoyed cooking, judging by the assortment of utensils jammed into a ceramic pot. She wondered if it was Karen, and instantly felt ruffled again. For the moment, she didn't want to think about Karen being asleep upstairs.

'So are you all friends, then? It must be difficult sharing with so many people.'

He laughed at her and grabbed two mugs from the heap of washing-up. An entire canteen of cutlery slid over the draining board and landed in the sink. He didn't seem to notice.

'I'm used to it. It's the price you pay for following your dream. I knew Ginger and Karen before we moved here. She's his sister, and he's been my best mate for years. The other two just turned up and refused to leave, which suited us. We needed the rent money.'

'And, er, is Karen . . .' Louise paused swiftly to phrase her question inoffensively. 'Is Karen jobless too?'

He stopped for a moment, a frown flitting across his brow.

'Karen's got her own income. So has Ginger. The rest of us here have to scrape by how we can.'

'Oh.'

'What I mean is, I haven't got a safety net.' She waited for him to go on. She knew what it was like, not to have a safety net. 'And the two of them have. It happens. I don't bitch about it. Ginger works anyway, but Karen doesn't. At the moment. She had a job in a bar, but she lost it.'

'Oh dear.' Louise rounded her eyes with sympathy.

'Don't feel sorry for her. She works to amuse herself when she feels like it. She pays her way, it just happens to be with her father's money. Grab a seat at the table. We can talk there.'

Louise pulled out a heavy wooden chair and sat down. The table was wide, solid and strewn with leftover Sunday newspapers. There was something in Ash's tone as he talked about Karen that intrigued her. It wasn't entirely respectful.

'So your parents don't have money?'

'My parents divorced me.'

'They did what?'

'I don't see them. Not any more. It's a really boring story. What about you?'

'Oh, er, my father died. My mum's in Kent. She works for a branch of the Health Service.'

'Really?' He stopped to look at her as he poured boiling water into the mugs. 'Was that recently?'

'My dad? Over a year ago. I try not to think about it if I can help it. He was a nice man. Fun, friendly, everybody liked him. He was always there, just being him.' She slipped off her coat and arranged it on the back of the chair, plucking at the jumper she'd thrown on that morning. Well, she'd thrown it on after taking an hour to decide which jumper to wear, and opting for the one with the V-neck that showed a little bit of cleavage if she leaned forward. 'I couldn't have a glass of water as well, could I?'

'Oh sure. Of course. You still feeling unwell?'

'Just a bit tired.' She watched him get her a glass and fill it with mineral water from the fridge. It wasn't what she expected. But perhaps it was Karen's.

'So Karen's your girlfriend then, is she?' she asked. He shot her a cool glance. She looked down at her bag quickly.

'She's Ginger's sister. She sings for us. And we've been seeing each other for a long time, yes.'

'Oh.' Louise opened the first newspaper and flicked through the pages quickly. A long time. That was not good news. She found the classified ads and tried to concentrate on them.

'She's got a great voice. Smoky, atmospheric, really sexy.' He flicked tea bags into a plastic bin and brought the mugs over.

'That's nice.' So, Karen was talented. That was even worse news. She focused on an advert for a town planner. He set the mug and glass of water in front of her and sat down. She took a sip of water, read the details of the ad several times, and frowned with concentration.

'I met her at Guildhall.'

'Oh.' She sniffed indifferently. Guildhall? What did he mean by that? At a gig?

'I met her through Ginger. We've got a good friendship. I value that.'

'Really.' Friendship. Even worse than lust. Friendships went on for ever. She opened her shoulder-bag, picked out a pen, and ringed the advertisement with great care.

'I've known them both for ten years now,' he said.

'Hmmn.' Ten years. Ten bloody years? They might as well be married.

'She's a great front woman. Gets the crowd going, you know.'

'Twenty thousand a year. I wonder . . .' What did he mean exactly by getting the crowd going? Did she get him going too, in her spare time? Of course she did. She was his girlfriend. Her eyes glowed as she read the job description for the town planner for the fifteenth time.

'I can't sing myself. I'm just a musician, really. Ginger can't sing either, but he has a go at harmonies. We need another woman, really. I don't suppose you can sing, can you?'

She looked up at him vacantly. She'd heard every word. She could have written it all down and read it back to him, but now was not a good time to demonstrate that.

'Pardon?'

'It was just a thought. You've got a smashing figure and

173

a great face. I bet you look really good in make-up. You know. Striking.'

'I am wearing make-up,' she said bluntly. Now she wasn't sure whether to be deeply flattered or desperately offended. 'And my singing causes people physical pain.'

'Can you play anything?'

She thought about her answer. She could be honest.

'Piano. But that also causes people physical pain.'

'Really? Do you?' He looked genuinely interested. 'How well?'

'Well enough to provoke frequent complaints from the guy who lives above me. By which I mean loudly and badly, but with enormous enthusiasm.' She mustered a dry look from her memory archives, delivered it, and turned her attention back to her newspaper. But he'd been interested in something she was doing, even if only for a moment.

'So,' he continued, nodding down at the newspaper, 'you've got a degree in town planning, have you?'

'No,' she said incredulously.

'I just wondered why you've ringed the ad.'

'I thought that was the whole point. If I apply for jobs I'm not qualified for I won't get them, will I?'

He smiled at her, lolling back in his chair. She picked up her mug and took a gulp from it. It was a good cup of tea.

'You've got to be cleverer than that. You've got to go for something appropriate but mess it up. The guys at the Jobcentre aren't stupid.'

'Mess it up? What do you mean?'

'I mean you've got to apply for the jobs, go for the interviews, but make damned sure you don't get offered anything. Just while you need to sign on, of course.'

'How do I do that?' She looked at him in alarm. The most gorgeous man in London was sitting across the table from her, true, but being pregnant, staying in her flat and coping with morning sickness all zoomed back to dominate her thoughts. 'I've always temped before. I don't know what you mean.'

'Basically, you have to tell them what they don't want to hear. If that's not enough, behave as if you're on the edge of a breakdown. And if that fails, fart loudly when it's all gone quiet.'

She gaped at him. That's what it all came down to? Breaking wind? He could have told her that in the café.

'Fart?'

'Fart,' he confirmed with a solemn nod. Then he smiled at her again. It was easy for him to smile. In fact, she suddenly had the urge to cry. Not on him, or even near him, but at him.

'It's all right for you to smile. But what if I end up being offered jobs all over the place? I'll be too ill to take them, I'll lose my flat and it will be a disaster. I've got to be able to offer something . . .'

She tailed away. It was so nice, so warm in this friendly, chaotic kitchen. She wanted to be like Karen upstairs, cuddled up in bed, with Ash downstairs making tea for her. Or she wanted to be in the bright, steamy café with him. She didn't want to have to go home after all this and be on her own again. Burning tears of self-pity suddenly appeared in her eyes. She tried to blink them away before he could see them.

'Hey.' He reached out to take her hand. This time, she didn't jump into the air. She let him hold her fingers until the urge to bawl began to slide away again. His fingers were warm. It was nice touching them.

'I'm sorry,' she issued in a strangled voice. 'It's just that everything's a bit difficult at the moment.'

'I know,' he said softly, standing up to walk around the corner of the table and put his hands gently on her shoulders.

'No, you don't know,' she mumbled.

'Yes,' he said with quiet confidence. 'I do.'

'No.' She turned to look up at him. His eyes were amazing. She could have climbed into them at that moment and asked for a lift home. It was as if he could see right into her. She gathered herself together.

'Ash, it's kind of you to think you know what's going on, but you don't actually. I suppose in some ways that's not very important. You don't need to know anyway. Why should you? It's got sod all to do with you. And I don't know why you're being so kind, but it's very . . . helpful.'

'Louise?'

'Yes?' she whispered.

'Shut up.'

Her mouth opened instinctively to argue with him, but words failed her. She closed it again. He squeezed her shoulders through her jumper.

'I'm here. I'll help you,' he said.

He dropped his head to hers and brushed her cheek with a kiss. She flinched, her eyes shooting open in shock. It was such a gentle action, a mere caress of his lips on her skin, and then he'd walked away again and seated himself back in the chair out of her reach.

'You didn't have to do that,' she babbled in panic. 'I don't know why you did it anyway, but there was no reason why you should. I don't need sympathy at all . . .' Her voice died. He was giving her that look again. 'Thank you,' she squeaked.

'I kissed you because I wanted to,' he said. 'Not because you're pregnant.'

'Oh.' She was relieved. 'All right then.'

She smiled at him. But then it hit her. She stood up and realised that standing up was silly. The last time she'd stood up, Rachel had expected her to say something earth-shattering. She didn't have anything earth-shattering to say. She sat down again. She couldn't lie, not when he was fixing her with his eyes in that way, but she had to say something.

'What do you mean?'

'Come on,' he said gently, ignoring her display. 'It's the only answer that makes any sense. It doesn't change my life, Louise, although I know it's changing yours completely. Relax. You've got to have someone to talk to about it, haven't you? You might as well be honest with me. What have you got to lose?'

She delivered several short, sharp breaths. She might have been practising for labour. Until she'd experienced labour, she could believe that this was more painful.

'Ash . . .'

He was being so – so reasonable. So sensible. So friendly. And so perceptive. There had to be something wrong with him. Surely nobody would behave like this, under these circumstances, unless it could come under the heading of 'weird'?

'Yes?' he said.

'I should make things clear to you. I'm having this baby because I want to, not because I have to. I don't need pity, and I don't need well-meant advice.'

'I know,' he said.

'And I don't need anybody to step in and be a substitute for anybody else. This – this has happened, and although I didn't expect it, I've come to realise that it's what I want. That's all there is to it.'

'I guessed that.' He nodded at her.

'And I'm only signing on until I don't feel sick,' she asserted.

'I'm not an expert on the process, but I'd worked that out for myself too.'

'What you should realise is that I'm determined to make something of this. Something positive.' He nodded again.

177

What was he doing, agreeing with her? He couldn't possibly know how she felt.

'You've never been pregnant!' she threw at him. He handled it very well, with an even more emphatic nod.

In the silence that followed, the defensive prickles subsided from her skin. It was very difficult to have a stand-up row with somebody who was so set upon understanding what you said. She leaned forward and lowered her voice.

'The thing is, I think I've finally grown up. I don't quite know why I'm telling you that.' She took another long breath. 'It's just that it's become so important. I've never signed on before, I've never had to think about my security before, and I've never dusted my ceiling before. Profound things are happening to me.'

His lips twitched, but his eyes remained steady.

'I've never eaten so much broccoli in my life.'

'I can only imagine.'

'I've never given up smoking before.'

'I believe you.'

'And I've never shared such private thoughts with a complete stranger before either.'

He laughed. He might have assured her that he wasn't a complete stranger. After all, they'd met a couple of times and got on pretty well. She mentally formed the possible answers he could give, but what he said was something she wasn't expecting.

'I bet you've never thrown up in somebody else's dustbin before either.'

She was horrified, but it wasn't even worth standing up and sitting down again. The man had seen her throw up in the dustbin. Feigning indignation at his accusation was pointless, but it had to be done.

'I'm not quite sure what you mean.'

'You do, but I don't mind if you don't admit it.'

She looked away from him and back to the local newspaper that she'd spread out on the table. He seemed to decide to stop teasing her and turn his attention back to why she was at his house in the first place. In truth, she herself had started to forget why she had come. She tried to concentrate. It was for his advice. Something to do with farting at job interviews.

'Got your CV?' he asked.

'Er, yes.' She crashed around in her plastic bag and found a handful of paper. She presented it to him. He shuffled through her CV quietly.

'What do you think?'

'There's plenty of potential here,' he said. 'I'll hang on to this and see if I can fiddle with it. Okay with you?'

'Yes.' She took a sip of tea while she studied him. 'Listen, I haven't heard from my sister yet. We had a bit of a row the last time I saw her. For all I know, she might have thrown your song away. I just thought I should tell you that. I did what I could.'

Any answer he might have given was interrupted by the thundering of footsteps down the stairs. Louise straightened. The footsteps careered through the hallway and arrived in the kitchen. They stopped behind her. She quickly pulled a newspaper from the pile in front of her and read the headline. She heard a lazy yawn.

'Hi,' a smoke, atmospheric and sexy voice drawled over her head.

'Hi there. Kettle's just boiled. This is Louise.'

Louise swivelled round in her seat ready with a cheesy smile. She saw a woman with impossibly glossy swathes of golden hair dressed only in a loose denim shirt. Karen pushed her hair out of her face to reveal kittenish brown eyes, a clear creamy skin and a wide, sensual mouth. And although she must have been around thirty, she only looked twenty-five. Louise hated her instantly.

179

'Ahh. So this is Louise.' Karen nodded at Ash and arched a delicate eyebrow. 'Great, great. I'll just get myself some tea and leave you both to chat.' She flashed a smile at Louise, proving that she could do happy-sexy and sultry-sexy equally well, and swayed over to the kettle, revealing her shirt to be rumpled at the back, half tucked into a pair of maroon satin knickers which were very high cut over the buttock.

Louise swallowed. The word 'bitch' flew into her mind. Why had Karen given Ash a knowing look? Why had she looked at him at all? And why had he turned round to look at her rear view as she bent down quite unnecessarily to pick up a stray piece of cellophane wrapper from the kitchen tile and dump it in the bin? Now he was pushing a hand through his brown hair and turning clear eyes back to her CV, as if he'd never given Karen's buttocks a second thought. Louise remained transfixed as Karen flicked the switch on the kettle, leaned back on the draining-board and performed a full stretch, her arms high, the few buttons which were fastened on the shirt straining to reveal an alarmingly full chest. Louise stuck out her swelling lumps competitively. Ash remained engrossed in her CV, making notes on it with a biro.

'So, are you musical too, Louise?' Karen asked huskily across the kitchen. Louise gave a curt smile.

'Not so's you'd notice.'

Karen nodded, flicking a tidal wave of hair out of one eye so that it fell endearingly over the other instead.

'They say these things run in families, but that's balls,' she said. 'I'm the musical one in ours. Ginger hasn't got a clue really. But he's mad, and that helps.'

'Right,' Louise said, willing the vision of gorgeousness to lose her footing and fall right down the waste-disposal unit.

'Ash's really talented,' Karen said, grinning at Ash's back.

'Fuck off, Karen. Haven't you got something to do upstairs?'

'But you are, darling, and you're just so coy about it, which makes it all the more charming.'

'Hasn't the kettle boiled yet?'

'He was brilliant at Guildhall. Blew everyone away. He could be professional now, but he's so single-minded it's scary. If only he wasn't so obsessed with the class war, he'd be up there with the best of them.'

'I said fuck off, Karen.'

'Oops, I'll shut up then.'

'Hang on.' Louise sat back and fiddled with her pen. 'Guildhall as in the music school?'

'Of course.' Karen daintily popped a tea bag into a mug and poked it around with her finger. 'Ouch. That's hot. Why, what's he been telling you? That he was dragged up in the East End and made his own guitar out of orange crates and elastic bands? Don't believe a word of it.'

'Karen!' Ash swung round and eyed her severely. She shrugged at him, flicked her hair backwards and forwards again, and pulled the tea bag casually from her mug.

'Okay, I'm out of here. Nice to meet you, Louise. See you upstairs when you've finished, working-class hero. Don't be long.'

Ash watched Karen's exit from the kitchen. Louise studied his expression with fascination. There was more than a flicker of irritation in his eyes. But they had known each other for ten years. They'd have got over showering compliments on each other by now.

'So?' Louise asked him as he heard Karen's footsteps fade up the stairs and a distant door swing shut. 'What was that all about?'

181

'Oh, she's just being a prat. Ignore her.'

'Guildhall School of Music? Not to learn how to play guitar with your teeth, I suspect. What did you do there?'

'Violin and cello,' he said, looking up at her again.

'But you're ashamed of that now, or what? I don't understand.'

He flicked a glance up at the ceiling while he pulled his tobacco from the pocket of his jeans. He turned his attention to rolling a cigarette, lighting it from a box of matches, and issuing a plume of smoke through his teeth.

'It's not what I do now. Not classical, anyway. I play electric violin. That's the sort of band it is. A bit unusual.'

'That sounds intriguing.'

'Yep. It's different.'

'So why the allergic reaction to what Karen said?'

He rubbed at his nose with his forefinger. He looked momentarily uncomfortable.

'I just can't be doing with the formality of it all. Regular stints in an orchestra, dressing up like a penguin, playing other people's music, toadying to some histrionic conductor, all that fucking ceremony. Treating music as if it's the property of the chattering classes. It's just not me.'

'So what—'

'And there are more worthwhile things to be doing than entertaining a bunch of socialites who don't give a fuck what you're playing as long as they can be seen with the right people in the interval.'

'But Karen—'

'Karen thinks that principles is a high-street store.' He gave her a humourless smile.

'So—'

'So can we get on with sorting you out? It's just that I don't want to explain it all. As I said, it's really boring.'

'But you did play in an orchestra, didn't you?' Louise attempted one final push. At last, she was getting a tiny glimpse of who Ash really might be.

'Yep. I was thrown out.'

'For . . . What did you do?'

He raised his eyes to her. There was a prominent glint of humour there.

'I mooned at the conductor halfway through the "Sinfonia Antartica".'

'And people saw you?' Louise's mouth dropped open.

'Couldn't miss me really. I was first violin.'

'And your parents didn't approve? Is that why they divorced you?'

Ash tapped his cigarette into his palm and rubbed the dry ash into the denim covering his thigh. She watched the action, mesmerised.

'My father was the conductor,' he said flatly. 'So shall we get on with your job applications now?'

'Why do you always do that?' Shaun asked as he leaned at a peculiar angle against the filing cabinets. Olivia looked up guiltily from Carol's chair.

'Do what?'

'That thing with the chair. You always lower it before you leave the office.'

'It's to bring old Cow-bag down to size,' Sarah quipped at Shaun, reaching up to ruffle his hair with her dark purple nails. He blushed violently, and opened his mouth as if trying to think of a suitable retort. 'Okay, I'm off now.' Sarah grabbed her leather jacket and winked at Olivia. 'Neal's picking me up. We're off to the family planning clinic this evening. It's time for my smear again.'

'Please spare us the details.' Shaun pulled a face at her.

'It's girl talk, Shaun. You don't mind that, do you? You're a big girl at heart, aren't you? See you tomorrow, Olivia. Hope you've got your scarf and gloves with you. You'll freeze your nipples off at the bus stop.'

'I'm sure my nipples will survive,' Olivia managed with only the faintest of blushes. They heard Sarah crash away down the corridor, yelling goodnights into the other offices, and disappearing down the stairs.

'That girl!' Olivia shook her head at Shaun. 'I remember my first job. I was so terrified of putting a foot wrong I hardly dared speak to anybody. But jobs used to last longer then. Everybody chops and changes now, don't they?'

'You can't blame people for that,' Shaun said, trying to stand up straight but remaining at an interesting angle. 'It's in our nature to change. We only become unhappy if we fight against it.'

'Ah, you're getting philosophical again.' Olivia made sure Carol's seat had dropped as far as it would go, patted it for reassurance, and wandered across to the coat stand. She wrapped her mac tightly around her and buttoned it right up to the chin. It was a horrible cold spell that they were experiencing. She only hoped that the bulbs wouldn't all be killed off. She was accustomed to crocuses in spring. Every year they had crocuses in the front garden. It would be strange if they weren't there next year.

'Look, Olivia, it really is freezing outside. Please will you let me give you a lift? I hate to think of you at that horrible cold bus stop on the hill with the wind whistling around your legs. You haven't even got trousers on.'

'Oh, I could never wear trousers to work.'

'So let me take you home. The car's always nice and warm, once it heats up. There's only a very small draught from the top of the passenger window, but you won't feel it in your coat.'

Olivia considered as she fitted her gloves over her fingers. She knew that Shaun was watching her for a response, his one long eyebrow raised in hope. Why he was so keen to help her all the time she wasn't entirely sure, but then again, he was a kind person. It was in his nature to help people.

'All right.' She put her head up and smiled at him. 'Thank you very much. You can take me home. And I can ask you something I've been meaning to ask you for the last couple of days.'

'Really?' His head bobbed around, his hair appearing to rise from his scalp.

'Don't look so worried. You can always say no.'

They walked out into the street and Olivia waited patiently on the pavement while Shaun played with the lock on the passenger door which refused to budge from the inside. Eventually, he forced it up, and grinned at her through the glass. In the dim light cast by the street lamps, he looked like a gnome. Poor Shaun. He was such good company, but so few women would take him seriously. Life was cruel. She slipped into the seat beside him, and after three attempts, managed to pull the door properly shut.

'People have love affairs with their cars, you know,' he told her as he repeatedly tried to start the engine. 'I've had Flossie for fourteen years. I wouldn't part with her if I inherited a million. I'm loyal like that.'

'Yes, I can believe it.'

'People don't value loyalty any more, do they?' He glanced at Olivia triumphantly as the engine fired into action. They lurched away from the old building, steering an uncertain course through a network of residential streets. 'It's a rare quality, that's what I say. You can spot it in people, you know.'

'You think so?'

'Oh, yes. People have auras. Some are almost visible, they're so strong. You're a very loyal person, for example. I can sense that.'

Olivia mused. Had her recent thoughts been loyal? Or disloyal?

'Carol's not. There's something very funny going on there, if you ask me.'

Olivia turned to look at him. His profile wasn't too bad, she thought passingly. His nose could be seen as Roman. He could always send a side shot of himself to a dating agency. It might get him over the first hurdle.

'Why on earth do you say that?'

'Dunno. She's so uptight, and she's supposed to have this great marriage, you know, two successful Health Service managers together, but there's something rotten there.'

'I don't really know anything about her husband. I just assumed he was exactly like her.'

'He's all right, actually. Works up near Bromley. I met him once at a regional do.'

'So why do you say she's not loyal?'

'Roger,' Shaun said, slamming on the brakes as they reached a completely expected junction. Olivia grabbed the dashboard as she was thrown forward.

'You don't mean Carol – and Roger?'

'Exactly.' Shaun ground the gears, and they stalled. He muttered something very polite under his breath, re-started the engine, and they shot away from the junction, almost into the back of the car in front. 'Sorry about that. It's the gearbox. You have to have a knack with it.'

'Yes.' Olivia fell into thought. While she was pondering the possible liaison between Carol, her manager, and Roger, the district manager, she held on tightly to the sides of her seat, and wondered if what she was intending to ask Shaun was tantamount to suicide.

'Sarah's a loyal one,' Shaun continued happily. 'But I'm not sure that Neal's the one for her.'

'Good grief!' Olivia laughed. 'Is this what you spend all

your spare time doing? Thinking about people at work and their relationships?'

Shaun didn't answer immediately, and Olivia's laugh trailed away. She stared straight ahead again. That was a tactless remark to make.

'Er, I do the charts, of course. That keeps me busy. I'm doing Sarah's for her now.'

'Of course.'

'And I read a lot. Especially poetry.'

'You do?'

'I do.'

'Oh, that's nice.' Olivia frowned ahead. She could hardly remember the poetry she'd studied at school. Poetry just wasn't a part of her life. Bob never—

'"Courage!" he said, and pointed toward the land, "This mounting wave will roll us shoreward soon." In the afternoon they came unto a land in which it seemèd always afternoon.'

Olivia looked at Shaun in shock. He had suddenly turned into John Gielgud. He grinned back. 'Tennyson. Great, isn't he?' He drove on quietly for a moment. 'You see, just because I don't spend every night clubbing, it doesn't mean I don't enjoy life. In my own way.'

'I understand, Shaun. I didn't mean to sound rude.'

'No, no. It wasn't rude at all. The truth is, I don't get out much. I don't really make the effort. I'm saving up, you see, for a holiday.'

'Oh.' Olivia stared out of the windows at the lights of the buildings they passed. They drove on up the High Street, past the beauty of Tonbridge School chapel, and out towards the suburbs of the town. A holiday. How long was it since she'd had a holiday? A proper holiday, not just for the sake of saying she'd taken time off, but somewhere she really wanted to go? She sighed. She'd never been where she really wanted to go. And now it felt as if she'd missed her chance.

187

'Just tell me where to turn,' Shaun said, building up speed as they approached the estate.

'Yes, if you slow down a bit, you need to pull off at this wide road here. It's just round the corner.'

'I'll try.' Shaun looked down at his foot, wriggling in his seat. 'Bugger it. The accelerator's stuck again.'

'What?'

'It's all right. It does this sometimes. It'll sort itself out in a minute.'

Olivia put both hands on the glove compartment, all pretence of calm jettisoned, as the car gained speed.

'We'll have to overtake this one, and come back in a minute,' Shaun said, not sounding at all alarmed. Olivia watched in horror as the Citroën swung out into the middle of the road, overtook the car in front, and headed off up the long hill which led to the country lanes.

'Ah, great. Uphill. That'll slow us down.'

'Good God, Shaun. You've got to get this fixed. This is a thirty-mile-an-hour limit.'

'It's okay.' He pumped his foot up and down on the pedal. The car responded by nosing ahead, then slowing again. 'There we are. No need for panic. Now, we just have to turn round somewhere, and we can go back and find your road.'

White-lipped, Olivia sat back in her seat and closed her eyes. She felt the car turning off, stopping, was aware of a three-point turn being enacted, heard a screech of brakes from outside and a long, angry blast of a horn, and sensed that they were now retracing their steps. She opened her eyes again once Shaun had pulled them off the main road and was safely mooching around her estate.

'Just – just there, please, Shaun. Turn left into that small road, and I'm the fourth house up.'

'Fine. These are nice houses, Olivia. Have you lived here long?'

'Since I got married.' Olivia released her seat-belt as the

188

car suddenly stopped, and let out the breath she had been holding.

'Pretty much all of your life, then?' Shaun had turned to smile at her pleasantly.

'No!' Olivia said harshly, her nerves stretched beyond politeness. 'Not all of my life. I had a life before I got married, and I shall have a life now. I did have other plans once, you know, other than to sit in a three-bedroomed semi in suburbia and wait for death. I was a person, once. With dreams, and ambitions, and visions of what I might do.'

'You sound like me.' Shaun nodded cheerfully, unfazed by the anger she had blasted at him. 'I've got lots of things I want to do. And you know what?'

'What?' she said, pulling back her head to look at him properly.

'I'm going to do them. That's what. Life's too short, that's what I say. So, Olivia, you were going to ask me something, weren't you?'

Olivia gathered the strap of her bag around her shoulder. She had been going to ask him something, yes, but now she was seriously unsure. But life was too short, that was what Shaun said. And if he couldn't help her, then who on earth could?

'Shaun, I'd like you to do something for me, but I will insist on paying you, and if you find the idea unpalatable, then you must say so. You must be honest with me.'

His eyes widened. He nodded at her stiffly, his fingers gripping the steering wheel.

'The thing is, I wondered if you'd like to teach me to drive?'

'Louise? It's Rachel. About your friend's song – find out when the band's playing, and I'll try to be there. Give me a ring, leave a message if I'm not here and I'll see what I can do for you. I can't promise anything. It depends on

189

how they are live, but I'll see them, just for you, okay? I'm sorry you're not there to take the call. Hope you're well. Love you. Bye . . . And, er, sorry about the other night. Of course I loved Dad, at least as much as you did. Let's not fall out over it.'

Louise rolled over on the bed, stared at the phone for several moments, then picked it up automatically and dialled Ash's number. She only realised once she'd pressed out the number that she'd remembered it by heart.

'Ash?'

'No, it's Ginger. Who's that?'

'Oh.' Louise bit her lip. She was sounding too keen. 'It's Louise. I met him at the Jobcentre.'

'Oh, Louise. Yeah, right. Hi there.'

'Hi,' she said, trying to picture this orange friend of Ash's, the brother of his girlfriend, and wondering what on earth she should say to him. 'Er, is Ash in, please?'

'Nope. He's got a darts match. Won't be back till pretty late.'

'Darts?'

'Yeah. Local pub. He's usually down there playing or practising. You could always catch him there if you wanted?' The name of the pub made Louise's lips twitch into a smile. It sounded like the sort of place Jon would never have gone into. Jon wouldn't have played darts either. He wouldn't want to be caught enjoying any activity that might be bad for his image. But Ash wasn't Jon, of course. 'I wouldn't go in there myself without a bodyguard,' Ginger continued cheerfully, 'but I'm sure you'd be fine. He's their star player, so if you say you're a friend of his you'll probably get free John Smith's all night.'

Louise laughed. She could picture him in the spartan bar in his tattered jeans, rolling a cigarette, cursing under his breath.

'No, I won't bother him tonight, but I've got something to tell him. Perhaps I could pop round tomorrow?'

'Just call by any time. If he's on the fiddle, you can always wait.'

'On the fiddle?'

'The violin.'

'Oh, yes. Thanks, Ginger. I'll just come by then.'

She rang off, feeling warm inside. Ginger sounded nice. He sounded rich too, but he was friendlier than his sister. Part of her wished she could just dash out now to the pub, arrive unannounced and watch Ash play darts. But she was so, so tired. And Karen might be there rattling her designer accessories at him in support. Tomorrow she would deliver the news that Rachel was interested in seeing the band. That would repay the favour he'd done her. The rest was up to him.

Chapter Eleven

Louise tapped tentatively on the green door at eleven the next morning. She'd left it long enough for Ash to have downed a handful of aspirins if he had been on the John Smith's all night. She wondered if his darts team had won their match. She wondered why she cared about his results or his hangover.

Eleven o'clock had given her enough time to feel sick, feel better again, and have a breakfast the size of a hearty supper. It was all right as long as she ate as soon as she felt nauseous, but she was starting to realise that afternoons were the worst. When she wasn't asleep, she was staring at the images thrown out by the television and trying to control a relentless buzz of nausea by eating. She had stopped watching *Ready, Steady, Cook* now due to the uncontrollable cravings that the programme brought on. The last time she'd watched it, she'd only just made it to Red Tomatoes being the winners before she was down at the Co-op piling into her basket the ingredients of honey-coated chicken breast on a bed of leek-and-red-pepper rice. It wasn't what she'd expected. She'd thought morning sickness was a quick gag while you were putting on your make-up followed by hours of normality. Nothing was quite turning out as she'd imagined it.

She waited, her hands jammed into her coat pockets. She looked smart today, for no other reason than that it made her feel better. She'd got her maroon boots on, and as long as she didn't take her coat off nobody would know that they clashed with her skirt.

The door opened and she forced a smile just in case Karen was about to appear in a lake of expensively conditioned hair. It was Ginger. She could tell that straight away, not just on account of his hair, but because he also had Karen's striking looks. She smothered her surprise. Her knowledge of red-haired men was limited to Ronald McDonald and Robin Cook. Ginger was living proof that red-haired, male and handsome could all fit together in the same breath. He was tall and solidly built, with a facial arrangement that could definitely be called cute. He immediately grinned at her.

'You must be Louise.'

'Yes, I am. I hope you don't mind me just turning up.'

'No problem. He's fiddling upstairs.'

'Oh look, I won't disturb you all if you're practising or something. Perhaps I can just leave a message?'

'We're not practising. Karen's gone to High Street Ken with a couple of friends and the rest are at work. I'm off myself in a minute. He won't be long, then you can talk to him yourself.'

He stood back for her and she entered the dark hall again, wondering what Karen would be shopping for with her friends, and musing on the merits of having wealthy parents. It must be odd to spend your days out spending money when other people were out earning it.

'She's a spoilt brat, isn't she?'

'Sorry?'

'Karen. It's what you were thinking. Ash told me you were signing on at the moment. I don't expect you've got much patience with people on private incomes.'

'Oh.' She gave him a cautious look. 'Perhaps I'd be shopping too if I had a bit more money.'

'She's all right really. Don't judge her too harshly. Ash gets intense about it, but it's not going to change the way she is. They're good for each other. They've got a chemistry, and it makes the band something special. They've been on and off like traffic lights, but ten years is a long time.'

He'd maintained a bright smile but beneath it she had the feeling that she was being warned away.

'Why don't you go up and let him know you're here? You can come back down and wait if you want.'

'Won't it disturb him?'

'Yes, but one of us tries to piss him off at least once a day.' Ginger winked at her. 'He's on the first floor. His room's at the front.'

He ambled away towards the kitchen, leaving her to it. She stood for a moment and gazed up the narrow stairs. Ginger hadn't said 'their' room, he'd said 'his' room. But then, if Karen was out, was that what he'd say anyway? She didn't want him to fling open his bedroom door, and be met with the sight of a double bed strewn with skimpy maroon silk knickers. But Ginger had vanished. She was only here to tell Ash that Rachel would try to see their next gig. Why was she so nervous, for heaven's sake? It was only a bedroom. Everybody had one. What went on in bedrooms could be exciting, but she had a bun in the oven and Ash had a girlfriend who made Pamela Anderson look frumpy. Nothing exciting was going to happen in Ash's bedroom.

She mounted the stairs. The first floor revealed a short corridor with several off-white doors leading away from it. She hovered like an indecisive burglar. A pair of traumatised nylon curtains hung from a rear window. Not Karen's choice of soft furnishings, she could guess. One of the doors was propped open, and she could see a towel draped over the side of a bath. The house was deep, and there was another floor. Probably enough rooms for Ash and Karen to have one each if they wanted.

She inhaled slowly. She was spying on him, but it was so difficult not to. She'd be in the bathroom in a minute, taking samples from the ceramic and trying to deduce forensically if they ever shared a bath. She should just find Ash's room, and knock. There were two doors leading to rooms which would face the front of the house. If he was playing the violin, she should be able to hear something, although the doors were pretty dense. A muted sound came from one of the rooms. She crept closer and studied the door from the outside. She raised her hand but froze with it in mid-air.

On her own in her flat, left to her fantasies, she had thought about Ash playing his violin. She had conjured up a romantic image of the lone, brilliant musician, seeking solace in the glory of his music. Karen had said he was really talented. She hooked her hair behind her ears and leaned closer to the door.

Slowly, surely, the sound of a violin drifted out to her. It started as a long, low, reverberating note, then it stopped. She shuffled closer to the door. There was a short silence, then the sound came again. It was even less convincing this time, a squawk of a sound, abruptly halting. She frowned.

She was unprepared for the blast of noise that suddenly assailed her. Screech after undignified screech. She'd never realised that a violin could produce such bizarre and appallingly tuneless sounds.

When Karen had said he'd knocked their socks off, was she being sarcastic? That would explain why he'd been so irritated. Louise felt it all slotting together. There was a friction between them which was difficult to define. Had she been trying to set him up? He'd said he'd played first violin in a prominent orchestra, if only briefly. But he couldn't have! This horrible noise couldn't be put down to improvisation. It was simple evidence that he couldn't play, and that he'd lied to her. Was anything else that he had said about himself true?

Bewildered, she crushed her ear right against the wood and leaned heavily against it. The sawing became unbearable. It veered off flatly, then suddenly stopped as abruptly as it had begun.

'Hell's bells!' she exclaimed, and snapped her mouth shut again. That had come out a bit loudly.

The door opened. With nothing to lean against any more, she staggered inside and toppled over. It was a moment before the shock of being discovered eavesdropping, together with the indignity of being in a heap on Ash's floor, began to dawn on her. With burning cheeks she struggled to her feet and turned to apologise effusively. Ash was standing with his hands on his hips. His hair was more dishevelled than usual, as if he'd been raking his hands through it compulsively. He looked like a sea urchin.

'Come in,' he said flatly.

'God, I'm sorry, I was . . .' She stopped. They weren't alone. A boy was sitting in the middle of the room perched on an old wooden chair opposite a music stand, a violin lowered on to his lap, his face a blank sheet of astonishment.

'Louise, this is Deepak.'

'H-hi Deepak.' Louise waved at him. It was ridiculous to wave. He was only a few feet away. But she didn't know what else to do. Deepak stared at her for a long, crushing moment, then looked up at Ash as if for clarification.

'She mad, or what?' he said in a thick London accent.

'I wish I knew,' Ash said, looking at Louise curiously. 'Deepak's my student, Louise. We've got another ten minutes to go before we finish, but you're more than welcome to wait downstairs.'

'I – er.' Louise knew her face was glowing now. She

might as well have had flashing light bulbs screwed into her cheeks too. She couldn't have gone any redder. 'I didn't know you had a student in here. I didn't know you taught music. I thought it was you playing.'

'Ah. That explains everything then,' Ash said with merciless sarcasm. 'I don't take money for private lessons, if you're wondering, so I'm not breaking any jobseeking rules.'

'Right. No, I wasn't thinking that.'

'We gonna finish this lesson then, or what?' Deepak gave Ash a hard stare.

Ash walked towards the door and opened it wide for Louise. She padded towards it across the floorboards, her shoulders stooped.

'He's keen,' Ash whispered to her. 'I like that. Why don't you put the kettle on for us, and I'll join you when I can?'

He ushered her out pleasantly and the door closed gently behind her. She stood on the landing, unable to move, her body alive with mortification.

'You two shagging then, or what?' she heard Deepak ask.

'Mind your own fucking business,' Ash's voice came back.

'She's a babe,' Deepak was going on. 'Nice arse. Shame she's mental.'

She couldn't wait to hear any more. She headed for the stairs, downed them two at a time, and threw herself towards the front door.

Ginger hailed her from the kitchen. 'Did you find his room?'

'Got to go!' she called over her shoulder, wrenched open the front door, and fled.

'Balls,' Sarah said loudly. Olivia looked up.

'What is it?'

197

'Oh, everything.'

Olivia left her desk and crossed the office to where Sarah was sitting. She was aware that Carol had glanced up. She straightened her shoulders and bent over Sarah, gazing at the computer screen.

'What's the problem?' she whispered. Sarah sniffed. Olivia could tell that it was something she didn't want Carol to know about.

'It's just this.' Sarah glanced up at Olivia, her heavily mascara'd eyes appealing for help. Olivia could see that she was trying to move files around on the computer screen without any real idea of what she was doing. Carol had sprinted through the functions of Windows 95 with them like Linford Christie being pursued by a rabid dog. It had left them both quivering with terror.

'I saved this file,' Sarah hissed. 'And I've lost the blimmin' thing. Where's it gone?'

Olivia pondered. Since their fleeting demonstration from Carol, they'd both been adding things to the computer, and now the screen, the *desktop* to be precise, was almost unrecognisable. She leaned over Sarah's shoulder and put her hand on the mouse, moving it aimlessly around to make it look as if she was trouble-shooting. Sarah suppressed a giggle. It was all for Carol's benefit, and they both knew it. If only she'd leave the office they could sit down and work out what had gone wrong. But Olivia wasn't going to give Carol another chance to tell her she was too old to cope with new technology. Privately, Olivia thought she was getting a better grasp of it than Sarah was, but that was probably because she was fascinated by it all. Sarah saw it as a hassle. Olivia was bewildered by the new images, but at the same time, in love with them. The computer brought contact with a new and exciting world to their small office.

'Problem?' Carol's voice hit them from the other side of the room like a well-aimed snowball.

'Not at all,' Olivia said casually. 'We've got it under control.'

She wiggled the mouse around the screen. She tried hard to identify the contents of the small icons dotted around. Sarah had been doing things she wasn't aware of. Carol let out a hearty sigh.

'Must I do everything myself?' she muttered in their direction.

'I'm sorry?' Olivia stood up.

'I asked you to copy this memo to the entire team, not just internally.' Carol waved a piece of paper in the air and set it back on her desk. Olivia thought carefully. She knew what her boss was referring to.

'I'm sorry, but you distinctly said it was an internal memo.'

'No, I didn't. I asked you to copy it to the team.' Carol didn't look up. 'I've had Roger on the phone today, asking why he wasn't advised about the proposals in advance of his meeting this afternoon. It was very embarrassing. Never mind.' She gave another sigh.

'But Carol, you did ask me to do an internal memo. I can remember clearly.'

'Yes, yes.' Carol waved a dismissive hand, her eyes down.

Olivia pursed her lips. 'Would you like me to fax the memo to Roger now?'

'No point now. Meeting's over.'

'But if he wants a copy I could fax it to him anyway, couldn't I?'

Carol lifted her eyes to Olivia's. She was not going to back down. She would never back down, even though they both knew that Olivia was right.

'I did it myself earlier, so you can relax and get back to

playing around on our two-thousand-pound computer, can't you?'

Olivia continued to watch Carol as her head bent back to her work. As she gazed at the constrained hair, the small, pretty features, she wondered what was going through her head. Roger, of course. Something that Shaun had said. She was having an affair with him. She turned back to Sarah.

'All right, Sarah, let's try this.' She moved the white arrow over an icon she hadn't seen before and double clicked on it.

'No-oo,' Sarah emitted in a long breath. 'Sh-i-t.'

'Sorry?'

'Nothing.' Sarah drew herself back in her chair tensely.

The previous screen had disappeared and the image of a man who seemed rather attractive imposed itself. She bent right over Sarah's shoulder for a closer look.

'I've seen him somewhere before. He's a footballer, isn't he?'

'Who's a footballer?'

Carol had left her desk, crossed the office in a series of elegant bounds, and was now examining the image with care.

'Michael Owen?' she said, at first, it seemed, in wonder. Then her voice hardened. 'What is Michael Owen doing on this machine?'

Sarah tutted sulkily and closed her eyes.

'Sarah, I asked you a question.'

'It was Shaun,' Sarah said, her head dropping.

For a fleeting moment it seemed to Olivia that all of Sarah's speculations about Shaun's sexuality seemed to be confirmed.

'He showed me how to download things from the Internet,' Sarah said. 'He was trying to show me how it worked. He said I wouldn't be so scared of it if I did something on my own, you see, so he asked me who I fancied. I said Brad Pitt, so he showed me how to get on to the Internet and download a picture of him. Then when I was here on my own the other lunchtime I thought I'd try it for myself. I thought of Michael. I tried to do what Shaun said, but it didn't work in the same way. He ended up as an icon. I don't know how it happened.' Sarah paused, her eyes widening as she studied Carol's angry face. 'I'm sorry, Carol.'

Carol stood up stiffly and smeared her hands over her hair while inhaling noisily.

'Let me get this straight. You and Shaun have been surfing the net on office time? On the office telephone bill? And for the purpose of setting miscellaneous men as wallpaper?'

'It was meant to be educational,' Sarah said.

'And in what way precisely did you think images of Brad Pitt and Michael Owen might be educational?'

Sarah's lips twitched as if she was going to come up with an answer but thought better of it.

'Delete this please, Sarah,' Carol instructed. Her voice had taken on the soft but deadly quality that Olivia had heard before. It was more chilling than outright shouting. 'I shall be looking into the issue of staff using the computers for social purposes. I shall also be speaking to Shaun about it. I think perhaps this matter should go further.'

'Carol,' Olivia inserted her voice gently, 'I know Sarah shouldn't have done this, but if Shaun was teaching Sarah how to use the computer, it could be seen as training, couldn't it? I know what Sarah means. You have to gain confidence on it before you can use it properly.'

'That's quite enough!' Carol's sharp ejection sent Sarah's face paling to white. Olivia took a step back. Carol's hands were clenched into tight balls by her side.

'How am I supposed to run this team with co-operation like this? Sarah, delete the images now. I shall be speaking to the agency this afternoon and asking for a replacement. You can spend the rest of the day tidying up loose ends, and making the situation as clear as possible for whoever comes tomorrow in your place.'

There was a stunned silence. Sarah's mouth had dropped open, a dark blob within the pallor of her skin. Carol's breath whistled in and out of her nostrils. She waited while Sarah fumbled with the mouse and began to click it in panic. Michael Owen disappeared. Everything disappeared. The computer made a low, reverberating sound and shut down. The screen went black.

'Now what have you done?' Carol's voice was deathly quiet.

'I don't know!' Sarah wailed.

Olivia's pulse raced. To her horror, Sarah's face crumpled and she started to cry. Instinctively, Olivia leaned down and put her arms around her.

'Come on, dear.'

Sarah buried her face in Olivia's blouse. Olivia stroked her head soothingly. The tears didn't stop. Carol's expression hardened. Olivia's heart was pounding inside her chest, five years of pent-up adrenaline bursting at her ribcage like flood waters hitting the wall of a dam. Carol stalked away to her desk. Olivia watched her. She was gratified to see that the fingers that picked up the Mont Blanc fountain pen were trembling.

'Come on, Sarah.' She ruffled her hair. 'I'm taking you to lunch.'

Sarah sniffed and sat up straight again. They both looked at the wet, black patches her mascara had left on Olivia's white blouse. Sarah gulped, somewhere between a laugh and a sob, and got shakily to her feet.

'You'll have to take staggered lunch breaks. I need somebody to man the phones.'

Carol hadn't looked up as she'd issued her order. Her eyes were burning into her paperwork, but Olivia could tell she wasn't reading it.

'Wait for me down in the hall, Sarah.' There was a firmness in Olivia's voice which surprised her. 'You go on ahead. I'll be down in a minute.'

Sarah grabbed her leather jacket and fled. The door in the corridor swung shut with a loud bang. Silence fell again in the office. Olivia approached Carol's desk.

'Not now.' Carol waved a hand airily, her eyes down. 'I'm busy.'

'Now,' Olivia stated.

Carol looked up. Her pupils were wide.

'What is it?'

'It's your job to make sure your staff are properly trained. If they aren't, and they subsequently make mistakes, it's your fault.'

Where she had got the courage to make that statement, she would never know. In five years she had never raised her voice. She had accepted, pacified, reasoned and put up with hypocrisy, but all without complaining. Yes, there was reason for Carol to look startled. Something had changed.

'Is that it? You've said your little piece now.'

Olivia smiled.

'I could put my thoughts in writing to Roger if you'd like the complaint formalised. He always welcomes input from the staff. I didn't think there was any need for him to know what the general feeling was in this team about your management techniques, but I'll do it if necessary.'

Carol drew in her cheeks as if she was sucking a powerful peppermint. Her eyelashes fluttered.

'However,' Olivia continued calmly, 'when I come back from lunch with Sarah, I expect you'll have thought again about replacing her. You might even have thought of arranging for a trainer to come in and show us around the new computer system. That way there'd be no reason to bother Roger at all.'

Carol drummed her pen on the desk in agitation. Apart from the irregular tapping, there was silence.

'Go to lunch, Olivia,' Carol said under her breath. Her face was white and strained. Olivia picked up her mac and made the point of not scuttling away by checking the contents of her bag and rearranging her desk before she made her way to the door.

'Olivia?'

She turned back. Carol was pretending to write something.

'I had no intention of replacing Sarah. She needed to be given a warning, that was all.'

Without a word, Olivia left the room, her breath bursting from her lungs as she cantered away down the stairs. She broke into a broad grin.

Sarah was shivering on the doorstep, her eye make-up streaked around her face where she had tried to wipe it away. Olivia held out an arm to her.

'Come on, you. I'm going to treat you to wherever you want.'

Sarah looked at the extended arm in surprise, but then linked hers through it.

'Better had as it's my last day. I didn't think things could get any worse, but that's always a bloody lethal thing to think, isn't it? My mum's going to go apeshit. She relies on my housekeeping money. This was supposed to be temp to perm.'

'You're not going to be replaced.' Olivia patted her arm as they headed towards the town. 'She was only trying to scare you. You'll have to be a bit patient with her. She's having a difficult time at the moment.'

'Is she?' Sarah whistled into the air. 'Hark at you. You can't stand the woman.'

'No, but I pity her. I don't think she's very happy.'

'Crikey, you should be the boss, not her. At least you care about people. Well, that's a bloody relief.' Sarah squeezed Olivia's arm. 'Thanks. I don't think I could have coped with any more disasters at the moment.'

'Why? What else is going on?'

'It's that rash on Neal's testicle.'

Olivia stopped in her tracks. Sarah's eyes were welling with tears again. She found a clean tissue in the pocket of her mac and offered it.

'I've got crabs,' Sarah said in a low voice.

Olivia brushed her fingers over the girl's hot cheek.

'There. Don't cry.'

'I – it was when I went for my smear. I knew something wasn't right, but I didn't know what. It was so humiliating.'

'Oh, Sarah. You poor girl.'

'So I rowed with Neal about it, 'cos I knew bloody well it wasn't me. Turns out he's been putting himself about all over the place.' Sarah laughed humourlessly and sniffed up into the cold air. Olivia tutted.

'I hope you told him what you thought of him.'

'Too bloody right. I told him I hoped his nuts dropped off.'

Olivia buried a smile as they slowly began to walk again. The mating game. Perhaps in some ways she'd been lucky as a young woman. Fate had excluded her from such anxieties.

'Then you definitely need to do something to cheer yourself up,' Olivia said. 'How about a little present to yourself? That's what I do sometimes.'

Sarah pondered as they reached the pedestrian crossing. She brightened suddenly.

'Can you stand the sight of blood, Olivia?'

'What?' Olivia paled.

'There's something I've wanted to do for ages but Neal talked me out of it. It wouldn't take long. We could do it in the lunch-hour, and I need someone to come with me, or I'll never have the courage to do it.'

'What the devil is it you want to do?'

'I want to get tattooed.'

Olivia stared at Sarah aghast.

'A bluebell, on my shoulder. What d'you think?'

'I—'

'Everyone's having them down now. It's really fashionable. Oh, go on. Come with me!'

Then suddenly she wanted to laugh aloud. What did she think? She didn't know what she thought. It was Sarah's life, her body and her decision. And she'd never been inside a tattoo parlour, although she'd seen one in a side street leading off the main road. This was a time in her life when she had made the decision to explore new ideas, not shut them out. Why shouldn't she go with Sarah? It was an unusual way to spend her lunch-hour. She usually took her sandwiches into the castle grounds and ate them there.

'I say we go to the tattoo parlour,' Olivia declared, astonishing herself for the second time in less than an hour. The red light at the crossing changed to green.

It was Ash.

But what was confusing Louise was that he was on her doorstep. She stared at him in bewilderment for a full minute before she was able to speak.

'Good grief!' she said.

He grinned at her.

'Hi.'

She was in an old grey floppy cardigan, a pair of yellow

and black leggings with a split in the crotch that showed her knickers if she bent down, and a pair of very thick socks. Her hair was everywhere. She tried to smooth it down without him seeing, but he was looking straight at her. She let her arms flop again.

'Erm, how did you know where I lived?' she asked, still hovering on the doormat.

'Your CV, remember?'

'Oh, of course.' He didn't seem to want to rush away. 'Would you like to come in?'

'Only if it doesn't put you out. It is fucking freezing out here, but I fancied a walk to clear my head anyway, and I thought I'd ask you why you ran off.'

That definitely involved him coming in. She mentally pictured the state of the flat. But it wasn't as bad as it could have been. Not since the contents had been introduced to the duster. She'd been sitting playing the piano when she'd heard the bell, and had gone through the usual panic that it might be Jon, but somehow she didn't feel as self-conscious about Ash seeing her flat as she always had when she'd dragged Jon home. Usually kicking, and screaming drunk, and by the buttons on his 501s. She shook the thought away.

'I'll put the kettle on.'

'And I just wanted to make sure you were all right,' Ash added as he wandered into the flat behind her. He stopped to stare at her wrought-iron candelabra. She saw him over her shoulder. He simply raised his eyebrows, then followed her through to the kitchen. He found himself a chair and settled into it. It was easy. It hadn't made her feel awkward. There was no need to say 'Do sit down, and don't mind the mess'. He seemed as relaxed in her kitchen as he had been in his own. It made her feel relaxed too.

'I'm really sorry I burst into your lesson,' she said,

arranging the mugs. He'd picked up the book of babies' names that she'd left on the table and was leafing through it with a smile on his face.

'Don't worry about that,' he said.

'Is Deepak your only student?'

'Nope, I've got about half a dozen at the moment. Two on cello, the rest violin.'

'Really? And none of them pay you?'

He glanced up at her.

'The money isn't the issue.' He was a bit curt. She looked at him in surprise.

'I didn't think it was. It's just a bit unusual.'

'Sorry.' He took a breath and then smiled again. 'I thought I was talking to Karen for a moment there.' But he could be blunt if the mood took him, that much was obvious. She didn't mind. It was quite attractive. 'I advertise locally for kids who can't afford to pay the full whack for private lessons. Word gets around, too. It's just to give them a start, really. They don't know what they can do because nobody gives them a chance.'

'But you do.'

'I try to. It's helpful, I think. I'm only introducing them to the idea. I've got one or two who are more advanced, but most of them are beginners. It pays off, but not financially, if you get my drift.'

He concentrated on the babies' names again as if he didn't want to discuss it any more. She made tea for them both and slid a mug on to the table beside him. She dropped into a chair on the other side.

'It was nice of you to call round.'

'No prob. It was you who called round to see me, remember? I just assumed you had something you wanted to say.'

'Oh.' She sat up straight, mentally slapping herself around the cheeks and splashing cold water on her face. It was happening again. Once she was in his company it was easy to forget what the point had been. Of course she'd gone round to see him. To tell him about Rachel. She cleared her throat quickly.

'I did have something to say. It's Rachel, you remember? My sister who works for the record company? Well, she rang and she's interested in seeing you play live. That's if you've got any gigs coming up.'

'Really?' His voice gained life. He chuckled. 'You mean, really? Hey, Louise, that's great. You never know what might come of that. It's a chance, at least.'

He stood up and paced around her floor, grinning to himself. Then he sat down again. She hadn't known many men who could be so grippingly entertaining just by getting up and walking around. Then he stuck his hands into his hair and pulled the strands into funny shapes. He didn't seem to be aware of doing it.

'D'you know I wasn't sure about your sister,' he said. 'It struck me that you'd lost the song and didn't know what the hell to say to me. I thought you were winging it.'

She blinked at him.

'You mean you thought I'd made it up?'

'Yep. You strike me as someone with a good imagination. I thought it was really funny. It kept me amused for hours. I didn't take you too seriously.'

He thought she was a congenital liar? She should be insulted.

'Still,' he continued, 'you thought it was me hacking away at the violin when you were listening outside my bedroom door, didn't you? You said so. So you must have thought I'd been lying to you, too. Call it quits. We're both honest. We know that much about each other, if not much else. Wow, this is great news for us,' he went on, playing with the book between his fingers. 'There's been so much bickering in the band lately, I even wondered if it was going to drive us apart. We'll have to get our acts together for this now.'

'Don't all good bands bicker?' Louise raised her eyebrows. 'I thought it was compulsory.'

'Not like we do, believe me. It's usually a good policy to sell a record or two before you go for the dramatic split.'

'Well, don't split up before your next gig then,' she told him firmly. 'Rachel might like you, and then God knows what could happen. I know for a fact she's set a couple of really good bands on their way.'

He tutted in disbelief again.

'We're playing at the Eye of Newt in Battersea this Friday. I expect that's too short notice for you, isn't it?'

'The Eye of Newt?' Louise perked up. She'd been there before with Rachel. It was considered a cult venue for upcoming bands. That would be something juicy to tempt Rachel with, even if it was short notice. And strong curiosity needled at her. What did this band sound like? Were they really talented? Would she be credited personally with discovering a rock legend? It made her want to wriggle with anticipation. 'You must be quite good then.'

'Don't sound so surprised. Some people think we are good. We've got a small crowd that follows us every-where. Loyal lot, they are. God knows where they ever came from, but they started turning up at all our gigs about a year ago. Can't get rid of the buggers now. So there'll be at least a dozen guys there who won't shout us off.'

'Oh.' A dozen? That wasn't many. She squashed her excitement. Perhaps they weren't any good after all. Even a place with the reputation of the Eye of Newt was allowed to make the odd mistake. She'd seen a couple there herself.

'But you'll need the song.' The thought suddenly

occurred to her. 'Rachel's still got it. I don't know how I'll get it back for you by Friday.'

'Don't worry about it. We had a row over the fact that I'd given it to someone to blow her nose on but we've got over it. Ginger rewrote it and the music's in my head anyway. It's better now. Sometimes it happens like that.'

'Great.' She smiled again and took a sip of tea. That was their information exchanged. What could they talk about now? She didn't want him to rush off just yet.

'So what's it to be?' he asked, holding up the book of babies' names with an eyebrow arched at her. 'Have you decided?'

She took another mouthful of tea to stop her smile spreading to her ears. Nobody had asked her about names yet. Nobody at all. She had been so desperate for someone to talk to about it. It felt wonderful. Would he mind if she rambled on about it? He didn't look as if he would. He was still grinning.

'Well,' she began slowly, 'it's all a question of—'

There was a sharp rap at her door. She looked through the kitchen at the tiny hallway and focused on it. Who? Why? And why didn't they bugger off? Ash waited quietly for her to do something. What she wanted to do was yell 'Hide!' and dive with him under the kitchen table until the intruder had gone away. But she couldn't really.

'I'll get that,' she said without moving. He nodded at her.

Stiffly, she stood up and walked to the door. She opened it.

'Oh!' she said.

It was Harris. She shifted uncomfortably. He wasn't smiling at her. He looked very serious. She'd been hammering on the piano a bit loudly earlier. She hadn't been thinking. It was about time that he dropped his amorous intentions and got back to telling her off. A man's unrequited lust could only last so many hours, after all.

'I'm really sorry, Harris. I'll play more quietly.'

He was fully clothed, and that also reassured her that he was there to complain. In fact, he looked as if he was about to go out. His hair glistened with gel, his chin was clean-shaven, and once again she was nearly knocked flat by the power of his aftershave. It was a smell that was growing on her, though. He might try slapping a little less of it on, that was all. He was draped in a white silk shirt and loose black trousers with a slim belt. She had to admit that he was a stunner, if hyperactive out-of-work actors were your style.

He cleared his throat elaborately, and put one hand casually into his trouser pocket. It stretched the material across his groin, and she fixed her eyes quickly on his face.

'Actually, Louise, I haven't come about your playing.'

'You haven't?'

'No,' he said. There was a pause. He gained a little colour in his cheeks. It made his eyes seem even darker.

'Oh.' She really, really hoped that Harris wasn't about to show her his private parts again.

'Although,' he added thoughtfully, 'I'm a bit tired of "Paint Your Wagon". Is there any reason it's your favourite this week?'

'Okay, point taken.' She frowned at him fiercely.

'I am here to ask you –' he paused again and fixed her with a stare that forbade her to move '– if you'd like to have dinner with me.'

'Dinner?' she echoed.

'Dinner,' he confirmed, actually blushing. It might even have been charming if Ash hadn't been perched in her kitchen at that moment and able to hear every word. She slid a shifty look along the hall. He had a leg crossed and was engrossed in babies' names.

'What – what sort of dinner?' She stood up straight, fighting with the colour rising in her own cheeks. What on earth did Harris see in her, anyway? Weren't actors used to courting women who floated around in acres of chiffon looking like Isabella Rosselini? He could probably have any woman he wanted. For a first date, anyway.

'I'd like to cook for you. In my flat. I've got a particularly fine bottle of red, and I'd like you to share it with me.'

'Oh, I see.'

She fiddled with the buttons on her cardigan, becoming more deeply embarrassed. Now it was clearer. He'd heard her thumping on the piano, realised she was in for the evening, thrown together a mountain of pasta upstairs, strapped himself in his glad rags, and shot down on impulse to lure her up to his den.

'What d'you say?' His eyes sparkled with hope. She crept an inch closer to him. Whispering at this juncture was futile. Even though Ash had started to sing 'I Talk to the Trees' very loudly. It was a gentlemanly gesture on his part, but she was sure he was still listening to everything that was going on.

'The thing is, Harris—'

But Harris was peering over her shoulder, his face contorted with concern.

'Have you got company?' he asked, his nostrils flaring in an inappropriately emotional manner.

'It's just that a friend's dropped round to see me. Now's not a good time.'

She fixed a pleading look on to her face. He put his head back and shook it, looking like a great, glossy stallion who had just been informed by the fattest mare in the field that she had a headache.

'We can talk about this another time, can't we?' She inched the door closed on him.

Then, as he looked as if he was about to stalk away, he

213

delivered her a very saucy wink and lowered his voice to a murmur.

'But you're in my thoughts, Louise. I'll be upstairs, and I'll be—'

'Burning?' she suggested hoarsely.

'Yes. Burning.'

'Okay then. See you.'

She closed the door on him quickly. She took a split second to recover herself, then danced back into the kitchen trying to look as if nothing had happened.

'That's just Harris,' she said brightly, laughing disparagingly. 'Don't mind him. He's an actor.'

Ash closed the book and laid it on the table. She could see that he'd finished his tea. He looked as if he was going to leave. Her spirits descended into an air pocket.

'"Paint Your Wagon"?' He stood up, the corners of his lips twitching. 'Really?'

'Not that you were listening,' she taunted him. It was better to be casual than petulant about him going. She still wanted to talk about names with him. But he had a life. She should just accept that.

'So you're musical enough to have a piano in your flat?'

'Bloody-minded enough, anyway.'

'I'd like to hear you play some time.' He was definitely aiming for the door.

'I'd like to hear *you* play. I'm sure that's much more fun,' she said, shuffling after him.

'You will. On Friday,' he stated.

He'd reached the door. He put his hand on the latch and left it there for a second. She tried to concentrate.

'I'm not sure if I can be there on Friday, but you must promise me you'll knock Rachel's socks off. She'll probably be lurking at the bar somewhere. That's what she usually does. So give it your all just in case.'

'Surely you want to see Ealing's answer to Oasis?'

'I – I don't think I'll be well enough. I get a bit tired in the evening.'

'Yep, I bet you do.' He gave her a sympathetic look.

'And you wouldn't want me vomiting during your act, would you?'

'Someone will. It might as well be you.' He twisted the latch. 'Don't worry about it. Thanks for this, Louise. And you stay on top of things, won't you? If you need any help, let me know. You've got my number.'

'Thanks.' She pursed her lips to stop herself pouting. It was a 'goodbye' sort of statement. He'd been kind to her, but he was obviously a kind man in all that he did. It wasn't that she was anything special. It was time to be grateful and see things for what they were. 'Really, thank you for your help, Ash. It's meant a lot to me.'

'Hey, no problem. Talk to you soon.'

And he was gone.

She drifted back into her kitchen after she'd heard the front door close behind him, and looked at his empty mug of tea and the book that he'd handled. She sat down. She cast a wary glance up at the ceiling. Somewhere up there Harris was smouldering. When they said that men were like buses – you waited for ages and then they all turned up at once – they never said that it would inevitably be at a time when you could do sod all about it.

She picked up the book of babies' names and settled down to study it again. There could be no earthly reason for her to prolong her girlish fantasies any more.

Chapter Twelve

'Sally!' Louise grimaced at the huddled figure standing in the dark on her doorstep. 'What the hell are you doing here? I'm just about to go out.'

'Where?'

'To a gig. Rachel's going to be there.'

'You're going out? Tonight? To a pub?'

'Yes.'

'But you're pregnant.'

Louise pulled Sally across the threshold and slammed the door.

'Do you mind not proclaiming that fact to the whole of Greater London?'

'I'm sorry. Can I come in, just for a second?'

'Of course, but I'd better not be late. I know what Rachel's like at these gigs. If I don't catch her early, she'll be getting sloshed with some stick-thin lead singer in leather trousers and then I won't get a sensible word out of her.'

Louise led Sally into her flat.

'That thing's still here, then?' Sally nodded distastefully at the candelabra.

'Why, did you think it might be taking two weeks off in Sorrento?' Louise tutted at her. 'And lay off my furnishings.'

She automatically went back to her bedroom to continue with her superhuman effort to look casually glamorous. Sally followed and sank on to the pile of clothes on the bed. Louise bent to her mirror and peered at Sally's reflection over her shoulder. Sally seemed very quiet. Louise waited for the apology that was inevitably forthcoming.

'Cold out, isn't it?' Louise paused with her lipstick in mid-air.

'Can't say I noticed.'

'Did you drive?'

'No, got the tube straight from work.'

'Not seeing Fergus tonight, then?'

'Oh, Fergus, Fergus, Fergus.' Sally cast herself back over the mound of clothes and lay spreadeagled on the bed, staring up at the cobweb on the paper lampshade. The slim auburn eyebrows met in a frown.

'Don't you ever dust in here?'

'Yes. Very recently, in fact.' Louise followed Sally's eyes up to the one cobweb she'd overlooked. It was sod's law that Sally would spot it. She missed her mouth and blobbed lipstick on the skin under her lip. She rubbed at it with her finger. Now she looked as if she had a worryingly contagious cold sore. Sally let out a long sigh. Louise turned round from the mirror and stared at her. 'What *is* the matter with you?'

'I just don't want to be on my own tonight. Can I come to the gig with you?'

Louise considered. There had still been no apology since their last phone conversation. It was only a minor detail, but she felt it was important.

'You're not exactly dressed for a gig, Sal. People don't tend to wear tailored suits to these things.'

'You could lend me something, couldn't you? You've got lots of tatty stuff. I always used to fit into your jeans. I bet I still could.'

'I assumed Fergus would be grilling rainbow trout for you tonight. It is Friday after all.'

Sally closed her eyes and groaned. It was odd that even

217

lying on the bed as if she'd fallen out of an aeroplane, Sally still looked remarkably professional. Her shoes were dangling from her feet, and peering at the insoles closely, Louise could see they were Russell and Bromley. She was holding the straps of her equally expensive handbag between her fingers. All the trimmings of a high-flying solicitor were there, just at an unusual angle.

'I can't talk about Fergus. I need to think. Think, think, think,' Sally chanted with her eyes shut.

'Oh dear.' Louise plucked a man-sized tissue from the box and rubbed at her smear of lipstick. 'I take it things have taken a dive then.'

'Hmmn.'

'Otherwise, I guess you wouldn't have come round like this,' she angled.

'Yep.'

'Not even, perhaps, to apologise for being such a cow on the phone,' Louise finished a little more firmly. Sally's eyes flew open. She cocked her head to examine Louise.

'Not still pissed off about that, are you? You've got something on your chin. Is it a rash?'

'It's lipstick.'

'Why did you put it on your chin?'

'Probably the same reason I asked the hairdresser to turn me into a summer vegetable.' Louise reached for the baby lotion and squirted it vigorously over another tissue. She clamped it over her chin. 'And I am still pissed off, yes.'

'Oh.' Sally stretched her amber eyes wide. Louise stared back adamantly as a trickle of lotion escaped from the tissue and began to run down her wrist. She raised her eyebrows at Sally, indicating that a fuller response was required.

'Louise, I was only saying what I thought. You wouldn't want me to lie to you, would you?'

'Yes.'

'Then I'm sorry. It's just that I saw what the girl I told you about went through. Although it was awful at the time, she said it was the best thing she ever did. She doesn't regret a thing.'

Louise turned back to the mirror with determination. She wasn't going to let Sally annoy her. She wanted to go to the gig. She was curious to hear Ash's band. He was gorgeous. She wanted to look at him again, perhaps for the last time.

'Listen, Sal, if you do want to come to this gig, you can, but I don't want you to keep going on about terminations, okay?'

'Okay.' Sally heaved herself up. Her gold clasp had fallen out of her hair, and the russet strands were now sensually ruffled around her shoulders. She couldn't help being exotic, even when she deserved a right hook. Louise clamped her teeth together and rubbed again at her red chin.

'So you're going to tell Rachel tonight about being an auntie, are you?'

'No chance.' Louise squinted at her face in the mirror. She slapped another palmful of foundation over her face. 'I know exactly where she stands on that issue, and you're not to say a thing. Promise?'

'Promise.' Sally did something odd with her fingers which Louise assumed was either a Masonic salute or something she'd seen on *Star Trek*.

'And I'm going to introduce her to an electric violin player.'

'You what?'

'Someone I met at the Jobcentre.'

'You're kidding.' Sally let out a loud laugh. 'Don't tell me, you're going to freelance as a talent spotter? I would have thought there might be more promising places to find talent than at the Jobcentre.'

'That's an ignorant comment, Sally. And anyway, it depends what you mean by talent.'

Sally gaped and pulled her shoulders straight.

'You've met someone!'

'Er, sort of.'

'At the Jobcentre.'

'Maybe.'

'Who plays the electric violin.'

'It's possible.'

'God, Louise. I thought you were going to have a baby!' Sally stood up and stared at Louise's reflection directly. 'You're serious, aren't you?'

'He's a friend, Sally, nothing more than that. Probably not even that after tonight.'

'A friend?' Sally looked sceptical.

'Think about it, Sal. I'm pregnant, he's got a girlfriend. Doesn't augur very well romantically, does it?'

'But you fancy him.'

'I'd have to be cremated not to.' Sally was still looking stunned. 'Well, I'm allowed to window-shop, aren't I? He's sexy, good company, and he's been very kind to me. He has no idea I lust after him, and more importantly, neither does his girlfriend. That's all. It's nothing more than that.'

'But – but you're going to have a *baby*!' Sally sat down again. 'Unless you've changed your mind. Is that it?'

'No, I haven't changed my mind.'

'Then . . .' Sally faltered. Louise abandoned the foundation seeing as she had satisfactorily turned her chin into a baboon's bottom, and dragged her brush through her hair again. She waited for Sally to compute the information in her own time. 'Then . . . having the baby isn't going to change your life. You're going to carry on as before.'

'Don't be daft. How can I?'

'So . . . what's going on? I don't understand.'

'So relax, Sally. Nothing's happening that needs passing by the board of censors. By the time my bump starts showing he'll be out of my life. It's just nice to dream a little. He's been thoughtful and I've done him a favour in return. That's all.'

'What did he do for you?'

'He picked me up when I fainted under the Catering stand.' Louise glanced at Sally. She seemed dumbstruck.

'And then what?' Sally still seemed to be finding Louise's situation impossible to grasp. Louise tossed her hairbrush to one side and put her hands on her hips.

'And then I become a single mother. Okay? Got a pigeon-hole for that one?'

'It's just that I thought that everything stopped when this happened. You know, men, flirting, life. Everything.'

'It's all going to change, Sal, but I'm not digging myself a hole. I'm still a woman, you know, baby or no baby.' Louise watched Sally a moment longer, and as she seemed to be in no danger of closing her mouth, scrabbled around to find a pair of jeans. She tossed them into Sally's lap. 'Do you want a top as well?'

'Louise, Fergus has asked me to marry him,' Sally blurted out, her face very white. Louise stopped rummaging and stood up, feeling giddy. Discussing things in theory was one thing. The reality was something else entirely.

'What, properly, you mean?'

Sally nodded, her lower lip caught between her teeth.

'Oh, why didn't you say so, you silly tart.' Louise was overcome with emotion. A surge of happy tears hovered in her eyes and then spilled over her cheeks. 'Congratulations, Sal. Come here. Give me a hug.'

Sally was stiff as Louise held her. Louise hugged harder. Sally became stiffer. Louise stood up again.

'The thing is,' Sally said, her eyes alarmed, 'I told him to sod off.'

The buzz was exciting as they pushed their way into the pub. It had been a cold and disjointed journey but inside they were assaulted by an earthquake of sound. The condensation dribbling down the windows was evidence of the heat produced by the wedged bodies. Louise hit the back of a leather jacket and reached behind her for Sally's hand. It was a cavernous venue, with two large rooms knocked into one on the ground floor. A heavy metal band was playing energetically in the far corner. Nearer the raised stage people were headbanging out of time to the music.

'Nightmare!' Sally yelled into Louise's ear. Louise glanced back at her. It wasn't exactly what she expected from Sally. If anything, Louise was the old fogey. Sally was always out, going somewhere, doing something. Louise thought she loved crowds.

'Bar!' Louise mouthed. They ploughed through a compound of leather, denim, suits and hair gel and reached the bar.

'Just tell me this isn't your band,' Sally said as they squeezed together and became mutually audible. 'Or your band's fans,' she added, pulling a face.

'They must be up next. They always do a couple of bands a night in this place from what I can remember. Anyway, I think my lot are all classically trained.'

'They'll go down a storm in here, then,' Sally said flatly.

'It's not their first gig. They must know what they're doing.'

Louise frowned as she called her order at the barmaid. She hoped they knew what they were doing. Rachel wouldn't take kindly to having her hectic schedule interrupted for a bunch of no-hopers. She had become more and more nervous about it since Rachel had said she would be there.

'What are they called, anyway?' Sally took her glass of wine and paused to fish a lump of cork from it with a polished fingernail.

'Er, I don't know.' Louise took a sip of Coke and edged away from the bar. 'I didn't ask.'

The wall of sound coming from the direction of the stage suddenly stopped. There were boisterous cheers. Louise thought that those coming from further back were of relief. The lead singer swung his guitar from his neck and gave an ostentatious bow. He grabbed the microphone, waving a sweaty arm in the air.

'Fuck you too!'

The four men stumbled from the stage to more cheers. Sally pulled Louise over to stand near a wall, where a gap had cleared in the bodies.

'I must be getting old,' she said, giving the band members distasteful looks as they grinned their way through the crowd to the bar. 'Those guys don't look old enough to swear. And I thought that was a load of tuneless crap.'

'You used to like AC/DC,' Louise challenged her. 'Don't you remember? It was your specialised subject. You even dragged me to a Radio Caroline roadshow because you said you felt stupid headbanging on your own.'

'It was only a phase I went through. I didn't headbang. I only pretended!' Sally protested. 'And I didn't go with you, I went with Guy.'

'Actually, fair-weather friend, you went to the first one with me before you met Guy. You drank lager and blackcurrant, and played air guitar all the way through "Touch Too Much". I was embarrassed to be seen with you.'

'Oh God.' Sally looked pale in the dim light. 'I think

you're right. I can remember throwing up in the loos afterwards. I never drank lager and black again. How did I forget all that?'

'Amnesia brought on by meeting a bloke. You suffer from it regularly.'

'I don't.'

'You do. What do you remember about getting home that night?'

'Er –' Sally looked confused. 'We just went home, didn't we?'

'I had to drag you back to the bus-stop to stop you getting off with some little bloke with a ponytail called Frankie who was admiring your Deep Purple badges.'

'God, yes, it's all coming back. I wonder what happened to him? He was really cute.'

'Sally! He was three foot tall, covered in spots and about nine years old. Besides which, you were arseholed. And you've got to stop wondering what happened to all the boys you knew when you were at school. You've got to think about the future.'

Sally shook back her hair and leaned against the wall. In Louise's jeans, a loose roll-necked jumper and a beaten-up suede jacket she'd borrowed, she didn't look like a terrifyingly good solicitor any more. And with her hair roaming all over her face and shoulders, she looked as if a good headbang might be on the cards.

'But that's the thing. The future does make me think about the past. All the time. Do you want to know what the first question was that went through my mind when Fergus asked me to marry him?'

'Er – "when", perhaps?'

'No, no. I thought, "Is Guy still living in Paddock Wood?" I swear to you, Lou, that was it. I was standing there with the tea towel in one hand and the garlic crusher in the other, and there was Fergus, down on one knee—'

224

'You never said he went down on one knee!'

'Well, he did. And I was looking down on him, at that lock of hair that always falls over his eyes, while he was presenting me with this tiny velvet box, and everything seemed to stand still while I thought of Guy and Paddock Wood. And then I thought of Nick. And Mark too . . .'

Sally sighed. Louise shook her head at her.

'. . . and Keith, and Lucien, and Peter. And Hans! I never thought I'd think of him again, but he came to mind.'

'Good grief.'

'. . . and David, and the other David, and David's friend Jeremy. They all came flooding back.'

'And all this time, poor old Fergus was on his knees next to the cupboard under the sink? Just how many days did you keep him in that position before you told him to sod off?'

'It was all over in a flash.' Sally tutted at Louise. 'It was like the Bayeux Tapestry, you know. They were all in different positions, as I remembered them.'

'So which one got stabbed in the eye then?'

'None of them.' Sally looked at her as if it was a stupid question. 'I've been stabbed in the eye a few times, but only when I was very drunk and I missed. And they'd never have embroidered that.'

'Obviously. So what happened?'

'Well, then I looked back at Fergus, at his big brown eyes, that floppy bit of hair, that straight nose, those lips of his . . .' Sally trailed away as she took a glug of her wine.

'And you wondered why on earth he fancied you?'

'He's too perfect,' Sally announced, snapping herself up straight. 'Something's wrong.'

'Apart from you telling him to sod off, you mean?'

'With him. There's got to be something I don't know. He must be hiding something.'

'A two-inch penis and balls like frozen peas?'

Sally pushed silky strands of hair away from her face. 'If only it were that simple. Sex is fine. But that's just it. It's all – fine.'

'I just don't understand you, Sally. Sorry, but there you are. I think one day you're going to think back to this time, realise what you could have done when you had the chance, and shoot yourself between the eyes.'

Sally paused, sipping at her wine and eyeing Louise steadily over the rim of her glass.

'I could say the same to you,' she said.

Louise was still searching for an answer when her shoulder was tapped from behind. She swung round, and brightened to see Rachel, in full gig mode. She knew how to turn up at these things looking important in a hip sort of way. Louise instantly felt frumpy and stupid again. But it was a huge relief that she'd made the effort to come.

'I've only just got here. Where's your bloke, then?'

'I don't know. One band's just finished, so I hope they'll be on next.'

'Topping the bill. That's a good sign. They don't take any old shit in here. They make them audition first. Good crowd, too. Have all this lot come to see your band?'

'God knows, Rachel. They look too trendy to be into electric violins.'

'Not in my experience.' Rachel cast a sharp eye over the bar. She pursed her lips and nodded. 'Yep, good mix. Lots of students, lots of young professionals, but an older crowd too. Not too much leather, plenty of T-shirts and just a hint of corduroy. Very promising. I'll get us a drink in, then. Sally! Lovely to see you!'

Louise watched as Rachel and Sally touched each other's shoulders lightly and exchanged air kisses.

'You're looking fab, as ever!' Sally enthused, running envious eyes over Rachel's tatty but sexy arrangement of black PVC trousers and rope-like tassel things that Louise was trying to disentangle from the clasp of her bag. 'You seem to get younger every time I see you.'

'And you're looking amazing.' Rachel gave a smile in return. 'All hair and eyes as ever. I don't know why you haven't been snapped up by now.'

'Oh, but she has –' Louise started, and winced as the pointed toe of Sally's boot made contact with her shin '– lost weight.'

'White wine, Sally, and a pint for you, Lou? You're not still on the wagon, are you? What's the matter with you? I'll get you a Guinness, that'll fortify you.'

Rachel gave Louise a further disconcerted glance and tried to head for the bar. She sprang back, waited for Louise to finish unravelling her top from her handbag, and carried on.

'She's stunning, your sister. I don't know where she gets all that dusky sex appeal from.'

'Yes, and brilliant at her job too. I should hate her.'

'You must have had a hell of a good-looking milkman.'

'Thanks,' Louise muttered, her shin throbbing. 'It skipped a generation, if you must know. My granny was hot stuff, allegedly, in her youth.'

'Your mum's nice-looking too, isn't she?'

'Yes, I suppose so.' Louise thought about it. 'In a sedate sort of way. I think she used to be quite a charmer, all long brown hair and big blue eyes, that's what Dad used to say, but she never had any old photos, and he was completely biased, so it's difficult to tell.'

'It was different then, wasn't it?' Sally said, her eyes roaming the heads of men milling round them, getting drinks in before the next set. 'It was easier for our mums. You just met someone, got on with them, and married them.'

'D'you really think that was easier?'

'I don't know.' Sally crumpled her face thoughtfully.

'There wasn't so much choice, was there? You didn't get the chance to try out so many men just to see if you liked the idea first. I mean, in those days, if you slept with someone, without the pill or anything to rely on, it was a nightmare, wasn't it? One false move, and—'

Sally stopped. She clamped her lips tightly and looked down at her drink.

'And you'd be stuck with a baby, whether you liked it or not?' Louise finished for her, her stomach churning. Perhaps once there was a baby to cuddle everyone around her would be deliriously happy, but for now she would have to make do with pity. In a week's time she'd see her mother again, and that was something that she could really look forward to. In the meantime, it would be nice if someone would fling their arms round her and squeeze her tightly. It was quite tiring being the only person who thought that everything was going to be all right.

'Louise!' She was grabbed from behind and engulfed in a hug. It knocked the breath out of her. 'You came! You're a fucking heroine, that's what you are. I need all the smiling faces I can muster up in this crowd. I can't see any of our regulars here. We're going to get killed, I'm sure of it.'

'Ash!' Her heart jumped. He was bristling with nervous energy, his hair all over the place, his eyes black with adrenaline.

'I'm just so pleased you're here.' He drew unsteadily on a Marlboro, his fingers trembling. Louise's stomach buckled with fear for him. He looked so nervous. She'd thought he would just saunter into it, as he sauntered into everything else, but he looked terrified. 'I just get jittery before we play. I've always been this way, you know, for live things.'

'It's going to be all right.' Louise squeezed his arm. 'Karen said you were really talented. Just remember that.'

'Yeah, well, Karen's off her face. She went to some impromptu wedding of one of her old school friends this afternoon and got plastered. I just hope she can remember the fucking words. Is this your sister?'

He stuck a hand out to Sally, who was stuck against the wall as if she'd just been nailed into place. Her eyes were like flying saucers.

'Pleased to meet you,' she breathed, shaking his hand limply.

'You too. Glad you could come. Hope we don't waste your time.'

'No, this is Sally, my best friend,' Louise explained quickly. Sally, at that moment, was looking as un-professional as she'd ever looked, her mouth gaping, her drink spilling over to dribble on to her boots. Louise didn't want him to think that this was the kingmaker she'd moved heaven and earth to get here for him. He'd realise Rachel was in the music business the minute he saw her. She had that powerful aura about her. Louise swivelled round to the bar. 'Rachel's just getting us a drink. There she is! Oh.'

All three turned to follow Louise's pointing finger. A few feet away, Rachel was locked into a deep-throated snog with a very tall, very blond man. His hands were roaming over her hips and spreading towards her buttocks. They all watched with fascination as he pinged her suspender belt through her trousers.

'Well, she'll be with us in a minute, I'm sure,' Louise mumbled, retracting her finger quickly.

'Right. Well, I'd better go and set up. We're on in a minute. Clap if you can bear it, and don't heckle me, for God's sake. I can't cope with hecklers.'

'If anyone heckles, just moon at them.' Louise grinned at him with a confidence she didn't feel.

'Thanks.' He smiled back at her. 'I really appreciate you

making the effort to be here. I know it can't have been easy for you.'

Louise watched him being swallowed in the crowd as he pushed back towards the stage. It was nice of him to say that. It made her feel warm that he'd even thought about how she might feel. But she felt fine at the moment, and was praying that her stamina would hold out. She glanced around. There were more people in the bar now than before, and shouts and laughs bellowed round the room. It was a big crowd for him to play to. Her palms became sweaty. Poor Ash, having to stand up there in front of all these suspicious people and get his violin out. She rubbed at her hot forehead.

'God, Louise. He's incredible!' Louise swung back to Sally. For a moment, she'd almost forgotten she was there, nailed to the wall.

'He's nice, isn't he?'

'Nice! I'd give anything to be on the end of the smile you just got.' Sally was staring at Louise with something like admiration. 'How did you do it?'

'Do what?' Louise asked coyly.

'Get his attention. I mean, I was here, flicking my hair around, rolling my eyes at him, and he didn't even know I existed.'

Louise thought about it. She could be smug, of course. Ash genuinely hadn't noticed Sally in a womanly way, or if he had, he'd hidden it incredibly well. But she also had to consider the fact that Sally was confessing to trying to flirt with *her* electric violin player. That wasn't fair.

'Listen, I never flirted with Fergus, so hands off.'

'Oh, you can have Fergus if you think he's so marvellous. It's sex appeal that I go for, and that guy's got it in lorry-loads. If only you could sleep with him.' Sally shook her head sadly. 'If only I could sleep with him.'

'Sally, for God's sake, you're spoken for. Get that into your head.'

'Right. Like Rachel is, I suppose.' Sally nodded over as Rachel detached herself from the tall blond man, whispered something in his ear, handed him a couple of glasses, and dragged him towards them.

'Hi, everyone. This is Benji. He's a doctor.' She nudged Louise. Louise wriggled out of nudging distance, throwing a brief smile in the direction of Benji's very orange eyes as she took the pint of Guinness he held out for her. 'This is my little sister, Louise, and her friend Sally.'

He was nice, Louise had to admit. He smiled at everyone, made suitably flattering comments, nodded understandingly at the answers they gave. Rachel's dark eyes were luminous with lust.

'Where's Hallam?' Louise hissed into Rachel's ear, pulling her to one side. Rachel frowned fiercely at her.

'At home. With the kids. They came over this evening.'

'Ah. Babysitting.'

'For his own children. It's his family, not mine. That's the whole bloody point I was trying to make to you.' She twisted herself out of Louise's reach and leaned against Benji's arm instead. Louise sighed with elaborate piety, but the impact was lost as a series of high-pitched squeaks flooded the room. The crowd jeered at the stage.

Louise turned around, her throat desiccating and her heart thumping. Please, please, be good, she entreated. Please don't balls it up. She threw a disapproving look at a man behind her who was yelling, 'Get on with it!' He stuck his tongue out at her, then seemed to think better of rudeness and wiggled it at her instead. He winked suggestively. She pulled a warthog face at him, swung back to the stage, and waited.

Karen appeared, being helped by several people up on

231

to the stage. A blast of shouts and wolf-whistles filled the air.

'Oh God,' Louise said to herself, closing her eyes. 'She's totally wrecked.'

She kept her eyes closed. Karen began a fumbling introduction, but the microphone squealed back through the speakers. There were more jeers. Then a click.

'Hi there, everyone. Same old ugly faces, I see.' Louise opened her eyes as Karen's sultry tones filled the room. Somebody laughed. Somebody said, 'Shhh.' Louise took a deep breath.

'We're Almanac. If you haven't seen us before, I'm Karen, and behind me we have Kerry on lead, Ginger on bass, Ned on drums, and Ash on violin.'

She stopped to sway sideways. Louise saw her hiccup violently, but her hand covered the microphone. There were more shouts. Louise's eyes smarted. She just couldn't turn round to see the expression on Rachel's face.

'Now if you're not going to shut up,' Karen said huskily, smiling seductively over the sea of faces, 'we're just going to have to shut you up, aren't we? Hit it!'

Louise backed against the wall as the sound hit them. She had been so afraid that it might be out of tune, out of time, with all the notes being played in the wrong order.

And it was.

'Stop, stop!' Karen clapped her hands. The instruments died away. There was an odd hush in the room. Of embarrassment. Louise's cheeks glowed. Karen seemed unfazed. She chuckled over the microphone, shrugging her shoulders.

'Ooops, that was my fault. I was supposed to count them in. Let's have another go. One, two, three, hit it!'

This time, the sound that hit Louise was incredible. A shiver crawled over her skin. Karen began to hop around the stage, kicking one leg out. Louise gaped at her over the

232

heads that were squashing forwards in front of her. She could see instantly why she was a good front woman. She had no fear, no inhibitions, and she was electrifying. Apart from a few staggers, she managed to throw herself around with a gazelle-like agility that Louise could only dream of. And then she began to sing.

'Fucking hell,' Louise heard Rachel eject behind her. She shot her a glance over her shoulder. She'd pulled away from Benji, who was too engrossed to notice, and was squinting sharply at the stage. She dropped her eyes on Louise, and bent forwards.

'Who is that girl?'

'Her name's Karen,' Louise shouted back. Rachel nodded, and pulled back again to watch with keen interest. Louise hugged her arms around herself with sheer delight and turned to drink in the scene. After several verses of the song, Karen sank back and allowed Ash to take centre stage, his violin clasped in earnest under his chin. Louise stared at him, willing him not to drop it. He drew up his bow, and began to play.

It was amazing. The sound he produced was a compelling mix of folk and hard-hitting rock. The drums pounded behind him imposingly. Louise couldn't take her eyes off him. She was fascinated, awed, overwhelmed with admiration. As he finished his solo the pub exploded into cheers. Foot stamping came from a small crowd at the back. Louise guessed that the loyal bunch of supporters had turned up after all. A solid lump wedged itself in her throat. It was corny, but it was true. Sally shook her arm.

'Are you all right?' she called into her ear.

'Yes.' Louise nodded until she felt faint, small fountains sprouting out of her eyes.

Of course she was all right. The most gorgeous man in London was not only sexy, kind, and great fun to be around. He was also obscenely good at playing the violin.

It didn't matter that he happened to be going out with the most gorgeous woman in London. He had come up to *her* when she'd arrived, given *her* a hug, and said that he was really happy that *she* was there.

She hadn't felt more all right for as long as she could remember.

Chapter Thirteen

Almanac played five more songs before Karen passed out
on the stage. It was a while before a caterwauling audience
took in the fact that she was out cold. Louise realised it
wasn't a stunt when the drummer sprang from behind his
drum kit, knocked the high hat flying, leaped forwards
and tried to revive her. Ash lowered his violin and stared
down at the glamorous pile of strawberry-blonde hair at
his feet, before putting his instrument to one side and
squatting down to pick her up and rest her on his knees.
The crowd began to surge forwards. Louise strained her
neck to see what was going on. Ginger took charge of the
microphone.

'Small problem, I'm afraid. We'll have to cut the set
short. Thanks for all your support.'

'Oh my God!' Louise clutched her untouched pint of
Guinness to her chest.

'What the hell's happened?' Sally was pushed against
Louise as people nudged their way towards the stage for a
good view.

It was clear that Karen was conscious again as she threw
her arms in the air and grabbed hold of Ash's neck. They
managed to get her to her feet, and she immediately fell
forwards against him. Pushing the drummer out of the
way, he hauled her into his arms and slowly carried her off
the stage. Louise watched with increasing dismay. Karen's
fingers were linked behind Ash's neck, her head flopped
against his chest as if it was a pillow. He carried her
through a clearing crowd with a grim face and manfully

kicked open a door leading to a private corridor. They both disappeared, the rest of the band following. The door swung shut, leaving the crammed bodies in the pub to speculate loudly while making a beeline for the bar. Louise felt herself jostled from all sides, and looked back to find Rachel. God only knew what Rachel would be thinking now.

Rachel was locked in eye contact with Benji while pulling on her jacket. She looked over at Louise and managed a brief smile.

'We're off now, Lou. Thanks for asking me here. I'll give you a call.'

'Hang on.' Louise heaved herself closer so that she could be heard. 'Karen's not always pissed. When I first met her she was as sober as a judge. She usually drinks mineral water, I'm sure of it. She's been to a wedding today, Ash said. She can't have known you were coming.'

'Who's Ash?' Rachel frowned.

'The violinist. He writes most of the songs as well.' Rachel looked distracted as she glanced towards the door that led out into the street. 'Rachel? Are you listening?'

'Right. Look, I've really got to go, Lou.'

'Aren't you at least going to speak to them?'

'I've told you, I've got to go. I would have had to leave early anyway, I just didn't get a chance to tell you.' Rachel's brown eyes were wide with appeal, and Louise gave up. Rachel always did what she wanted to, dissent or no dissent, and what she obviously wanted to do now was to go somewhere with Benji and bonk him to the last inch of his life. All the excited anticipation seeped out of Louise's body. She glowered at Benji. He looked away from her and pretended to be fascinated by something over by the door. She looked back at Rachel.

Just a tiny word of support, Louise implored as she gazed back at the deep brown eyes which could be so distant. You're my sister. You're the only one I've got and you're going to be an auntie, like it or not. In a parallel universe, you would stay with Hallam, adore his children, and fall about with happiness at the thought of having a little niece or nephew. But of course, she reminded herself, this was reality.

'Go on, then,' Louise said, trying to smile. 'Have a nice night.'

'I'm going straight home!' Rachel declared indignantly. 'I'm just dropping Benji off on the way.'

'Fine. Have a nice drive, then,' Louise said.

'See you soon, little one,' Rachel said, suddenly grabbing Louise's shoulders and planting a kiss on her cheek. 'You take care of yourself, and if you need a loan or somewhere to stay while you sort your life out, you only have to ask.'

She watched them both as they headed away from the bar, out of the door and into the cold night. It was odd that Rachel had called her 'little one'. She hadn't done that for years, and even then it had only been in rare moments of affection. And odd, too, that she was offering the home she shared with Hallam as somewhere to stay. She'd have to stay there herself to invite her sister to come and crash over. She became aware that Sally was standing beside her, a fresh glass of wine in her hand.

'I didn't get you a drink. I knew you'd say no, and I didn't want to draw attention to things. Has Rachel gone, then?'

'Yep.'

'With Benji?'

'Yep. She said she was just going to drop him off on the way home. I don't know why she said that. I don't know why she didn't just say that they were going off to have rampant sex. I don't know why she didn't tell me outright that she had no interest in seeing the band, but that it was a brilliant excuse to meet up with Benji. It was so obvious.

'That's that, then.'

'Yep. And the band was crap anyway, so it was a pretty failed mission, all in all.'

'How can you say that?' Sally turned round aghast. 'They were brilliant. I haven't seen such a good band for years.'

Louise faced her blearily.

'Karen collapsed because she was pissed. It's not very professional, is it?'

'Oh, don't worry about that.' Sally shook her head. 'They all do that. All the interesting ones, anyway. Rachel's probably really impressed. It's probably sealed their fate. She's rushed off to phone the big boss about them now, I bet you.'

But now Louise felt totally miserable, and to make things worse, she was overcome with tiredness. The chaotic noise of the pub was crashing in on her. All she wanted now was to be at home, in bed, with a cup of hot chocolate, but first she had to fight her way back across London. Her face set into a sulk. It had all gone wrong, and the final straw was that Sally would leave her halfway down the District line and she would have to rumble on down the Piccadilly line to the unfashionable part of Ealing and dash home through the dark streets on her own. That would underline the fact that it was all over. No excuse to see Ash any more. Just herself, her flat and her pregnancy.

'Cheer up,' Sally said breezily. 'Shall I get you a Coke or something?'

'No,' Louise muttered. 'I don't want a sodding fizzy drink. I want to wake up and find I've been living somebody else's life.'

'Don't worry about Ash.' Sally concentrated on pulling another lump of cork out of her glass. 'They don't know how to open wine bottles in pubs, do they? That's the third one in this glass. I don't think it meant anything. The way he was holding that girl.'

Louise gazed at Sally in surprise.

'What do you mean?'

'I know what's pissing you off.' Sally looked at her directly. 'He picked her up and carried her off the stage. Quite heroic. I was moved.' Sally looked unmoved. 'Somebody had to do it, Louise, and he was the closest. And she was only clinging to him because otherwise he'd have dropped her. You shouldn't read so much into it.'

'Of course I'm reading something into it, Sal, she's his girlfriend! And I wasn't pissed off. It's totally natural that he should carry her around when she passes out.'

'Yes, you were. I could tell you were feverishly jealous when you were telling me about her on the tube. Frankly I expected her to be more fantastic than she was. I don't think they're sleeping together. I bet if you went out the back now, you'd find him giving her a serious bollocking for making a tit of herself. I don't think there's any love lost between those two, I really don't.'

Louise was silent. How could Sally say all the wrong things so much of the time, then suddenly say all the right things?

'But having said that,' Sally continued airily, 'you're not on very solid ground yourself, are you? Even if he's not sleeping with her, even if it's one of those relationships that's just waiting to be over, and even if he likes you . . .'

'Yes?' Louise craned her neck.

'What the hell are you going to do about it?' Sally asked.

Louise pondered. A string of flippant replies came to mind, followed by a string of more serious ones. The confusion hit her again, as it was gaining the habit of doing when she thought of Ash.

'I want to go home, Sally,' Louise said.

'C'mon then.' Sally pulled her jacket together and dumped her glass on a table as she took Louise's arm and shunted her forwards. 'And I'll come home and stay over with you.'

'You will?' A silly smile spread over Louise's face.

'Of course,' Sally said in a practical voice. 'I've left all my clothes in your flat.'

'Okay, so let's run through it again. Accelerator, brake, clutch. ABC. Accelerator, brake, clutch.'

Olivia nodded, pointing her toes at the pedals in turn. One, two, three. It was easy.

'No, you have to do them with different feet. Watch mine again.'

She concentrated at Shaun's feet in the half-light. In the passenger seat beside her he seemed very unmanly. But that was only because she was used to seeing a man in the driving seat.

Shaun had offered to take her out to the industrial estate for her first lesson. She had thought it was a bit odd to do it in the dark, but he'd assured her that it was well lit by street lamps, and that they would only go round the car park, and he'd pointed out that if she wanted lessons in the daylight they would only have the weekends. What's more, he'd said that he wasn't doing anything on Friday night, and as she never did anything on a Friday night, it seemed like a good idea.

But they'd been here over an hour now and Olivia was itching to get on with some driving. When they'd arrived he'd motioned her into the driver's seat, and she'd felt a deep thrill of power sitting in front of the steering wheel. He'd run through the controls, some of which, she refrained from saying, were bleeding obvious, then he'd shown her all the gears, and she'd changed them with the engine off.

Then, as she'd been twitching to get the engine going and drive around, he'd decided to run through the principles of the Highway Code. They were still sitting in the middle of the empty car park, illuminated by yellow lights, with the engine off, and she was still pointing her toes at the pedals, like Margot Fonteyn but sitting down. It was very elegant, but it wasn't what she'd been excited about when they'd set out on their adventure.

'Look, Shaun, I know the theory is very important, but since we're here now do you think I could actually drive the car?'

Shaun sat back in his seat, rested his arm over the back, and looked at her.

'Do you feel ready for that? I thought you might like to gain a bit of confidence first. It's very difficult, I know, when you're a little more mature to learn something for the first time.'

She smiled at him indulgently.

'I've been inside cars all of my adult life. I watched Bob drive for nearly forty years. And I tested both the girls on the Highway Code when they took their tests. The thing I've never, never done, which I really want to do, is to be in control.'

Shaun cocked his head at her. He pulled his arm back into his lap and tutted at himself. 'Yes, that was stupid of me. Of course you'd want to have control of the car. It's obvious. Simple, but totally obvious.'

'Shaun? Can I start the engine?'

'Oh, absolutely. You go ahead. Let's do something positive.'

He sat back, placing his hands firmly on his knees, and waited, staring straight ahead.

'So . . . so, I'll just twist the key then.'

'You go right ahead.'

'Just give it a little twist.'

241

He nodded, his eyes on the logo of the printing company across the car park.

'I'll just . . .' Olivia swallowed. She reached out her fingers, and touched the car keys in the ignition.

Her fingertips tingled. Bob had handled these keys over and over again. It had felt strange to hand them over to Shaun, but not nearly as strange as touching them herself when they were in position, waiting to be turned, to fire the engine into life. She had never tried to drive this car. She'd had the bus, and there was nothing wrong with the bus. And before the bus, she'd had Bob.

But this was a different chapter of her life. Now, she only had herself. She fingered the stiff plastic stem of the key once more. Once she had driven the car, she knew she could never go back. She twisted the key.

As soon as she heard the engine moan into life, instinct took over. She thrust her right foot at the accelerator, and pushed it to keep the revs going. The engine screamed back. She pulled her foot away quickly and the engine died away. It stalled.

'Oh,' she said, disappointed.

Shaun cleared his throat. His hands were still clamped purposefully over his knees.

'I – I'll just do that again,' Olivia decided aloud.

When the engine screamed the next time, she pulled her foot away, but not so violently. She touched the pedal gently, pulled away, and put pressure on it again. She began to smile.

'That sounds all right, doesn't it?' she called to Shaun. He nodded without looking at her. She waited for him to tell her what to do next, then, as no direction was forthcoming, turned back to her controls.

'Right then. Right. I'm going to put the clutch down, and put the car into first gear. That's what I'm going to do. I've seen it done loads of times. I can do it.'

She slowly raised her foot from the accelerator. The engine seemed to be running smoothly now. She lifted her left foot in the air, and elaborately brought it down on to the clutch pedal. She pushed it right to the floor. That's what Bob had told Rachel when he was teaching her. Right to the floor. She reached out with her left hand, and took hold of the gear lever. Now that the engine was running it was a lot more daunting than shifting it about before. She drew in a breath, and pushed the car into first gear.

She sat silently, rooted to the spot. The car park remained empty. The yellow lamps beamed down on the Ford Escort in the middle of the vast expanse of tarmac. Shaun whispered something to her that she didn't catch.

'What?' she whispered back.

'Handbrake,' he repeated in a hoarse voice.

'Oh yes. Handbrake. Of course.'

She released it and returned to her crouching position over the wheel. The car didn't move. The tarmac was perfectly flat. The engine hummed, her left foot was glued down to the floor, her two hands gripped the wheel. Her right foot strayed over the pedals, and hovered in the air over the accelerator.

'Ready?' Shaun whispered out of the side of his mouth.

'I think so, yes.'

They waited. Shaun said nothing. Olivia said nothing. She wasn't capable of saying anything, or of moving. She was just thinking very hard, of all the things that she was supposed to do next, then when she had got them all in the right order, she thought of them all again.

'Olivia?'

'Yes?'

'We're not going to move unless you take your foot off the clutch.'

'I know.'

243

'Do you want to do it, then?'

'I'm not sure.'

To his credit Shaun neither sighed nor tutted. He just sat quietly as if he was thinking about something else.

'Driving a car's a bit like life, except that it's encapsulated in a car, if you see what I mean,' he said finally. 'You have to decide what sort of car you want, and where you want it to take you, and how quickly you want to get there. But most importantly you have to know in your heart whether you want to be a passenger or the one with your hands on the wheel. What I'm really saying is, do you want to be driven, or do you want to be the driver?'

Olivia turned to look at him from her crouched position. He hadn't said, 'That's what I say.' He was still staring at the logo in the distance as if it was really interesting. She steeled herself.

'Right then.'

She lifted her left foot, stage by stage, from the clutch. Suddenly, she felt the car engage. She panicked and slammed the pedal to the floor again. She issued a string of short breaths to hype herself up.

'This time it's going to happen.'

She tried again, her foot moving more fluidly. When she felt the engine jump, she pushed down on the accelerator. The car began to move.

'Oh my God. I've done it. Look, we're moving!'

She concentrated. She wouldn't let the car stall again. Shaun would think she was an idiot. She would keep it going for as long as possible. The car lurched forwards.

'We really are moving. Look, Shaun. I'm driving!'

She gripped the wheel as they chugged across the smooth tarmac. The logo of the printing company ahead grew mesmerically closer and closer.

'It's fantastic!'

'Okay, I think we could turn the wheel now.'

'I really am driving. I'm in control. Why didn't I do this before?'

The kerb rimming the car park appeared in the headlamps.

'We need to turn the wheel,' Shaun said, glancing at Olivia as she embraced the steering wheel. 'Olivia?'

'The wheel. I'll turn the wheel.' She yanked it round as far as it would go. The car swung sideways and careered off towards a concrete stump.

'Brake, now, Olivia! Brake! Take your foot off the accelerator and push the brake!'

The concrete stump was suddenly directly in front of them. Olivia's throat clamped. Her hands were stuck on the steering wheel, her feet paralysed into position. Shaun threw himself bodily over her and took hold of the wheel. The tyres squealed.

'Take your feet off everything. Just lift them into the air!'

'I – I can't move.'

'Yes, you can.'

'No, I can't.'

'For God's sake, Olivia!' Shaun's voice lost all of its gentle persuasion and became a bellow. 'Will you stop being such a bloody wimp and take control? Is it what you want, or isn't it?'

Olivia's feet levitated into the air. The car rolled into the centre of the tarmac again, Olivia's mind sharpened like acid by Shaun's incredible loss of temper. Instead of just letting the car stall, she remembered to put her foot on the clutch as it slowed down. And she put her right foot on the brake. They came to an abrupt halt, and lurched forward in their seats. The engine remained humming as Olivia reached for the gear lever and pulled it back into neutral. She wrenched the handbrake up, making it click the way Bob used to do when he was in a bad mood. Then she sat

back in her seat and swivelled round to stare at Shaun ir
anger.

'How dare you call me a wimp? You hardly know me.'

She heard Shaun expel a long breath. Then, when he
turned to look at her, she saw that he was smiling. No, i
was more than a smile. His lips were spread into a wide
grin.

'You're laughing at me,' she said, ruffled.

'Not in the slightest,' he laughed.

'You are. Listen to you. Laugh, laugh, laugh.'

Shaun put his head back, opened his eyes to the roof of
the car, and laughed loudly. Over and over again. Olivia
began to smile. It was difficult not to. He had a funny
laugh, one that made you want to laugh as well.

'*Half a league onward!*' Shaun called into the air. '*Into the
valley of Death!*'

'I drove, didn't I?'

'Yes,' he said, dropping his eyes on her.

'I really did. I drove the car.'

'Yes. You drove the car.'

'And I didn't stall it.'

'No, you didn't.'

'Because you shouted at me. You knew if you called me
a wimp, I wouldn't stall it. Didn't you?' She nudged his
arm playfully. 'You knew, didn't you?'

Now she couldn't stop laughing. She slapped her hands
on the steering wheel in triumph.

'Can you see me, Bob? I can do it! I'm not hopeless. I'm
not a bag of shopping. Rachel? Louise? I drove the car! I
drove the blimmin' car!'

'It's brilliant, Olivia. You've made fantastic progress
tonight.'

'Yes.'

Olivia stopped laughing and stared out into the
deserted terrain around them. Flat, open spaces and big

empty buildings, all dependent on people to arrive, and to give them life. But she wasn't an empty building waiting for other people to give her life. She had been, in the past. She had always been the solid, unmoving thing that the moving things anchored themselves to. But now she was a moving thing herself. She smiled again, a more confident smile, one brought about by knowing that the direction she was travelling in was the right one.

This week she was driving the car. Next week she would do other things. Another week before the dinner. By the time she saw Louise, she would have things to say to her, and things to show her that would surprise her. And delight her.

'So,' Olivia said, beaming happily at Shaun, 'shall we do that one more time?'

Louise and Sally crashed through the front door.

'Shhh!' Sally put her fingers to her lips. 'You don't want to wake anyone up, do you?'

'Fat chance.' Louise dragged Sally through the hall and pushed her into the flat. 'Harris will either be out bonking or in bonking. There's nobody else to offend.'

'Harris.' Sally savoured the name. 'Sounds like a man with a big bank balance.'

'He's got a big something.'

'It's just so long since I've stayed over with you. I'm almost excited.'

'I'll put the kettle on.'

'Ho, hum.' Sally followed Louise through to the kitchen and swayed against the units. 'Lovely place, this. I just love all this white Formica. It's especially good at picking up grimy fingerprints. Why do you pay so much for such a dumpy flat?'

'Because I'm a silly cow. Just to save you expressing your opinion.'

247

'You're a silly cow,' Sally said as if the thought had newly occurred to her.

Louise filled the kettle and plugged it in. Sally sank into a chair and picked through an assortment of baby and toddler magazines strewn across the table.

Sally has insisted on stopping off for a few drinks on the way back, saying that if it wasn't closing time she didn't feel normal being at home. Louise knew what she meant, and seeing as she hadn't got to go home alone tonight, she felt less tired. But Louise had been surprised at how much Sally had thrown back. Tonight she'd seemed determined to get steaming drunk.

'Where did the flowers come from?' Sally frowned across the room at the bucket sitting on the floor. 'I didn't see those before. They don't look very well. You ought to water them.'

'They're in water. And I don't really care if they die anyway. They came from Jon.'

Sally sat up straight and pulled a dramatic face.

'Jon?'

'Yes.'

'*The* Jon?'

Louise gave Sally a patient smile while she organised the mugs.

'They're a get-well-soon present.'

'Oh. Have you got any brandy, or anything?'

'I drank the brandy before I knew I was pregnant. There's some white wine left in the fridge, but it's been there a couple of weeks.'

'You see,' Sally said as she lumbered over to the fridge, 'that's the thing about being pregnant. It's good for your health. You give up smoking and drinking, eat salads and lots of fibre, and the best thing about it is that you don't do it because anybody tells you to. You do it because you can't do anything else.'

248

'That just about sums it up.' Louise doled coffee into the mugs.

'And it would be really good if you could make yourself feel like that, just at will.' Sally took the wine bottle from the fridge, found herself a glass and sloshed out a measure. She took a large sip. 'But you can't. And apparently when you're pregnant you think that you're going to give up all your vices for ever, because suddenly you can't see why you ever had them all. Hang on. What's happened to your fridge?' She lunged at it again, opened the door and stuck her head inside. Louise waited patiently. 'And it's not just your fridge.' She flicked the door shut and gazed around the room with wild eyes. 'It's your whole flat. You've had a personality transplant.'

'Yes.'

'There are green things in there.' Sally pointed at the fridge accusingly. 'And you've done the washing-up. And you've hoovered or something. And,' she paused and took in a noseful of air, 'I can't smell curry. When did you last have a take-away?'

Louise gave her a self-satisfied smile in response.

'See?' Sally waved her hands. 'This is pre-cisely what I'm saying. When you're pregnant, they say you do lots of things that are good for you, and go off all of the silly things. All of them. Dropped like a ton of bricks.'

'Apart from sex,' Louise said. 'If you want to count that as a silly thing.'

'Apart from sex. Although you could really go off that as well. But the horrid thing is that when you're not pregnant any more, you want to indulge yourself in all the vices again. All that common sense that dawns on you in a burst of hormones just disappears.' Sally threw her hands in the air. 'Just like that. Boof! Gone! And you're back to being a stupid, self-destructive old bag again.'

Louise turned round with the kettle in her hands.

'Just who are you calling a stupid, self-destructive ol
bag?'

Sally sat down again and stared at the tiger lili
hanging over the side of the bucket.

'You, of course. So why did Jon send you flowers? D
you think he wants a reconciliation?'

Louise laughed loudly.

'He wanted to make himself feel better, that's all.'

'Oh.' Sally sniffed and flopped over the table, he
auburn hair swirling. 'Fergus sent me flowers. All th
time. It really got on my nerves.'

Louise glanced at Sally, before bringing the mugs ove
to the table and sitting down.

'Sal? Why are you talking about Fergus in the pas
tense?'

'It's obvious, isn't it?'

'Not to me. I like Fergus. He's a decent, good-lookin;
friendly, intelligent bloke. I don't understand what
wrong with him.'

'Hmmn.' Sally dipped her nose alternately into her mu;
and her wineglass. She stuck her head in her hands an
stared at Louise. '*You* don't like it, do you?'

'What don't I like?' Louise wished whole-heartedly tha
she was as drunk as Sally. Then she might be able to follov
her trajectories.

'Being told what to do. When people suggest somethin
to you that they think's good for you, you just go off an
do the opposite.'

'What?' Louise thumped her mug down. 'You can
honestly be suggesting that I'd have a baby just to g
against popular opinion?'

'Well, no, not exactly,' Sally reasoned. 'But in a way, ye:
Not the baby, exactly, but other things. It's as if you'v
always got to make up your own rules. It's as if you loo
at the well-trodden path, and have to go somewhere else

250

'That's so stupid.' Louise wanted to laugh at the serious look on Sally's face. 'It's not planned.'

'But that's it. My life has been planned, you see.' Sally seemed focused, if only momentarily. 'I thought about it tonight. When you were talking about headbanging. That was the last time I really did anything different. I don't think I've really let myself go since then. I used to throw myself around with some sort of abandon then. I don't any more. You always did. You had fun, didn't you?'

Louise raised her eyebrows but said nothing.

'And perhaps there are things that I'd like to do, things that you might do, that I wouldn't,' Sally said, nodding at Louise and proving by the extremely sincere expression on her face that she was very drunk. 'Things that you have the balls to do, that I don't.'

'Oh, come on. I'd never have had the guts to fight through a law degree with the dedication that you did. That's why you've got a brilliant career. That's why I haven't. You're a bloody hard worker. You turn up at your office every day looking fantastic, and do your job excellently. That takes balls.'

'It doesn't,' Sally said, sliding upwards again.

'It does.'

'No, I disagree. Balls are what you need to do something different. Something people don't expect you to do.'

'No, no. Balls are what you need to persevere. I've never had those kind of balls.'

'No, I don't accept that we've had different kinds of balls. I think that you've had them, and I haven't. I know I'm good at my job, I know I'm professional, and I know that Fergus wants to marry me. But that's not what balls are all about.'

Louise put her mug down. She stood up and walked around the kitchen. She allowed a silence to fall between

251

them while they both thought about what had been said. She turned back to Sally, resting against the sink.

'It almost sounds as if you envy me, Sally,' she said. 'That can't be what you mean.'

Sally shifted herself in her chair. She fingered a strand of her hair and glanced away at Louise's untidy mass of paperwork.

'Well, perhaps I do envy you.'

'Why?' Louise ejected. Then she laughed. 'For God's sake, woman, I envy *you*. Don't you realise that? You're beautiful, professional, high-incomed . . .' Was there any need to go on? Sally still looked doubtful. 'And you've just been proposed to by a beautiful, professional, high-incomed man. Isn't that what we all dream about? Get a grip, will you?'

'But you . . .' Sally swayed over the table, her eyes revolving in different directions. 'You've never even had to lift a finger to have men falling all over you. You know how to laugh, don't you? You even make other people laugh. You just wing it, and you defy all the bloody rules.'

'What rules?'

'The rules. You know. The things I abide by. I've done it all in the right order. I should be feeling totally smug. And look at us! You're the one who's up the spout with no job, no money and no man, and you're the one who's happy!'

Louise was increasingly convinced that Sally was not just drunk, but poleaxed. It was a miracle that she was still sitting up straight.

'No, really. Think about it. I'm pregnant, the man responsible doesn't want to know, I've lost my job, and I'm on a knife-edge until I can sort out a proper career for myself. I'm going to find a way through it, but this isn't by any means how I would have wanted it to happen.' She stopped and allowed herself time to think. Sally was being frivolous. It was fine, as long as she didn't push it too far. 'I've got a lot on my plate, Sal. Don't envy me, whatever you do.'

They looked at each other. Sally's eyes stopped rotating. She picked up the book of babies' names and opened it upside down.

'Sorry.'

'It's okay.'

'You can come and stay with me, if you want,' Sally said in a small voice. 'If this flat's too expensive for you. I've got room.'

'Thanks, Sal, but the last thing you need at the moment is a woman who can't decide whether to crave or honk lurking about your house.'

Sally snorted.

'We've been through a lot of things together, and we could survive this. I'm pretty sure of it.'

'That's really sweet of you.' Louise approached Sally and touched her shoulders. 'Don't take offence, but it's not like your woman at work. When you've got to be around it all day and night it's not just theory. And what would you do when I'm a beachball on two cocktail sticks?'

'I'd take the piss out of you, obviously.'

'And after that? When I go into labour? When I yell and scream and sweat a lot?' Louise chortled at Sally. 'And what about a poohing baby making your house smell like a cowshed? I think that just might cramp your style a bit.'

'I'd open the windows. And I could babysit for you.'

Louise stopped laughing as she looked into Sally's eyes. For a moment, it seemed as if she was completely serious. Then Sally smiled and her eyes began to rotate again. Louise was relieved.

'I'm a bit pissed,' she confessed. 'Don't get me to sign anything, will you?'

'Course not.'

'Is that your phone ringing, or have I got Almanac still buzzing in my ears?'

253

Louise concentrated. The phone was ringing. She looked at her watch quickly. It was far too late for anybody to call her. Unless it was Ash.

She sprinted through the hall and ran into the bedroom without stopping to explain anything to Sally. He would have got home now, and he could be ringing to say that Karen was all right, and that when he had clasped her to his chest, it had only been the decent thing to do, but that in the débâcle that had followed they'd decided to split up. Even though Louise was pregnant, he'd loved her from the first moment he'd seen her, and he was on his way over in a taxi with all his worldly goods. But then she would have to explain that he couldn't possibly stay over because she'd have nowhere to put Sally. But that wouldn't be important, because she had an old Lilo that could be aerated at high speed and covered with a duvet. And Sally was so obliterated, she wouldn't notice anyway. But at the same time, she would have to make it clear that she wasn't reliant on him for anything, and that she was intending to branch out into a new career as soon as she stopped feeling sick. He did know that anyway, but she'd have to make it clear if he had his bags packed ready to come round. She dived on to the bed, apologised mentally to the bunch of cells in her stomach for the shock, and hoiked up the receiver.

'Yes?' It came out as a pant, but she wasn't that bothered. She just had to hear his voice again.

'Louise?'

'Yes!' She rolled over on the bed, grinning up at the dusty cobweb, all of the adrenaline that had been building up exploding into a fireworks display of happiness. And now that he was on the phone, all that mattered was that he'd thought of her, and he'd called. He didn't have to move in at all.

'How are you?'

She dropped her grin, her eyes still fixed on her cobweb. Something wasn't right.

'Ash?'

'Er, no. It's Jon.'

She was silenced. The cobweb wiggled around in the draught caused by Sally who had decided to come into the room and lie down next to her on the bed, her face a perfect picture of drunken repose. Louise shuffled over to make room. Sally groaned and snuggled up to the pillows.

'Have you got someone with you?' Jon asked.

'Er, not really.' Louise was too numb to think of a great answer to that one.

'Right. Okay. So, did you get the flowers? I thought I might hear from you.'

'Yes. Tiger lilies.'

'I know you like them.'

'Right.'

Sally began to snore. She threw an arm over Louise which hit her in the face. Louise swore at her under her breath.

'You have got someone there, haven't you?'

Louise sniffed back her indifference to the question.

'Okay, can you just hear me out?' Jon continued. He was on a sales roll. If it got too nauseating, she'd just hang up. She was too tired to fend him off. 'The reason I rang is to ask you how it went, and to see if you needed anything.'

'It's all fine.'

'Right. And I wanted to apologise to you as well.'

'Hmmn.'

'Louise? Did you get that? I was a shit, and I know it. It was something that happened between us, and I should have been there for you. I realise that now. I've talked to a few people about it, and not one of them has stood by me.' He gave a self-deprecating laugh. 'In fact I've been to hell and back, if you must know. The women at work have practically sawn my balls off because of this. I realise I was wrong, Louise.'

'That's good.' Sally's snoring was getting louder. Louise pulled her head up and stared at her in amazement. Hadn't Fergus ever spent the night with her? Why did he still want to marry her?

'So . . .' Jon seemed hesitant. Louise pushed the receiver back to her ear.

'I'm sorry, were you saying something? You commissioned MORI to conduct a poll for you and the results were surprising.' She heard his sharp intake of breath.

'I deserve that. Louise, I wanted you to know that I'm really, really sorry. I treated you abominably, and it'll live with me for ever. When I think about what you've been through, with only your girlfriends there for you, it makes me feel appalling. It wasn't their job, it was mine, and I should have been there.'

'Right.' Louise felt her eyes closing. It had been such a long day.

'And I wondered if I could make it up to you in any way. Perhaps I could take you out to dinner. Somewhere really fantastic. You just say where, and I'll make the booking.'

Louise opened her eyes again. Her stomach started to rumble.

'What, anywhere?'

'Yes, Louise, anywhere. The thing is . . . I've been thinking. Perhaps it was a mistake for us to split up in the first place. Perhaps we had a good thing going, but I just didn't realise it.'

Louise smiled at the ceiling, and held the receiver towards Sally as she snorted, turned over and farted.

'Louise? Have you got someone—'

'Jon? I'll call you. Bye now.'

She put the receiver down, rolled over and fell asleep next to Sally.

Chapter Fourteen

'What's wrong with your mouth, Rachel?'

Rachel grunted and turned over. She felt her shoulders being shaken. She groaned, swore and buried her face in the pillow.

'Rachel? Are you going to play on the computer with us now?'

'Shhh, Ricky. She'll play with us when her mouth gets better.'

Rachel peered through slitted eyes at her pillowcase. She could see through blurred vision that Hallam's side of the bed was empty. That would explain the smell of bacon drifting up from downstairs. But his pillow was dented. That was because he had actually slept next to her, it was just that she had crept between the sheets and gone into a temporary coma and couldn't remember him being there. She could remember getting home now. But Hallam hadn't woken up. And he was so used to her coming in after him, just as she was used to lying there, waiting for him to come home from a delayed flight, or an extended dinner, that neither of them thought anything of it. Another unearthly voice whispered over her slumped form.

'Rachel, if you're not awake, just say so, and we'll go away.'

Ricky. He couldn't help being seven. He couldn't help coming out with the sort of comments that cut through her veneer and cracked her face into a smile. Even when she'd only been asleep for a couple of hours.

'I'm not awake,' she rumbled through the pillow.

'Okay, we'll go away,' the whisper responded earnestly. 'We'll come back with a cup of tea later to make your mouth better.'

Glen erupted into a shriek of laughter.

'You're stupid. She's awake. How can she talk if she's not awake?' The shrieking went on. Rachel stirred protectively, sat up and shook her hair around her head. So much for video classification. These two boys had seen more horrifying images in this bedroom on a Saturday morning than they could ever encounter on celluloid.

'Don't be a smart-arse, Glen. Ricky's trying to be thoughtful.' Her voice emerged as a croak. The leaden feeling of guilt hit her. She shouldn't be smoking so much. Not now she was in her mid-thirties. Now it was serious.

She surveyed the two faces. Ricky's, small and delicate, broke into a delighted smile as if he wasn't sure what she'd said, but knew she was on his side. Glen looked cautiously at her for a moment, then sprang away, shouting as he headed for the stairs.

'I don't care. I'm going to tell Dad you've got a bad mouth.'

'A bad mouth?' Rachel pushed her fingers into her hair and squeezed a handful into shape. She pressed her lips together. They felt swollen and numb. She put a tentative finger up to her face, and opened her eyes in alarm. Her mouth felt huge, as if she'd got mumps from her chin up to her nostrils.

'Ricky, go and help Daddy with the breakfast. I promise I'll come down and play on the computer with you if you give me a chance to get up.'

'Okay.'

He cast a final, fascinated glance at her face, then fled.

'And close the door after you!'

The door remained open. She heard him career down the stairs unevenly.

She lay back against the pillows. Her thighs were sore. Her breasts were sore. Her mouth was sore. What had happened with Benji last night had been totally anticipated in some ways, and a complete shock in others. She'd meant it to happen. She'd planned it, even to the point of arranging to see Louise's friend's band. Hallam couldn't have complained at her going out on one of his rare Friday nights at home when she'd explained how vulnerable Louise was at the moment, not having a job, worrying about money, and all the trimmings. She hadn't meant to be so calculating, but fate had just stepped in and offered her the first opportunity since she'd been living with Hallam to start an affair.

And now that she'd started one, how did she feel? She stretched her legs under the soft cotton of the duvet, and traced a hand over her body. She felt exhilarated with sexual pleasure. Benji had been harshly passionate, and it had been amazing. She waited for guilt to consume her. The only sinking sensation came from her lungs which felt like two sacks of flour. She thought about Hallam. No guilt arrived. She wondered how Benji felt this morning, waking up to the memory of their lovemaking. He had said it was unique. She believed him. Was it any more than that? Did it matter if it wasn't?

Hallam's resonant voice echoed through the floor. The boys were both talking at once, demanding his attention. He was playing the diplomat, as ever. It had been so exciting when they'd first met. He had his career, she had her career. They'd got to know each other better. She learned about his failed marriage. He had his career, and his children. She had her career. Now he had been made redundant. Now he had his children. She had her career.

She got up, stopping to lean against the bed to allow the

dizziness of exhaustion to pass, and walked slowly through to the ensuite bathroom. She pushed the door closed with a bare foot, and looked at herself in the mirror.

A bolt of shock transfixed her. What had Benji done to her face? She'd realised he had a layer of stubble. Of course, she'd felt it last night, and not just on her face. It had been thrilling, electrifying, a violent sensation of the moment. But the only time she'd ever looked as disfigured as this was when she'd had her four back molars out to make room for her wisdom teeth, aged fourteen, and Louise had crammed a handful of marbles into her mouth to show her what she looked like. And then her skin hadn't been bright pink.

'Oh my God!'

She met her own wide black eyes in the mirror. She started to laugh. What would Louise say now? She was so judgemental about the whole thing. She straightened her face.

Louise didn't understand what was going on in her own sister's head. It was as simple as that. Louise, and everybody else, could be as censorious as they liked. Nobody was ever going to take her side in this situation. Everybody loved Hallam. Everybody thought he was the right sort of man for her to be with. Everybody saw it through Hallam's eyes. Nobody stopped to consider what she herself could see.

She doused her face in cold water and mopped it with a soft towel. Whatever the new woman used in the washing machine was doing the trick. Everything she touched these days had a faint aroma of lavender, and was like silk to the touch. She was worth the money Rachel paid for her to come in, to clean, to wash, to get everything together again. And there lay the irony, Rachel thought, stepping back to look at her lips in the mirror again and trying to convince herself that her chin didn't look like a pizza.

Everybody thought that it was Hallam who kept Rachel together. This new woman – what was her name? Kathy, or something – was doing more to keep Rachel together than Hallam could. It was, in fact, Hallam who was splitting her down the middle. She considered her disfigured excuse for a mouth and frowned. Men. They always had to impose themselves, to take up more room, to imprint their personalities. They tried to edge you out of the way, on the tube, on the pavement, in the pub. Even on your own bloody face.

She threw on a silk wrap, ruffled her hair, and wandered down the stairs. Hallam was standing in the hall. He looked up at her. She stopped, her throat tight. He was an elegant man, even in jeans and a jumper. Her heart stuttered as his eyes roamed her face. He blinked, and then he smiled before going back into the kitchen.

'I'm just going to make a phone call, Hal.'

'Fine. Breakfast's ready when you want it,' he called back.

She stood in the hall for a moment, listening to the scramble of voices in the kitchen. Of course Hallam wouldn't make anything out of the gravel rash on her face. Of course he wouldn't suspect anything if she wanted to make a phone call. Why would he? Wasn't life just perfect, redundancy excepted? The inconvenience was only temporary. He'd get another job in a short time. He was a senior manager, with experience that would be worth another good salary in another international company as soon as he floated his skills on the market. No, apart from this minor blip, everything was in place as far as Hallam was concerned. He saw his children when it suited him, he had a good relationship with his ex-wife regardless of anything she threw at him, and he had a doting live-in partner who herself was totally fulfilled as far as he could see. Rachel listened a moment longer, wondering if one of the boys would come out to the hall, find her and force her to play on the computer. They seemed to be busy with other things now, and she heard Hallam saying something about a walk. She bit her lip, and wandered away to find the phone. She flicked through the Filofax on the table until she found the number she needed. She took a breath and dialled.

'Is that the Eye of Newt? Oh hi, Keith, it's Rachel Twigg. Sorry I didn't get to speak to you last night, but that last band you had on, Almanac . . . Yes, I thought so too. Have you got a contact number for them?'

She picked up a pen and waited. A squeal of laughter came from the kitchen. Ricky. Hallam was pretending to be the electric fence in *Jurassic Park* again.

'Hi, Keith, yep.' She scribbled down a number. 'Gotcha. See you soon, then. Cheers.'

She hesitated by the phone. She could have got the number from Louise. She would have liked to talk to Louise properly and tell her what she was really feeling about Hallam. When she'd talked about it before it had come out all wrong, as if she was bored with him, and it wasn't that at all. But Louise's life was so different from her own. She'd only make snap judgements, and she couldn't handle any more lectures. She wandered back through to the kitchen in time to see Hallam helping the boys into their coats.

'We're going for a quick stroll,' he said, glancing up at her. For a moment she thought his eyes were troubled, but they cleared and he was smiling at her. 'There's a bacon sarnie there for you.'

'Well . . .' Rachel rubbed at her hair. 'Just give me a sec to throw some clothes on and I'll come with you.'

'Come on, Dad,' Glen was saying, pulling at his hand.

'Okay, okay. Listen, we'll only be half an hour or so. It'll give you time to sort yourself out, won't it?' Hallam said.

'It's no problem. I can just bung my jeans on.'

'But we're going now, Rachel. And you look like you need a shower.'

Rachel hesitated. This was exactly the problem. Once again she was being treated as the outsider. If she could have sat Louise in the kitchen right now and shown her what was happening perhaps then she'd understand. But although her heart was sinking, she wouldn't let the boys know.

'Oh. All right, then.' Rachel grinned at Ricky quickly. He was acutely sensitive. He was looking from Rachel to Hallam, his round eyes worried. 'I'll set the computer up, shall I, Ricky? You can thrash me at whatever you like when you get back.'

There was a pause. Hallam zipped the front of his Barbour.

'Actually, I was going to take them to the pictures later,' he said, not looking at Rachel. 'There's something they really want to see.'

'Great!' Rachel forced herself to sound bright. She casually slipped on to a stool and picked up her bacon sandwich. 'That gives me time to get on with some work, then.'

'Won't you come to the film?' Ricky said, his bottom lip dropping.

'Can't, love. Sorry.' Rachel pulled a hideous face at him, and he giggled. 'You lot buzz off then and leave me in peace. I've got some things to sort out.'

She took a bite of her sandwich and flicked over the front page of the paper as they crashed down the hall, all talking at once, and left. The front door slammed shut. They were too excited to shout a goodbye. She put the sandwich back on the plate and sank her chin into her hands. There was still tomorrow. She had been honing up her skills at *Quake* during the week and she was dying to see the expression on Ricky's face when she showed him. She'd got a surprise for them both, too. A game that they'd been talking about for weeks. Even Hallam didn't know yet that she'd bought it for them. He'd be pleased. Tomorrow they could hole up in the house and have a day playing games together. She was looking forward to it.

The house was uncomfortably quiet without the boys. She got up and wandered through to the living room, clicking on the stereo and twisting the volume so that the CD blasted out. Benji had urgently wanted to know when he could see her again. She draped herself on the sofa and closed her eyes. She wouldn't ring him yet. She'd think about it.

Olivia locked the garage door and tested the handle, humming to herself. Another successful session with Shaun, this time out on a deserted country track. She'd even got to change gear from first up to second.

He seemed so much more ready to listen to her today. She'd explained that she'd been absorbing the details for years, not sitting next to Bob like a crash dummy. She may not have spoken her thoughts aloud, but every time he'd changed up, changed down, braked or swerved, she'd been making mental notes. Perhaps not because she thought she would ever do it herself, but just because it always made the drive more interesting. And as Shaun had dropped her off he'd surprised her by giving her a book. She'd been reluctant to take it at first. She had no idea why. Something to do with an old adage about accepting gifts from strangers, but Shaun was no stranger. It had been wrapped in a plastic bag and sellotaped down but in her hands she'd felt that it was a hardback, small and dense. She'd wondered whether to open it there, with him watching, but he'd said that he was in a hurry and asked if she wouldn't mind opening it later. So she'd got out of the car, opened the garage, and Shaun had steered the Escort inside. He did it differently from the way Bob used to. Shaun had steamed in at great speed and slammed on the brakes an inch before he hit the back wall. Bob used to edge the car in, always slowing as he reached the back wall and rolling the last couple of inches.

Not knowing what to say to Shaun about her present, she'd thanked him for the lesson, and he'd seemed happy to hand over the keys to the Escort, leap over to his Citroën, give her a cheerful wave and disappear. That was it for now.

It was a wintry day. She stopped on the short drive to squint up at the lifeless sky. Not even clouds to give it character, just a pale grey wash. There had been a few days when snow threatened, and it looked as if it might come soon. But inside she was bubbling with excitement. It was Saturday, which meant she didn't have to face Carol at work, and it also meant that this time next week Louise would be on her way down to Kent for dinner.

She'd rung Katherine Muff. She stopped to giggle quietly. It helped her mentally to bring Katherine down a peg or two. She might have been the class success story, but at least Olivia now realised that she'd got a silly name. She'd kept the call to Katherine very brief to stop her gloating on about her job, her family, or whatever it was she would gloat about if she was given half a chance. She'd told her she'd be there, and was bringing her daughter. Katherine must know about Bob, and that he'd died. Somebody must have told her.

Olivia stopped. At least, she assumed she must know about Bob. Anyway, she thought as she walked briskly through the cold to her front door, her book clutched in her hand, the point was that by this time next week, she *would* have interesting things to say about herself. In fact, she intended to put the others to shame. Just one more week, and her list of answers to the politely posed question, 'And what are you doing now, Olivia?' would be long enough to bore them all into the grave.

'Yoo-hoo! Olivia! How are you?'

She turned as she approached her front door and frowned at Diane Fisher, standing in the porch of the adjoining house huddled in a cardigan. She should smile, but there had been bad feeling between the families ever since the Fishers had questioned Bob's fee for building that bloody porch for them. Olivia knew he'd undercharged because they were neighbours and friends. It was the sort of thing he would do. But they had come back with their own grossly inadequate estimate, and to save trouble, Bob had let it go. That was at a time when the bills were only just being met, and Bob shouldn't have given in. He'd always been too kind.

She smiled anyway.

'Diane. How are you?'

'I haven't seen you for so long!' Diane hopped out of the porch and over the lawn to stand on her side of the diminutive wooden posts that held the low linked chain in place. 'I was wondering if you were all right. You mustn't stay inside and mope, you know. If you need anything, anything at all, some shopping doing or something, you only have to ask.'

Olivia swallowed a hearty sigh and obediently crossed her own front lawn to stand on the other side of the chain. Diane's pity was something she didn't need. She gritted her teeth and hoped that it wasn't visible.

'It's very kind of you, Diane, but I tend to get the shopping done in my lunch-hour.'

'Of course. Well, if you ever need a lift anywhere, to get the heavy things, I can drive you.'

Diane had always been able to drive their Metro. But she shouldn't feel resentment now, only understanding, she

told herself. She was entering the land of the geo-
graphically independent herself.

'How's Paul? Do you hear from him often?'

'Oh yes.' Olivia could tell from the way Diane's small
blue eyes flashed that she was lying. Perhaps it took a
mother to recognise bravado when she saw it, but it was
there, no question. 'Yes, he's always on the phone, telling
me how he's doing. He's been in Italy, you know, on a
business trip. Doing really well. I said to him, when he told
me how much he was earning, but what are you doing
with it all?' Diane laughed loudly. 'I don't know. They just
don't seem to struggle like we did, do they? I don't think
they know what it means to struggle.'

'No, they don't really,' Olivia agreed.

'What about your girls? Still living the high life up in
London?'

'Oh, yes. They love it up there. Lots of action, they say.
They think it's dull here.'

Diane relaxed her shoulders as if she'd decided not to
stay in character any more.

'Paul says that too. It was good enough for them when
we brought them up, wasn't it? I don't know.' She gazed
down at the strip of dry earth on her side of the chain
which in the summer contained a row of marigolds. She
laughed suddenly. 'When I think of all that fuss over the
caravan.'

'Yes,' Olivia said, smiling. She could remember the
caravan incident as if it was yesterday. Louise had
blamed Paul, Paul had blamed Louise. At the time, the
absurd notion had even passed through her head that
they would be lovers when they were older. But it had
never happened. Now they both had their own paths to
follow.

'And Paul's still not married,' Diane said, drawing a
deep breath. 'You'd think he might do that for us,

267

wouldn't you? I'd like nothing better than a little grandson, tottering about. You know how it is.'

Diane gave Olivia a sad, complicitous look. Olivia thought about it as she obediently returned the rueful smile. Did she know how it was? What about her plans? What on earth would any grandchild of hers think of her intentions if one had ever existed? It was just as well that there were no complications of that nature. She was in no frame of mind to potter round handing out toffees.

'Anyway,' Diane said, looking cold and shuffling in her slippers, 'I just wanted to say hello. And if you need anything, you only have to ask.'

'Oh yes, Diane. Thank you. And if you need anything at all, just let me know.'

'Me?'

Olivia had turned to go, seeing as Diane seemed to be about to skid back across the lawn in her slippers, but the question stopped her.

'Yes. You know. If I can ever get you anything in town. Seeing as I work there.'

Diane nodded. She pulled her cardigan around her body.

'I don't go into town much now.'

'Don't you?'

'Not really. There doesn't seem much point. We've got all we want local. I sometimes see you going off really early, wrapped up in that mac of yours, and I think, poor Olivia. What a life. Cold bus stops. Nine to five. You know.'

'Yes. What a life!' Olivia smiled again and waited for Diane to be struck by lightning.

'Still.'

Something else occurred to Olivia as she contemplated Diane. She looked unhappy. She had her husband around her still, and he had always been a nice man, but she still looked unhappy.

'Well, give my regards to Paul next time you speak to him, won't you?' Olivia said. 'He was always such a nice boy.' It was a lie, but it didn't matter. She could still remember all the fuss when Louise had slapped him in the caravan. At the time, she'd been proud of her daughter although she hadn't let her know it. Somebody had to slap Paul Fisher, and she could never have done it herself. Diane scuffed the toe of her slipper on the grass.

'And you say hello to your girls from me.' Olivia noticed she didn't comment on how nice they'd been as children. Particularly Louise. She hid a smile. 'I'd better be off now.'

'Oh yes, I'd better get on too,' Diane said with sudden urgency. 'The hall needs doing. You just put it off, don't you? You've always been as houseproud as me, Olivia. We always understood each other there, didn't we? Home and family. They always came first. They always will, won't they?'

Olivia watched as Diane scooted away, stopping to remove her slippers and examine the bottoms carefully before putting them under her arm and disappearing back into her porch. Olivia turned back to her front door and let herself in. She stood in the hall and gazed around the small space. Did her hall need doing, she asked herself, standing quietly in the gloom and surveying it. Home and family. Doing the shopping local. The world was in danger of getting smaller. At her age, at her stage in life, the world should be getting smaller. This was what they were all saying.

'Oh rest ye, brother mariners, we will not wander more.'

She crossed the hall and sat on the stairs. Shaun had been quoting from his favourite poem all through their session together. That line had intrigued her, and she'd asked him to repeat it, over and over. Eventually, he'd sat back and recited as much of the poem as he could remember, but she was fairly sure that he improvised in certain places. It was one reason they'd been out for much longer than they'd intended. Poor Shaun. She'd held him up, and it was no wonder he'd shot away the moment he'd dropped her off. But he'd told her that the lines were from 'The Lotos-Eaters', and had gone on to talk about his love of Tennyson for a good fifteen minutes before they remembered that it was supposed to be a driving lesson.

She'd done 'The Lady of Shalott' at school, and for some reason, Shaun lapsing into poetry like that had re-awakened a longing she used to have for beautiful words. Bob had never really been moved by words. He used to like the songs she played on the piano and would sing along with the lyrics, but would get them wrong just to make her laugh. They used to play records to each other, too. If she ever pointed out a lovely line to him, he'd say, 'That's nice,' and really mean it, but he'd never have looked something up, or memorised a piece of poetry, let alone think to recite it to somebody else.

Olivia gazed around her spotless hall. Was this it, the land of the Lotos-Eaters? Was this the final resting place? It would be easy to stay, to be complacent, to refuse to wander from it. But when Shaun spoke of the land of the Lotos-Eaters, it was because it was somewhere he wanted to go, not somewhere he already was. And he'd said something about sunset-flushed mountains and dropping waterfalls which produced a picture in Olivia's mind so majestic that she'd felt strangely emotional. Wherever the sunset-flushed mountains were, Olivia knew for sure that they weren't in the suburbs of Tonbridge.

She pursed her lips. Through the wall she could hear the faint sound of Diane hoovering her immaculate hall.

She stood up again and laid the plastic bag containing the book on the hall table. She would look at it when she was in the mood to sit down. For now, she wanted to keep moving. She twitched her handbag back on to her shoulder. It was still early afternoon. She would get the bus into town now and do some of the things she'd promised herself, before she had the chance to talk herself out of it.

Louise wasn't imagining it. *Madame Butterfly* was blasting through her door. She'd been reading an article called 'One Step at a Time' and was so engrossed with guessing the age at which her baby would learn to walk that the noise had washed over her at first. The dilemma seemed to be whether baby bouncers perpetuated jumping reflexes or instilled confidence in small wobbly legs. She was still sitting on the fence over the issue when she caught herself trilling along to an aria. She'd stopped, looked up and realised that the aria was continuing without her.

She wandered to the door with the magazine in her hand. The music was so loud it had to be coming from the hall, but that wouldn't make any sense. She leaned against the door and listened hard. She stood back in shock. There was definitely a radio or cassette player at full volume out there. The landlord hadn't warned them about having workmen in, but it was taking things a bit too far. It was Saturday afternoon. If she'd been at work all week, she'd be very annoyed. She was annoyed anyway. She fumbled with the catch and yanked open the door, ready with a severely cross face and a stinging rebuke.

Harris was lying on the floor outside her door. Next to him was a portable cassette recorder. He was wearing Ray-Bans and had his arms comfortably tucked behind his head. He looked as if he was sunbathing. He inclined his head in her direction, and gave her a slow smile.

'Hello, gorgeous!' he said.

She was struck dumb. She stared at him while paralysis gripped her, the baby magazine dangling from her fingers.

271

He was in jeans. Black ones, and a tight black T-shirt. It showed off a sturdy torso and solid biceps, but then she already had graphic details of his physique branded on to her brain. His arms were bare and covered in goose-pimples, which was inevitable seeing as the hall was colder than an igloo.

'You stupid bugger!' she expelled at him. 'What the hell are you doing?'

'Serenading you.'

Her mouth flapped open and then closed. She decided just to look at him for a minute or two while she worked out what she was going to do about it. He seemed comfortable enough, and he obviously had no intention whatsoever of getting up, goose-pimples or not. He maintained his smile, and while she could only see her own reflection in his Ray-Bans, it was obvious he was looking her up and down.

'Harris,' she sighed at him, leaning against the door. 'I think it's time you and I had a little talk.'

'Talk?' He stretched his legs.

'Yes, I think so.'

'No, I don't think so. I don't think we should talk. I think we should make love.'

She thought about it even harder. She hadn't thought to make public pronouncements about her situation, but Harris did really seem to be intent upon conquering her. And she had a moment's pity for him as he lay there in the Arctic, pretending not to shiver under a thin layer of cotton. He could be proffering his genetic material all over the place. It was a waste of his time to be displaying it to her.

'Harris,' she sought for words. 'What have I ever done to deserve this?'

'You want me, too!' He grinned at her. 'You can't pretend you don't. You came up to my flat and practically threw yourself at me.'

'But—' With resignation she held open her flat door for him. 'Look, why don't you come in?'

'Sure.'

He sprang up as if he had been catapulted from the hall carpet, grabbed the cassette recorder and readied himself to enter her flat.

'To talk,' she clarified.

'If you say so.' He shrugged in reluctant agreement and she stood back to allow him in. He bounced past her and headed for the bedroom.

'In the kitchen!' she instructed loudly.

'Can't we talk in here?'

'No.'

She leaned into her bedroom, gave him a determined look, and marched on to her kitchen.

'Kitchen then.'

'And turn the music off. Lovely as it is, I can't think with it so loud.'

The music suddenly stopped. She draped herself over one of her kitchen chairs and waited for him to give up and join her. She still had the baby magazine gripped between her fingers. She tossed it across the table. She'd have to find a way to explain things to him that was tasteful. Waving a magazine in his face wasn't very subtle, and he had recently put a lot of effort into seducing her. A man had to maintain his pride. And Harris was an actor. His ego was a significant consideration. She braced herself.

'Harris?'

It had all gone very quiet. She hooked her hair behind her ears. He was still in her bedroom. Not asleep, surely? Or going through her knicker drawer? Surely not. She stood up and yelled.

'Harris! Get your pert butt into this kitchen right now, or I'll throw you out!'

She inched herself towards the bedroom as no response was forthcoming, dreading the worst. Not naked sprawled on the bed. Please, no. She jumped as he emerged from her bedroom just as she reached the open door. He was holding out the book of babies' names. She'd left it on the bedside table, having browsed through it once more before she'd fallen asleep the previous night. His fingers pinched the edge of the cover as if it was a used potty. His face was contorted, as if he was suffering an acute attack of dyspepsia.

'Give me that.' She snatched it from him. She stalked back into the kitchen and thumped it on the table, turning to him ready to put the situation straight once and for all.

With his other hand he proffered a pair of diminutive knitting needles which were gummed together by a wedge of yellow wool. The pair of booties that she'd attempted to create. She hadn't left them on the floor by the bed? Yes, evidently, she had. Together with the knitting pattern with the cutest baby in the universe on the front which he then produced for her and waved in her face. Paul Daniels would have been impressed. And by the meshing of his eyebrows and the dilation of his nostrils, she could tell that it was a deeply painful discovery for him. But it was his fault, wasn't it? Had she given him sufficient encouragement to warrant the distraught body language that he was displaying? She knew she hadn't.

'Look, Harris, none of this is really your business but I feel I should tell you that—'

She stopped. She couldn't really do anything else. He had whipped away his Ray-Bans and demonstrated to her clearly that he was crying. She staggered back against her kitchen table. Tears were dribbling profusely over his cheeks. It was difficult to know what to say.

'It's so beautiful,' he said in a choked voice, holding out her knitting.

274

'No, it isn't,' she said factually. Nobody could call a blob of yellow knots 'beautiful' even if they were inclined to overreact. She knitted in the way that bricks float.

'This!' he asserted, waving the cutest baby in the universe in her face.

'Oh, that. Yes, he's sweet, isn't he?'

'You!' he said, thrusting out an arm and pointing at her as if he was directing the traffic.

'Me?' That was pushing it too far. She'd never quite understood why she attracted male attention, but it wasn't because she was beautiful. 'No, I'm not.'

'Mother!' he announced.

'Oh I see what you mean.' That had been much easier than she thought. He'd got the point amazingly quickly. 'Yes. Me, mother.'

She frowned at herself. Me, mother. You, Tarzan. Who did she think she was talking to? King Kong? She smiled at him in a civilised way and started again. 'Yes, Harris, I'm expecting a baby, you see. It's all a bit of a surprise, but I'm very happy about it now it's happened. I probably should have told you before but I didn't feel I knew you that well and—'

She was silenced by Harris lunging at her. She tried to dodge him, but he'd obviously played rugby. He captured her in an embrace that winded her. She struck a rigid pose, mostly due to shock, but after several minutes had passed and he seemed in no immediate danger of releasing her she decided it was easier to relax and be cuddled instead. And his arms were warm, and it felt very nice to be hugged so strongly.

'Thanks,' she muttered throatily into his shoulder. He set her away from him and looked at her with dark, bleary eyes.

'God, it's overwhelming, Louise. I'm so happy for you. I'll look after you!' His announcement was so triumphant,

275

she didn't have the heart to explain that she was intending to look after herself. She patted his biceps.

'It's nice of you to think so, Harris.'

'I can give you anything you need,' he said without apparent fear of contradiction. 'All you have to do is ask. What a woman!'

He engulfed her again, giving her a fleeting glimpse of what it felt like to be a strand of bacteria smothered by a white corpuscle. Later, she would explain that she was actually fine. For now she allowed herself to sink against his chest, and just experience what it felt like to be pregnant and embraced by a man at the same time.

Chapter Fifteen

'It's so good to see you, Louise!'

Louise gave Jon a short smile which turned into a long smile. It was difficult not to be generous. There was nothing that he could say that would alter her feelings. She'd rung him and asked him if he'd like to meet at very short notice. He hadn't even pretended that he'd got something else planned, which was odd as it was Saturday night. He'd sounded pleased that she'd phoned him at all. So she'd dressed herself up, and this time she hadn't scalded herself in the shower, put lipstick on her chin or smudged her mascara. She'd even produced a co-ordinated outfit, a striking royal blue velvet shirt with a figure-hugging skirt to match. The whole process had been quite fluid, and she'd hummed her way through it, squirting a puff of Opium on each wrist, and smiling at her own radiant image before leaving the flat.

'You're looking good, Jon.'

'Thanks.' He flicked back his hair.

She'd chosen a bistro in Kensington which was light, airy and buzzing with activity. Jon had already been at the table when she'd arrived. Yet another inconsistency. Usually he made a point of being at least half an hour late. In the past he'd always let her feel as if he'd come from somewhere else to meet her, and was on his way to somewhere else afterwards. Tonight it almost felt as if she was at the top of his agenda.

He picked up the menu and ran his eyes over it. He was still a gorgeous-looking man, and she could see why she'd

fallen for him. He had a boisterous aura about him, a sort
of masculine energy combined with impishness. It
showed in the quirk of his lips, or just a slight sparkle in
his eyes. He was engaging, and it was why he was so at
home in sales. She dwelt on the gleaming chestnut
highlights in his hair. Would the baby have them? Would
his brown genes and her blonde ones be wrestling it out
down there? Or perhaps the baby would be more like her
father – bald and rugged. Or even like Jon's parents? That
was a thought. What the hell did they look like? She hadn't
got a clue. If she'd planned this she might have demanded
to see the family photo album in advance. What if they all
had Prince Charles ears and Jon had spent his childhood
having corrective surgery? She'd never thought to ask.
You wouldn't, under normal circumstances. She peered at
his skin closely for signs of scars.

'Lou? You're not even listening, are you?'

'Sorry?'

'I said, Chardonnay all right with you?'

'You don't usually check with me first,' she smiled
pleasantly. 'But I'll just have a weak spritzer, please.'

He gave her a teasing look.

'Your liver giving you gyp at long last?'

'I'm on a new regime. I've given up smoking, and I'm
down on drinking. I feel a thousand times better for it. You
should try it.'

Jon tried to ease the unlit cigarette in his hand
surreptitiously back into the packet.

'But you do what you want,' she continued airily. 'I'm
not out to convert you.'

'No, well, perhaps you're right. Perhaps it's about time I
thought about giving up anyway. Hell, why not? I'm going
to start a new regime, right now. It's all part of the new me.'

'Really?'

'Yep.' He surprised her by winking at her. 'You'll see

what I mean as the evening goes on, Louise. I've changed. I'm not the same person you used to know.'

Louise opened her menu while Jon ordered their drinks from a waiter who was sniffing with indifference as he took the order, and contemplated what a new Jon could be. Perhaps any minute now he was going to lean across the table intimately and ask her to call him Janet. The waiter departed, yelling their order across the restaurant. Jon leaned across the table intimately. She waited for him to speak with bated breath.

'So how did it go, Louise? Don't talk about it if it's too painful.'

She realised that the clawing of his fingers in her direction was an attempt to take her hand. She squashed her hands firmly into her lap.

'I'm not sure why you want to know. It's all over, as far as you're concerned.'

He sighed deeply. That wasn't one of his usual sales pitches. Sighing just wasn't his style. For a moment she thought he almost looked sad.

'I wish I'd handled it better,' he said. 'There were even times when I wished I'd persuaded you to keep it. Perhaps we could have made a go of it. It's been upsetting for me too. That baby was half mine, you know.'

She was speechless.

'Oh, I know what you're thinking. It's bloody arrogant of me to think I could have persuaded you one way or the other. And it is. I'm sorry. But sometimes these things just jump up and bite you. You don't plan them, you don't mean them to happen, but just like that,' he clicked his fingers, 'your life changes for ever.'

'I'm with you so far.'

'Well, my life has changed through this, even though it's been dealt with. It made me think about where I am, what I'm doing, what it's all about.'

The drinks arrived. She took a small sip of her spritzer while Jon went through the motions of trying the wine, savouring it, considering his decision carefully, and finally nodding to the waiter who rolled his eyes to the ceiling disdainfully before filling the glass and drifting away again.

'So, what are you saying?' she asked casually.

'I'm saying that if I could do it all over again, you meeting me in the pub, dropping your bombshell, me saying what I did . . .' He took a deep gulp of his wine and swallowed thoughtfully. 'I'd do it differently.'

'How, exactly?'

He looked at her squarely. It was the first time they'd made extended eye contact. She felt a shiver of guilt. Should she be telling him about the baby right now? But she was intrigued. She didn't want him to stop talking. Not just yet.

'I'd be more understanding,' he said. 'I'd ask you what you felt. And I think I'd have talked to you about marriage.'

Louise's glass thudded back on to the table. Her voice emerged as a whisper.

'Sorry?'

'Well, you know.' If she hadn't known Jon better she'd have thought he was blushing, but she'd never seen him blush before. He shifted in his chair, glancing quickly over his shoulder. He was only momentarily distracted by two women in thigh-length boots wandering past their table.

'You're not serious, Jon. Tell me you're not serious.'

'I don't know. It did make me think about it. I'm in my thirties now, so are you. Neither of us is getting any younger. We're that sort of age, aren't we? I mean, why do any two people get married anyway? What reason is there other than starting a family?'

'I did think there might be something about love squeezed in there somewhere.'

'Of course, of course. This is all coming out wrong.'

The waiter reappeared as Jon was settling into another long sigh. He sat up straight, rearranged his jacket and regarded the menu seriously. He put on a formal voice that was as new to her as everything else he was producing.

'Louise? Are you ready to order, or shall we tell him to go away for a few minutes?'

'You can *ask* 'im to go away, but you'll be bloody luck if ee comes back again.' The waiter smiled down at Jon without humour. 'It is Saturday night, sir.'

'I'm ready.' Louise pondered her menu once more. She settled on a first course and a hefty main dish, and placed her own order. The waiter gave her an ironically grateful look and scribbled it down. They both looked at Jon, who was staring blankly at Louise.

'You never have a starter!' he said.

'How do you know?' she asked pleasantly. 'Are you ready?'

Jon looked back to his menu, flustered. He ordered a main course for himself and flapped the menu closed.

'Thank you so much.' The waiter grimaced at them, gathered the menu and tutted loudly before sashaying away.

'This is so unlike you, Louise. Can you really get through all that?'

'You'd be surprised,' Louise said, picking at the edge of her bread roll and popping it into her mouth. 'I've been eating like a horse recently.'

Jon sipped his wine again, as if for sustenance.

'There's something about you, Louise. You've changed. No, it goes right back to the pub, when you told me about all this. You were – I don't know – odd. It wasn't how I thought you'd react.'

'Odd?'

'Calm. In control. Just different from how you usually are.'

'So I'm usually out of control, then?'

'No, I didn't mean that.' He laughed at her. 'But you're a bit chaotic. You know you are. It's charming. It's why I fell for you in the first place. But it's almost as if you've . . .' He stopped to choose a word.

'Grown up?'

'Well, something like that. It wasn't meant to be an insult, though.'

'Never mind.' Louise gazed around the restaurant idly. It was filling up. Plenty of couples, of groups, of friends out together. How many of them were pregnant, she wondered, eyeing the women curiously. She knew now that you couldn't tell.

'I just thought you'd be more upset. But you don't seem it. You don't seem flustered at all.'

She turned her attention back to Jon and tried to concentrate on what he was saying.

'Sorry?'

'And I think it's because you've got someone else.' Jon put his glass down, folded his arms, sat back in his chair, and gave her one of his direct stares. She stared back at him.

'Was that a question?'

'If you like. Louise, have you got somebody else?'

She considered for a moment, munching on another piece of bread roll. She frowned.

'I'm not sure I understand the question.'

'Somebody was snoring when I phoned you,' he said bluntly, raising an eyebrow at her.

'The thing is, Jon, it's the word "else" that's confusing me. That would assume I had somebody, and then had somebody else. Do you see what I mean?'

'Look, this is difficult enough.' He pursed his lips. 'I'm

really trying to be friendly here but you seem set on putting me down. Is there something you want to say to me? About Kelly? Is this about her? Because I can tell you, Louise, that's all over, and there's no point raking over dead ground. Is that what's bugging you?'

'Erm,' she tried to think. He'd slept with Kelly, the very single one in his office. But she'd always known that. She shook her head. 'Nope.'

Jon threw his hands into the air.

'Then I don't know what it is with you. You have got someone, haven't you?'

'And if I had someone, why would you have a problem with that?'

'Have you?'

'Have you got a problem with it?'

'So you have?'

'It's none of your business.'

'There was someone there in your bedroom when I phoned you. I need to know if it's important to you. Please tell me, Louise. Have you got someone else? Yes or no.'

She thought carefully about her answer. If she said no, he'd think she was free and waiting for him to make amends. If she said yes, it would be the first time he would have contemplated the concept of another man finding her attractive. She thought of the tiger lilies. Her get-well-soon present.

'Louise?'

'Yes, Jon. Yes, if you must know, I'm in love with somebody, and it's not you. All right?'

Jon blanched. Louise stopped munching on her bread roll and watched his face pale to the point of transparency. After a moment of inertia he fiddled with his chair and refilled his glass with wine. He pushed a hand through his hair. He stopped to pull a cigarette out of his packet, light

it and inhale deeply. He blew a ragged jet of smoke into
the air.

'Jesus,' he said finally. He rested his head on one hand
and tapped the end of the cigarette into the ashtray
without looking at her.

Her attention was gripped now. There was something
badly wrong with him. He was behaving out of character
in every possible way. Now he had dropped any sem-
blance of cool and was muttering to himself as he smoked
and drank heavily in front of her very eyes. It was as if
he'd forgotten she was there. She studied him until he'd
almost finished the bottle of wine. She leaned forward.

'Jon?'

He looked up at her with distant eyes.

'Hmmn?'

'You were saying something, weren't you?'

He scratched his head, as if he was genuinely having
problems remembering their conversation. His cheek
twitched.

'I don't think it's important now. Don't worry about it.'

'Talk to me. What's the problem?'

He sat up straight in his chair.

'That question is the problem. This is the problem, all of
it.'

'I don't understand.'

'No. You don't. Because I'm too late.' His voice was
unusually soft. It took her aback. 'It doesn't matter what I
do now, does it? That's why you're calm. It's because you
don't care about us any more. I mean, you *really* don't care
about us, it's not just an act.'

'I never did put on an act with you, Jon.'

'No, you didn't. It's what made things so good between
us, although I didn't realise it. You always talked straight.
I'm so surrounded by bluffers at work, and socially too,
and then there was you. My breath of fresh air.'

Her eyes widened. He shook his head again and let go of a long breath. 'And we did have some fantastic times, didn't we?'

She nibbled the inside of her lip, not daring to answer. Yes, they'd had some fantastic times. He was teasing the memories out of her. They made her feel odd, almost regretful, but that wasn't what she'd expected at all.

'And I thought I could put things right before it was too late,' he went on. 'But voilà. Too late.'

'Voilà!' echoed the waiter, bringing Louise's starter and placing it in front of her with a flourish. 'And sir would like another bottle of wine?'

'Why not?' said Jon without looking round.

'And a straw to drink it through, perhaps?'

The waiter grinned at Louise and was gone. Jon stood up and glared after him. Louise reached for his arm.

'Hey, Jon, sit down. This place has a reputation for rudeness. It's part of the entertainment. You must know that? That's why it's so popular.'

'Arsehole!' Jon sat down, hunching his shoulders. 'He'd better watch it, or we'll be out of here without paying the bill.'

'Calm down,' Louise said.

'Why should I be calm?' Jon drank heavily from his glass again. His voice was intense. 'It's a bloody mess, that's what it is. I've realised I'm in love with you, and you don't give a toss. For the first time in my whole life I've actually fallen in love with someone. God knows how it happened.'

'In love?' she gulped.

'Yes. With you! And your Dad's a brickie, for Christ's sake.'

'*Was* a brickie,' Louise corrected, stunned.

'My parents wouldn't even let me play with the council estate kids. God knows what they'd make of me falling in love with one.'

Jon emptied his glass, poured the remaining splash of wine from the bottle into it and drank it. 'But there you are. That's fate for you. That's the classless society. We all get a good education, we all live in London, we all meet, get drunk, and bonk. So you just don't know who you're going to fall in love with, do you? I mean, you can't plan it like they used to.'

Louise sat very still. She wasn't surprised by what he was saying. She'd heard him say similar things before, but not aimed at her.

'It's all a big jumble now.' Jon sniffed and looked over his shoulder. 'Where's that other bottle of wine?' He looked back to Louise's plate. 'God, sorry. Do eat, won't you. Don't mind me. I'll just have another fag.'

He lit up again, and Louise saw that his fingers were shaking.

'The thing is, Louise, I've never been in love with anybody before.'

'So you said,' she whispered. Her food stayed on the plate, untouched.

'I can't sleep, I can't eat, I'm drinking and smoking too much.' He gave her a whimsical smile. 'It's so corny, it makes you want to stick your fingers down your throat. At least, that's what I always said. That's because I've been immune before. Right up until now.'

Louise swallowed.

'It's a shock.' He blinked his eyes wide open. No more than a few weeks ago she'd have been crawling under the table with pleasure to receive such a look. It would have been a shade of his intentions towards her. But now there were no shadows, only spotlights. It was interesting to see what was revealed. He'd made comments about her family and her background that she wasn't prepared to hear. Not from anybody.

'Jon, I think I'm going to go.' She took her napkin from

her lap, folded it and placed it on the table.

'You can't go,' he said flatly.

'Yes, I can.'

'No, you can't. We haven't finished our meal.'

'Jon, if I want to go I'll just walk out of here. That's the way it is these days.'

'I don't want you to. Please don't. Not yet. I haven't explained anything properly. God, Louise, what I'm trying to say is that all the things I thought I wanted were crap. I mean all that stuff about moving up in the world was bollocks. I didn't realise what I really wanted until I didn't have it. You say you're in love with somebody else, but at least hear me out. We were together for over a year, weren't we? I mean, I was around when your father died, wasn't I? That was pretty heavy stuff.'

She had known Jon then. He'd comforted her with a couple of answerphone messages explaining that he was working late, but was thinking of her. The good times they'd had were in pubs, restaurants or in bed, not when she'd needed him.

'What I'm saying is we have a history. You can't have built up that sort of relationship with somebody in the last couple of weeks. I just want you to hear me out. Please?'

His eyes were shining at her pleadingly. Could it possibly be that he had been profoundly moved by what had happened? Really? It had changed the way she saw her own life utterly and completely. Was she being arrogant to assume that it might not have had a similar effect on him?

'All right.' She sat still again and waited. The occupants of the tables nearest to them were glancing over. He wasn't aware that his raised voice was attracting attention. 'What do you want to say, Jon?'

'I want to say this.' He reached out for her hand. Reluctantly, she extended it for him. He clutched it in his.

His palms were warm and damp. 'Louise, I'm sorry. I'm so bloody sorry for everything. I've been a total bastard.'

She swallowed. He had tears welling in his eyes. He seemed to have lost all ability to control himself.

'Louise, I love you. I *love* you, don't you see? You're not like anybody else. You're unusual. You're funny. You're honest. You're a complete loony. But I've seen a new side of you these last few weeks. You've got dignity, you've got self-respect. I didn't understand that before, but now I do. Now all those others, Kelly, Matty, Helen, they're all irrelevant.'

'Matty and Helen?' Louise's eyes stretched open. Her hand was caught fast.

'And so,' Jon continued with determination. 'I'm going to give you this. Throw it in my face if you must, but I came here intending to give it to you, and I am going to give it to you. Then you can leave if you want. No, hold still.'

She watched, mesmerised, as he fumbled with one hand in his jacket pocket whilst maintaining a secure hold on her with the other.

'No, don't pull away. Because look!'

Shock pelted through her at breakneck speed as Jon produced a small velvet box and placed it in front of her. She could see their neighbours peering over with interest.

'See?' Jon went on, tightening his grip on her hand so that she couldn't even wiggle her fingers. 'And look what's in here.'

He flipped open the box and showed her the ring. It was a solitaire. Tasteful, discreet, probably quite expensive. She lost the power of her muscles. Her hand became limp in his.

'But I thought you said . . .' She was inaudible. She could still see tears in his eyes. She felt an answering swell.

'Louise, I know I've been a sod, but I've realised that I

love you. And,' his voice broke, 'I came here intending to ask you to marry me. So I'm going to do it. Will you marry me?'

Louise sat motionless while the world kaleidoscoped around her. Around them people were watching eagerly. She couldn't take her eyes from Jon's. His stayed firmly fixed on hers, drilling into her, demanding forgiveness.

He'd asked her to marry him, even though he thought she was no longer having his baby. He thought that he loved her. There was no other reason. He sat opposite her, his soul bared in his eyes, the father of the baby she was having.

'Louise?' he mouthed at her across the table.

The whole restaurant was hushed, waiting for her response. She dropped her head so that she didn't have to look at the desperation in Jon's face. The tense silence around them was shattered. She looked up sharply and realised that her action had been taken as a nod. Saturday night exuberance crashed in on them as people laughed with relief and glasses chinked. Someone clapped.

Jon slipped the ring on to her finger. He gave a disbelieving laugh. He stood up, reached over the table, pulled her up into his arms and smacked a kiss on her lips.

Should she patronise him? Reason with him? Hit him? By now their audience was too enthusiastic to be disappointed. She tried to smile at him. This was no time to talk anything through. The momentum had overtaken them.

'Yay! She's happy!' somebody yelled.

'You've never proposed to me,' a male voice muttered.

'Well, smell you, sweetie!' another male voice parried.

Jon let her go. She plopped back into her seat.

'She said yes!' Jon turned round and threw his arms out to his audience. Louise watched him perform. Something profound had happened, but she wasn't sure what it was.

She could even feel tears on her cheeks. She was vaguely aware of the waiter bustling through to stand by her elbow.

'Congratulations, madam. Would you like a glass of champagne, or a valium. Either way, it's on the 'ouse.'

Olivia stood at the back door, peering out at the garden. It was black outside, and when she readjusted her eyes she saw only her own reflection in the smooth sheet of glass. She took a step back. Was that really what she looked like?

She smiled at herself as an experiment. Her own indistinct image was ten years younger, the rebounding light unable to capture every worry-line on her face. It was very satisfying. Her eyes looked bright and almost pretty again. She'd been thought of as very pretty when she was much younger. Like Louise. She was lovely, although she'd never seemed to be conscious of whether she was or not. She had more in common with her youngest daughter than Louise could imagine. They had both become adrift, gone off the rails, at some point in their young adult lives. The thought made her turn away from her reflection, almost as if to stare at it any longer while thinking such thoughts would will upon Louise the same destiny that she had found herself.

She poured herself a glass of wine and sat at the kitchen table with it, pondering the plastic bag taped around Shaun's present. It was silly to have put off opening it for so long but she liked to have something to look forward to at the end of the evening. A glass of wine at a certain time, the news, a phone call to Louise or Rachel, perhaps.

She pulled the bag towards her and unstrapped the plastic folds. She peered inside and removed the dusty-looking book. It was blue, a lighter, faded blue around the edges as if it had been exposed to the sun. She turned it over in her hands to read the spine. The gold print read *Tennyson's Poems*.

She stared at the book, confused. She couldn't understand why she'd assumed the book would be something else. *Russell Grant on Astrology*, or a collection of *Learning to Drive* jokes. The thing that was so surprising was that it was only today, out in the car earlier on, that she'd told Shaun she liked him quoting Tennyson. But he'd come to meet her today with the book already wrapped and ready to give her. How could he have known?

She opened the cover and a note slipped out. She unfolded it, and tried to read his looped scrawl.

'Dear Olivia, I bope you enyoy these. I bave put a blip of paa-per in a coulple of palaces – places for you. But it's op to yov to see what you hike. No, like. With Shergar. Shergar? *Regards*. Shaun.'

She took another sip of wine and laid his note on the smooth surface of the table. It was well creased and soft as if he'd pondered over it for some time. It was a blast of humanity laid against a cold veneer. Something stirred inside her.

She got up, walked under the plaster arch that Bob had built which led into the living room, and aimed for the stereo. That stereo hadn't been touched for so long. Once it had become clear that he was ill neither of them had wanted to hear music, and nothing had been played on it since. She squatted down on her haunches and opened the smoky glass front to the unit. Louise and Rachel had both laughed at it. Louise said she could take it along to the Antiques Roadshow in a couple of years, but only the old stereo would play the records she and Bob had collected. She thumbed through the edges of the album sleeves and slid out the Mamas and the Papas. She set the record deck to play on thirty-three, and carefully looked over the list of tracks. Reading the titles again after all this time set the pit of her stomach fluttering, but she had to do it. She laid the record flat and guided the needle over to the track she wanted to hear. The speakers crackled as they were awakened from sleep. She walked back to the kitchen and picked up her glass of wine.

Olivia wandered over to the back door again with her glass. Her reflection forced her back in. But there was a world out there concealed by the blackness. She didn't want to be forced back inside her small house. If she could go out there in the cold and dark and stand in the garden, it would prove it. She twisted the key in the door as the track began to play its stirring introduction.

It had been their song, if it was ever possible for them to have a song seeing as they never courted in the way that other couples did. But later, once they were married, and once they had realised that there was love between them, it had become their song. It still was. Olivia opened the back door and stepped out on to the even paving stones of the patio. The haunting melody of 'Dedicated to the One I Love' floated out to her.

She gazed around the garden trying to adjust to the darkness while she stood in the arc of light cast by the kitchen. Still, she thought, I stay within safe boundaries. She wandered to the edge of the patio and dipped a toe on to the damp grass. And what if she were to walk all over the grass, wet as it was, in the middle of the night, with the stereo blasting, and with the kitchen door wide open? Just what would everybody think? Diane's bedroom looked over the back. She might well see Olivia flitting around with a glass of wine. She'd assume the doctor had put her on happy pills.

She threw her head back and gazed right up into the night. The clouds had cleared. It sent a cold rush of excitement over her. She could see the stars! And there was a moon, a crescent moon.

Her exhalations coming in white streams, she rolled her head back as far as it would go. And this sky, these stars, this moon, were being seen all over the world. All she had to do was become like one of the stars, then she could shine down wherever she wanted.

She took another glug of her wine and began to spin around, her arms outstretched, very slowly, with the crescent moon as her focus. The song dug like a trowel into her chest. She had to endure it.

She saw the light go on in Diane's bathroom. The blind was pulled down huffily. Olivia stopped spinning. She heard a loud cough from behind the blind. She heard the blast of the tap and the clink of Diane using a bottle of something as her nightly routine. It was no use trying to pretend she was a star when her neighbour was gargling so loudly.

She walked back up the garden and into the house. She closed the door firmly behind her. She went back to the table, sat down and pulled Shaun's note and the book towards her. She opened it at one of the pages he had marked. He had put a pencil scribble in the margin to show that he wanted her to read a verse of a poem. She glanced at the title of the poem. 'In Memoriam'. Her pulse slowed. She read.

> I sometimes hold it half a sin
> To put in words the grief I feel;
> For words, like Nature, half reveal
> And half conceal the Soul within.

'My God,' she uttered, throwing the book down on the table. Shaun's note had fluttered to the floor. The Mamas and the Papas had gone on to sing a rock song. What did Shaun think he was doing, for God's sake? Did he think that she thought it would be sinful to talk about her grief?

Did he think she *should* talk about it? What did he mean, and what did it have to do with him? This was the second time he'd trespassed on territory which was very private.

She sat still as the album played to its conclusion. So, it seemed, she thought finally, as she left Shaun's book on the table where it had been flung and made her way up to bed, her slippers mesmerising her with each step, it was still impossible for her to cry for Bob. She'd played the song that would have made it happen if anything could, and still nothing. She undressed and thought of all her new ideas. She climbed into bed and curled up under the covers. But it was a blessing that she couldn't cry, because if she did, all of her plans would probably come crashing down around her ears.

Chapter Sixteen

'Good God!' Louise stooped to pick up the bouquet of roses as she fumbled with the key to her flat door. Jon collapsed against the wall beside her. She led them both into the flat, wandering through to her kitchen to examine them in the light. A dozen red roses left outside her door. Her heart flipped over as she found a small card. Ash? Could it be?

'From your other boyfriend?' Jon asked behind her back.

'God, no!' She laughed edgily. 'I expect they're from . . .' She fumbled with the envelope and pulled out a message. 'Harris.' She shouldn't feel so disappointed. It was a lovely gesture. So thoughtful of him.

'Harris? Not the luvvy who lives upstairs?'

And where would she put them now? She'd used the bucket for the tiger lilies. She ignored Jon and began a search of her cupboards for something elegant enough to stand a dozen roses in. There was a measuring jug. It wasn't very pretty, but it would have to do. She arranged them calmly, giving herself time to think. It had been the obvious thing to do, to invite Jon back to her flat. They weren't going to be able to talk in the restaurant after he had swallowed his second bottle of wine. Outside, he'd hailed them a cab and insisted on paying. All the way home he'd clutched her hand and exchanged mother-in-law jokes with the cab driver. It hadn't seemed to matter that Louise herself was unable to speak. She plucked and poked at the roses, but they insisted on trying to fall out of the jug. Eventually she propped them against the wall and turned round purposefully.

'Jon, we need to talk.'

'Certainly, my dear. Once I've found your brandy.'

Louise leaned back against the kitchen table and turned her hand over slowly. The solitaire glinted under the harsh strip-light. She twisted it round until the stone had disappeared and all she could see was a thin gold band around her finger. Her wedding-ring finger. She wrenched the ring round again. It felt odd. Jon didn't know who he was asking to marry him. She pulled at the ring until it was halfway off her finger.

'Where is that bottle?' Jon reappeared and leaned against the door-frame. He grinned at her lopsidedly. 'You can't have guzzled the whole lot. There must be alcohol somewhere in this flat. There always is.'

She slid the ring back into place. They must talk, first.

'It was Sally. She was on a bit of a bender when she came round. She pretty much cleaned me out of booze.'

'Sally?' He straightened his face and raised his eyebrows. 'What was she doing here?'

'She's my friend. Why shouldn't she be here? She needed to talk about something.'

'Really?' His eyebrows seemed to crawl even higher. 'Bitching about me, were you?'

Louise decided not to answer. He ambled back into the kitchen and yanked open her fridge door.

'Don't answer that if you don't want to. I'll have a beer then. Blimey, no beer and only half an inch of wine. And food everywhere. You really are serious about changing your lifestyle, aren't you?' He pulled out the nearly empty wine bottle and tipped the contents into a glass. His eyes roamed her kitchen and rested on the drooping heads of the tiger lilies hanging out of the plastic bucket on the floor. He frowned. 'Not a very prominent place to display them, Lou.' He focused on the roses on the table, to make a point.

But then, she wanted to say, the tiger lilies were to congratulate her on her termination, whereas the roses were to congratulate her on her pregnancy.

'Jon, I need to tell you something.'

He pulled out a chair and draped himself over it, loosening the collar of his shirt. It made him look rakish. She felt a reluctant stir of attraction.

'You'd better tell me all about you and Harris, hadn't you?' he said.

'What? He's a neighbour, nothing else.' Jon strained his eyebrows disbelievingly. 'He saw me looking a bit down the other day. The flowers must be to cheer me up. We've got to know each other quite well.' The eyebrows were starting to irritate her. 'Well, it's just as bloody well I've had some friends, Jon, seeing as you disappeared like a rat down a sewer.'

'Okay.' He smiled instead. 'In which case, you'd better tell me about the guy you thought you were in love with. That way we can wipe the slate clean and start afresh. It's the only way, Lou.'

Louise slowly sat down on a chair and faced him across the table.

'It's not about anybody else. It's about me. There's something you should know, something I didn't have a chance to tell you in the restaurant.'

'Blimey, you're not pregnant, are you?'

He stretched his eyes in fake horror, then collapsed into giggles, his glass to his lips.

'Sorry, Louise. I couldn't help it. It's just the look on your face.' She stared back at him solemnly and he buried his smile quickly. He sat up more elegantly and crossed one leg over the other. 'I'm really sorry. That wasn't funny. Not after what you've been through. I just thought laughing might do you good. You look as if you haven't had a good laugh in a while.'

She let him squirm. In fact, she had laughed a lot recently. With Sally, with Ash, even with Harris. He'd suggested she call the baby either Gordon or Wendy, after his parents. That had made her laugh. Jon rubbed at his face uncomfortably.

'No, I really am sorry. You see, I have changed, Louise, and I'm sure you have too. It's been a very maturing experience. I'm sure it's been twice as profound for you, especially at your age. You must be wondering if that was your only chance. Don't mind if I smoke, do you?'

It didn't surprise her that his vow to give up smoking had been forgotten. That was Jon.

'Actually, I'd rather you—' He had already lit his cigarette and was rifling through the scattered papers on her table. 'What are you doing?'

'Looking for an ashtray.' He stopped as he picked up a leaflet. He squinted at it. Her pulse began to thud quietly in her ears. 'What's this?'

'Just some details.' She leaned over and took the leaflet from his fingers.

'Jesus, Louise. You don't want to cling on to all this stuff. It's morbid. You should throw it all out now.'

She stood up and looked into his eyes. They were sad. Genuinely sad. He slipped one arm around her waist.

'Hey, come here.'

'I'm going to make some coffee.'

'Hey!' His eyes smiled at her. 'Come and sit on my knee. Coffee can wait. And don't give me that look, I know sex is out of the question. I just want to hold you. I need this all to sink in.' He chuckled again. 'Show me that ring again.'

He pulled her on to his lap and reached out for her hand. She looked down too. Her hand in his, the engagement

298

ring binding them together. Except that the ring was only a trinket. It could be taken off, flung into a distant garden, flushed down the toilet, hurled into a skip. The thing that bound them together was growing inside her, and was going to last a lifetime.

'Jon, I'm still pregnant,' she said, freezing into position on his lap like a garden gnome perching on the edge of an ornamental pond. She felt his muscles tighten under her.

There was a long silence. She tried to get up, only to find that his arm was still clamped around her waist. A column of ash fell from his unsmoked cigarette and scattered on the lino.

'Say that again,' he said quietly.

'I—' She swallowed. She was not going to apologise. Not to him. Not to anybody. 'I'm still pregnant. I haven't had a termination.'

He cleared his throat. He still seemed unwilling to release her from his lap.

'And – you're saying that it hasn't happened *yet*, or what?'

'It's not going to happen. I'm going to have the baby.'

His arm dropped from her waist. She glanced at him quickly. He seemed deluged with his own thoughts. She got up and busied herself with making a mug of coffee. She couldn't turn round and look at him. Not just yet. It was too much to face the man who had just found out that he was really going to be a father, not just for the next five minutes, but for ever and ever until he keeled over and died. Even after he'd died, in fact. Her father was still her father, scattered over the Weald of Kent as he was.

'I, um . . .' She stirred the coffee frantically, words piling in on her. 'I was going to tell you, at the right time. But there hasn't been a right time yet.'

'When did you decide on this?' he asked. She dragged herself away from the collage of past and future and back to the present. She pretended to be preoccupied with refilling the sugar bowl.

'Er, a little while ago. Not immediately. I wasn't sure what I was going to do at first.'

'And you're sure about this? Or are you going to change your mind again in another couple of days?' She swung round on him. 'I only ask that, Louise, because you're turning my fucking head inside out.'

She watched him, her pulse thumping. His head. His life. His feelings. What about hers?

'I'm going to have the baby, Jon. It's my decision, and I'm happy about it. I'm not asking you to be happy. I'm just telling you what's going to happen. You can have as much access as you like after the baby's born.' She paused and added, 'If you want it, that is.'

He looked up at her, his eyes showing surprise again. For over a year, she'd been quite unable to surprise him with anything she did. She'd tried so hard. She'd strained until she'd gone blue to be enigmatic. Tonight, it was on the hour, every hour. She almost felt sorry for him.

'You were planning to do this on your own, then?'

'Of course. There's no need for you to be involved. You're still a free agent.'

He stared at her open-mouthed. Well, what did he expect? Tears? Recriminations? Tiger lilies rammed down his throat? She was in control of her situation. There was no need to make him eat his flowers. She found him an ashtray and slipped it on to the table beside him, sitting down with her coffee.

'I expect you'll want this back.' She twisted the ring from her finger and laid it on the table top. 'I didn't actually say yes, you know. It was all too fast, too sudden. I think you misinterpreted me.'

He dropped his eyes to stare at the ring. His mouth still hung open in concentration. He looked like Ronnie

O'Sullivan taking aim with the snooker cue. A dashing figure, too dashing to be bogged down by everyday concerns, except when his arse was on the line.

'I, um, I'm very flattered you asked me, Jon, but a restaurant wasn't a very private place to talk things through, was it? Not in view of what's been happening.' She felt she should say something else. 'I'm sorry this is a shock for you. I wasn't expecting to see you again so soon. I certainly wasn't expecting you to propose.'

He chewed on his lip. She was starting to feel very uncomfortable. It was completely unlike him to be silent for so long. Banter was the tool of his trade, and he was good at it. It had been what had brought them together.

'So I—'

'The baby's going to need a father around, Louise,' he said slowly, breaking his silence. 'You know how important that is. Look at the relationship you had with your own father.'

It wasn't what she expected him to say. By now there should be skid marks on the lino where he'd sprinted for the door. But he was still there, and he looked remarkably sober all of a sudden.

'This isn't an ideal world,' she said.

'No, but we can do our best for the child, can't we?'

'I always intended to do that, from the moment I made my decision. It's my priority now. Anything else is going to come second.'

'Like a man?'

She gave him a sharp look.

'If necessary, yes. That depends on the man.'

'I see.' Jon's crossed leg was bouncing, his brown DMs twitching. 'So you're making way for this other bloke then, are you?'

'Other bloke?' She gripped her mug. 'What do you mean?'

301

'Bloody short memory you've got,' he said. 'You are quite sure I am the father, I suppose? You don't seem to be able to remember the men in your life from one week to the next.'

'What?'

'There was Andrew at work. He always had the hots for you. And greasepaint features upstairs who sends you roses. And some other bloke, too, that you don't want to talk about.'

'What the hell—'

'Or are you going to shave your head and get a set of dungarees and bring it up in a teepee? With a big sign outside. "No penises allowed."'

She thumped her mug down in anger.

'Just bear with me, Louise. I'm not being the sod you think.' He stood up suddenly and walked over to her window. He flicked up the roller blind. It left their reflections staring back.

'What did you do that for?'

He heaved a breath. 'I needed to have control over something. I've always hated that blind. It's the crimson daisies on it that have always annoyed me. You just don't get crimson daisies. They don't exist. It always really bugged me that someone would be spaced out enough to think they'd be a good idea for a blind.'

'I never thought you paid so much attention to my soft furnishings.' Louise looked at him curiously. 'I didn't think you noticed anything about this place.'

'You'd be amazed at what I notice.'

'Oh yes? Like what?'

'Well, you've had a bloody great spring-clean since I was last here. All the fluff's gone from the skirting-boards, the big pile of newspapers has disappeared from the bedroom and there are no cobwebs. The sheet music's been put in a neat pile on the piano. And you've got an oversized torture implement in your living room.'

'The candelabra, you mean?'

'That's what they told you, was it?' He shook his head at her. 'Salesman's dream, you are. *The Moor's Last Sigh*'s still by the bed. You've still only got to chapter three, but you don't want to give up. And you only really keep it by the bed because it hides the book on compatible star signs under it. You consult that one regularly.'

'I don't!' she protested.

'Yes, you do. And you've got an odd fetish for wicker. A wicker basket, wicker little shelves and things. A pot from Corfu with your toothbrush and toothpaste in it, and a mat you bought from Oxfam.'

'Jon . . .' Louise pushed back her hair. She had to think and tiredness was engulfing her. 'What's all this about? Where's this leading?'

'I think what I'm saying is that I still want to be with you,' he said. He walked over to the table and carefully picked up the delicate gold ring that was lying there. He turned it over under the light. 'This is so typical of me, isn't it?' He gave a disparaging laugh. 'I go charging in with fanfares and banners, and all the time I could have been talking to you, putting things right. It didn't need this, did it?'

She felt oddly moved by his behaviour. He took the ring and slid it back into the small velvet box. It snapped shut. He tucked it away inside the pocket of his jacket. 'Maybe another time.'

'Yes. Maybe,' she said.

'Lou?' he began hesitantly. 'Do you think I could stay here tonight, with you? It's just – I don't want to go.'

She watched him scratching his chin, shifting awkwardly as he waited for her response. It was a different Jon she was seeing now. One he had hidden from her in all the time that they had been together. If only this was the real Jon. There was only one way to find out.

'Stay tonight, Jon,' she said. 'If we're going to get to know each other, we might as well start now.'

Rachel smiled as she heard the front door banging.

'In here!' she called from the study.

Hallam had asked her that morning if she'd mind him taking the boys out to McDonald's for Sunday lunch. When she'd protested about their going out without her for the second day running, he'd explained that he was worried about Ricky. It was the first she'd heard of it. Apparently, Anne was concerned that Ricky was becoming confused about his maternal role model, or some such psycho-babble. He was too quiet at school, and was having nightmares. Rachel had pointed out to Hallam that he didn't have nightmares when he stayed with them, and she suggested that it was seeing Anne's face looming up to him for a goodnight kiss that set him off. Hallam hadn't laughed. He'd asked for her understanding, and requested politely to be allowed to take his own children out on his own. They hadn't rowed about it. They never did row. But Hallam was surprisingly firm. As he'd left, he'd commented that it would give her time to make a few private calls.

Ricky came racing into the study. Rachel hopped away from the computer.

'Tum-tum-TARA!' She flung her hand out to indicate the boxed game which she had wrapped and placed next to it. Ricky's eyes opened wide.

'Another one!' he breathed.

Glen piled into the room, pulling Hallam after him. They were both laughing.

'Now!' Glen was begging. 'Please, can I put it on NOW!'

'All right, all right, you persistent little bugger. You can play it now, but you'd better make sure Rachel doesn't need the computer to work on this afternoon.'

Rachel absorbed the scene around her. Glen was swinging a plastic Virgin Megastore bag from his hands, Ricky was still gawping at the wrapped present Rachel had left on the desk. Hallam smiled at her briefly.

'Hi, Rach. Get much done?'

'I'm not working this afternoon,' she said, failing to keep the irritation from her voice. 'I told you that this morning. I thought we could all play a computer game. In fact, I thought that's what we'd planned.'

'We *are* going to play a computer game.' Glen glanced at her as he edged his way on to the chair and pulled a box from the red bag. 'A brilliant one. Dad's bought it for us.'

'Yes. Brilliant.' Ricky slid on to the chair next to Glen and tried to elbow him along the seat.

Rachel stared at the game that Hallam had bought as Glen pulled off the lid and emptied the contents on to the desk. He pushed the instructions to one side and grabbed the CD, slotting it into the computer.

'Shouldn't take long to load,' he said, his eyes stuck to the screen.

Bitterness swelled inside Rachel. It was a strange mixture of unreleased sorrow and anger. Hallam was leaning over Glen's shoulder, squinting at the screen as the loading information appeared. His eyes fell on Rachel's present.

'Hello, what's this?'

'It's nothing,' Rachel snapped, thrusting herself forward and yanking the box out of sight.

'Rachel?' Hallam stood up and gave her a quizzical look.

'It's fucking nothing, okay?' she shouted at him. She stared at Hallam venomously, gritting her teeth together, not daring to open her mouth again. There was a long, deathly silence. Ricky was gazing up at her in something like awe. Even Glen had taken his eyes off the screen, and was watching Hallam for a reaction. There was none.

'Dad?' Glen whispered. 'She said "fuck".'

Rachel fought with her angry tears. She had to maintain control, for Ricky's sake, if nobody else's. Ricky tapped her leg, and slipped his hand into hers.

'It's all right, Rachel,' he said, his eyes luminous. 'We can play your game too.'

'Oh—'

Something inside her broke down. She gave a wrenching sob and fled from the room. She raced up the stairs, not daring to stop or look round. She hurled herself into the bedroom and on to the bed, the present gripped in her hand. She hammered it against the duvet, wishing it was a mallet and the duvet was Hallam's skull.

'You bastard. You bastard. You bastard!'

She gave up and buried her face in the cotton. The smell of lavender teased her nostrils. It made her cry with greater anger. The door to the bedroom clicked shut. She stiffened. Hallam was standing there behind her, watching. She could feel it.

'Am I the bastard?' he asked quietly.

She took several ragged breaths before sitting up sharply and flinging the box across the room at him. It bounced off his head and into the laundry basket. He looked confused for a moment, then rubbed at his forehead.

'I'll take that as a yes, shall I?' he asked.

She hauled herself up and marched around the room, her fists clenched.

'I bought that same bloody game for them. It was meant to be a surprise. I wanted to show them that I'd listened to them, that I knew what they liked. I was showing that I cared, don't you see? And you *ruined* it!' She glared at him, unable to stop pacing.

'Why didn't you tell me?' he asked.

She stared at him incredulously. She tried to control her breathing, and lowered her voice to seethe at him instead.

'Because then it wouldn't have been a bloody surprise, would it?'

'I see,' he said, leaning back against the door. 'Now I know what the problem is.'

'Don't . . .' She shook her head in frustration. 'Just don't make me feel stupid.'

'I'm not trying to,' he replied, meeting her fiery stare. 'I thought you might be tired, that's all.'

'I'm not sodding tired!' She began to cry again.

'No?' He inclined his head. 'And yet you got so little sleep on Friday night.'

She stopped pacing and looked at him. He turned and let himself out of the bedroom, pulling the door quietly closed behind him. She heard his footsteps on the stairs, and his voice rising from the study as he joined the boys again.

She thumped her fist against the closed door.

'So why don't you bloody well ask me about Friday night then?' she issued into the white gloss, thumping the door again for good measure.

'Ash!' Louise was unable to stop her delighted grin from spreading to her ears. 'What are you doing here?'

It was a fair question, seeing as she was in Totz baby shop.

But it was just so wonderful to see him that she couldn't disguise it. He was in his denim jacket, his jeans and his thick black jumper. His hair was in more disarray than usual. It looked as if he'd been teasing the strands mercilessly with his fingers. He was looking more and more like Bjork every time she saw him.

'I, um . . .' A flush touched his cheeks. He lowered his

eyes and fingered a small teddy bear he was clutching. 'You've caught me out, haven't you?'

'Buying teddy bears? Certainly looks like it. What is it, band mascot or something?'

'Oh, no, not really.' He fiddled with the bear, twisting it around by the ears. 'What do you think of this one? Is it cute, or does it look like a psychopath? I can't decide.'

He twirled it at her with such agitation that it pinged out of his hands. She caught it deftly and examined it.

'Psychopath.'

'Good. That's what I thought. I prefer the bunnies really, but they're more expensive.'

'The bunnies?'

'The blue and white ones, over there.' He pointed over to a counter of soft toys.

She folded her arms and gave him a firm look.

'Just how long have you been in here?'

He glanced at his watch, raising his eyebrows.

'Blimey, nearly an hour now. Time flies when you're in your local supplier of baby goods, doesn't it?' He smiled at her suddenly, and she felt as if summer had arrived. 'So, how are you keeping? Did you get back from the gig okay? I came to look for you, but you'd gone.'

'I'm sorry about that. I had a sudden attack of tiredness.'

'But I'd have made sure you got home. We could have dropped you off in the van.'

'No, no, Sally came home with me and stayed over. I was well looked after, thanks.' His concern touched her.

'So, um.'

'Right.'

They spoke at the same time. He grinned at her. 'Go on, you first.'

'I just wondered if Rachel had been in touch with you?'

He took the bear from her fingers and began to fiddle with it again. She watched with concern. If he wasn't careful, the ear was going to come right off.

'Well, you can't expect her to be seriously in: ˙rested in us, can you? It was a bit of a fucking fiasco.'

'Oh.' She was disappointed, but it was as she'd feared. She clenched her fingers inside her gloves, trying to think of something to say that would stop him from running away. Dwelling on his blown opportunity wasn't the best tactic. He looked awkward as he stood in front of her as it was. And what was he doing in Totz anyway? She was itching to ask. She could even dare to hope that the reply might have something to do with her. But then again, if she and Jon were going to try to forge a relationship, she shouldn't be hoping anything of the sort. She should be telling him right now that Jon had stayed at her flat for the weekend and that he was planning to drop by several evenings in the week. It was the way they'd agreed to start things off. But when she opened her mouth, what she said had nothing to do with Jon.

'I came to look at prams.'

'I'm not rushing off if you want a second opinion.'

'Would you mind? I know it's early days, but I just thought I'd check them out.'

They wandered over to the selection of prams. Louise fingered the handles and squinted at them.

'Hey, this one's cool.' Ash pulled out a light buggy and fiddled with a series of levers. 'Folds down into a sofa-bed. You can put all your friends up too. Plenty of room for your shopping.' He squatted down and patted the tray beneath. 'You can fill this up and use it as a paddling pool when the baby gets older. Handy slot attachment on the side.' He put his hands on his hips and stared at it. 'God knows what for.'

'Hair dryer?'

'Must be. All you need is go-fast stripes and alloy wheels.'

'No way!' she laughed at him. 'And no furry dice.'

'Not even a *Feu-orange* hanging from the hood?'

'Nope.'

Louise nearly fainted as she turned over the price tag. She dragged Ash down the line of prams towards the budget range.

'Let's just forget about being flash for the moment. There. What's wrong with this one?'

'It's okay, I suppose.' Ash looked unimpressed. 'Bit difficult to tell without a baby in it.' He put the bear on to the mattress and looked at it from all angles. 'Well, it fits teddy, but I think your baby's going to be a bit bigger than that when he arrives.'

Louise fell into thought while Ash put the bear into a number of different poses to check out the features of the pram. It was stupid of her even to look at bottom-of-the-range baby products while she still had no reliable income. She watched for a while longer until the assistant came up to them with a forced smile and confiscated the bear from Ash.

'Is there anything I can help you and your wife with?' she asked with a simplicity that left them both staring back at her blankly.

'No.' Louise snapped herself into action and linked her arm through Ash's. 'We've found out what we needed to know. Thank you.'

She carted him out of the shop. His legs were almost dragging with reluctance.

'But I was having fun.' The stiff wind assaulted them. 'And at least it was warm in there,' he said ruefully.

'Warm, and poignant. I can't afford any of it. Not now, and certainly not when the baby's born. Not unless I get my act together pretty damn quickly and do something about it.'

He nodded at her. His eyes were serious now. When

she'd talked about her career plans to Jon, he'd just waved them away with good humour and talked about the money he'd earn once he had an MBA under his belt. She still felt he wasn't thinking things through. But it was up to her to do the thinking. She'd promised herself she'd do this independently, and she wasn't going to let herself down.

'Do you need to talk it over with someone?' he asked. 'I've just got enough for a cuppa if you can face the greasy spoon again.'

She was about to protest, but she stopped herself. He was being friendly. There was no harm in that. And with Ash she really could think. It was as if her head cleared when he was around.

'Well, all right,' she said. 'If you really don't mind. I won't keep you for long, though. The last thing you want to spend a Wednesday afternoon doing is listening to a pregnant woman trying to plan her—'

'Louise?'

'Yes?'

'Shut up.'

'Okay,' she squeaked, and took the arm that he extended to her.

Chapter Seventeen

'Here y'are, love. Late delivery. It come apart, this one did. You want to tell your friends to wrap things up properly. And there's a letter for you too.'

The postman handed Louise a heavily sellotaped brown package and a flat envelope that looked like a bill. She tucked the envelope under her arm and concentrated on the parcel. It was ripped at one end and the pointed toe of a garish slipper was sticking out. She was tempted to observe that someone must have given it a hell of a bashing to get through the wrapper and find out what was inside, but she bit her tongue.

As the postman whistled away down the path she leaned on the door-frame, pulling the offending slippers from the paper. She dropped them on the ground and slipped her feet into them. Together with her yellow socks they looked amazing. She laughed quietly. Identical to the first pair of circus clown slippers, only newer, stiffer and even more pointy. They really were hideous. She felt inside the remains of the paper and pulled out a folded Marks and Spencer's bag. Inside was a thermal vest edged with frills. She shook it out. It was huge. Her mother had a habit of buying everything for her at least four sizes too big, as if she couldn't get over the idea that Louise would grow into things. She didn't know how right she was at the moment. She pulled the vest over her head to test it. It stretched easily over the polo-necked sweater she was wearing. Louise left it there. She'd change into a skirt in a minute so that she looked like a woman when Jon came over after work.

She took a deep breath of cold air. It wasn't exactly fresh, but it was invigorating. She gazed down her path at the main road. The afternoon rush-hour traffic was mounting, but it didn't annoy her. Life was extremely bearable at the moment. She was only going to take things one day at a time, and since the weekend she had tentatively been feeling more settled. Jon was surprising her more and more. He'd even asked if she'd mind if he got a key cut to her flat. It was odd now, knowing that he could come and go as he chose. As if they were living together. He'd rung her from work each afternoon to ask if she'd mind if he came back for the night. It was the end of the week, and he'd spent all of his free time with her since Saturday night. He was still protesting his feelings for her, and she allowed him to say what he wanted without gushing back at him. There was a chance that love would grow between them. She'd been besotted by him once. She owed it to them all to try.

She turned her attention to the envelope and ripped it open. Her eyes widened with surprise. It was a cheque from Party Animals. She read the amount again and grinned with sheer pleasure. It was much, much more than she might have expected. Dear Andrew. Perhaps he was still nourishing his soft spot for her after all. And there was a note attached to it. She squinted at it.

'Please find enclosed the salary we owe you, plus a bonus to help you through Christmas,' she read in a murmur. 'Good luck with your job hunt. Sorry about everything, Andrew.'

She looked at the cheque again. It was only money, and money didn't usually have the power to stir her into euphoria, but this was security. It would cover the phone bill and next month's rent, and it would keep her head above water while she moved on with her plans. It was another step towards independence, and if Andrew had been around, she'd have jumped into his arms and kissed him to death.

She glanced at her watch. She should have a quick bath now. Jon could be here any minute. She nudged the door to close it, but caught sight of a figure turning into her path. Damn it. It was Jon, and she still looked like a wreck. But the cheque had lifted her spirits, and in a burst of spontaneity she threw open the door, rushed down the path at him, and waved the cheque in front of his eyes.

'Louise!' He looked almost disturbed to see her. But it was her house. Who did he expect to be rushing out to greet him? Linda Lusardi?

'Look, Jon, it's money. From Andrew. Money they owed me!'

'Fine.' He held her away from him with a frown. He glanced around, as if to be sure they weren't being watched, and edged past her quickly towards the door. She stood on the path and watched him trying to distance himself from her.

'I thought you'd be happy. It means I'm not as destitute as I thought.'

'Terrific,' he said, heading for her hallway without turning round.

She looked like a wreck. That would be the problem. Jon wouldn't want to be associated with her in public until she'd done her hair and slapped a bit of make-up on. She hadn't had time for a bath, and . . . She looked down at herself in horror. She had a frilly vest on over her jumper, and was sporting a pair of long, thin slippers on her feet with labels sticking out at the sides. It was no wonder Jon was so embarrassed.

'Jesus!' She turned to get herself inside as quickly as possible.

'Louise! Hey!'

She swivelled round. Excitement and shock stampeded
over her.

'Ash!'

She shot a fearful glance over her shoulder. Jon was now
standing on the doormat inside the hall and was leaning
against her wall casually, watching.

'Um . . .' She looked back to Ash, who was striding
towards her with a wide smile, his eyes bright, his hair a
tangle of brown knots. He looked as if he hadn't slept for
a week. He reached her on the path and enveloped her in
a hug which knocked the remaining breath out of her
lungs. It struck her that he couldn't have seen Jon
languishing in the shadows of the hall. In fact, she sensed
that Jon had dropped back, perhaps deliberately. She
squirmed within the forceful embrace.

'Ash, what – what – why are you here?'

'Your CV, remember? I said I'd bring it round for you.
And I have to talk to you. Is now a good time?'

'For – for what?'

'For this.' He winked at her, then, to her shock, planted
a kiss directly on to her lips. His mouth was so warm, so
insistent, that it was difficult to pull away, but she had to.

'God, Ash.' She pushed him away in a fluster. 'What did
you do that for?'

'You're brilliant. Fantastic. It's all sorted, and I've never
been so happy.'

'What—' She looked quickly over her shoulder to see if
Jon was still in the hall, but she hadn't left a light on inside,
and it was too dark. She had an instinctive feeling that he
was hiding round the back of the door. It wouldn't be very
dignified, but it was something he might do. Ash was still
holding her tightly. He laid his cheek against hers, and
waltzed her up and down her path. She laughed
nervously.

'You've sorted my life out for me, Louise, and you don't

315

even know it. And I want to take you out somewhere, celebrate. On me.'

'No, stop it!' She shook him away. 'What's going on?'

'Rachel, your sister.'

'Yes?'

'The one who works for the record company?'

'Yes, I know who she bloody well is. What is it?' H
eyes stretched open in anticipation. 'She called you?'

'Yes, but it's not what you think. She called Kare
They're not interested in the band, just her. It looks li
Karen's going to make it. On her own, of course, but the
that's what she's best at.'

'What?' Louise stepped back, horrified. Ash w
nodding cheerfully.

'It's just great, the way it's worked out. We had a tota
destructive house row, everybody fell out with everyo
else and she left and went off to live with a mate of he
instead. So there you have it. The band's split up, Karen
fucked off, and Ginger's not talking to me any more, b
he'll get over it. I've never been happier.' He grinned
prove the point. He glanced down at her body, allowed h
eyes to roam right down to the yellow socks and slippe
complete with labels and back up again to the frilly ve
over her jumper, then grinned even more broadly. 'You'
totally fucking mad, do you know that?'

'Er—'

'And I want to ask you out. I'm free. I'm going to sta
all over again, doing things I really want to do from no
on. And that includes asking you out to dinner. What d
you say? It'll have to be somewhere cheap, though. Yo
won't mind, will you?'

Louise's mouth dropped open. She delved deep insid
for some sort of word, anything would do just to tid
things over, but nothing came. She just stood in her ve
and slippers and gaped at the most gorgeous man i

London who had just asked her out on a date.

'Uh . . .' A lorry crashed past, but she hardly heard it.

'Can we go inside and talk about this? Bit noisy out here, isn't it?' Ash grimaced as the lorry was followed by a series of double-decker buses.

'Um, you see, the thing is . . .' She swam in his pale green eyes, wishing that the world would vanish and leave the two of them alone.

'The thing is, she's pregnant.' Jon's harsh voice cut across them from her doorstep. Louise knew without turning around what his expression would be like. She watched Ash as he glanced over her shoulder in Jon's direction. 'And it's mine,' Jon finished firmly.

Slowly Ash took his hand from Louise's shoulder. She watched his eyes for a sign of disgust. What she saw there was closer to dislike.

'So you're back,' Ash said bluntly. Louise's eyebrows shot up to her hairline. That wasn't what she expected him to say at all. A thousand questions squirmed around in her head, none of them capable of making sense. Ash glanced at Jon again, then dropped his eyes on Louise. His expression softened.

'If you need me, you know where I am.'

She nodded dumbly.

'She won't,' Jon stated. Louise could sense that he had left the doorstep and was walking slowly towards them. Surely not a fist fight, on her path, right in front of the bus stop? Over her? A pregnant woman with flyaway hair in a vest and slippers? What the hell had she done to merit this?

'Relax,' Ash said calmly to Jon as he reached them and drew himself up to his full height. Jon was slightly taller than Ash, but Ash was more solid. 'I realise this is a private matter. I'm going now. I said what I came to say.'

He turned and walked away, very slowly, as if to show

317

Jon that he wasn't intimidated. He didn't look back.
Louise stared after him. He disappeared from sight. That,
without doubt, was the last she would ever see of him.
Now she should go inside and attempt to explain it all to
Jon. Her arms and legs wouldn't move. She gazed around
herself at South Ealing on a wintry Friday afternoon. The
traffic was still crawling past in the twilight as if nothing
had happened. She met eyes with two women standing at
the bus stop, clutching shopping bags and watching
avidly. She swallowed.

'Come on, Lou,' Jon said at her elbow. 'Let's get back in.
You look a mess.'

She turned to look at him. He had gripped her elbow
firmly and was hauling her towards the door. She shook
his hand away.

'I know which way my house is, thank you.'

'Christ, Louise, what's got into you!' he hissed at her.
'You look like a lunatic standing out here dressed like that.
Get inside, for God's sake.'

He stalked ahead of her into the shadows of the hall, and
waited for her at the door to her flat. She followed him at
her own pace. Once she was inside the main hallway, she
pushed the front door shut and leaned back against it. She
flicked the light switch, squinting as the naked bulb above
her head dazzled her. Jon glowered at her, then turned his
attention to his keys.

'Whatever that was all about, it's over now, Louise. I
want to get in here, have a shower and a beer. Then you
can explain it to me.'

She sniffed and put her head back to look at him
properly.

'And you'll tell me all about Matty and Helen as well as
Kelly then, I assume.'

'Who?' He blinked innocent eyes at her. He must have
been even more plastered than she'd thought in the

Kensington bistro. He'd obviously clean forgotten about
it.

She jumped as the doorbell blasted suddenly over her
head. She put her hand to her chest, her heart diving for
cover.

'God Almighty, that startled me!'

'If that's him again—' Jon took a purposeful step down
the hall.

'Jon, just stop playing Fred Flintstone, will you?' she
snapped. What she really wanted to do was slap him hard
around the face, but she didn't know why. 'Just let me get
the door, then for heaven's sake let's get into the flat.'

She pulled the door open roughly, her emotions
churning.

'Yes?' she bellowed at the figure standing on her path.
Recognition dawned. It was three years since she had
seen this man, and she'd forgotten that he looked like
Mr Tumnus. If she'd remembered that, she'd never have
written to him suggesting oral sex. Her spirits crumpled
into despair.

'Louise!' The eager smile on Giles the accountant's
bearded face was failing rapidly. 'I – I got your letter and I
was driving home from work this way. I – I thought we
could . . . perhaps . . .' His voice tailed away.

'Hasn't anybody heard of the telephone?' she cried at
him in disbelief.

'I – I would have rung, but I can drive home this way,
you see. If I take the A307 from Kingston I can avoid the
A3 completely—'

'Oh, just go away!' She slammed the door violently in
his face. She blew out sharply, her nerves in tatters, and
swung round to face Jon. He was frozen into position, his
key pointed at her door. His expression had flattened out
into total astonishment.

'Right then,' she said, striding across the hall in her

319

slippers. 'I think that's my past dealt with. Let's go and talk about the future, shall we?'

The conversation had not exactly resolved anything, Louise thought on Saturday as she sorted through her wardrobe with one eye on the time, and tried to find something that might be appropriate to wear down to Kent. Something suitable for her mother's reunion dinner which would also do for her announcement. What would her mother like to see her daughter in at the moment she found out that she was going to be a grandmother? She raked through the coat-hangers again. She could hear Jon in the kitchen, washing up. He'd never washed up in her flat before. It felt strange. All of it felt strange, and even stranger since Ash had winged up the path, made a series of dizzying statements, and winged back down it again.

She sank on to the edge of the bed. She had told Jon exactly what had happened between herself and Ash. The fact that he had been there to give her advice about signing on, that they'd met several times and that she'd asked Rachel to go and see his band to return the favour. She'd omitted the part where they'd surveyed the prams in Totz. She gazed at the pair of turquoise leggings in her hand. What she hadn't told Jon was how she felt about Ash. She wasn't even sure herself what she felt. All she knew was that when she thought about him she felt uplifted. In another life, she and Ash might have started something. Who could say where it might have ended up? Perhaps nowhere. She snorted at herself.

'At least let me drive you down.' Jon was standing in the doorway with a tea towel in his hand. She wondered if he'd been there long enough to hear her ungainly snort. 'You're going to miss the train at this rate, Lou. I don't like the idea of you cavorting across London and down to Kent in your state.'

She frowned at him. 'I'm not in a state. I've eaten and I don't feel sick. I'll be fine.'

'Not much time,' he said, tapping his Rolex. It was fake, but not many people knew that. 'And you. Not a very good combination.'

He almost looked affectionate. She pushed thoughts of Ash from her mind. In a few weeks, the memory of his shining eyes and disastrous hair would fade. In a few months, she would start to forget the way he said, 'Louise? Shut up.'

'I'm nearly ready,' she lied, standing up again and throwing a bundle of clothes on the duvet.

'No, you're just taking everything out of your wardrobe and putting it on the bed,' Jon chuckled at her. 'Let me drive you down. I'd like to see your mum again anyway. We got on like a house on fire the last time we met. I'd like to be there when you tell her about us and the baby. I'd love to see the expression on her face.'

'No, Jon. I really need to see her on my own first. Maybe you can come down another time?'

Louise forced a smile and fixed it in place. She was also wondering what the expression on her mother's face would be when she told her. There was the baby, and there was Jon. She had a feeling that her mother's reactions to the two distinct developments were going to be somewhat different. The two of them had met when Olivia had come up to visit Louise in London. Louise had cooked a meal and Jon had joined them. Jon had talked about his career prospects for three hours without taking a breath. Even Louise was falling off her chair with boredom by the end of it. When Olivia hugged Louise goodbye, she suggested it was a little odd that Jon hadn't talked about their relationship at all. Louise had laughed it off then. But her mother, annoyingly, had been right about Jon, not so much in what she said, but what she didn't say.

Louise stuffed the turquoise leggings into her holdall with sudden vigour. How could she be saying that his mother was right when she was going to have his baby and was contemplating a life with him?

'So do you want a lift to Charing Cross, at least?'

'Oh no, don't worry about it. I quite like travelling on my own. It gives me time to think.'

'Plenty to think about, eh?' Jon nodded at her. 'Just make sure your mother knows I asked you. I don't want her to think I let a pregnant woman paddle around London on her own without offering help.'

'I'll tell her.' Louise jammed some thick tights and a pair of knee-length black boots into her bag. She didn't like the inelegant image Jon had conjured up. It wasn't how she felt about herself.

'Great. And, er, you won't mind if I stay here for the weekend then?'

She looked up at him.

'Do you want to?'

He shrugged. 'I might as well now I'm here. It'll make me feel closer to you, Lou, just being around your things. If you don't mind.'

'No, I don't mind.'

'And you won't mind if I use your washing machine? Mine's on the blink.'

Louise piled her make-up into a foam bag and zipped it up firmly.

'Go ahead.'

'Great.'

'At least I'll know where you are if things go horribly wrong,' she said with a flicker of nerves. 'I'll be able to ring you, won't I?'

'Yeah,' he agreed, fondling the tea towel. 'Although I might go out tonight, so don't worry if you don't catch me.'

'Oh. Okay. People from work?' She wandered around the room, trying to decide what else she should be taking with her.

'I thought I might see a few friends. I mean, I can't just disappear off the face of the planet without explanation, can I? They'll be wondering where I am. It'll give me a chance to explain.'

'Explain?' She finished her circuit of the room and rested her eyes on him.

'That I'm with you now.' He drew her into his arms and gave her a brisk hug. 'That my life is changing. That I've got responsibilities now, ones that are important to me.' He kissed the end of her nose. 'That I'm putting the past behind me and moving on. Just like you are, you wicked woman.'

'Wicked?' She screwed her nose up at him. 'What do you mean?'

'C'mon, Lou, a string of men arrive at your house not expecting to find me here. The red roses. The huge cheque from Andrew. I know what you've been up to.'

She studied his eyes seriously.

'No, you don't. I explained it all to you last night. It was all theoretical.'

He tutted at her.

'You've been a lot naughtier than I gave you credit for, but if you don't want to admit it that's fair enough.' He softened his voice. 'I understand why, Louise. You want to reassure me that I'm the father of the baby. I know that. I believe you.'

'Listen, Jon.' She stood away from him, trying to see into his mind. It wasn't a happy experience. 'I haven't been as naughty as you think. In fact, I haven't been naughty at all. Andrew was a colleague, nothing more. Harris is just an actor. He can't help making dramatic gestures. Ash is a kind person who helped me when I was on my own. When

323

I wrote to Lenny and Giles I thought I was single. I was on the rebound. I don't think I'd have done anything about it even if I hadn't found out about the baby.'

'Lenny too?' His eyebrows shot up. 'You didn't mention that. Blimey, Lou, if it weren't for the baby I'd wonder if you'd got someone down in Kent as well.' He gave her a mockingly severe look. 'You are quite sure that it's your mother you're going to see, aren't you? Not some old flame I should know about.'

'No, you don't understand.' She gave up. He was twinkling at her as if her imaginary misdemeanours had sent her up in his estimation. Her irritation was rising. Not once during their conversation last night had she been able to get him to talk about Matty, Helen, and Kelly and God knew who else. But she kept telling herself it was the past. They had to think about the future now.

'Now you'd better get a bloody move on. Isn't your mother supposed to be meeting you from the train?'

'Yes, I'm nearly ready.'

'And when shall I expect you back?' He almost looked eager for her return. She took comfort from it.

'Probably pretty late on Sunday. I think we're going to have a lot to talk about.'

'You just take as much time as you need.'

Louise glanced at her watch as the phone began to ring. 'Shit, who's that?'

'Another admirer perhaps?' Jon smirked at her.

'Leave it out, Jon, it isn't funny. I'll have to leave it on answerphone. If it's Mum, I'll pick it up.'

She raced through to the bathroom to gather her toiletries together. She yanked her toothbrush from the pot from Corfu, stuck a couple of bottles and a bag of cotton-wool balls under her arm, ran out, went back for her shampoo, ran out again, then listened to the odd sound that was coming through her answering machine.

324

She walked slowly through the kitchen and listened harder. It sounded like a child whining down the phone. No, it wasn't a child. It was somebody crying. What was even more of a shock was that Louise suddenly realised it was Rachel.

'Louise? Louise, are you there?' Rachel's voice trailed away into tears again.

Louise dropped her toiletries on the kitchen floor with a clatter and grabbed at the phone.

'Rachel, I'm here. What's wrong?'

'Oh, Louise.' Rachel started to sob uncontrollably. Louise felt her skin go cold. Had somebody died? Rachel was in a terrible state. 'It's Hallam.'

'What's happened, Rachel?' Louise asked firmly. 'Take a deep breath and tell me.'

She heard Rachel take a deep breath.

'I've told him about Benji. He said we should split up. He offered to leave but I couldn't let him, so I've left instead.'

'What?' Rachel was crying again. Louise glanced up at on who was standing in front of her and tapping his watch. She shook her head at him. 'Go on, Rachel.'

'So – so I've left,' Rachel said.

'Okay.' Louise nodded at the phone, surprised at how calm she was. 'So—'

'And I haven't got anywhere to go!' Rachel's voice became a wail. Louise sank to her knees on the lino and rested her head against the Formica cupboard door. She couldn't remember the last time she had heard Rachel let herself go like this. Not even at their father's funeral. When they were children, probably. She got angry, yes. But floods of tears? It wasn't Rachel's thing.

'What about Benji, Rachel? Have you told him you've left Hallam?'

'No,' Rachel gulped. 'No, he doesn't know. He wouldn't

325

want to know. It's only sex, nothing more. I can't tell him'
Rachel's voice broke into tears again. 'So I'm all on m'
own. I just grabbed a few things and left.'

'Right.' Louise thought quickly. Jon had given up o'
tapping his watch and wandered away. It was obviou'
now that she was going to miss her train. She'd have t'
ring her mother and explain. She'd understand. Or woul'
she? She'd promised she'd take her to the dinne'
Otherwise she'd have to go on her own. But Rachel was o'
her own, and she'd never been this much in need of help'

'Oh, Lou!' Rachel cooed.

'It's all right, Rachel, everything's going to be fin'
You're not alone. Just tell me where you are.'

'I'm in my car.'

'Fine. Where is the car?'

'In your road,' Rachel said, her voice cracking. 'Outsid'
your house.'

'Oh.' Louise stood up.

'And there's a traffic warden walking towards me'
Rachel finished, her voice becoming a sob again.

'Okay. Now you're going to start the car before you ge'
a ticket, take it round to a side road and park it. The'
you're going to come to my house, and the door's going t'
be open. We'll take it from there,' Louise said.

'Okay,' Rachel sniffed.

'All right?' Louise confirmed, squashing the receiver t'
her ear to reassure herself that Rachel was taking som'
sort of action. If not, she'd have to dash outside and sort i'
out herself.

'Yes,' Rachel said in a small voice.

'So start the engine then.'

'I am.' Louise heard the engine revving. She realise'
that Rachel was not going to put the phone down. Sh'
hung on.

'Piss off, you old bag. Can't you see I'm going?'

'Rachel?'

'Yes.' The voice was small again.

'Did you get a ticket?'

'No.'

'I'm putting the phone down now. I'm going to the door and I'll be there when you get to the gate. Will you be okay without me?'

'Yes,' Rachel said. 'I'll ring off first, though.'

'Okay, you do that.'

'And Lou?'

'Yes?'

'I love you.'

Louise nodded, a lump rising in her throat.

'I love you too, Rach.'

She placed the phone down, heaved an exhausted breath, and looked around for Jon. She found him in the sitting room, watching *Grandstand*. He glanced over his shoulder.

'Everything all right?' he asked.

'Slight change of plan.'

Chapter Eighteen

'Just don't tell Mum I was crying. I don't want her to worry,' Rachel said as they climbed out of the BMW and stood on the tarmacked driveway next to their bags. 'Let me just finish this fag, then we'll go in.'

Louise took several deep gulps of air. It was a miracle that she hadn't thrown up in the car. Rachel always drove everywhere as if she was trying to get a good starting position for the Grand Prix, and with a cigarette between each finger. The world was coming back into focus again. Astronauts probably felt like this when they came back to earth.

Most of the lights were on at home, a few lights at the Fishers' house too. She turned full circle and allowed the familiarity of the estate to envelop her. The evenly spaced houses and neat gardens were orange in the street lamps. There was no jarring thunder of lorries and buses. It was so peaceful. She was home and somewhere in the house her mother was waiting. It was a lovely, familiar comforting feeling. It was how she used to feel when she came home from school. Everything in its place, as expected. Rachel was looking up at the pebble-dashed façade of their old house as she dropped her cigarette and ground it under her heel.

'Weird coming back, isn't it?'

'I expect Mum heard us arrive,' Louise urged. 'We haven't got much time to change. We'd better knock hadn't we?'

'Let's go for it. And remember, not a mention of me

and Hallam. Poor Mum's got enough on her plate, and I'll only get a lecture about it. I can't cope with that right now.'

Louise knew. She'd realised how little Rachel could take on board while she'd been listening to her in the car. It hadn't been the right time to tell her about the baby. Later, when they could sit down together as a family, she'd let them know what was really happening. Then if Rachel had anything scathing to say to her she'd have her mother here to support her.

'Mum'll just be happy to see you,' Louise said, taking Rachel's arm as they gathered their bags and marched up to the front door together. 'She sounded thrilled that you were coming too.'

'But worried about table placements, I know.'

'She's only worried about what the others will think if she turns up with one extra.'

'I told you. I can just sit at the bar with a bottle of wine. I'll be fine.'

'They'll squeeze you in,' Louise said as they both reached the doormat and stood on it without ringing the bell. 'And if they don't, I'll come and sit with you separately. It won't matter if we can't join in.'

'Huh!' Rachel held on to Louise's arm. 'It'd be a real busman's holiday for me to be left out of things. Still, at least this way you both get a lift. I can't believe you were going to get the bus there. There are such things as taxis, you know. Even down here.'

'It's just habit. You know what Mum's like.' Louise lowered her voice just in case their mother could hear them through the door. The house was very quiet. 'You've got to be nice to Mum. She's got her own way of doing things. There's no point having a go at her.'

'I wasn't going to have a go at her.' Rachel looked at Louise indignantly. 'Why, were you?'

'No!' Louise exclaimed back. 'I'm just making sure tha[t] you don't.'

'Right. And if anyone's going to be a bitch, it's me. I[s] that it?'

'You can be a bit outspoken, that's all.'

'Bloody hell, give me a break, will you?'

'Rachel,' Louise said slowly, 'all I'm saying is tha[t] Mum's Mum. She's not going to change now. She's set i[n] her ways, but I think that's something we should b[e] grateful for.'

'Grateful? When she's so depressed?'

Louise stepped away from Rachel and reached for th[e] doorbell.

'She's not depressed.'

'Oh, really? Work? Home? Perhaps she feels a burst o[f] high spirits on the bus in between the two?'

Louise sighed. 'I know it's not ideal at the moment, bu[t] she'd going through a grieving process which is totall[y] natural. She'll be fine. We've just got to give her time.'

'Right,' Rachel said, stiffening in the cold. 'Are yo[u] going to ring that bloody bell or not?'

'I'm doing it.' Louise pressed the bell and moved close[r] to Rachel. She gave her arm an impulsive squeeze. 'Grea[t] to be home though, isn't it? Thank God there are still som[e] things that you can rely on.'

They both watched through the frosted glass as [a] shadowy figure approached the door. Louise felt tear[s] prick at her eyes. She had anticipated this moment for s[o] long. Her lips spread into a smile as she saw their mothe[r] fumbling with the catch on the door. The door swun[g] open.

'Surprise!' their mother called at them, spreading he[r] arms wide and curtseying in the hall. She giggled, and di[d] a turn for them.

Rachel and Louise had both opened their mouths, read[y]

with an affectionate greeting. They shut them again. Neither of them moved. Olivia giggled again.

'Well, aren't you going to say anything?'

'You've changed your hair,' Rachel said vacantly.

Louise ranged her eyes over the elegant figure who was now striking model poses under the British Home Stores lampshade. She had changed her hair. That was probably the easiest fact to get a grip of. Instead of the loose, soft wings that had framed her head, her hair was now cropped into a chic cut, high around the ears, with a light fringe that emphasised her eyes. But her eyes were different too. She'd changed her make-up. It was usually a smear of blue for special occasions, but tonight her lids were covered with creams and browns that made her irises glow blue. Her lipstick was dark, and matched the deep cherry of a pair of bold clip-on earrings. And she was wearing trousers. She never wore trousers. These were fashionable ones, of a soft suede material, with a pair of ankle boots brushing the hems. A loose silk top of a muted gold was tucked into a thick leather belt, and she was wearing a casual jacket which matched the trousers and swung jauntily around her waist. The complete ensemble knocked ten years off her.

'Mum, what have you done to yourself?' The stark comment was out before Louise could stop it. Olivia straightened her face and gave Louise a chiding look.

'Is that all you can say? You'd better stop shivering on the mat and come in. I've got lots to tell you.'

They stepped inside. Olivia shut the door behind them, rubbing at her arms.

'It is horrible out there, isn't it? They've forecast snow in the next day or two. I've got a coat to throw over this for getting there. Have you both brought something nice to change into?'

'Hello, Mum,' Rachel said, recovering herself and

pressing a kiss to her mother's cheek. 'You look absolutely fantastic.'

'Have you been drinking?' Louise asked, still unable to stop staring. It wasn't just how her mother looked, it was how she was acting. She seemed light-hearted, flippant, dizzy. It wasn't the sedate, steady atmosphere that she had expected to walk into.

'Oh, hark at you!' Olivia slapped her daughter's arm playfully, and danced through to the living room. 'Just dump your coats and bags in the hall for now and come on through. We're going to have a glass of something together, then you two can go on up to your rooms and get changed. The water's hot if you want showers or anything.'

Louise glided into their old living room and gazed around. She was expecting the *Changing Rooms* team to have done a make-over, but thankfully it was the same as ever. The navy blue sofa, the two chairs, the low coffee table with the plant placed with geometric accuracy in the centre, the row of photographs on the mantelpiece and the polished piano were all achingly familiar. It was a relief. Olivia had already trotted through the archway into the kitchen. The fridge door opened.

'Now, Rachel can only have a tiny sip of this seeing as she's driving,' Olivia breezed on. 'But Louise can have as much as she likes. She can keep me company, then she can't make rude comments about me drinking on my own.'

Louise glanced at Rachel. The two of them had come to a standstill in the middle of the living room. Rachel raised her eyebrows and said nothing. Louise led the way into the kitchen. Her mother was struggling to open a bottle of champagne. She had set three fluted glasses out on the table. Louise couldn't remember the last time they had been used.

'Here, let me.' Rachel took the bottle gently while Olivia flushed and waved her hands.

'I'm sure I could have done it.'

'Yes, but I've got it down to a fine art,' Rachel smiled at her mother. Louise sank back against the cupboard doors and watched. Rachel glanced at the label and let out a whistle of surprise. 'Real champagne! What's got into you, Mum?'

'What hasn't? I've got so much to tell you both. I'm so pleased you've come too, Rachel. I never would have thought to ask you. I thought you hated coming home!' She rushed at Rachel and gave her a tight hug. 'And you, Louise.' She sighed in happiness. 'It's so, so good to have you both here.'

Louise opened her mouth to say something. She wasn't sure what she would say. She couldn't remove the frown of confusion from over her eyes. Olivia flitted past and into the living room.

'I nearly forgot!' she exclaimed, yanking open the stereo door and prodding a button on the tape deck. 'I found this among your old tapes, Louise. I thought we could listen to it to get us in the mood.'

'Mood for what?' Louise said in a low voice, turning to Rachel for an answer.

'Shhh!' Rachel hissed. 'Don't put the dampers on things.'

'I'm not—'

They both stopped and stared at their mother as a familiar introduction boomed out from the cumbersome speakers.

'Ding de ding de de ding!' Olivia sang, hopping back to the kitchen. 'Have you got that bottle open yet, Rachel? Call yourself a dipso? You're hopeless!'

The champagne cork flew out of the bottle, hit the ceiling and skidded across the floor. Olivia hummed to herself as she held out the glasses one by one, ignoring the fact that a spume of champagne had erupted from the bottle and was now dripping off the edge of the table and on to the lino. She didn't grab a J-cloth and tut as she cleared it up. She just let it drip. Louise was becoming more confused by the second.

Olivia began to wiggle her hips and sing at the top of her voice.

Louise gripped on to the edge of the kitchen unit behind her for support. Rachel threw her head back and let out a shout of laughter. Olivia jived over to Louise and handed her a glass.

'Go on,' her mother said. 'Have a sip. It'll relax you.'

'Mum, what has got into you?'

'I'm going to tell you. Take this first.'

Louise took the glass with wooden fingers and gripped on to the stem. Her mother was dancing and dishing out champagne while Cyndi Lauper was bellowing out through her father's old speakers. She was wearing trousers, earrings and make-up, and she was looking and acting like someone who really believed that girls just wanted to have fun. It wasn't very – grandmotherly. Louise swallowed.

'Right!' Olivia declared. 'What shall I tell you first? Shall we sit down?'

'Yes, let's,' Rachel agreed cheerfully, pulling out a chair for herself and giving Louise a nod to indicate that she should do the same. Louise drifted over to the chair she'd always occupied when she lived at home and sank into it.

'Okay then.' Olivia perched opposite them and gazed at them both. Her cheeks were flushed, and her eyes were sparkling. They gaped back at her in silence.

'Well, the thing is—' Olivia stopped. She looked from one daughter to the other with less certainty. 'I – I was hoping you'd be happy for me.'

'Mum,' Rachel took her hand patiently. 'Unless you tell

us what's going on we can't know whether we're going to be happy or not, can we? Just take a deep breath and come out with it.'

'Well,' Olivia laced her fingers together on the table. 'I've done a lot of thinking recently. Very recently, really. It was after Katherine bloody Muff's phone call. I thought of all those women, and what they'd all done with their lives. I thought of myself, and what I'd done. A wife and mother. That was it.'

'But – being a mother's so important,' Louise asserted. 'You should be proud of it.'

'I am proud.' Olivia held up a hand to Louise. 'But I had Rachel very young. There were things I always wanted to do, and I never did them. So – so I thought I could do some of those things now.' She stopped to take a sip of her champagne. 'In fact, that's not quite accurate. I thought I'd do all of those things now.'

They both stared. Rachel leaned forward, her face full of anticipation. She seemed to have forgotten her own problems.

'So what are the things, Mum?'

'Well . . .' Olivia hauled in a deep breath and blurted at them, 'I'm learning to drive the Escort, I've told Carol to get stuffed, I'm going to resign from work and take a trip abroad. Round the world, in fact. Via India. I've always wanted to go there.'

Olivia looked startled now as both her daughters sat bolt upright at the table.

'And I've joined the Liberal Democrats,' she finished breathlessly. She picked up her glass of champagne and finished it in one gulp.

There was a long, long silence. Louise was unable to move, even to twitch her fingers towards her glass, much as she needed to drink it now. Rachel stared in amazement.

'Bloody hell!'

'Can't you just vote for them?' Louise asked weakly.

'I didn't want to just vote for them. I wanted to join the party, and I have.'

'But you're not political!' Louise's protest was faint. 'You never take any notice of what's going on.'

'How do you know?' Olivia asked, her face elaborately quizzical. 'Tell me how you know what's been going on in my head all these years?'

'But you never said—'

'Ah!' Olivia put up a finger. 'That's different. Saying and thinking are two different things.'

'Bugger the Liberal Democrats, what's this about going round the world?' Rachel had started to laugh. 'I thought you were afraid of flying, Mum.'

'It was Bob, don't you see? He never wanted to go abroad. It was simpler to agree with him. How can I know if I'm afraid of flying or not? I've never been inside an aeroplane. You two have. It can't be that difficult.'

'When?' Louise voiced. She could feel the blood draining from her cheeks. 'When are you going away?'

'I'm not sure yet, but soon. There's a nice little travel agent in Tonbridge, and they're going to help me sort it out. Sarah came with me and helped me too. She's a nice girl really. I didn't think I liked her, but I do.'

'Sarah?' Rachel raised her eyebrows.

'From work. She's got crabs and Carol's been awful to her. But it's because she's having an affair and she's not happy either. So I told Carol not to sack Sarah, and she didn't. That's when I stood up to her.'

Louise's eyes widened even further. Her mother had said 'crabs'.

'That old bag's having an affair?' Rachel blinked.

'Well, you haven't seen her,' Olivia told Rachel reasonably. 'She's actually very attractive when she's not issuing orders.'

'Who's got crabs, Sarah or Carol?' Louise asked in bewilderment.

'Oh, it doesn't matter who it is. The point is I stood up for myself.'

'Good for you!' Rachel sat back and gave a burst of applause. 'About bloody time too.'

'And you're driving the car?'

'Oh, yes. Shaun's teaching me. One of the social workers. We've had a few lessons now. He says I'm coming on really well. He recites poetry to me, you know.' She gave her daughters a shy look. Rachel chuckled back. Louise could feel her face dropping further and further into her lap.

'But – Mum – what will you do for a job when you come back? What about security? I thought that was important to you.'

'I've been secure for nearly forty years, Louise,' Olivia said abruptly. 'And Bob's insurance policy left me well looked after. I'll do something else when I come back. I don't know what yet. I'm not going to plan that far ahead. For once, I'm going to try to – to wing it.'

'Wing it,' Louise echoed.

'God, Mum!' Rachel rested her chin in her hands and gazed at her mother in admiration. 'I didn't think you had it in you. You've astounded me, you really have.'

'You mean that you thought I was a wimp!' Olivia blushed.

'No, never.' Rachel took her mother's hand and squeezed it. 'But I knew you were unhappy.'

'Well, I'm not unhappy any more,' Olivia said with quiet certainty. 'I've never been more sure of what I'm doing. It doesn't mean I don't have fears. Of course I do. But I'm going to carry on in this direction now.'

'Bully for you, Mum. It's brilliant.'

'Oh!' Olivia glanced at her watch. 'Look at the time.

We'd better hurry up and get on our way. And I've got one last thing to show you.'

She stood up, her face reddening again, then suddenly slipped her jacket down over her shoulders. She pursed her lips together as if she was trying to stifle a laugh. Louise squinted at a small, red patch on her mother's upper arm. It looked like a scab.

'You fell over?' she offered.

'Mum, you didn't! I don't believe it!'

'It was Sarah who put the idea in my head.' Olivia frowned down at her arm. 'It was a bit of an impulse thing.'

'Okay, now I really am dreaming!' Rachel stood up and clasped her mother in her arms. She smacked a kiss on her forehead. 'You've been a closet loony all these years, and we never knew it! At least we know who Lou gets it from now!'

Louise gazed at her mother and sister, hugging and laughing. She felt as if she was watching a film except, unfortunately, she couldn't flick a button to change the channel.

'It looks disgusting at the moment, I know,' Olivia said. 'But when it all clears up it's going to be a little crescent moon. That's what they put on there. Sarah got a bluebell, you see. I went through it with her, and I thought, well, if Sarah has the courage to do that at her age not knowing what life may bring her in the future, then there's no reason for me not to do it. I'm not going to have enough time to really regret it, am I?'

'You've got a tattoo?' Louise emitted faintly. She was devoid of feeling. She was prepared to believe anything now. If her mother had suddenly announced that she'd been the sixth Beatle but had never thought to tell them, she would have just nodded.

'Do you think it's tacky?' Olivia gave Rachel a worried look. 'I thought so at first. It was different in my day. But

Sarah said it was really trendy now. She said all the girls were having it done. I wanted to know what it felt like. It's – it's sort of symbolic really.'

'As long as you don't whip your clothes off and show us your pierced nipples as well,' Rachel guffawed.

Louise stood up. She put her chair carefully back under the table, where it belonged. She wandered away through the living room, listening to her sister and mother exchanging jokes.

'You going to get changed, Lou?' Rachel called.

'Yes,' Louise said robotically.

'Don't use all the hot water. I'll be up in a sec.'

'And we'd better all hurry up,' Olivia said. 'I can't wait to wipe the smug smile from Katherine Muff's face. I'm just dying for her to ask me what I'm doing now. We don't want to be late for my grand entrance, do we?'

Louise sat in the back of the car as they drove into the town. It suited her to sit sulking in the back while her mother and sister chatted at high volume over the gear lever in the front.

'Not just one, but two glamorous escorts!' Olivia exclaimed after she had directed Rachel into the restaurant car park and Rachel was trying to find a space to squeeze the car into. 'And I'm arriving in a silver BMW. Really, Rachel, you should have dropped us off at the front just in case somebody was watching!' She laughed at herself. 'And you both look so gorgeous. I'm going to be so proud tonight. My lovely daughters! I thought I'd be struggling up the road from the bus stop, on my own, in my mac. Life changes so quickly, doesn't it? One minute you're one sort of person, the next minute you're someone else. It's exciting, isn't it?'

'Have you stopped yet, Rachel?' Louise snapped from the back. 'I need to get out. I'm feeling a bit sick.'

Both Rachel and Olivia turned in their seats to look at Louise. She stared back mutinously, strapped in by acres of seat-belt, feeling like a toddler.

'And you look so lovely,' Olivia said reassuringly, her eyes uncertain as she studied her youngest daughter. 'I like your boots especially. Where did you get them, dear?'

'A shop,' Louise said, hating herself for being difficult, but unable to co-operate. 'Why, Mum, thinking of getting a pair for yourself?'

'Well, they're very practical, aren't they?'

'Mum, you're not eighteen any more,' Louise heard herself say as she fumbled ineffectually with the door handle.

'Well,' Olivia said, wide-eyed, 'neither are you, Louise.'

Louise sank back into her seat. Rachel cleared her throat.

'I tell you what, I'll drop you two off at the steps, then come back and park the car. How about that? Then if Katherine Muff's watching she'll be blown away.'

'Oh. Okay, dear.' Olivia smiled and turned away from Louise.

Rachel swung the car round and veered back to the front of the restaurant. She drew up with a screech of tyres that sent them all flying towards the windscreen.

'Can we get out now?' Louise asked with assumed patience.

'Yep.'

'Take two daughters into the restaurant? Not me!' Olivia chanted happily. 'I just – oh, hang on, that should be the other way round, shouldn't it? Take one daughter into the restaurant? Not me! I—'

'I think we get the drift, Mum.' Louise wrenched open the car door and crawled out into the night. She inhaled cold air into her lungs. Olivia snapped the passenger door closed and tapped spiritedly on the roof. Rachel squealed away, waving a hand at them, and rounded the corner into the car park. Louise heard her mother give a deep sigh.

'Louise?'

'Yes, Mum.' She began to walk towards the double oak doors of the Steak House.

'Louise, hang on.'

She stopped and turned round to wait for her mother. Olivia was patting at her hair and blinking widely into the gloom as if she'd dislodged a contact lens.

'I think my eyes have stuck together. It's this non-stick mascara Sarah made me buy. Let me just sort it out. I don't want them all to think I've got a nervous tic. Especially that bloody Katherine.' She straightened herself. 'Louise, you said you had something to tell me when you came down. Some good news.'

'Oh, it's not important right now, Mum. Maybe later.'

Louise looked at her mother illuminated under the multicoloured bulbs which were draped around the door of the restaurant. She watched her fiddle with her handbag, her scarf, the lapels of her coat. Her heart softened. Olivia was extremely nervous, that much was obvious. And she was doing courageous things, wonderful things. She couldn't know that her timing was particularly bad for her youngest daughter. And in their own ways, they were both ignoring public opinion and doing their own thing. Perhaps it even gave them something in common.

'Here, Mum,' Louise held out her arm. 'If you want to make an entrance, why don't you grab hold of this.'

Olivia hesitated, then stalked forward in her ankle boots to take Louise's arm. She beamed at her.

'I'm not used to walking in heels. I feel like Dick Emery.'

'Just don't wear them round the world, then.' Louise kissed her cheek. 'I'm proud of you too, Mum. I'm sorry I've been so quiet.'

341

'It's all right, dear. I know what the problem is,' Olivia said, reorganising her scarf once more ready to mount the steps.

'You do?'

'That boyfriend of yours.' Olivia nodded. 'Good riddance to bad rubbish, that's what I say. Good Lord, I sound just like Shaun!'

Louise absorbed the remark without comment. Agreement was on the tip of her tongue, but it couldn't be. That wouldn't make any sense.

'Who's Shaun, Mum? You mentioned him before.'

'He's a very nice man. I have a feeling he understands me very well. Very well indeed. Odd, isn't it? Come on then, shall we trip the light fantastic?'

'Yes, let's.'

Louise stopped as they heard footsteps hurrying towards them in the darkness.

'Oh, hang on, Mum. I think that's Rachel.'

Olivia glanced over her shoulder. 'Is that you, Rachel?'

'Who's that, then?' came an answering, breathless voice. Louise let go of her mother's arm and they both turned to examine a woman who was trotting across the concrete, grabbing at an umbrella and raising a red, harassed face to them.

'It's, er, I'm Olivia. Who's that?'

'It's one of your old crones,' Louise whispered into her mother's ear, and heard her stifle a giggle. 'And the years haven't been kind either.'

'Shhh!' Olivia pinched Louise's arm through her jacket. 'Hello there! I must know you, I think. Are you here for the reunion?'

'Olivia!' The woman reached them, panting uncomfortably. 'Just let me get my breath back. I'm late, I know it. I expect the others are all inside by now. It doesn't do to be late, does it? But the trains are so unreliable.

Public transport's just getting worse, isn't it?'

'We wouldn't know,' Louise entered smoothly on her mother's behalf. 'We were whisked here in a BMW.'

'A BMW?' The woman coughed and gave a broad smile. Louise regretted her boast when she registered the wiry greyness of the woman's hair, blown into chaos by the wind, her huddled shoulders within her thin coat, and the tired look around her eyes. 'Oh, that's nice. I can't drive myself, but it's lovely to get a lift, isn't it? This must be your daughter, Olivia. I'm so thrilled to meet you.' She shook her head. 'What a beautiful girl. You must be so proud.'

Olivia had walked away from Louise, leaving her standing stupidly with her elbow extended, and towards the cold woman with the flyaway hair.

'Good grief!' she issued in a breath.

'And you look wonderful!' the woman said. 'But you always were a beauty, Olivia. I used to be so jealous of you. Not that you'd ever have known it. But we should get inside really, shouldn't we? They must be wondering where I am.'

Olivia surprised Louise, and the cold woman judging by the startled expression on her face, by suddenly enveloping her in a hug.

'Oh, yes,' she panted at Louise over Olivia's shoulder. 'Let's do this, shall we?'

'Katherine!' Olivia gulped aloud. 'It's so – so wonderful to see you!'

'And you too, but we'd better go in, hadn't we?'

'Katherine Muff?' Louise voiced her surprise aloud.

'Stacey, actually.' Katherine coughed again. 'We mustn't stand out here in the cold.'

'Oh, and here's my other daughter!' Olivia exclaimed, standing back to welcome Rachel as she arrived jangling her car keys, and sauntering in an impossibly sensual way

343

towards them. 'I hope you don't mind me bringing one extra. Rachel, this is Katherine.'

'Katherine Muff?' Rachel reached them and raised her dark eyebrows expressively.

'Stacey,' Katherine corrected. They stood and stared as Katherine put her head to one side and seemed to deliver them a series of winks. It was a moment before Louise realised it was a nervous tic.

'Let's go in,' Olivia said quickly, allowing Katherine to plod up the steps ahead of them, and giving both of her daughters long, warning looks before following.

Chapter Nineteen

'This is driving me mad,' Rachel whispered to Louise as she dug an elongated spoon into her Strawberry Heaven. Louise bit back a sympathetic smile.

'Never mind. Nearly over.'

But Olivia was enjoying herself. Louise cast her a sideways glance. The sixteen women were seated along a row of narrow mahogany tables which had been pushed together for the occasion. They had added a place for Rachel at the end, and Louise had managed to slip herself on to the corner next to her. Most of the women hadn't brought guests, but those who had seemed to have opted for sisters or friends rather than husbands. It was a zone devoid of testosterone apart from a doe-eyed young waiter with floppy brown hair who brought on a flurry of airy giggles every time he approached the table. It had occurred to Louise that she and Rachel might behave the same way on sight of a desirable young male thing once they were well into their fifties. It would all depend on who you had at home waiting for you.

Katherine Muff was at the far end of the table, engrossed in conversation with a pale woman who was pecking at her bread roll like an undernourished sparrow, despite the fact that they were on dessert. Olivia was opposite a woman called Geraldine, whose eyebrows spread from her eyelids to her hairline, and whose breasts were comfortably resting on the table. Louise sipped her Coke and smiled down at her mother's animated profile as she waved her hands in mid-explanation. She looked fantastic.

By far the most vibrant of the women at the table, although one of her earrings had slipped off and was resting on top of her Banana and Chocolate Supreme. Louise felt a surge of pride. Her mother had so much to talk about, because so much was happening for her. And it was about time, too. Rachel had been right.

Louise turned back to her Pineapple Delight and stabbed at it again. It had been comforting to think that her mother would be there for her. Even while Jon was battling to prove to her that they could make it work as a couple, she had always felt that there was a safety net. If it all went wrong, she could dive back into her old bedroom, baby in tow, and sort herself out. She'd even wondered if her mother might be keen to babysit while she forged her way in a new career. She sucked on a mouthful of cream. When she made her situation clear, later, when they were alone together, would Olivia abandon her plans and offer to stay? Would it ruin the new life she was charting out for herself?

But if she explained that she and Jon were going to stay together then Olivia would still be free to explore her new ideas. Perhaps that was it, Louise decided, brightening. She should explain that she wasn't relying on her mother for anything, and then they could all be happy about it. All, she thought, casting a look at her sister while she pulled a disbelieving face at her twelve-inch-high dessert, apart from Rachel, of course. Rachel had talked incessantly about Hallam's children on the journey down, and how ill-equipped she felt to be a stepmother. No, there would be no joy on Rachel's behalf. But she couldn't have everything.

'Girls?'

Louise swivelled round. Her mother had crept down the table and put a hand on her shoulder. She spoke into Louise's ear, loud enough for Rachel to hear. 'Just to let you know, I've spotted someone I know at the bar.'

Louise wondered how this could be interesting information to them when they hadn't got a clue who anybody at the dinner was anyway. Rachel abandoned her fight with her Strawberry Heaven and looked up without interest.

'Who's that, then?'

'Carol!' Olivia ducked behind Louise's back as if she was dodging a bullet.

'Mum?' Louise twisted her neck painfully to find her mother squatting on her haunches and snorting silently to herself. 'Carol who?'

'Carol from work!' Olivia rasped, her face flushed, putting a finger up to her lips. It struck Louise that she was somewhat the worse for wear. 'She's sitting on a bar stool over by the green ice bucket. But don't look now!'

Rachel and Louise swung round to stare. There was a petite woman in a tight skirt and high heels teetering on the edge of one of the high, red-trimmed stools placed along the bar. She was smiling into the eyes of a tall man with grey highlights who was sitting alongside her, and who, judging by the expression on both their faces, was showering compliments on her. Louise was surprised. The woman didn't look like someone who could put the fear of God into her employees. But then, you never could tell.

'That dwarf's her?' Rachel exclaimed in loud disbelief.

'Shhhh!' Olivia rounded her eyes reprovingly. 'I just thought I'd point her out. Don't let her know we've seen her.'

'Mum's the word!' Rachel said, a smile spreading across her face. 'Is that her lover?'

'SSHHHH!' Olivia hissed. 'It's Roger. The area manager. They mustn't know I'm here!'

'Why not?' Rachel said, arching an eyebrow. 'Won't do any harm for them to know, will it? You could blackmail her. She'd have to be nice to you then.'

Olivia shook her head wildly.

'But, Mum,' Louise reasoned, concerned at the sight of her mother crouching on the carpet. 'If you're resigning anyway, none of it matters, does it?'

'That's not the point!' Olivia said, lurching to one side as the young waiter appeared. He glanced down, shook his head, and proceeded to the end of the table where Katherine Muff was beckoning him coquettishly.

'Mum, stand up. You can't stay down there,' Louise said.

'I just wanted you to see her,' Olivia mouthed as she began to inch back towards her chair.

She slipped back into her seat, leaned over her dessert to stare down the table at her daughters with a suggestive expression, then nodded earnestly at Geraldine. Geraldine hadn't seemed to notice that she'd been away. Louise watched while her mother delivered a spoonful of dessert to her mouth, realised that she was chewing on her earring and delicately put her napkin over her mouth to retrieve it. She turned her attention back to Rachel. Rachel still seemed to be fixated on the image of Carol at the bar.

'What a cow,' Rachel ejected. 'When you think of all the crap she's put Mum through. She deserves a broken nose. I'd love to be the one to give it to her.'

'Hmmn,' Louise agreed.

'Oh, hold up. She's going to the loo.'

Louise glanced up with more interest. 'How can you tell?'

'She's patting his arm and pulling her handbag on to her shoulder. Unless she's leaving, but I don't think so. No, I was right. Heading for the ladies. Probably going to put her Femidom in right now.'

'God, Rachel. You're making me feel sick.'

'The food's doing that, Lou, nothing to do with me. Right then.'

348

Louise looked up in surprise as Rachel got to her feet.

'Where are you going?'

'India,' Rachel said with a straight face.

'You're not . . .'

'I need a wee. Is that all right with you?'

'No, Rachel. No violence!' Louise frowned at her vigorously. She'd seen that odd look on her sister's face before. It meant trouble. It had been twenty-three years ago, when Rachel had declared fervently that she would tickle Louise without mercy until she relinquished Sindy's caravan and let her keep it for ever.

'See you in a tick.' Rachel had calmly picked up her bag and was already walking down the low carpeted steps from the restaurant area to the bar.

'No!' Louise stood up and immediately sat down again. She smiled reassuringly at the woman called Audrey sitting opposite her, who had looked embarrassed at regular intervals for no reason that Louise could put her finger on. 'She's going to the loo,' Louise explained comfortingly.

'Ah,' Audrey said, nodding. 'They're nice toilets. Very clean. Plenty of paper.'

Louise nodded back.

'She – she should be fine then,' she smiled.

'Yes,' Audrey said, and blushed again.

Rachel pushed her way into the ladies and took in her surroundings. Five cubicles, only one of them occupied. She allowed the door to swing shut behind her and leaned back against it. It was stuffy in there despite the cold outside. Typical of such a place to have the heating on too high, even in the winter. There was a row of basins set into a unit of beige and green, and a long mirror spread over them. She heard a self-conscious sniff from the occupied toilet and sucked at her cheeks to stop herself smiling. She stood still for several minutes. Let her sweat. There was silence from the fenced-in compartment in which Carol, she hoped, was desperately trying to force herself to have a wee despite the fact that somebody could hear her. She heard another deep sniff, and the sounds of Carol rummaging in a handbag. That old chestnut. She would just give it long enough for Carol to think that she must have imagined that somebody else was in the ladies with her, and then she would act. She froze into position, breathing softly, for another minute.

Rachel dabbed around with a lipstick, pushed the tap to wash her hands, and put on another layer of mascara. She knew that Carol was waiting for her to leave but she wasn't going to give way. Eventually she heard the toilet-roll holder spinning, a series of loud coughs, and the flush being pulled. Rachel watched in the mirror as the cubicle door was opened, and the small, neat figure of her mother's tormentor emerged and headed for the basins.

'Hello,' Rachel said in a deep voice.

Carol glanced furtively over her shoulder as she picked up the soap and rubbed it between her hands under the hot water. She focused on Rachel as if seeking recognition. Rachel gave her a long, seductive smile. Carol turned back quickly to the business of washing her hands.

'Hello,' she said, a little nervously.

'You don't know me, do you?' Rachel said, draping herself over the sinks and batting her eyelashes.

'No,' Carol said firmly, avoiding Rachel's eye and fumbling inside her handbag for a lipstick.

'I'm another of Roger's lovers,' Rachel said. She waited for her words to be absorbed, forcing back a smirk. Carol eyed herself in the mirror, her lipstick halfway to her mouth. Then she turned round to look at Rachel properly. Rachel wiggled her eyebrows at her. 'Didn't he tell you about me?'

'I don't know what you mean,' Carol said at last. The colour had fled from her cheeks.

'He'll deny he's had others,' Rachel said factually. 'You can't blame him really. Got it all his own way. Devoted wife and a handful of mistresses.' She stretched herself erotically, squirming back to her own reflection and brushing her hair back behind her ears.

'Who are you?' Carol demanded.

'I didn't mind the fact that I wasn't the only one,' Rachel said philosophically to her reflection, ignoring the question. 'But can you put up with that?'

She glanced at Carol's profile in the mirror. Two bright red spots had appeared on her cheeks.

'The one before me couldn't.' Rachel pouted at herself. 'But you have to accept that not everyone's into the things Roger's into. It takes a broad mind to accommodate him.' She flashed Carol a dazzling smile. 'If you see what I mean. Perhaps that's why he stayed with me for so long.'

'What things? I mean, what do you know about Roger?' Ooh, she was losing it, Rachel thought with satisfaction. She was diving on the bait.

'Well, the last mistress – I'm sorry, you don't mind if I call you that, do you? – wouldn't put up with the role-playing.' She shrugged. 'But then, she was a bit strait-laced. I always thought so.'

'Role-playing?' Carol squinted at Rachel in alarm.

'You know. Doctors and nurses. Air stewardesses. Whatever. I must admit, the first time Roger told me that he wanted to be the nurse I was a bit surprised too. Especially when he asked me to go out and buy the kit for him.' She glanced at Carol in indignation. 'I mean, do you know how difficult it is to get a nurse's outfit with a chest forty-four and a thirty-eight waist? And Dolcis don't do black stilettos in a size twelve, let me tell you. You have to order them specially.'

Rachel awarded herself a point. Years of experience had paid off. She could estimate a man's size at a glance, and judging by the way that Carol was gripping the edge of the basin with white knuckles, she'd been pretty accurate. Now it was time for the kill.

'But don't make the mistake the others do,' Rachel went on, wagging a finger. 'Don't wait for him to ask you. It embarrasses him so much. Take my advice, Carol—'

'You know my name?' Carol whispered.

'Listen, sweetheart, I've heard about them all.' Rachel pulled a rueful face at herself and hoisted up her knickers. 'If you want to keep him, surprise him. That's what they never learn. I'm sure that's why he kept coming back to me. But you've got to make sure he thinks it's your idea.'

'My idea?'

'Absolutely,' Rachel confirmed. 'The last one got it all wrong. He feels so –' she searched for the right word, 'patronised if he thinks you're doing it just for him. You have to say to him, firmly, "Roger, this is what I want you to wear!"' She regarded Carol seriously. 'He'll pretend to be shocked. He'll even struggle. But for him, you see, that's part of the fun. You have to let him go through the motions. Make it clear it's what *you* want, that your sex life is incomplete without it, and you'll be fine.'

'God!' Carol leaned heavily on the basins and met her own eyes in the mirror.

'The truth is, Carol, I've met somebody I really like. If only Roger had another woman who could understand him the way I did we could say goodbye for good. It was only sex between us. He didn't really care about me.' She pursed her lips nobly. 'I always knew that. If he could find somebody he really admired who could share his sexual tendencies too . . . well, then I think he would have found the woman of his dreams. That would free me up – and

Roger would be all yours. That's why I'm telling you all this.' Rachel put out a hand and touched Carol's arm lightly. 'One woman to another.'

Carol nodded, her jaw clenched.

'Don't let him know we've spoken.' Rachel said sincerely. 'If I were you, I'd get him out of here before he sees me.' Rachel shook her head, biting on her lip emotionally. She gathered Carol into her arms. 'He's yours for the taking, Carol. You know what to do now!'

Carol was stiff and small within her embrace. Rachel felt a flicker of doubt running through her, but brushed it away. She thought of the five years in which her mother had been ridiculed and belittled under Carol's rule. Olivia may have thought that her predicament had gone unnoticed but Rachel had been aware of it. This may have been her first chance to act, but her protective instincts had always been strong. Ricky's face flashed into her mind as she patted Carol on the back. She was good at protecting others. At fighting other people's corners. Perhaps one day she'd be good at fighting her own too.

'Good luck, Carol.' She flashed a smile at her. 'I think you deserve him. I really do.'

Carol gave a brief nod, gathered her bag and stalked away. She stopped at the swing door and looked back at Rachel, her dark eyes bleary.

'Thank you for being so honest with me. It's a good thing when women can stand together like this. It's so hard out there, trying to prove yourself in a man's world, trying to be strong for everybody. Putting a bit too much energy into it. As if you're compensating. For not being a man, for not being a mother.' Carol gave a half-laugh. 'I hate myself sometimes, if you want to know the truth.'

Rachel nodded slowly, her smile fading.

'You'd better get out of here, Carol.'

'Yes.' Carol gave an embarrassed laugh. 'Thank you whoever you are.'

'Don't thank me.'

Rachel watched her go. The door swung shut behind her. After she was sure that her mother's boss was not going to run back and put her head round the door with another pertinent observation, she began to relax. She also began to feel distinctly uncomfortable. She leaned heavily against the basins and stared at herself. Her own guilty face stared back. She wasn't sure how much time elapsed as she confronted her own image, but her isolation was destroyed as the door to the ladies was shoved open, and a breathless voice assailed her.

'Rachel!' It was Louise. 'What the hell did you do? I sat there for ages thinking you two were beating each other to death with your Filofaxes, then Carol came out looking as if she'd seen a ghost, grabbed Roger, and they both left. What the hell did you say?'

Rachel pulled her handbag on to her shoulder.

'Have they gone?'

'Yes. It was all very subdued. What have you been doing?'

'What have I been doing?' Rachel slipped her arm into Louise's and walked her back to the door. 'Being a total hypocrite, that's what.'

'But you told her where to get off?' Louise asked wondrously.

'Not so much where to get off as how,' Rachel said shortly. 'And we must be allowed to go home now, surely?'

'We're going to give Katherine a lift home,' Olivia announced to Louise in the lobby. Rachel had already gone to extricate the car and bring it round to the front for them seeing as a freezing rain had started to fall.

'We are?' Louise glanced around her. At the door, people were saying goodbye in a much more tactile fashion than they had said hello. She wondered whether the wine had anything to do with that, or whether all of the women had turned up to the reunion gripped by the same fears as her mother.

'Yes,' Olivia said distractedly, grabbing one of her rediscovered friends in a farewell hug and stepping back to look around. 'Ah. Here she is!'

'I can get the train,' Katherine was saying as she crossed the lobby being helped into her coat enthusiastically by the doe-eyed waiter. 'It's very kind of you to offer, Olivia, but it's right out of your way.'

'Nonsense!' Olivia said firmly. 'It's a small detour, and besides, I've hardly had a chance to talk to you all evening. I don't know what you've been doing.'

'No. Well.' Katherine smiled gratefully at the waiter as he propelled her purposefully towards the door. 'Thank you, young man. And we'll definitely be coming back here. We've decided to do this every few months, you see. But I'll let you know when. I've got the card.' She winked at him several times and twitched her head. His smile tightened.

'Let's get outside,' Louise said, nudging her mother's elbow. 'Rachel won't want to be kept waiting.'

'Oh yes,' Katherine huffed chestily as she trotted across the carpet, her coat halfway up her body. 'Your other daughter. Quite stunning, isn't she?'

Louise sighed as her mother stopped in her tracks to wait for Katherine. For a moment she'd thought she could get all three of them through the door and down the steps in one fluid motion. They began a discussion about Rachel's looks.

'Is that Rachel hooting?' Louise wrenched at Olivia's coat. 'Yes, it is. We'd better hurry up.' As they made it out

355

on to the porch, Louise hissed into her mother's ear, 'If it takes you this long to get out of a restaurant, how many years is it going to take you to go round the world?'

'Oh, be quiet you. Rachel's waiting.'

They jogged through the rain to where Rachel had stopped the car. Louise dived into the back and shuffled her way along the seat. There was a long wait while the rain hammered at the car roof and Louise and Rachel waited for Katherine to stop protesting and get in the front. Finally Olivia pushed her into the seat, closed the door on her, and slipped into the back. Rachel paused with the keys in the ignition.

'Where are we going?'

'Hildenborough,' Olivia said assertively.

'It's very kind of you.' Katherine shook her rain-spattered hair in Rachel's direction. 'You're both such lovely girls. I was telling Olivia how lucky she was.'

Rachel pulled away from the restaurant and out into the traffic in the main road.

'You need to take this fork, Rachel,' Olivia said, leaning between the two front seats and pointing at the wind-screen. Louise gently pulled her back into her seat.

'She knows, Mum,' she said quietly. 'You're forgetting, we used to live here too.'

'Oh, you!' Olivia muttered with a hint of annoyance. 'When are you going to stop telling me off, Louise? I'm the mother, not you.'

'It's like that, isn't it?' Katherine contributed, settling into her seat, although Louise noticed that she reached for her seat-belt and gripped it with iron fingers as Rachel decided it was time to hit warp drive. 'It all changes when you get older. My sons tell me off all the time.'

'Oh yes, tell me about your family!' Olivia squeezed her head between the two front seats. 'I'm dying to hear all about them. And about you. What did you do after school?

Somebody told me you trained to be a journalist. That must have been exciting.'

'If you don't sit back I'm going to elbow you in the face, Mum.' Rachel met Louise's eyes in her driving mirror. Louise hid a smile.

'You just drive the car, Rachel. I'm going to talk to Katherine,' Olivia insisted.

'Well, I did some training. I had it all worked out then. I wanted to be a foreign correspondent. Can you imagine that now?' Katherine peered down at herself bleakly. 'But then I got married and the boys came along, and it never really happened how I'd planned it.'

'You were always good at languages,' Olivia said supportively. 'You were always good at everything. You need to turn off here, Rachel. I used to think you might be a translator or something.'

'You were good, too,' Katherine said. 'If you hadn't left—'

'Here, Rachel!' Olivia banged Rachel's shoulder. 'The back way's quicker.'

'I speak four languages,' Katherine confirmed as the car swung off the main road and they all grabbed hold of the nearest luxury fitting for support. 'But I've never really used them. The boys have travelled. Greg's in Australia now, and Mark went to California. He's a scientist, you see, and that's where the facilities are. We used to go to France a lot as a family, but that was when Graham was alive. I don't go there any more.'

Rachel drove on into the rain. The roads became darker and narrower. They seemed to be heading out into the country.

'Are you sure this is the right way, Mum?'

'Yes, dear, just keep driving. So Graham isn't – isn't with us any more?' Louise frowned at her mother's clumsiness. Olivia's expression showed that the words hadn't come

357

out quite as she'd intended. There was a pause. Katherine swallowed noisily and gave a small cough.

'He – um. I lost him four years ago. I—'

Katherine startled them all by choking back on a violent sob. Rachel was so shocked she swerved, mounted a low bank and scraped the car along a hedgerow before bringing them back on to the road again with a thump. Louise grabbed hold of the seat in front. Olivia sat forward, putting a hand on Katherine's shoulder.

'Slow down, Rachel,' she urged in a low voice.

'Right,' Rachel said, casting a look at Katherine which was for the first time, tinged with concern. 'Are you all right Mrs Muff?'

'Stacey,' Katherine corrected in a wobbly voice. 'Just call me Katherine, please. I'm all right. I'm sorry. I really am sorry.'

She delved into the pocket of her coat and pulled out a handkerchief. Silently, she mopped at her cheeks. Rachel slowed the car to a crawl.

'Rachel?' Their mother's voice was uneven. 'Pull over please, in the next safe spot.'

'We're in the middle of nowhere, Mum. There might be werewolves around.'

'Just stop joking and do as I say. Find a lay-by or a passing place or something, and pull the car right off the road.'

Rachel flicked her eyes to Louise in the mirror. Louise regarded her sombrely. The car purred on until they reached the entrance to a field with a five-bar gate set back from the lane. She edged off the road, pulled alongside the gate and stopped. She slipped into neutral and the engine died away to a low hum. It was quiet apart from the whirr of the heating fans and an odd stifled sound coming from underneath Katherine's hanky.

'Mum?' Rachel whispered.

'Shhh!' Olivia shot her a severe look. Rachel bit her lip and sat still. Louise waited.

In the warmth and peace of the car, Louise felt as if she was picking up the vibrations coming from Katherine's heaving chest. Even Rachel's dark eyes were unusually melancholy when she glanced at her again in the mirror. For several moments, the four women sat, alone with their thoughts. Olivia broke the hush.

'Katherine?' She rubbed at the huddled shoulder. Louise turned to look at Olivia in surprise. Her own mother's voice was trembling, as if she was close to tears. But she hadn't seen her cry since her father had died. 'Do you want to talk about Graham?'

Katherine nodded, pulling her handkerchief away from her face. Louise could see a stream of tears cascading down her chin.

'Nobody lets you talk about it, do they?' Olivia said, struggling with her words. 'Since I lost Bob I haven't been allowed to talk about him to anybody. I can think about him, but I can't let it out.'

'I know!' Katherine turned in her seat and looked back at Olivia. Louise watched her mother's face crumple. A bolt of shock paralysed her. Olivia was going to cry, and judging by the distortion of her face it wasn't just going to be a dribble of tears.

'Graham was such a lovely man. I loved him so much!' Katherine said in a high voice. 'We used to do everything together. After he retired, we had so many rows. He became so difficult, but I never stopped loving him. He was my companion. And now he's gone and I'm so alone. Life's so empty now.'

Louise clamped her teeth together. If she wasn't careful she was going to cry too. Olivia drew in a deep breath beside her, tried to speak, then let out a long wail. Louise stuffed her hands into her pockets and fumbled for a tissue. The one she produced was old and frayed around the edges, but she bunged it along the seat to her mother. Olivia took it and cried into it as if her heart was breaking. Louise cleared her throat and glanced quickly at Rachel in the driving mirror. To her shock, Rachel's eyes were brimming.

'I loved Bob,' Olivia gulped, 'and he loved me, too. He was so kind. And I felt so guilty when he died. I still feel so gu-guilty.'

'I wish I'd been nicer to Graham when he was ill.' Katherine smothered her face with her handkerchief. 'I snapped at him sometimes. I didn't mean to. He became very d-difficult.'

'And it's too late now!' Olivia rammed Louise's tissue into her eyes.

Louise gazed up at the cream leatherette ceiling. The two older women cried and cried. The fans whirred. Beyond the windows, rain dripped from the spiked twigs of the beech hedge. She closed her eyes and swallowed the hard lump in her throat. From the driver's seat, she could hear Rachel sniffing loudly. She opened one eye in time to see her sister bend her head over the steering wheel and release a long sob.

'I – I'm so s-sorry,' Katherine emitted.

'It's not you,' Olivia wept forcefully into the stringy tissue. 'It's me.'

'It's me.' Rachel brushed jerkily at her face with her hand. 'I've left Hallam. But I love him. I love him so much. I wish I'd never left him!'

Olivia clamped her hand on to her daughter's shoulder and gripped it.

'And – and I'm pregnant!' Louise contributed. Without warning, she too burst into tears.

Olivia moved her hand swiftly from Rachel's shoulder to Louise's knee. She squeezed it until it hurt. Then, as if

Louise's words had sunk in, she gathered her youngest daughter into her arms in the back seat and they hugged as if they couldn't let each other go.

The inside of the car suddenly seemed to get brighter. Louise stiffly pulled away from her mother and squinted. Somebody was shining a torch at them from the outside.

'Rachel?' Louise whispered in alarm. Rachel raised her head from the steering wheel, her make-up everywhere except where it should be. She blinked into the torchlight as somebody tapped on the driver's window. She pressed a button and the window dropped with an electronic whine. Louise craned forwards.

'Oh hello, officer,' Rachel swallowed. 'How can we help you?'

'I wondered if everything was all right in here.' Louise could see a uniformed policeman peering into the car. Now she could see the squad car that was parked a few yards up the lane ahead of them. They hadn't heard it drive past or pull over.

The four women nodded at him mutely, stifling sobs. He regarded them for a moment longer in fascination, then flicked off the torch.

'It's not a very safe place to stop, madam. I'd suggest you move on from here. The lane widens out as you get into Hildenborough.' He paused as they all seemed to choose the same moment to wipe their eyes. 'There's a large lay-by about a mile ahead if you want to stop and – chat.'

Rachel nodded and gave him a weak smile.

'Thank you.' She stabbed the button and the window zipped up again decisively, leaving his transfixed face staring at them all a moment longer. Then he wandered away towards his car. They watched him in the head-lamps. The squad car moved off and rounded the corner out of sight.

Olivia drew in a long breath and let it out again slowly.

They all followed suit. Louise felt as if she'd been un
strapped from a whalebone corset and could breathe
freely again.

'Well,' Olivia said at last. Katherine made a noise o
agreement. Rachel and Louise nodded. Rachel readjusted
her seat-belt and put the car into gear, dropping the
handbrake. She glanced around her.

'Are you really pregnant, Lou?'

'Yes,' Louise admitted.

'Fuck me,' she breathed.

'Language!' Olivia and Katherine ejected as one. Rache
turned back to the wheel.

'Right then. Are we all ready to move on now?'

Chapter Twenty

'It's just so incredible!' Rachel grinned, lobbing her glass at her mouth and sucking up the contents. 'I still can't believe it. Me, an auntie! A real live auntie!'

'It's still incredible to me too, Rach.'

Louise was becoming confused. She was sitting at the kitchen table sipping on a cold glass of water, Rachel was emptying the bottle of wine she'd brought with her into her glass, and Olivia was standing at the kitchen door, gazing at her own reflection.

She'd expected to get two contrasting reactions to her announcement. On that count, she'd been dead right. But what was confusing her was that it was her mother who had started to look as if she was sucking lemons while Rachel was bubbling over with excitement.

'But what does it actually *feel* like? I can't imagine it.'

'Well, it's weird. It's not like anything else you've felt before. It's like being a chauffeur. You just drive around wherever you're told to go.'

'I can try to imagine that.' Rachel looked vague and took Louise's fingers in her hand. 'I'm just so sorry I was a cow to you before. I wish you'd told me.'

'I needed time to work it out on my own.' She smiled back at her sister.

Olivia drew an audible breath. 'You surely don't mean you're going to keep it?' she exclaimed.

'Oh yes!' Louise nodded at her forcefully. 'Yes, I am.'

'Thank God for that.' Rachel clutched at her chest. 'I was

already planning complimentary tickets to Hanson concerts.'

'Louise,' Olivia sat down with them and laid her hands flat on the table. 'I don't think you've thought this through.'

'I have.' Louise folded her arms across her chest.

'It's not as easy as you think,' Olivia said with emphasis. 'Having a child on your own's a terrible thing.'

'Terrible?'

'You'll have no life. You won't be able to go out. You'll be stuck inside, frustrated and unhappy. You won't be able to form friendships or relationships. Your life will come to a standstill.'

'Mum,' she said, biting back her disappointment, 'I've thought about it very carefully. I've got plans and ideas. I don't need you to bail me out. I need your moral support, that's all.'

'I can't give you that!' Olivia looked as if she was going to burst into tears for the second time that night. Both Louise and Rachel were stunned. 'You don't know what you're doing. Good God, Louise, what's the matter with you? It's not difficult to sort it out these days. Not like it was when I was young. It was illegal then, don't you realise that? If you got pregnant, you were stuck with it. And him, whoever he was. Single mothers were stigmatised. You were labelled everywhere you went as a disgrace.'

'*Plus ça change,*' Rachel muttered.

'I—' Louise sought in her confused brain for answers. 'I'm not going to be a single mother. I'm going to stay with Jon.'

'I thought you two had split up?' Olivia looked increasingly distressed.

'We did, but we got back together again.' Louise stumbled over her inadequate reply. She'd never seen her mother look so overwrought. 'We're going to try to be a family. If that doesn't work out, I'll—'

'You're going to marry him?' Olivia's voice soared. 'Because of the baby?'

'Well, no. Well, yes. Not really. I'm not sure. He wants to marry me anyway, I think.'

Olivia stood up. She paced across the floor, wrenched at the key in the back door, and threw it open. A blast of December air assaulted them. She took several short, sharp breaths and closed the door again.

'What are you doing, Mum?' Rachel asked.

'Savouring the big wide world. It's all out there, you know.' She turned round. 'Louise, I can't let you do this.'

'You really can't stop me.'

'I'm telling you that I won't be there for you. You can't rely on me for financial support, or to help you bring up the baby. You can't expect me to play the role of the doting grandmother. I've been around for you both to lean on for too long. I've got my own life to lead now. You just can't be this – this selfish.'

Louise was aware that Rachel was gripping her hand tightly. She squeezed it back. She had an ally, if an unlikely one.

'I don't expect you to do anything, Mum. Nothing's going to change.'

'How can you say that?' Olivia pleaded. 'Everything will change. I'll have to do the right thing now, won't I? You'll need me. Jon won't stick by you. If you won't face it, then I will. I can't leave you all alone with your baby. You'll need somewhere to stay, and a babysitter while you sort your life out. Who else is going to do that for you?'

'You've only met Jon once,' Louise asserted. 'He's changed. You haven't seen him now. He's really happy about this. I owe it to the baby to try.'

'You're talking about marrying a man you don't love!'

365

Olivia protested, waving her hands in agitation. 'You'll spend the rest of your life regretting it. That's if you stay together. And if you don't, you'll be alone with your child anyway. I – I had such hopes for you. For both of you. And look at you. All you seem to want to do is destroy yourselves!'

'That's enough, Mum,' Rachel said in a low voice.

'No, it isn't enough!' Olivia thumped her fist down on to the table, making them both leap off their chairs in shock. 'You don't understand! I married a man I wasn't in love with, don't you see? I wasn't in love with him! stayed with him for years knowing that because of you two girls.'

Louise stared. Their mother? Not in love with their father? How could this be?

'What do you mean? Of course you loved him. You've just had too many glasses of hock. You're getting maudlin.'

'I mean I *had* to marry him. Don't you understand?' Olivia hurled at her.

'What do you mean, you *had* to?' This was ludicrous.

Rachel sipped her wine without comment.

'Because of her!' Olivia pointed at Rachel. 'Because I was pregnant, and because in those days you had the choice of dying on the table of a back-street abortionist, or getting married. That was it! But it's not the same now. You've got a choice. Why can't you see that? Why can't you take advantage of the way things have changed?'

Louise gaped at her own mother. She felt as if she'd been Tangoed.

'You okay, Lou?' It was Rachel's soft voice in her ear. She nodded.

'I just don't understand what's going on.'

'Do you want to go to bed? You look tired.'

Louise looked down at Rachel's hand stroking hers.

'No, I've suddenly got a second wind. I wish someone would explain all this to me.'

Olivia stood up abruptly, marched over to the kettle and waved it in the air. Her face was still strained.

'Coffee, anyone?' She filled the kettle from the tap and plugged it in. Rachel shook her head woefully at her mother's back.

'Poor Mum,' she said under her breath. 'All these years. It's no wonder you've been so unhappy.'

Olivia collected crockery from the cupboard and crashed the cups on to the saucers. She pulled a handful of teaspoons from a drawer and banged them down on the unit.

'I'm fine,' she sniffed. 'I'm sorry that I had to tell you like that, Rachel. I didn't mean to throw it in your face. I've never regretted having you.' She concentrated on arranging the teaspoons in the saucers. She grabbed at a jar of coffee and yanked off the lid. Louise and Rachel followed the resulting explosion of granules down to the kitchen tiles.

'Mum?' Rachel said softly. 'I knew it all anyway.'

The teaspoons clattered.

'You can't have done,' Olivia said, patting at the side of the kettle to see if it was warm.

'I did. Dad told me.'

'He did?' Olivia scratched at her head and played with a teaspoon that catapulted through the air and landed in the sink. She replaced it with another one.

'Yes, he did.'

'When?' Louise's voice was a squeak.

'A long time ago. He made me promise not to tell Mum knew.'

'Then – then why didn't he tell me? We talked about everything.'

Rachel's expression seemed to harden as she looked at Louise, but then she squeezed her hand again.

'I know you and Dad were bosom buddies, but this wa
something that didn't involve you. It was because Mun
was depressed at the time, and seeing the doctor. I wante
to know why, and he told me.'

'Depressed?' Louise looked back to her mother fo
confirmation. 'I don't remember you ever being de
pressed!'

'That's the advantage of being the youngest,' Rache
explained. 'At the time you were busy drooling ove
Starsky and Hutch posters and playing Abba albums. You
were too young to notice.'

'Mum?' Louise wanted to run around the room with he
hands over her ears, shouting – but she wouldn't have
known what to shout. Everyone was behaving as if these
revelations were true. Olivia didn't answer. She banged
open the cupboard and pulled out a pack of biscuits.

'Jammy Dodger, anyone?'

'She's in denial,' Rachel told Louise in a low voice as i
their mother had just been sectioned. 'And if she won't tel
you why, I will.'

'Why?' Louise mouthed.

'Mum? Are you going to explain?' Rachel pressed.

'Explain what, dear?' Olivia proffered the pack o
Jammy Dodgers. They both shook their heads.

'You want Lou to do the things you didn't do,' Rache
began. 'When you were in the sixth form at the gramma
school you had your life ahead of you. Bright prospects
good qualifications, and supportive parents. But then i
went horribly wrong. You left early without a word o
explanation to anyone. Suddenly, it was all over.'

'No. I—'

'Your supportive parents threw you out on the street.'

Olivia's face was like chalk.

'My mother didn't understand. Things were differen
then.'

'You had no choice. You were on your own. You had to marry a brickie.'

'I—'

'She threw you out?' Louise looked at her mother in horror. 'Granny?'

'She was a prize bitch, Lou.' Rachel's black eyes flashed. 'She'd never have let us know, but she abandoned Mum when she needed her the most.'

'Oh God.' Olivia dropped the Jammy Dodgers and put her hands over her face.

'So it's not Mum's fault that she sees the same things happening to you.' Rachel's grip on Louise's hand was so tight it had started to hurt. 'In fact, she's manufacturing the same situation. It's all she knows.'

Louise tried to pull her hand away. She wanted to rush to her mother and put her arms around her. How could she possibly have guessed at some point in their lives they might both have been alone, bewildered and pregnant? But Louise was happy and excited about it now. That was something they hadn't shared.

'Mum—' She stood up.

'Not now, dear,' Olivia said, taking her hands from her face. 'I – I'll talk to you tomorrow. I'm going to bed now. I need to be on my own.'

'But—'

'You go on to bed,' Rachel inserted. 'It's all right, Mum. We're all too tired tonight to think anything through. We'll see you in the morning.'

Olivia nodded. Her eyes were glassy. She touched Louise lightly and held out her cheek for Rachel to kiss. They watched her drift away as if she was walking through water. The door to the hall clicked and they heard her footsteps as she mounted the stairs.

Rachel emptied the bottle of wine into her glass. She let out a long breath, and raised her eyebrows. Louise had the feeling that she was going to say something meaningful.

'Shall we scoff all the Jammy Dodgers now Mum's gone?'

'Oh, Rach.' Louise lunged towards her and engulfed her in a hug. 'You've been so amazing. I'd never have thought you'd be my champion. What would I have done without you?'

'I just think it's about time we were all honest with each other.' Rachel returned the hug. 'Hey, it's a profound moment, finding out you're going to be an auntie. Probably much, much more profound than knowing you're going to be a mother.'

Louise gurgled at her happily. 'Whatever you say, big sis.'

'No, really. Think about it. By the time your baby's sixteen, he or she is going to hate you with a passion for no other reason than because you're Mum. But I'll escape all that. I'll be the maverick auntie. I'll do the jokes, you do the nagging. Suits me fine.'

Louise sank back into her chair and gazed at her sister fondly.

'You've been so strong. You're always strong. I don't know how you do it.'

'It happens when you're the eldest. You grow up fast. I got told things while you were still making stools out of cotton reels and Fablon for Sindy's caravan.'

It probably wasn't a good moment to remind Rachel that she'd extorted Sindy's caravan from her. Louise pushed her hands under her clothes and felt for her stomach. It was an unconscious gesture, but she felt better with the warmth of her fingers over her skin.

'I'm so happy for you.' Rachel's eyes had dropped to Louise's stomach too. 'And if you get bored, you can offload it on me.'

'I thought you hated children.'

'I don't hate children at all.' Rachel gave a wobbly smile.
'I love the boys, you know. I really do. Hallam kept
shutting me out. I felt like a total outsider. It's difficult
trying to be a good stepmother when nobody will let you
in. That's all it was, but it was so important. I've got
maternal instincts, too, you know, if only somebody will
give me a chance to show them. I should have explained it
to him, but I didn't. I threw a painting at him and ran
away. Stupid, defensive cow that I am.'

'A painting?'

'The woman with three breasts. He bought it in Finland.
I've always hated it.'

Louise chewed on her lip. Annihilating Hallam's taste in
paintings could be put off for another time.

'You're going back to Hallam, then?'

'If he'll have me.'

'You really do love him, don't you?'

Rachel nodded. 'Unadulterated Richard and Judy. I
never realised how much until I left. He's everything I
want. I – I think it's really important to be with the man
you love, Lou, whatever packaging he comes in.'

'How do you know, though?' Louise frowned. 'You
have to weigh it all up, don't you?'

'Nope. That's too clinical. You know in the pit of your
stomach. That's it. I think Mum's right about that. You
shouldn't tie yourself to Jon unless you're very sure about
him. You might meet someone in the future who you can
really love. What would you do if he walked into your life
and you were already married, for all the wrong reasons?
It'd be a mess. You've got to think about that.'

Louise tried to form her doubts into sentences, but she
couldn't. She'd thought that she'd be able to talk through
her feelings with her mother, but Olivia had fled. It was up
to her two daughters to make sure the house was secure

and turn the lights out. The younger generation had assumed control while their mother had scooted off to the safety of her bedroom. Life had moved on.

'Rachel, there was just one thing I was going to ask you.'

'Shoot,' Rachel said.

'It's just about work.' Louise stopped. 'It's, um—'

'There's going to be a temping slot coming up in January in promotions. One of the assistants is leaving, and we usually try out a temp first to see what happens. It'd be totally up to you to prove yourself, of course, but if you're interested in that for starters, it'll get your foot in the door. If you can impress the right people you could have a break waiting for you after the baby's born.'

Louise felt a warm rush of pleasure. She hadn't even had to beg, and Rachel wasn't going to make her feel stupid for turning down opportunities in the past.

'But I'd have to be interviewed.'

'Of course.'

'I – I'm not sure how good I'd be. I'm not dynamic in the way you are. I wouldn't want them to think they'd got another Rachel Twigg turning up.'

'You'd be treated on your merits along with the rest, Lou. This isn't nepotism, just pointing you in the right direction. I reckon you'll be fine, though. All you've lacked is motivation. This department would be perfect for you. You've got a good eclectic interest, imagination, and you're a charmer. You're a smart cookie, and I think the company will snatch you up.'

'God, it almost sounds as if you like me.'

'Don't push it.'

Louise beamed at her.

'Aren't you going to be smug and unbearable?'

'Nope,' Rachel smiled. 'But I will say it's about bloody time. Music's always been your thing. It's the right career

372

for you. And I say that as a highly perceptive woman, not just as your big sister.'

'Thanks. This means so much to me.'

'Go to bed now. You look bushed. We can talk about it again when you've had a good night's sleep.'

'Aren't you coming up too?'

'I just want to finish my glass of wine and pop into the garden for a fag. You use the bathroom first.'

'Okay.' Louise stood up.

'Lou?' Rachel grabbed her. 'I'll be the best auntie you could ever wish for.'

'I know you will. What with you and Sal I think this baby's going to be spoilt rotten. Until you both have your own babies, of course.'

Rachel shook her head.

'It's not for me. I love my job, and I love the family I've already got. You bring up a baby. I'd still rather bring up a wine box.'

Louise left Rachel in the kitchen and made her way through the hall and up the stairs. She stopped on the landing. Her mother's door was ajar. Louise listened. She could hear breathing, but she wasn't sure if she was asleep or not. She nudged open the door. A shaft of light fell across the flat bedspread. Olivia was sitting at the window, holding open the curtain and looking out at the sky. She seemed to sense somebody was in the room and turned round.

'Oh, Louise. I was just watching the clouds. They always fascinate me.'

Louise padded across the carpet and stood behind her mother.

'You never really see the sky in London.'

'That's a shame. I like to see the sky. It's always changing, always moving on to somewhere else.'

Louise kissed the top of her mother's head.

'You'll see a different sky when you travel. It will be wonderful. You'll have to write and tell us all about it.'

'I will.'

'I'm really excited for you, Mum.'

'And I'm excited for you, too, dear. You know when something's right. You can feel it.'

'Yes, you can.'

'I can feel it now, and I think you can too. It was wrong of me to try to tell you what to do.' Olivia's face was concerned. 'I hope you forgive me.'

'Hey, let's say no more about it. Tomorrow we'll start all over again.'

'I'm tired. You must be too. Good night, dear.'

Louise wandered away. Now she wanted to be in her old bed, to rest and not to have to think.

'Louise?'

'Yes, Mum?' She turned at the door.

'I'm sorry, darling.'

'It's all right. I understand.'

'I was thinking.' Olivia looked ghostly in the gloom. Like a spirit freeing itself from an earthly body. 'You could stay in the house while I'm away. It – it's a family house really. You and the baby could come here.'

Louise leaned against the door. 'Thanks, Mum. It's nice of you to offer, but it won't be necessary.'

'Yes, and that way, you don't have to marry . . .' Olivia's voice trailed away. She twitched the curtain again as the moon appeared from behind the clouds.

'Good night, Mum,' Louise said, pulling the door closed behind her.

'Nurses' uniforms?' Olivia paused on the doormat, giving Rachel an astonished look. Louise dumped her bags next to the car. 'Good Lord! You are an amazing girl. I had no idea you had it in you!'

'Well, we're all full of surprises, aren't we?' Rachel gave her mother a kiss. 'Go back in, Mum, you'll freeze out here. It looks as if it's going to snow sooner rather than later.'

'I wish you didn't have to leave so early. I was hoping to have you both all day.'

'I know, but if it does snow the traffic's going to be a pig.'

'I understand,' Olivia said regretfully. 'And you're sure you don't want to ring Jon to tell him you're on your way, Louise?'

'God, no!' Louise laughed. 'He's probably sleeping off a hangover. I expect he'll still be in bed when we get there. But you'd better go inside, Mum. You're shivering.'

'I want to wave you off. I'm not going to see you both until Christmas.'

'Oh, yeah, and that's years away.'

'And you will come down with Hallam and the children if he has them this year, Rachel? I thought it might be nice to have a big gathering this Christmas.'

Rachel nodded. 'If it works out, we'll come down together. I'll ring you and let you know.'

'I thought I might invite a few friends too,' Olivia said hesitantly. 'Just perhaps, you know, from work maybe. And I thought Katherine might like to join us for Christmas dinner. What do you think?'

'I'll wear my run-proof mascara.' Rachel headed for the car.

'You wouldn't be talking about Shaun, would you?' Louise teased as she leaned on the car. Olivia's cheeks went pink.

'Heavens, I don't know what he'll be doing, do I? It's not as if he hasn't got a life. He's got all sorts of plans. It's just that he's been so helpful and I feel I should repay him somehow.'

Rachel glanced over her shoulder at Louise. They

exchanged overt knowing looks just to make their mothe
squirm.

'Go on with you.' Olivia waved her hand. 'And driv
carefully.'

'I will.'

'Come here, sweetheart.' Olivia impulsively cantere
forwards to hold Louise tightly. 'I'll ring you all the time
and if you need anything you just have to ask. You know
I'm here every evening. Just pick up that phone if you
want to talk.'

'Thanks, Mum, but don't worry. I'll be fine.'

'And you'll be back for Christmas.'

'Of course.'

'And you remember what I said.' Olivia ruffled Louise'
hair. 'The house is yours if you want to stay. You onl
have to let me know. And use that cheque I've given yo
for heating. You mustn't be cold, you know.'

'How could I be cold in a brand new pair of fleec
slippers and a thermal vest?' Louise widened her eyes.

'They arrived!' Olivia said happily.

'And it took you this long to ask!' Louise laughed
'You've really surprised me this weekend, Mum. I'm s
proud of you.'

'And I'm proud of you, too.' Olivia's eyes misted over
She clutched her younger daughter to her chest.

'Time to go.' Rachel jangled the car keys.

Louise and Rachel chatted sporadically on the journey
home. Rachel declared that she was determined to beat th
weather, and before Louise could blink they'd sped round
the M25 and were enmeshed in the tangle of Londor
streets near her home. Everything seemed so cluttered, s
chaotic. But she had to keep a clear head. Now she had
plans, and even bright prospects. Her family understood
And Jon would be waiting for her in her flat.

'Will Hallam be at home when you get there?' Louise

asked as they turned into Pope's Lane and Rachel looked for a place to pull over.

'I bloody hope so.' Rachel expelled a ponderous breath, as if she had been thinking of nothing else. 'I'll be stuck if he isn't. I threw my door keys at him in a fit of self-destruction.'

'If not, I'll put you up.'

'I know. Thanks.'

She slid the car smoothly into a space and applied the brakes. She turned to Louise as the engine stilled and the buzz of London reverberated around them.

'Are you going to be all right, Lou?'

'Of course.' She smiled at Rachel. 'I've got the new Jon at home waiting for me, and whatever you and Mum think, we're going to try and make a go of it.'

Rachel put out a hand and stroked Louise's hair.

'I quite like Jon, you know. He can be a snobbish twat, but he could get over that. Kids change you, once you accept them. They break down all your barriers. He might be a really good father after all. You just can't tell. Look at Mum and Dad. They were great parents, weren't they?'

Louise gathered her bags, kissed Rachel, and waved as the BMW shot off and out of sight. They were great parents. She turned the phrase over in her mind. Yes, they were. But at what cost?

She carted her bags along the pavement and trudged down her front path. She paused with her keys in the air. Should she ring? It was an absurd thought, but she wasn't used to arriving unannounced. She took a deep breath, and pictured Jon as he usually was, late on a Sunday morning. Hair ruffled, just a hint of a five-o'clock shadow, in jeans and a shirt carelessly thrown over his body. She smiled. It was when she found him most attractive. With any luck he would still be in bed and she could slip in beside him. A warm cuddle was just what she needed.

She quietly let herself into the hall, put her bags on the floor next to her flat door, and fiddled with her keys until she found the right one. She heard a giggle as she was inserting the key and twisting it. She shook her head in the direction of the stairs. It hadn't taken Harris long to find himself another distraction. She pushed the door open. As she did, the giggle came again, very loudly, followed by a male chuckle. The noise had come from inside her own flat.

She came face to face with Jon, as she'd expected, dishevelled in jeans and a half tucked-in shirt. He was sitting astride a woman on the floor, her clothes looking equally rumpled, and he was tickling her. Louise allowed the door to swing shut behind her, staring into Jon's eyes in disbelief. It was some moments before she had the presence of mind to focus on whoever it was squirming under him. She did so when the woman sat up abruptly, pushing Jon off, and shook back her auburn hair.

It was Sally.

Chapter Twenty-one

'Jesus!' Jon sprang away from Sally and fell against the piano whilst he hurriedly attempted to tuck his shirt back into his jeans.

'This isn't what it looks like,' Sally said urgently, struggling to her feet and holding out both of her hands in appeal.

Louise took a moment to absorb the scene completely. In any case, she was totally incapable of speaking. She leaned back against the door and gazed at them both. Sally's face was redder than Jon's but the flush over his chin was spreading up to his cheeks.

Louise blinked. She opened her mouth and closed it again. Sally squatted down quickly to retrieve her hair clasp from the floor and gathering her hair behind her head, snapped it into place. She was pursing and un-pursing her lips. Louise watched her put a finger up to the corner of her lip and wipe the skin there. But Louise hadn't needed to see that small gesture to know that Jon had been kissing her. He had a tiny but visible smear of lipstick just under his mouth.

'Sally came round to see you,' Jon stated, standing up straight now. 'She hasn't been here long. I was going to make her a cup of tea and tell her about our plans. It seems you hadn't got round to telling her about us yet, Lou.'

She looked at him. His expression was an attempt at a playful reprimand, but his eyes were startled. She ignored him and looked back at Sally instead.

'It's true, Louise. You must believe him. I brought the

Sunday papers round for you. I wanted to see how you were, and I thought if I rang you might try to put me off. I had no idea you were away. I didn't think Jon would be here, did I?'

Louise felt her pulse rising. It was as if the reaction had been delayed by shock. Now her heart was thumping painfully inside her ribcage, but still the words wouldn't come.

'C'mon, Lou,' said Jon, brushing back his hair in a swift gesture and resuming his appealing stare. 'Don't make more out of this than it is.'

'I—'

'I know how paranoid you can be,' Jon continued in a soft voice. 'I've known you for long enough. Don't let it get the better of you now. We were just having a laugh, that's all.'

'I'm sorry, Louise,' Sally gushed. She was picking at her clothes, fingering her hair. Her hands were trembling. 'I'm really, really sorry.'

'I should have rung.' When Louise found her voice finally, it came out as a croak. 'I should have rung you to say I'd be early. Then I wouldn't have seen this.'

'Yes, that's it, Lou.' Jon started to walk towards her. 'You wouldn't have seen this, and you wouldn't have been able to make something more out of it than it was. I was just tickling her. I shouldn't have, I know, but we were just messing about. There wasn't anything in it. Christ, you don't need me to tell you that, surely?'

Jon put out a hand and touched Louise's arm.

'Let's not ruin things. Not now.'

'Please remove your hand from my arm,' Louise said breathlessly, her chest starting to heave. He withdrew it instantly. She took several short breaths, then found the strength in her legs to move away from the door.

'Which one of you would like to leave first?'

'Oh, come on!' Jon's voice rose impatiently. 'Your boy-friend and your best friend? What planet are you on, Lou?'

'I will,' Sally mumbled. Jon watched her silently as she gathered her jacket and her handbag and made it to the door. She turned to Louise as if she wanted to say something else.

'One question, Sal,' Louise managed. 'Is this the first time?'

There was a long pause.

'Yes,' she replied.

'Now go,' Louise said in a whisper.

Sally let herself out. They heard the front door close after her. There was a brief silence in the room. Then Jon erupted.

'For God's sake!' He began to pace around the room, pulling at a tuft of his hair. 'This is so like you!'

'And this is so like you,' she replied. Now that Sally had gone she felt calmer. Now at least she only had to deal with one of them, not both of them.

'Listen—'

'No, *you* listen!' she instructed with such force that he stopped dead in the middle of the room and stared back at her, mute. 'I'm going to go into the kitchen and I'm going to make myself a cup of tea. I want you to gather anything of yours that you can see and leave. I don't expect you to interrupt me, I don't expect you to come into the kitchen for any reason at all. If you've left anything in the bathroom it's just bloody well tough.'

'But—'

'No, Jon. That's it. The next sound I expect to hear on account of you is the front door closing on your way out. Leave the keys where I can find them.'

She gritted her teeth, determined not to say more. She held his gaze stonily and with absolute determination. In response his shoulders dropped, as if he finally realised that he was in a situation he couldn't talk his way out of. He looked defeated.

She swiped at the handle to her bag and heaved it up. She made her way to the kitchen door and pushed her way inside, then stopped as she was about to close it behind her. Jon was watching her, his face dejected. His shirt was still loose around his chest, and it suddenly occurred to her that he looked puny.

'You're a shit,' she said.

'I know,' he replied.

She closed the door.

'Hallam?' Rachel shivered inside her long coat on the doorstep. 'Can I come in?'

He stood for a moment on the threshold, barring her way, but then he stepped back and leaned against the wall, kicking open the door. Rachel was shocked at his appearance. His shirt was unbuttoned halfway to his waist, his hair looked as if he hadn't bothered to comb it and there was a distant look in his eyes. For the moment at least, he had abandoned the elegant, poised bearing that had seemed so much a part of him.

She caught the aroma of whisky on his breath as she walked into the hall. He straightened himself and walked away, turning into the living room and leaving Rachel standing in the hall with the front door wide open. She closed it.

At least the boys weren't here this weekend. It was just the two of them. Rachel chewed on her lip. She'd clarified her feelings in her own mind now, but there was a long way to go before she would be able to make him understand. That was if there was a chance that he would forgive her. She took off her coat, draped it over the peg, and walked straight through to the living room. Hallam was crouched on the sofa, a bottle of whisky in one hand.

He was in the process of refilling his glass. He glanced at her and held out the bottle.

'Want one?'

She shook her head.

'Course not. You're driving, aren't you?' He tossed back the contents of his glass. 'Or are you? Has he given you a lift here?'

'Who?'

'Your doctor.'

'Oh.' Rachel reclined against the door while she watched him. 'No, I'm on my own.'

'Well, go right ahead.' He cast out an arm. 'Help yourself to what you want. I haven't packed for you. I couldn't bear to do that, but you won't mind doing it yourself, will you? I can't remember exactly who bought what. You'd think I'd have learned, wouldn't you, after the last time. We should have kept receipts, Rachel. That way there'd be no argument. Oh, what the hell!' He tipped another measure of whisky into his glass. 'Take what you like. I don't give a toss.'

She walked slowly around the coffee table and sat down on the armchair opposite him.

'What's up, Rachel? Thought you had the monopoly on getting rat-arsed? You should have patented it, my dear, if it was going to concern you this much.'

'Hal, I want to talk to you.'

'Fine!' He smiled at her unevenly. 'Tell me all the reasons you're leaving me. I'm waiting. In fact, I have a feeling I've heard it all before somewhere. You won't mind if I watch a video while you unload your conclusions on me, will you?'

Rachel stood up. She clenched her fists.

'Hallam, you're being pathetic.'

He sat back, shocked, and focused on her.

'I am?'

383

'I said I want to talk to you, and I am going to talk to you.'

'Talk away.' He flung a hand out and laid it to rest on the arm of the sofa. 'I can't wait to hear what you've got to say.'

Rachel sat down again. She had never seen him like this. It was daunting. But she had to be honest with herself, and honest with him. It was the only way forward. For the moment, at least, his attention was on her. He flicked his ears with his fingers so that they wobbled, something he did sometimes to make the boys laugh.

'I'm all ears,' he said.

'You've been an insensitive, inconsiderate bastard. You've made assumptions that you never should have made. You never stopped to ask me what I thought, or what I felt. It's been a sham.'

'But you,' he said, pointing an unsteady finger at her, 'went off and slept with somebody else. I never did that.'

'I know,' Rachel said, her colour rising. 'And I wish I hadn't. I wish I'd had the courage to be honest with you and tell you why I was so unhappy, but I ran into someone else's arms instead. I'm not proud of myself. I'm ashamed, if you really want to know. But it's too late. I can't undo it. At least I told you about it. You need never have known, but I wanted to tell you. I wanted to be honest with you.'

He sat back in the cushions, gazing at her.

'Go on.'

'I—' She stood up and clasped her hands together. 'It was because you already had a family. A ready-made one. And you always assumed that I was happy with that. You took one look at me and said, "Career woman. That'll do nicely," but you never stopped to ask what I really wanted. You thought the kids got in my way, but they never did. I had to protect myself, don't you see? I became

384

fond of them, but you always put yourself between us, as if I had no right to love them too. And it made me doubt everything I'd built up for myself. You just—' She put out her hands to him expressively. 'You thought you knew what I felt, but you never asked. You never heard it from my lips.'

He cleared his throat. He pushed away the bottle.

'I thought the boys were an irritation to you. I just assumed—'

'That's exactly it!' Rachel cried at him. 'You just assumed, and assumed, and assumed.'

'But you love your job, don't you? I always thought it came above everything else.'

'I do love my job!' she exclaimed, standing up again to walk around the armchair and stare at the painting of the woman with three breasts that he'd hung back up again, if at a slightly odd angle. 'But I'm a woman too, Hal, don't you see?' She turned to implore him with her eyes.

He stood up too. He self-consciously did up a button on his shirt and tucked the tails into his jeans. It was as if he was suddenly aware of how he looked.

'Rachel, I—' His brows were drawn together in concentration. 'The thing is, I was trying to protect you. I just thought the boys got on your nerves. I thought they got in the way of your work.' He sounded completely sober now. 'I tried to do what I thought you wanted. If I was wrong, I can only say that I'm sorry. I thought you disliked children, and there was every reason to believe that my children from my former marriage would be an intrusion into your life. It's the impression you gave me.'

Rachel tutted with impatience.

'I thought you wanted them all to yourself. I wasn't going to get in your way. I tried to be all the things I thought you liked about me. Independent, free,

385

interesting. I thought if I started going on about the kids you'd think you had another ex-wife on your hands.'

'And I was trying to be all the things I thought you liked about me. I thought you wanted me to give you space.'

'Well, it looks as if we both got it wrong then, doesn't it?' Rachel snapped at him.

There was a silence. Hallam rubbed his fingers around his chin.

'Does this mean you're not about to walk out? I just need you to warn me so that I know how to feel about this.' He pushed his hand through his hair. 'I've missed you so much and I couldn't believe that it was you at the door. I was so happy to see you.'

'That was you doing happy?' Rachel smirked at him.

'I can—' He cleared his throat noisily. 'I can do a better happy if you like. But first you have to tell me that you're not going to go.'

Rachel ran her tongue over her upper lip while she thought.

'I'm not going to go. I'm going to stay here and work this through with you.'

He looked away from her as she spoke. 'And what about the doctor?'

'He's nothing, Hal. He was never the issue. Forget him if you possibly can. I have.'

She waited as Hallam walked across the room to the stereo and leaned against it while he gazed at their pile of CDs. She inclined her head curiously.

'What are you doing?'

He held a finger up to her as he found what he was looking for and slipped it into the machine.

'I know I'm not very good at expressing myself,' he said over his shoulder, his eyes still not meeting hers. 'But I love you, Rachel. I love you very much. I think you should know that.'

He pressed a button and walked towards her as the introduction played. She felt her heart melt as she saw the intense look of longing in his eyes. He reached her, but seemed unsure of himself. Her skin prickled. He had played this song for her when they had first fallen in love. If anything, she loved him more now. And he was mouthing the words to her, as if he was unable to form them himself.

'Anything you want, you got it.' He touched her face cautiously.

She drew him into her arms.

'If you ever go silent on me again, I'll nail your testicles to a turntable.'

'Promises, promises!' He lowered his mouth to hers.

Louise saw Sally as soon as she entered the restaurant. She was sitting at a table in the corner with her head in her hands. She was wearing sunglasses which, given the flurry of snow in the air, were causing others to cast her curious looks. Louise marched to the table and sat down opposite her. Slowly, Sally raised her head. Her mouth was pale and devoid of lipstick, her cheeks white.

'Louise—'

'Shut up. It's good of you to meet me for lunch, but I haven't come here to listen to you. I've got some things to say. First of all, I've been thinking about this. I know this wasn't the first time, so don't lie to me any more. I've had all day yesterday to think about it, and I've put it together. Your reactions when I talked about Jon, his when I talked about you. There was an undercurrent there, something I was too stupid to put my finger on. Even your reactions about the baby were to do with Jon. When you said Jon and I would be tied together for the rest of our lives you were horrified, but not on my behalf. On your own.'

She stopped to take a breath. An Italian waiter offered them menus. Sally didn't move. Louise took them both and gave him a curt smile.

'Can you give us a few minutes alone, please? I'll call you over when we're ready.'

'Certainly.' He departed silently. Louise pursed her lips and laid the menus flat on the table. Sally nudged her sunglasses up her nose.

'It explains why you didn't want to marry Fergus, and why you seemed to envy me. It explains everything. So can we start from that basis, please? I'm going to leave if you feed me a load of bullshit.'

Sally ran her tongue over her top lip. The skin there was cracked and dry.

'Nothing had ever happened before this weekend,' she said.

Louise smiled sardonically at her own reflection in Sally's sunglasses. 'There's not much reason for me to hang around then, is there? I'm not going to have my intelligence insulted any more.'

She stood up. Sally shot out a hand and hung on to her arm.

'I haven't finished, Louise,' she said. 'Sit down.'

Sally had a firm grip on her sleeve. Louise considered shaking her away and storming out but she sat down again.

'I – listen, Lou, I need a drink.'

Louise waved a hand at the waiter. He approached them cautiously.

'Two glasses of house white, please,' she instructed.

'I'll have the same,' Sally said.

He glanced at them both for clarification. Louise nodded at him. She laced her fingers together on the damask tablecloth.

'Go on then, Sal. You'd better speak fast.'

'He made a pass at me. Some time ago.' Sally swallowed, her face twitching. 'A heavy pass. It was that night we all went out together, a few months ago. We were all drunk. I – I suppose I was quite flattered at the time. But I was shocked too. I've never had a fling, not with anyone who's involved with someone else.'

'It must have been exciting.' Louise gritted her teeth.

'I – you two seemed to be drifting apart. I thought you were better off without him, and I didn't want to hurt you by telling you, although I think he thought I would. Especially after you split up.'

'It would explain why he was so twitchy about you,' Louise said, her heart thumping.

'I haven't been like you, Louise, you see.' Sally pulled off her glasses and folded them in her hands. She opened her mouth to continue but stopped as the waiter appeared with four glasses of wine balanced on a tray. He placed them one by one on the table with elaborate precision.

'Thank you,' Louise said. He drifted away again. Sally picked up one of the glasses. Her hands shook violently, but she got the rim to her mouth and took a deep gulp. Louise studied her face. She was wearing no make-up at all today. Her eyes were small and pink within her pale skin, her lashes light brown without mascara. She looked like the girl she'd known at school.

'I've always done the sensible thing.' Sally's lips wobbled. She bit them between her teeth. 'You see, I've had problems to deal with too, but I buried them under the surface. I got on with what had to be done. I always did that. Just took the straight line to wherever I was going.'

'And it got a bit boring, did it?' Louise suggested. She took a sip of wine, wincing at the acid taste, but as it went down her muscles relaxed.

'I – the girl at work. The one who had the termination.'

'Yes?' Louise said with feigned interest.

389

'That was me,' Sally said in a small voice.

Her eyes were downcast as she drained her glass. She picked up the second and started on it. Louise sat back in her chair and assessed Sally from a distance. She was fidgeting with her cutlery, shifting the wineglasses around the table. Anything but look at Louise.

'When?'

'About a year ago.'

'Who was the father?'

'Fergus.' Louise raised her eyebrows but said nothing. 'It was what we both wanted then. It made sense. I'd just been offered the partnership. He had opportunities in his career. It wasn't the right time.'

Louise blew out. She didn't want her feelings to soften towards Sally. She hated her for what she'd done. She wanted to throw a punch across the table and knock her flat. But she sat still, turning her words over in her mind.

'I know it was the right thing to do,' Sally went on in a low voice. 'I don't regret it. But it's killed any feelings I had for Fergus. Perhaps if he'd been less sure of what we should do himself I might have thought about it differently, but it's too late now. I just feel this dreadful sadness. It won't go away. You – you can't know how this feels. I hope you'll never know.'

'And then he asked you to marry him.'

Sally nodded. She lifted her wine to her lips and drank until the glass was empty. She put it back on the table heavily and slid the third glass in front of her.

'I'm not making excuses, Lou. I don't expect you're ever going to want to see me again after this, and I don't blame you.' It wasn't a question, Louise realised. Sally's voice was devoid of hope. 'On Sunday I think I had a moment of total madness. It was the first time I'd ever done something that broke the rules. I don't know what I was thinking. Nothing logical. Nothing that I can explain. It'd just been so long since I'd done anything spontaneous. It was only flirtation. And you have to know that there was a kiss. Just one. Even if you hadn't walked in, I'm sure I wouldn't have let it go further than that. But I know it was still a shitty thing to do to you. I suppose as it was happening I was trying to justify it to myself. I thought of you and Andrew—'

'Whoa. Hold it right there.' Louise put up a hand. 'Me and Andrew?'

Sally raised her eyes.

'You slept with Andrew. You told me. I'm not even sure now that the baby's Jon's. Are you?'

Louise froze, shocked. She tried not to erupt, but to understand instead what had been going through Sally's mind.

'Two months ago, Sally, when Jon was treating me like a doormat, I went for a drink with Andrew. We went back to my flat, fumbled a bit, then he left. At no point did his – his apparatus leave his trousers. If you must know, I think he was too drunk to get it up. Is that graphic enough for you?'

Sally sat up straight.

'But you implied—'

'No, that was your imagination working overtime. I felt guilty because I was still theoretically going out with Jon at the time and I'd played with the idea of sleeping with someone else. It never happened.'

'God, Lou. Sorry.'

Louise snorted, grabbed her wine, and took another swig of it. She forced it down. It was making her feel sick, but she needed the anaesthetic, otherwise she was indeed going to lay Sally out with an almighty thump.

'So you thought that I could be lying to Jon about all this, presumably because he was my best option.'

'Hell, I just didn't know. I said I'm sorry. I – I

391

understood your confusion better than you think, you see. I've been there. I know how bewildered you become when you're pregnant. You turn into a different person. Every possible combination of solutions goes through your mind. You can think desperate things.'

'Oh, Sal.' Louise could not keep the sadness from her eyes. 'I thought we knew each other, but we don't at all, do we?'

Sally didn't answer. She picked up her napkin and rubbed her moist palms with it.

'And you didn't tell me when you were in trouble,' Louise went on ponderously. 'I wonder why not.'

'I didn't tell anyone apart from Fergus. I just swept it under the carpet. If – if I'd talked to anyone else, they might have influenced me, and I knew what I had to do. I couldn't bear to be distracted.'

Louise considered Sally. She was a wreck. The unwelcome swell of affection that she had been fighting back loomed again. She surprised herself by reaching a hand out across the table. Sally stared at it in surprise. Louise flexed her fingers.

'C'mon, give me your hand.' Sally cautiously put her hand in Louise's. 'You're a complete bitch, Sally.' Sally looked away. 'I hate you for what you've done.'

'You – you don't love Jon,' Sally said quietly. 'I don't know how this is going to make any sense, and I don't expect you to believe me, but if you'd loved him, it – it never could have happened. I would never come between you and . . .' She tailed away.

'And?'

'And someone you really loved. Or who loved you.'

Louise released Sally's hand. She pushed back her hair and tried to think clearly.

'Will you see Jon again?' she asked directly.

'No. Never. Will – will you?'

Louise gave a humourless laugh.

'That depends on how good a lawyer he gets himself.'
She tutted under her breath. 'I don't mean that really. The
baby's still his. He'll have rights.'

'But you won't – I mean, you're not going to try to . . .'
Sally left her sentence unfinished.

'Have a meaningful relationship with him?' Louise
suddenly wanted to laugh. The image of Jon skulking
around her living room with his shirt-tails flapping flitted
across her mind. She had felt so relieved when the front
door had banged for the last time. She was angry, yes.
Furious. But with Sally. Jon seemed unable to stir her
emotions any longer.

'I'll take that look as a no,' Sally said, twisting her lips
ruefully.

'Absolutely. From now on, I'm on my own. And it feels
bloody good, I can tell you.'

Sally looked exhausted, but the corners of her lips
twitched into a dry smile. 'That makes two of us, then.'

'You won't be on your own for long, Sal. You'll meet
someone. It won't matter about Fergus, and Jon, and all
that history then. You'll put it behind you.'

Louise was amazing herself. Where had this
munificence come from? She was sitting down to lunch
with her best friend, who that weekend had been
discovered frolicking on the floor with the man who was
supposed to be fathering her family. It was so odd. It
wasn't that it didn't matter, because it did, and it would
have consequences. No doubt in the future she'd flash
back to the shock, the pain and the anger she'd felt. Maybe
she'd even think twice about trusting Sally with a
boyfriend again. But that could be dealt with. Sally had
been trying to prove something to herself. Jon hadn't been
relevant to what happened. Louise herself hadn't even
been relevant. It had been a way of breaking free of the

393

bonds Sally had created for herself. In one, destructive act she had exploded the shroud of pretence they were all hiding under. Louise didn't love Jon. Jon didn't love Louise. The truth of it had always been there, but now it was exposed.

And Sally was still her best friend. Louise picked up her glass and chinked it against Sally's.

'I'm going to make you suffer for this, Sal.'

A muted light appeared in her friend's eyes.

'You mean you're not going to disown me?'

'I'll let you sweat about that for a bit, but probably not. I need you. And you need me. Men come and go but friendships don't. You're a bloody idiot for trying to throw what we've got away.'

Colour flashed into Sally's cheeks. Louise decided to say nothing. It was for Sally to wrestle with her own conscience. She wasn't about to make it too easy for her.

'Tell – tell me about your weekend. How was your mother? Is she keeping well?'

Louise tried to keep a straight face, but failed. Sally's voice had been peculiarly polite, as if she was trying to impress Louise with her best behaviour.

'Well, let's just say you're not the only one showing signs of lunacy at the moment.' She dropped the façade and grabbed Sally's hand again. 'I've got so much to tell you, and you're just not going to believe any of it.' She glanced at her watch with a sudden thought. 'But how much time have you got? Won't you have to be back at work soon?'

'Fuck it.' Sally drained the third glass of wine and eyed Louise's covetously. 'I'm not going back. I'm going to play truant. That'll shock them all, won't it? They'll just have to manage without me this afternoon. I'm going to spend the day trying to win my best friend back instead.'

'Can you do that?'

394

'Just watch me. You've lasted longer than any job I've had, and I'm not about to let you go now. So you can start by handing over that glass of wine. You shouldn't be drinking in your condition, and you damned well know it.'

'You're not going to win me back by bossing me about,' Louise protested, but nudged her glass towards Sally.

'Yes, I am,' Sally declared firmly. 'It's about time you had somebody nagging you and I've decided it's going to be me. That way, if you get together with a man you'll do it for the right reasons instead of all the wrong ones.'

'Man? What man?' Louise laughed incredulously.

'That's another thing we've got to talk about this afternoon. But first we're going to eat something, otherwise your baby'll be stunted and I'll pass out.' Sally flipped open the menu and concentrated on it. 'And you're not allowed to have shellfish, so don't even think about ordering it.'

'I assume you're paying.'

'Of course.'

'Good. I might just allow you to buy your way back into my affections.'

'That was my intention.' Sally peered across the table.

'Great.' Louise grinned. 'In that case, after we've eaten we can pop over to Mothercare. You have got your cheque-book with you, I suppose?'

Chapter Twenty-two

'I love it up here,' Shaun said, coming to a halt next to a bench. Olivia rubbed at her fingers through her woollen gloves. The castle grounds were her favourite lunchtime venue, especially in the summer, and sometimes in the winter too. Today she had felt the need to get right away from work, away from the town, and climb the twisting pathways which spiralled up the old castle mound. Shaun had been hovering in the office as she was putting on her coat so she'd asked him if he wanted to walk with her. He'd agreed readily and brought his sandwiches with him. Olivia had a ham roll and an orange in a bag swinging from her arm, but she didn't feel hungry as she gazed down at the town from their vantage point.

'So, shall we sit here then?'

'Plenty of benches to choose from,' Shaun noted, pulling his thick jacket around his body. 'We seem to be the only ones braving the weather today.'

'Oh, are you cold?' Olivia looked at him in concern. The tip of his nose was red but he shook his head bravely.

'No. Not at all. It's nice to be out. With you,' he added in a quiet voice.

Olivia sat down, feeling warmer for his comment. Shaun rustled his plastic bag beside her and embarked on his first sandwich. A sparrow hopped towards them, his head cocked in hope.

'Oh, go on then.' Shaun picked off his crust, crumbled it in his fingers, and tossed it out over the concrete path. His action brought a handful of birds swooping down from the trees. 'Poor things. They need it more than I do. Don't hog what you don't need, that's what I say.'

'Hmmn.' Olivia smiled to herself.

'Not hungry?' Shaun glanced sideways at her.

'Oh, yes. I'll eat something in a minute. But first I've got some things to say, Shaun. I wanted to tell you first, before anyone else at work knew.'

He sat up straight. He had crumbs on his lips but he didn't seem bothered by them.

'I don't quite know what order to put things in.'

He swallowed his mouthful of sandwich, watching her avidly.

'Nothing you do ever surprises me, Olivia.'

She laughed, flattered and pleased by his comment. But she was going to surprise him, she was sure of that.

'No, Shaun. Even with all your insight, I don't think you can anticipate this.'

'Ah!' He put up a gloved finger. 'But I've done your chart, remember. You've got no secrets from me any more.'

'Oh, the chart.' She felt a prickle of worry. She'd forgotten about that. But perhaps that was a good place to start. 'I've got a confession to make about that. The day that we went to the pub, when I said it was my birthday?'

'Yes?'

'It wasn't my birthday. I don't know why I let you believe that it was. I was just in need of some attention, I suppose. But I'm sorry, Shaun. The chart you did was all wrong. You had the wrong date of birth, you see.'

He took another bite out of his sandwich, and noticing the thickening group of grey birds around them, crumbled up another large portion of crust and tossed it out.

'I knew that,' he said.

'You did?'

'Yes. I did the chart for your real date of birth, not the one you gave me.'

She turned to him in astonishment.

'I should have owned up, but I thought you might be offended. You know, see it as an intrusion of privacy, or something.'

'Good Lord.' She laughed at him. 'I thought I was the one who was going to surprise you. You've taken me aback. I underestimated you, obviously.'

'Yes,' he said. 'I think you have, but never mind. The thing is, I notice everything about you. I have done ever since I joined the team. Your husband was still alive then but it didn't mean I didn't notice you.' He played with his plastic bag in agitation. Then he stopped fidgeting and looked out into the distance. 'I knew enough to know exactly when your birthday is. I know every mood you have, every expression your face is capable of.' His voice died away.

'I – I don't know what to say,' Olivia said, when she could speak again.

'Don't say anything.' He pulled a second sandwich from his plastic bag and lobbed it directly at the birds without bothering to take a bite out of it. 'I didn't tell you that to embarrass you or to make you say something back. I know how things are.'

'Thank you, Shaun.' Olivia patted his hand. 'I like you very much too. I mean, very much,' she insisted. 'You always make me happy. When I think back over my time at work it has always been you who cheered me up. When Carol was at her worst, when I thought I couldn't deal with it any more, you'd come into the office to dump some papers or pick up some files, and before I knew it, it would all be bearable again.'

'Glad I've helped.' Shaun slid her a sideways look. He seemed to think better of eye contact and pretended to be fascinated by a thrush who had appeared to elbow the sparrows out of the way. 'But that's not so important any

398

more, is it? Carol seems to be making a real effort to be nice to everyone suddenly. Well, everyone's entitled to a transformation aren't they?'

Olivia allowed herself a private smile. What had passed between herself and Carol would remain just that. Private.

'She does seem happier, that's true.'

'And you're not going to be around for much longer anyway, are you? So you won't need me to cheer you up.'

'How do you know that?'

'You're talking about work in the past tense. My guess is you've got another job.'

'Another job?'

'Well, you've got a different set of clothes and you've changed your hair. You know what they say. When a woman changes her hair, it's not all she's changing.' He nodded at her meaningfully. 'So tell me what's happening.'

'It's not a job, Shaun. I'm going away.'

'Away?' He raised his unified eyebrow. His features seemed less strange now. She'd got used to looking at them. They were a part of him.

'I'm going to go abroad for a few months.'

'Really?' His face was a mixture of delight and disbelief.

'Yes, really. To the land of the Lotos-Eaters.'

'Wow!' His mouth was open in wonder.

'And beyond.'

'Really?'

'Yes. I'm going to stop off at a few places, but by the time I come back I'll have flown around the entire world. Can you imagine that?'

'Gosh. I've been saving all this money to go away myself but you're the one who's gone ahead and done it first.'

'We must be kindred spirits.' She nudged him. He smiled.

'You know—' He jammed his hands in his pockets and

399

straightened his shoulders. 'You don't have to go alone Olivia. Not if you don't want to.'

'Don't I?'

'No. It's just that – I mean, say if you want me to shut up It would be up to you, of course. But if you wanted companion. Someone to travel with. You know.'

She let him struggle for a moment longer, but her hear softened towards him.

'I know, Shaun. And it's very kind of you to offer. Bu I'm not going to be travelling alone.'

'You're not?' His eyes were disturbed as he turned to look properly at her newly cut hair, her animated face. 'Ol I see. I've been dense, then. I'm sorry.'

'I met up with her again recently. It turns out we have a great deal more in common than we thought. She's alone now, and I'm alone, so we've decided to go together. I'm going to go away with my old schoolfriend Katherine.'

'Oh!' Shaun looked entirely relieved. 'Oh. That's nice fo you both. Yes, very nice.'

'We'll probably end up murdering each other, but you never know. We might have a lovely time. And then I'l come home, Shaun. When I've been away, and visited the places I want to see, I'll come home.'

'Oh, yes. I suppose you will.'

'And when you've travelled, and you've visited the places you want to see, you'll come home again too, won't you?'

'Well, yes. I will.'

'Yes.' Olivia beamed at him. 'And when we're both a home together again . . .'

He looked at her with hope in his eyes. The wind caught his hair and blew it sideways. She reached out and very gently patted it down again. He jumped at her touch and blinked erratically.

'Then you might want to ask me out to dinner. And I might say yes.'

'Oh. Oh, I see.' He took his hands from his pockets, stretched them out in front of him and rested them on his knees. His cheeks dimpled into a secret smile.

'But that's a while off,' Olivia continued. 'And if you don't mind, I'd still like you to teach me to drive, and I'd love you to come to Christmas dinner with me and my family if you'd like to. That's if you don't have any other plans.'

A squall of wind blasted them both into a shudder, but he turned with confidence and smiled at her. A glow spread from her stomach to warm her whole body.

'If you're sure I wouldn't be intruding.'

'Not at all,' she said. 'As long as you don't mind the others intruding on us.'

As she looked at him, at the unashamed love in his eyes, the straightness of his lips, his upright demeanour on the low park bench, she wondered why she had never seen him as attractive before. There was nothing to be laughed at in the look he was giving her now. One of discovery, elation and understanding. The sort of look a man gave a woman at the moment when he realised that his feelings were shared. It was rare, and it was to be treasured. She would carry the memory of it with her while she was away and hold it to her heart like a talisman. It would bring her home safely. Back to him.

'Louise?'

Louise turned at the mention of her name, but she didn't need to see Ash to know it was him. He hadn't tapped her on the shoulder this time, but had spoken her name softly next to her ear as if to avoid making her jump. She had been loitering next to the Office and Secretarial board, examining the cards with solemn intent and wondering if it was possible that he might appear. He had to, at some point. She'd been in the Jobcentre nearly all day every day since Jon had left.

'Oh, hello.' She smiled at him.

'Hi. I just saw you there. So I thought I'd say hello.'

Her smile widened. They looked into each other's eyes. Somebody had to say something.

'And what brings you down to the Jobcentre?' she asked. 'Got your thermos flask, have you?'

'Not today. It's my signing day today. But I shouldn't be signing for much longer, thank God.'

'Really? What's happening then?'

'I – have you got time to talk?' He glanced around as if to confirm that Jon wasn't with her.

'Yes, all the time in the world.'

'Do you want to get a cup of tea?'

'Why not?'

They walked out of the Jobcentre together. The woman at the reception desk glanced up, her bob swinging. Louise winked at her as they left the building.

'Fucking freezing out, isn't it?'

Louise laughed as they pounded the icy pavement.

'I'm all strapped up in a thermal vest and sixteen layers of jumpers. I can't feel a thing.'

'Shall we go in here?' Ash stopped as they reached the glass front of the greasy spoon. 'We're almost regulars now.'

'It'll do fine.'

They pushed open the door. Louise approached the counter.

'Oh no, I'll get this,' Ash said, patting at the pockets of his jeans as if to work out how much change he had on him.

'No, this is on me,' Louise said.

'No, I'll pay for it.'

Louise put a hand out as Ash fumbled for loose change

They were both awkward. It was difficult to find a way round it.

'Listen. Why don't we each buy our own? It's simpler that way, isn't it? Neither of us can afford it really.'

'Right. Well, you order what you want then, and I'll go and bag us a seat.'

She ordered two teas and some toast for them both, and followed Ash over to the table he'd chosen. It was the one next to the window with the ripped plastic seats. She sat down opposite him.

'So!' he said, running his eyes over her. 'You look good. Really good.'

'I do?'

'Yes.' He scrutinised her more closely. 'You've changed something about you. It's not just in your face.'

Louise raised an eyebrow but kept silent. Finally Ash chuckled under his breath.

'It's your hair. You've had a different cut.' He laid his hand on his chest in relief. 'Thank God I worked it out. It's a capital offence not to realise when a woman's had a haircut, isn't it?'

'I think I'd commute your sentence to life imprisonment,' she said. 'But it's nice of you to notice. I did have something done. Not that I paid, of course.'

'Oh, right. Of course. It was a present.' Ash nodded. He gave her a tight smile.

'My friend paid. Sally. You met her, didn't you?'

'The ginger one.'

'Yes.' Louise waited while a short man delivered their tea and toast to the table and delivered her a hefty wink. She picked up her tea and warmed her hands around the mug. She liked the fact that Ash had referred to Sally as 'the ginger one'.

'I shouldn't have let her pay really, but she insisted. She's being particularly nice to me at the moment.'

403

'Is she? Why's that then?'

'She snogged my ex-boyfriend. He's the one who was standing in my hall imparting information to you when you came round.'

Ash put his mug down carefully.

'Your ex-boyfriend?'

'Well . . .' Louise fingered a piece of toast longingly, then succumbed and took a large bite out of it. 'Sorry. I'm just so hungry. Don't mind me being a pig. At least you know why I'm being a pig, don't you?'

He smiled.

'The thing is, I knew what Jon was like but I thought he'd turned over a new leaf. But he hadn't, so now he's gone, and Sally's spending lots of money on me.' She crammed the remains of the toast into her mouth and chewed on it. 'I don't really need her to do it but I'm emotionally blackmailing her to make sure she never does it again. I'm starting a new job after Christmas, you see. A proper job. I'm going to earn a decent amount and save up for a pram with go-fast stripes.'

'Are you?' Ash seemed increasingly surprised by Louise's announcements.

'So.' She swallowed her toast. 'What are you doing now?'

'Hang on, Louise. I can't keep up with you.' He laughed under his breath and held out a hand. 'It's like this every time I see you. There's always something new. I don't know how you do it. You make me dizzy, you know.'

Louise followed her toast with a mouthful of tea.

'It's not as complicated as it sounds.'

'You make me feel boring. I've never met anyone who made me feel boring before. It's quite a revelation. I know how my friends have been feeling for years now.'

'Look. I'll explain. I'm staying in my flat. It's big enough, it just needs tarting up. I've talked to the landlord and he says I can give it a lick of paint. I've had a cheque from my old employer and at last some money's come through from signing on which is going to tide me over until I start a new job. See? All sorted. When it's time for the baby to be born I'm going to stay with either Sally, Rachel or my mother until I'm over the birth, then I'm going back to work. Mum will be back from going round the world then.'

Ash sat back against the plastic seat. He looked stunned.

'Your mother's going round the world?'

'It's what she has to do,' Louise informed him.

'By balloon, or what?'

'Pardon?'

'Your mother going round the word.' Ash broke into a grin. 'And when I say by balloon, I mean in the sense that she might be hanging on to a piece of string and hoping the wind will take her the rest of the way.'

'You haven't met my mother.'

'Nope,' he admitted. 'But I've met you, and you must get it from someone.'

Louise tried to be ruffled but she couldn't. It was such a relief to be with Ash. She could put the memory of Jon's mock sincerity behind her and just be herself. She didn't need to assert her independence with him either. He'd always understood that. She could joke about it with him without having to thump her fist on the flimsy table or get red in the face.

'I'll have you know I have a promising career in the music industry at hand.'

'You do?'

'I do.'

'I envy your child, Louise,' Ash said sincerely. 'For what it's worth, I think you'll be a great mother.'

'You really do?' Louise swelled with pride at the thought.

'I really do.'

405

'Thank you.' Louise beamed at him in gratitude. 'That's the best thing anyone's ever said to me.'

'No problem.' He picked up his mug and drained his tea. He looked thoughtful for a moment, then pushed the mug to one side. 'Well, I'd best be off.'

'But you haven't told me what you're doing.' Louise shot out a hand to him. She pulled it back again self consciously. 'I mean, you said you probably wouldn't be signing on for much longer.'

'It's nothing really.'

'Please go on.'

'Well, it's just that I've been thinking about things. And I've had to be frank with myself. It was after that last gig.' If Louise hadn't known him better she'd have thought he was blushing. 'It's about stage fright, really.'

'Stage fright.'

'Yes. Pretty prosaic next to what you've been doing, know. But that's what it boils down to. I'm not a performer.' He played with the handle of his mug. 'If I'm honest, it's probably why I struggled with the band. It's probably why I've struggled all along with music. I'm no a front man.'

'Oh, I see.' She remembered his pupils, dilated with fear when he'd been about to play at the pub. He'd been terrified, but then he'd gone on to deliver a fantastic performance.

'I know what you're thinking.' He gave a small smile. ' was all right once I was on stage.'

'I thought you were amazing.'

'But it was miserable. I hated it. Just like I used to hate i when I played in the orchestra.'

'But Ash, you can't give up music. You're so talented.'

'I'm not going to,' he said. 'I'm thinking of taking professional qualification so that I can teach in schools The sort of schools where I can really do some good

406

Where I can enlighten kids who've never heard the sound of a violin in their lives. Where I can bring something good into their lives.'

She rested her chin in her hands, moved by his words. He glanced away from her dismissively.

'I'm being nauseous, I know.'

'I'm not Karen,' she stated boldly. She even held his eyes when he looked at her.

'I know you're not Karen.' He lowered his voice. 'I didn't mean that.'

'But you don't have many people around you who understand how you feel, so you assume I'm gong to take the piss out of you.'

'No. I thought you'd be the one person who'd understand.' He shuffled in his seat and reached a hand up to play with his hair. By the time he'd finished he looked like a Viking with two distinct light brown horns sticking out of his head.

'I – well, I wish you luck, Ash. I envy your children.'

He looked up at her, startled.

'What children?'

'The children you're going to teach.' She patted his hand reassuringly. 'Unless you know about any others out there?'

He laughed in an unrestrained way that made her feel happy.

'So!' She buttoned up her coat ready to face the cold. 'We'd better pay for this delectable experience, hadn't we? It looks as if we both have a lot to get on with.'

'Yes, I'd better get back. I've got a student coming later.'

They paid at the counter and wandered outside. The door swung shut behind them. Louise stamped her feet on the pavement to prepare herself for the walk home and glanced up at the sky. She'd told her mother that they

never saw the sky in London, but she could see it clearly
now, a strip of silver far above the reaches of the leaden
buildings lining the road. A soft, cold snowflake landed on
her nose. She brushed at it with her finger.

'Odds on for a white Christmas?'

'Well, we can dream, can't we?'

She fumbled in her pockets for her gloves and pulled
them on.

'So,' she said.

'So,' Ash echoed. He suddenly enveloped her in his
arms. She held her breath as her body was pressed against
his. Then he released her. He stood back, rubbing his
hands together. 'Well, good luck, Louise. I'm really glad I
banged into you.'

'Yes, and me you. I wanted to thank you for everything
you did. You were so kind.'

'It as nothing. It really was . . .' He squinted along the
road, as if he had already left her and was several paces
away. 'Nothing. See you.'

She watched him walk away. She hadn't meant to,
because she'd thought she'd be the one to walk away first,
but she'd been wrong. He strode into a small throng of
shoppers. She turned quickly on her heel. She faced the
way she had to go, and walked away too.

She began at a brisk pace, but there were too many
people in her way. She slowed down and calmed herself.
Then she stopped completely. It was no good, striding
around Ealing like this. She had the baby to think of, and
she had her own frame of mind to think of, too.

She looked around at the gaudy combinations of
Christmas lights and cotton-wool snow cluttering the
shop windows. A flutter of dissent rose up inside her, then
died away again. Ash was a lovely man. He would always
be a lovely man. She had his phone number, and he had
hers. There was no point in them both being strangers to

each other. Why should they be? Before too long she would ring him.

She walked on, a smile touching her lips. It would have been unusual to start a relationship with such total honesty. There was nothing they could pretend to each other now. And if there could be no relationship, there was a friendship, one that she would value. It had shown her how things could be, and for that she would always be grateful to him whether he knew it or not.

She turned the corner. Her body was grabbed from behind. She was swivelled around by a pair of strong arms and her lips were crushed with a kiss. It was a kiss that seemed to go on for ever. She opened her eyes in shock. She recognised the two light brown spikes sticking out of his head. His kiss deepened. She put her arms around his neck to keep her balance. Eventually he released her.

'Jesus!' The minute she was free she slapped his arm in agitation. 'Don't you ever, ever do that to me again, do you hear me? I nearly had a heart attack!'

Ash was grinning at her, a dusting of snow sitting on his head.

'I just wondered if I could walk you home.'

'You said you had a lesson!'

'I lied,' he said without shame.

'Well,' she puffed at him. 'If you're going this way anyway, I suppose you can walk with me.'

'I'm not, but I will.' He offered his elbow to her. She considered it with due care, then threaded her arm through his.

'I wouldn't mind the company. But you shouldn't read anything into it.'

'Oh, I won't,' he said. 'I'll just walk back with you, drop you at the door, and be on my merry way.'

'That's right,' she said firmly. They began to walk

409

together. 'Unless,' she added after a few paces, 'you just want a cup of tea to warm up once we get there.'

'Well, it depends what sort of tea you have. Naturally.'

'Happy Shopper do you?'

'You're a woman of impeccable taste, Louise. I always knew it.'

'And you promise that you're not going to startle me with any more surprise kisses?'

'Sort of promise.'

'That's not good enough.'

'I promise I'll offer to leave after a cup of tea and stay only if you want me to stay, but I can't promise not to kiss you again. How about that?'

'I'll think about it,' Louise said. 'But I'll let you know as we go along. That suit you?'

'I think I can work with that.'

'The thing is, the flat's a bit of a mess and last night I cooked up a huge pan of broccoli. I'm sure the smell's everywhere now, and I haven't had a chance to open the windows so you might think—'

'Louise?'

'Yes?'

'Shut up.'

'Okay,' she said, as the snow thickened.